In the darkest hours of Sar Akka, when the Light is threatened with extinction, the Dream Warrior will arise. Look to the signs, for this warrior heralds the beginning of the Great Battle that will decide the fate of all the Peoples.

Other Books by D. J. Conway

The Ancient & Shining Ones
Animal Magick
Perfect Love (formerly *Astral Love*)
By Oak, Ash, & Thorn
Celtic Magic
The Dream Warrior (fiction)
Dancing With Dragons
Falcon Feather & Valkyrie Sword
Flying Without a Broom
Lord of Light & Shadow
Magickal, Mythical, Mystical Beasts
Maiden, Mother, Crone
Moon Magick
The Mysterious, Magickal Cat
Norse Magic
Warrior of Shadows (fiction)

Warrior of Shadows
The Final Battle

D. J. Conway

1998
Llewellyn Publications
St. Paul, Minnesota 55164-0383 U.S.A.

FIRST EDITION
First Printing, 1998

Cover art by Kris Waldherr
Cover design by Anne Marie Garrison
Book design and editing by Jessica Thoreson and Rebecca Zins

Cataloging-in-Publication Data
Conway, D. J. (Deanna J.)
Warrior of shadows: the final battle / D. J. Conway.—1st ed.
p. cm.
Sequel to: Soothslayer.
ISBN 1-56718-178-3
1. Psychics—Fiction. I. Title.
PS3553.05455W37 1998
813'.54—dc21 98-5868
CIP

Llewellyn Publications
A Division of Llewellyn Worldwide, Ltd.
P.O. Box 64383, K178-3
St. Paul, MN 55164-0383

Printed in the United States of America

In memory of Sharon Elizabeth
1959-1975.

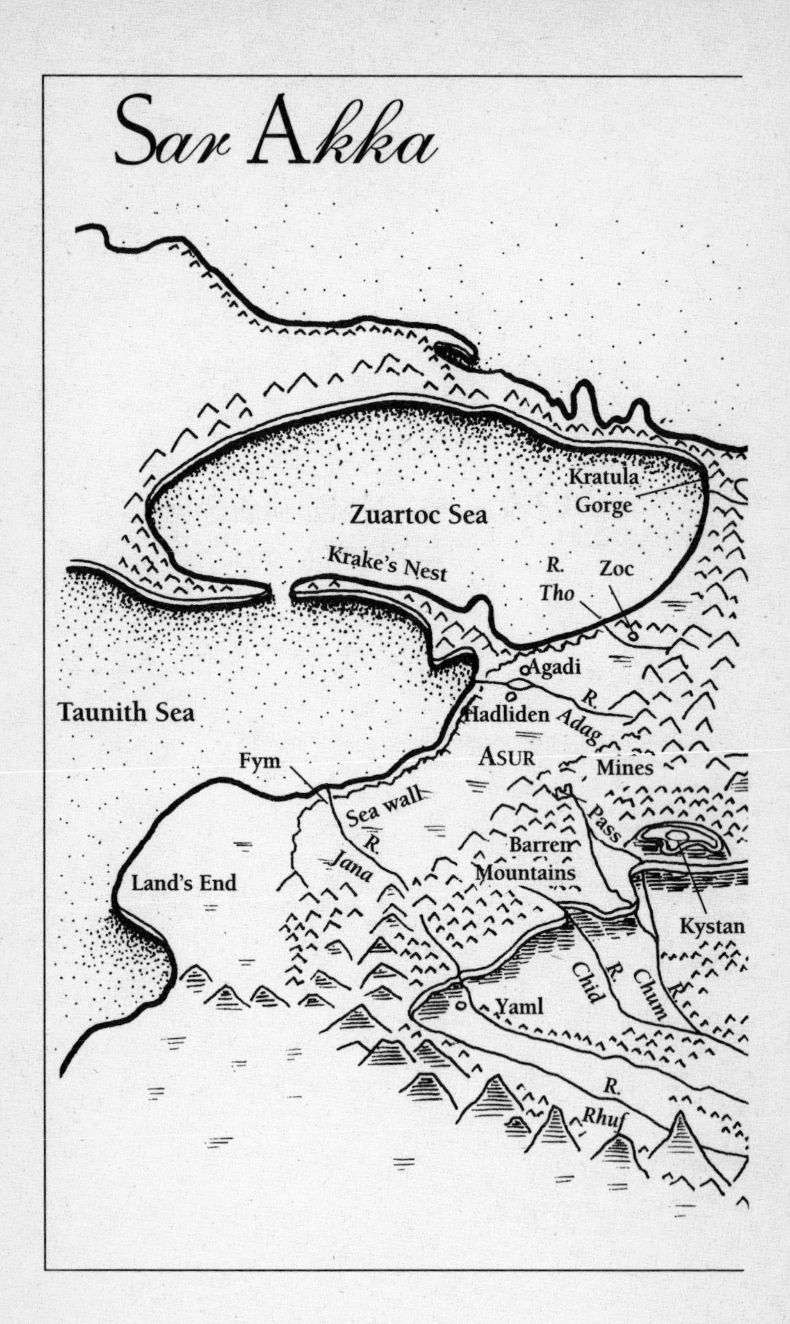
Sar Akka
Zuartoc Sea
Kratula
Gorge
Krake's Nest
R.
Tho
Zoc
Agadi
R.
Adag
Hadliden
Taunith Sea
Asur
Mines
Fym
Sea wall
Pass
R.
Jana
Barren
Mountains
Land's End
Kystan
Chid
R.
Chum
R.
Yaml
R.
Rhuf

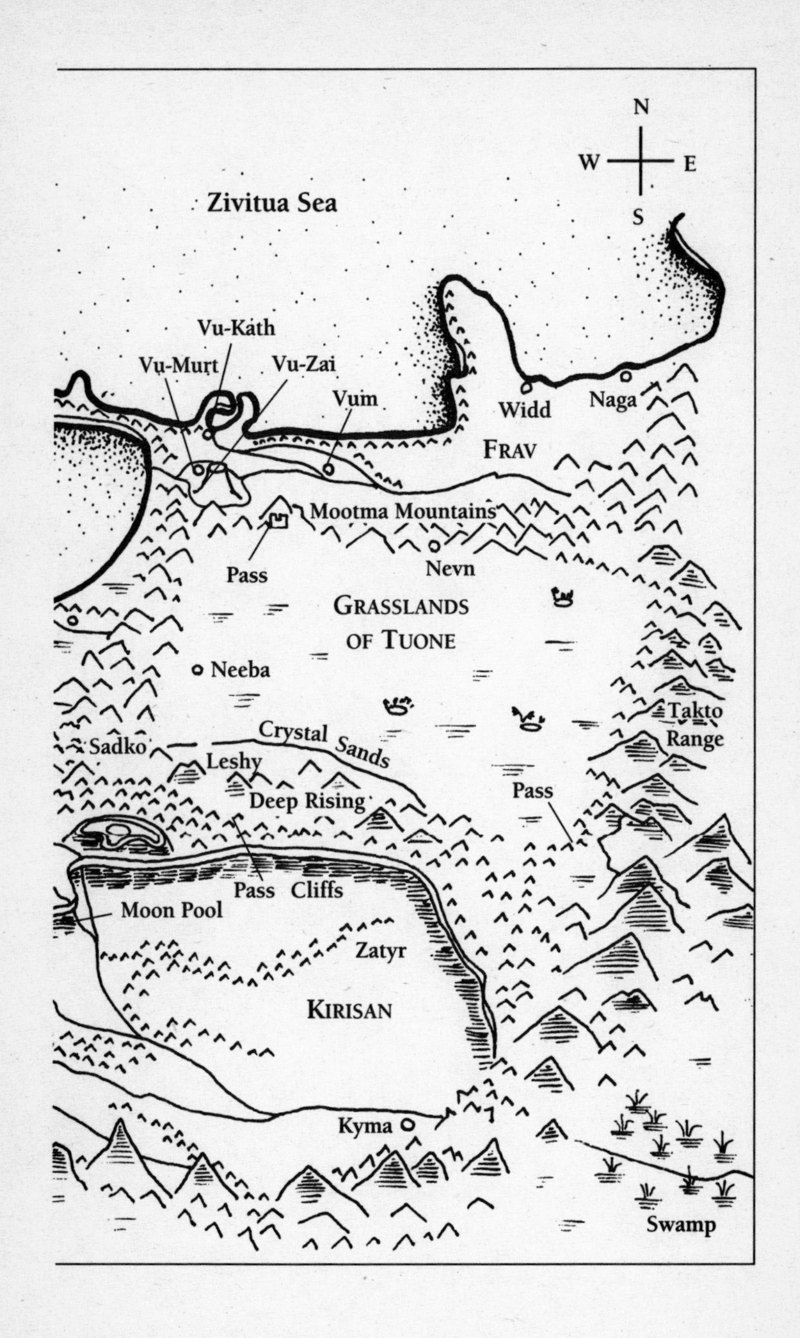
N
W
E
S
Zivitua Sea
Vu-Kath
Vu-Murt
Vu-Zai
Vum
Widd
Naga
FRAV
Mootma Mountains
Pass
Nevn
GRASSLANDS
OF TUONE
Neeba
Takto
Range
Crystal Sands
Sadko
Leshy
Deep Rising
Pass
Pass
Cliffs
Moon Pool
Zatyr
KIRISAN
Kyma
Swamp

Pronunciation Guide

Adag: Aye´ (long "a")-dag
Agadi: Ah-gah´-dee
Asperel: Ass´-per-el
Asur: Aye´ (long "a")-sir
Athdar: Ath´ (as in "am")-dar
Ayron: Aye´ (long "a")-ron

Baba: Bah´-bah
Babbel: Bay´-bull
Balqama: Ball-kah´-mah
Barsark: Bar´-sark
Breela: Bree´-lah
Burrak: Burr´-ack

Cabiria: Cah-beer´-ee-ah
Cassyr: Cass´-seer
Charissa: Chur-iz´-zah
Chid: Chid (as in "kid")
Chum: Chum
Cleeman: Clee´-mon
Clua: Clue´-ah
Corri: Core´-ee
Croyna: Croy´ (as in "troy") -nah

Daduku: Dah-doo´-koo
Dakhma: Dahk´-mah
Druk: Druk (as in "truck")

Fenlix: Fen´-licks
Feya: Fay´ (long "a")-yah
Fravashi: Frah-vah´-shee
Frayma: Fray´ (long "a") -mah
Friama: Free-ah´-mah
Fym: Fim

Gadavar: Gad´-a-var
Gertha: Grr´-thah
Geyti: Guy´-tee
Gran: Gran (as in "bran")
Grimmel: Grim´-ell

Hachino: Hah-chee´-no
Hadliden: Had´-li-dan
Halka: Hall´-kah
Halman: Hall´-mon
Hari-Hari: Har´-ee
Hindjall: Hind´ (as in "hinge")-yall

Imandoff: im´ (as in "imp") -an-doff
Iodan: Ee´-o-dan

Jabed: Jah´-bed
Jana: Jah´-nah
Jehennette: Gee´-en-et
Jevotan: Jay´ (long "a") -vo-tan
Jinniyah: Gin-ee´-yah

Kaaba: Kay-ah´-bah
Kaballoi: Cab´-ah-loy (as in "toy")
Kanlath: Can´-lath
Kayth: Kay´-th
Keffin: Keff´-in
Kirisan: Kier´ (as in "tier") -i (as in "it")-sahn
Korud: Core´-ud (as in "thud")
Krake: Krake (as in "brake")
Kratula: Kraw-too´-lah
Krynap: Cry´-nap
Kulkar: Kool´-kar
Kyma: Ky´ (as in "eye")-mah
Kystan: Ky´ (as in "eye") -stan

Leshy: Lesh´ (as in "mesh")-ee
Limna: Lim´ (as "limb")-nah

Magni: Mahg´-nee
Malya: Mahl´-yah
Medha: May´-dah
Melaina: Mee-lane´-ah
Menec: Men´-ek
Merra: Meer´-ah
Minepa: Min-e´ (as the "e" in "egg")-paw
Minna: Mee´-nah
Mootma: Moot´-mah
Morvrana: Morv (as "more")-rah´-nah

Naga: Nah´-gah
Natira: Nah-tier´-rah
Neeba: Nee´-bah
Nevn: Nev´-n
Norya: Nor´-yah
Nu-Sheek: New-sheek´
Nu-Sheeka: New-shee´-kah

Odran: O´ (as in "oh") -dran (as in "bran")

Qishua: Kish´-oo-ah

Rhuf: Rough
Rissa: Ris´-sah
Roggkin: Rog´ (as in "dog")-kin
Rushina: Roo-shee´-nah
Rympa: Rim´-pah

Sadko: Sod´-koh
Sallin: Say´-linn
Sejda: Say´-dah
Shakka: Shah´-kah
Sharrock: Shar´-rock
Shilluk: Shill´-uck
Simi: Sim´-ee
Sussa: Soo´-sah

Taillefer: Tal´ (as in "alley") -ee-fur
Takra: Tahk´-rah
Takto: Tahk´-toe
Tamia: Tay´-mee-ah

Taunith: Tow´ (as in "ow") -nith
Taymin: Tay´-men
Thalassa: Thal (as in "alley")-ass´-ah
Thidrick: Thid´ (as in "kid") -rick
Tho: Tho (as in "throw")
Tirkul: Tur´-kull
Tujyk: Too´-yek
Tuone: Too´-own
Tuonela: Too-oh-nell´-ah
Tuulikki: Too-oo-lee´-kee

Utha Unop: Oo´-thah Oh´-nap
Uunlak: Oo´-un-lack
Uzza: Oo´-zah

Vairya: Vair´-yah
Varanna: Var-ah´-nah
Vayhall: Vay´ (as in "way") -hall
Vu-Murt: Voo´-murt
Vu-Zai: Voo-zai´ (as in "eye")
Vum: Vum (as in "come")

Wella: Well´-ah
Wermod: Were´-mode
Widd: Widd (as in "lid")
Willa: Will´-ah

Xephena: Zeh-fee´-nah

Yaml: Yam´-el
Yngona: In-go´-nah

Zaitan: Zai´ (as in "eye")-tan
Zalmoxis: Zal (as in "alley")-mox´-iz
Zatyr: Zah-tier´
Zingas: Zing´-gahs
Zivitua: Zi (as the "e" in "egg")-vi´ (as in "it") -too-ah
Zoc: Zock
Zuartoc: Zoo-are´-tock

The Prophecy of the Dream Warrior

From the Bahrhatta, the Ancient Book

In the darkest hours of Sar Akka, when the Light is threatened with extinction, the Dream Warrior will arise. Look to the signs, for this warrior heralds the beginning of the Great Battle that will decide the fate of all the Peoples.

Dissention and evil will appear in places of wisdom. A key will open the hidden door to long-lost tombs and secret help. The wall with no gate will be broken and cannot be rebuilt. Silent death, long buried, will stalk the land. But in the warmth of love will beat new hearts, hearts that hold the unborn voices.

Ancient globes of power answer to both a child and a shaper of illusion, while an army fights upon a black plain. An evil shadow rides the night, bringing with it visions of fear and despair. Another lost key can seal the door to hell.

Armor from the sea can protect in the maze of the Place of Fire. Two serpents must die that one greater can be reborn. The Moon loses its light, while the black abyss opens wide.

Jinniyah will strive to control the Dream Warrior through the blood. Only if the Warrior listens to the voice that is not a voice can Jinniyah be defeated and Varanna come again.

Scribe's notes: This portion of the Prophecy was given by Serrati, the Oracle of the Temple of the Great Mountain, as she lay upon her deathbed in the year of the Krynap, tenth Turning after the Journey.

The Ancient Lay of Destruction

From the secret cave the treasure came,
carried by one of great fame.

The warrior crossed the bridge with one
who fought with five and carried one.

He dared the flames and Footed Snake
to reach the altar, melt and break.

The black disk shone there, key to the door
of evilness, corruption, more.

Yet forth he strode and slammed it down,
the plaque into the evil crown.

It melts and boils, the two are one,
and she who dreams the battle done,

Shall risk her life for victory
and in her flight shall set us free.

Chapter 1

The resinous odors of fir and pine hung spicy and thick in the summer air around the mountain camp of Frayma's Mare. The warrior women not on duty guarding the border with Frav lay in the shade of tree and boulder or sparred with the wooden practice swords.

The only man in the camp was stripped to the waist, his white-streaked black hair tied back with a leather thong. The blue-stone buckle on his belt winked in the bright sunlight as he whirled and danced, darting in and out of sword range of the Tuonela woman facing him. The woman wore trousers and a laced vest of soft leather, her bare arms browned from the summer sun. Her shining blonde braids whipped from side to side as she ducked and danced in swordplay.

It is difficult to remember that Takra is with child. Corri Far blood watched her friend Takra Wind-Rider parry and thrust with Imandoff, the father of Takra's child. *She barely shows at all. Only a fullness of breast and a little thickening of the waist.*

Corri winced as Imandoff gave Takra a welt-raising blow across the arm. The sorcerer immediately stepped back, his wooden weapon drooping in his hand.

"Now I have you!" Takra Wind-Rider yelled a battle cry and lunged at Imandoff, her practice sword a blur of motion. Suddenly, both swords touched heart-level at the same time. Takra and Imandoff stepped back, perspiration pouring down their faces.

"Never spare me in practice, Silverhair," Takra said, her oval face red with exertion. "No Fravashi will."

The tall sorcerer threw his arm around the Wind-Rider's shoulders as they walked to the shade, where Corri sat watching.

"I will not ask you to forego this battle because you are with child." Imandoff splashed water from a bucket over his face. "But I will not practice with you again unless you wear body-armor that covers the babe." His gray eyes were determined as he watched Takra rubbing the welt on her shield-arm.

Takra brushed damp strands of her pale blonde hair off her face and nodded. "I have no wish to miscarry our child, Imandoff, but I must keep my skills sharpened. The Harvest Moon is less than three moons off. And I will be at Corri's side when she fights against Kayth! No one will stop me from that. Besides, you know the way of the Tuonela women during times of war. And every warrior able to lift a sword will be needed in the times ahead."

Imandoff Silverhair flexed his long-fingered hands as he stretched. A red mark shown plain on his pale chest where Takra's wooden sword had marked him in the last thrust. "I know you love our babe, Takra, but I wish there were some way to keep both of you safe, far from the battle." He sighed and gently touched her cheek. "But you are right. The loss of one warrior may turn the tide of battle against us."

"I worry about you, Takra." Corri watched her friend as the tall woman sat down with her back against a tree. "Perhaps you should guard the healers. That way you would not be in the thick of battle." *You would do that when the moon lands in the sea.*

"Corri, do not ask that of me." Takra held Corri's gaze without a blink. "If the battle is lost at the border, the child and I will be killed as soon as the Fravashi invade the grasslands. Knowing how the Tuonela love their freedom, the Fravashi will not leave one of us alive."

And you love Imandoff as much as I love Gadavar, Corri thought. *You want to be at his side whatever happens. I cannot fault you for that. I would demand the same.*

"I know, but I do not want to lose my Sister-Friend." Corri turned her attention to Imandoff. "Have you heard how Thidrick fares?"

"Thidrick still guards with Kulkar's men," Imandoff said as he dropped to sit beside Takra. "He speaks little of Frav, except of his hatred for the Volikvis and Trow."

"He lost a sister to them. Can you blame him for his hatred? I cannot. Their use of women reminds me too much of Grimmel." Corri scratched idly in the dust with a twig. "What of Tirkul and Balqama? Will her father change his mind, Silverhair?"

"I talked with the trader. He has declared his daughter dead. He will not allow her name to be spoken among the family." Imandoff retied the thong around his dark hair. "And Tirkul and the girl are finding little welcome among the Tuonela Clans. The Tuonela and Fravashi are old enemies." He sighed and leaned back against the tree by Takra. "One cannot change tight-closed minds, only avoid them."

"Tirkul heals?" Takra asked, trying to get comfortable. "His wounds from the Fravashi torture were small to his body, but great to his mind."

Imandoff nodded. "Balqama says each day he is stronger."

Takra sighed as she loosened her belt and the tight vest laces. "It will be not much longer before I have to get looser clothes, thanks to you, sorcerer." She smiled and laid her hand lovingly on the sorcerer's knee.

"You will be a beautiful mother, Takra." Imandoff pulled her into the circle of his arm.

Takra leaned against his muscled shoulder, a faint smile on her lips. "Who do you think our daughter will look like, Silverhair?" Her eyelids lowered slowly as she tried to stay awake.

"She will likely have my black hair and magickal abilities, but undoubtedly your eyes." The sorcerer's voice softened, then fell silent as they both dozed off.

Corri smiled at her friends, then took her whetstone from her belt pouch and quietly began to sharpen the various knives she kept concealed about her person. *What would it be like to have a child with Gadavar?* she thought as she glanced at the sleeping pair. *What would that child look like, be like?* Her thoughts turned to the tall, dark Green Man, far away in the forested hills of Deep Rising. *Do you think of me, Gadavar?* As if in answer, she felt the Green Man's love and strength surrounding her.

Her hand froze in mid-stroke as she caught the faint cries of a baby at the edge of her hearing. For a moment Corri thought there was a baby in the camp, an impossible thing, she knew, in a group of fighting warrior women. Then she felt a strange inner tugging at the center of her being, as if an invisible cord connected her with this far away child. Her skin prickled as a tiny spark of possibility burst into her mind.

Takra said she knew she was with child when her moon flow stopped and she became sick each morning. I have not been sick. She wrinkled her forehead as she thought back over the time period from the Trial of the Mask to the present. *But my moon flow has stopped. And I keep hearing this baby cry inside my mind. No,* she shook her head in denial. *It is simply all the tension of preparing to meet Kayth at Harvest Moon. Even though Gadavar and I made love, it was only one time. The child I hear must be*

Takra's. She closed her eyes and thought back to the night in the Green Man's arms. *Whatever happens, I will always remember that night, Gadavar. What I feel for you is far deeper than anything I felt for Tirkul. I will love you till I die.*

She shook away the reveries and began once more the rhythmic draw of the knife across the stone.

"Rider coming!" The sentry's call alerted all within the forest clearing. Imandoff and Takra were instantly awake. The women of Frayma's Mare leaped from their resting places to grab at spears and swords while the sparring pairs dropped the wooden weapons and reached for the deadly killing swords.

The Tuonela horseman rode slowly into the camp, one hand held out shoulder-high. He nodded to the armed women as he slid to the needle-covered ground.

Norya, the shakka of Frayma's Mare, waited silently beside her tent-wagon as the rider unsaddled his horse, then rubbed it down before giving the reins to a waiting warrior. The man's dark eyes scanned the campsite, coming to rest on the ramrod-straight form of the old shakka.

"I bring messages," he called as he strode toward Norya, one hand drawing a small roll of parchment out of his belt pouch as he walked.

"For whom, and who sends?" Norya's quiet voice carried clearly in the silence that fell over the camp.

"From the Baba and the Oracle to the shakka Norya and to the Dream Warrior and her companions." The man looked over the crowd, then nodded as he saw Corri step to the shakka's side.

Norya took the curl of parchment in her wrinkled hands, a frown puckering her brow as she unrolled it to look at the scrawl of writing on it.

"I cannot read Kirisani," she said, motioning to Imandoff, "but give me the Baba's message."

The Tuonela warrior stood straight, his dark eyes closed, as he repeated the message from the Tuonela religious leader. "I have seen a dream of the great Varanna. She told me that the Dream Warrior must be fully clothed in the ancient armor for the last battle. The Tuonela have no knowledge of its whereabouts. Seek among the old records at the Temple of the Great Mountain."

Norya nodded. The rider nodded back, then walked toward the stew kettle simmering over the fire. "You can read this?" Norya asked Imandoff as he stepped to her side. She handed him the roll of parchment.

The sorcerer scanned the message, his gray eyes serious. "It is from the Oracle. She, too, has had a dream about the ancient armor of Varanna." He closed his eyes and touched the parchment briefly to the center of his forehead. "I feel her frustration in not having the armor, her puzzlement as to where it now lies." He looked down at the parchment in his hand, then turned to Corri, who stood at his side with Takra. "I think we should return to Kystan. Perhaps the most ancient Temple records hold a clue that the Oracle has not found."

"The Harvest Moon is not far off." Corri shaded her blue-green eyes with one hand as she peered up at him. "Do we have time for this quest?"

"And what if we do not find it?" Takra tucked her thumbs into her belt, clasping her strong hands together.

"I think you must!" The shakka's hazel eyes were bright, their fans of wrinkles deepening as she glanced from Imandoff to Corri. "The Baba and the Oracle always dream true. Varanna's armor might well hold the key to victory in this battle."

"Then we must go to Kystan." Corri turned and strode back to her campsite with Imandoff to gather their belongings.

Takra moved close to the shakka as the warriors dispersed, their voices and the whack of wooden swords once more filling the warm mountain air of the camp.

"Shakka, I would ask a question." Takra scuffed one boot nervously in the dry dust. "Can you see if the child I carry will live through this battle?"

Norya paused, her eyes looking far beyond the scene around her, as if listening. "I can see nothing beyond a scene of you and the Dream Warrior standing at the stone bridge which reaches into the evil city of Vu-Zai." She blinked, then shook her head. "This does not mean you will die; it does not mean you will live. It means that a wall has been cast across the future, a wall that keeps me from seeing beyond. Perhaps this is the work of the Volikvis and the man Kayth. Perhaps it means that the Goddess has not woven your fate, Wind-Rider."

"Then I must walk as a warrior, trusting in the Goddess." Takra nodded and left to join Corri and Imandoff.

"May the Goddess bless and protect both you and your daughter, Wind-Rider," Norya murmured as she watched the Tuonela warrior woman walk away.

"I forgot how hot it can be out on the grasslands." Corri wiped the perspiration from her face with one hand. "How much farther to Leshy?" She waited until Takra filled the water flasks from the small spring under the lip of a bank before allowing the horses to drink.

"You can see the glare of the Crystal Sands ahead." Imandoff shaded his eyes as he looked to the south. "We will have to wait until dark to cross. We should be inside the city of Leshy about three hours after dark. It will be cooler there."

"I must be getting soft." Takra yawned and blinked her eyes. "I look forward to a bath and a bed in an inn this night." She grinned at Imandoff.

"I hope we can get rooms at the White Boar," the sorcerer said, smiling back at her. "This is the busiest time of the caravan season. The merchants will be out in great numbers while the weather holds. When the grasslands' storms of autumn break, there is little if any travel."

"The storms of summer are no better." The memory of such a violent summer storm rose in Corri's mind as she looked around at the tall grass bending in waves with the ceaseless wind. *I have changed so much since I rescued Tirkul's little sister from the flash flood caused by such a storm. That storm was the beginning of so many changes in my life, but I do not regret a one of them.*

"We will rest a while here," Imandoff said as he spread a blanket in the shade of the bank. He sat down, pulling Takra beside him.

Corri sat, chin on bent knees, gazing out over the rolling grasslands as Takra slept beside the sorcerer. The horses grazed nearby, their ears and tails flicking at the clouds of insects hovering near the tiny spring. She watched Imandoff gently touch Takra's cheek as she slept, her blonde head on his chest.

Will I ever know that kind of love? I thought I had it with Tirkul, she thought. *If I live through the battle, I want to build a love like that with Gadavar.* Her glance fell to Takra's hand that lay protectively across her belly. *Oh Goddess, keep my friends and their child safe. If a life must be sacrificed for victory over Frav, take mine!* Her head drooped as she fell asleep in the afternoon's pressing heat.

The key lies in Deep Rising. Corri awoke with a start at the voice in her dreams. Imandoff and Takra had just wakened in the bank's shade, stretching and rubbing their eyes. The sun was sinking in the west, casting long shadows over the undulating grasslands of Tuone. The air was still heavy with intense heat.

The key to what? Corri shaded her eyes as she stared toward the Crystal Sands. *It was not the voice of the Lady, but who? If I must hear voices in my dreams, at least I should get clearer answers.* Corri dusted off her leather trousers as she went to saddle Mouse. *No need to say anything to Imandoff or Takra until I puzzle out the meaning.*

"By the time we reach the Sands, the glare will be gone." Imandoff folded the blanket and tied it behind Sun Dancer's saddle. "We should reach Leshy just before they close the gates."

"What if the inns are full?" Takra saddled Lightfoot, then swung up onto the gray-speckled black horse.

"Then we might have to seek lodging at the Mystery School." The sorcerer patted the roan's neck as Sun Dancer pranced in the lowering rays of the setting sun.

"I would rather spend the night in an inn or sleep in a stable." Corri turned Mouse toward the Sands and the mountains of Deep Rising. "I like Jehennette," she said over her shoulder, "but there are other initiates there who may not think as she does. Remember the trouble I found in that School the last time I stayed. I prefer a place I can get out of if and when I choose."

"I am with you on that, Sister-Friend," Takra said and sighed. "I just wish the roofs of inns were closer to the ground."

"We should not have to take to the roofs this night, Wind-Rider." Imandoff's teeth were bright in his dark beard as he smiled at the warrior woman.

"I have yet to spend a night in an inn with you, sorcerer, that we did not have to climb over roofs and down drain pipes," Takra growled as she touched her heels to Lightfoot's flanks.

Corri smiled as she rode behind Takra. *Your growls and frowns are just a cover for your fear, my Sister-Friend. Even Imandoff knows that.* She smiled again when the sorcerer turned and winked at her, as if he heard her thoughts.

They rode up the caravan trail and into the city of Leshy just as the great gates were closing for the night. The streets were empty, except for a few furtive figures that stayed in the shadows of alleys. As Corri had feared, the White Boar had no rooms; neither did the Golden Sharrock. But the stable boy at the Sharrock directed them to a small inn, the Cup and Sword, set back from the others on a narrow side-street.

"At least this one is closer to the ground." Imandoff grinned as Takra patted Lightfoot's nose and gathered her saddlebags.

"Do they have a bath house?" Takra sighed and brushed at her leather trousers.

"Of course. And our rooms are only on the second floor." Imandoff threw his arm around her as they followed Corri into the Cup and Sword.

The common room was nearly half-full of people, but no one gave the trio more than a passing glance. They followed a maid up the stairs to their rooms and left their saddle bags.

"I am ready for a drink," Imandoff said as Takra asked the maid the way to the bathhouse. "I promise not to drink as much as I once did. I have the child to think of now." He was answered by Takra's smile.

"See someone you know, old man?" Corri grinned up at him. "Most of them looked pretty disreputable to me."

"Silverhair's friends are mostly shadow-lurkers, Farblood. The kind you and I would take care to avoid. But he manages to find out all sorts of things from them." Takra waited, her arms full of rough towels. "Keep one hand on your dagger," she said to the sorcerer. "Some of the men below look to be the kind who would cut your throat for your belt buckle."

"I will take care." Imandoff gave the Tuonela a quick kiss on the cheek, then disappeared down the stairs to the common room.

Corri and Takra took another stair that led outside to the back of the inn, where they found the bath house. The door to the small building creaked and grated on its one remaining hinge when Corri pushed it open. A mineral scent of hot spring water wafted through the dark room.

"Here is a tallow dip." Takra took a rough-made candle from her load of towels, holding it out to Corri. "I do not enter strange dark buildings without a light."

"Nor do I." Corri concentrated and snapped her fingers to light the tallow.

The two women cautiously peered inside, then entered and wrestled the door shut. In the center of the room was a wooden tub large enough to hold four grown men and reached by a step-platform built around the outside of it.

"Not used much," Takra commented as she unlaced her leather garments and laid them beside her sword. She shivered as she glanced up to the shadowed rafters, festooned with dust-laden cobwebs.

"I doubt that those who frequent the Cup and Sword care much about bathing." Corri slipped her mother's ring and Gadavar's silver amulet into her belt pouch. She laid aside her own clothing and climbed the platform to look down into the steamy water. "Must be connected to a natural hot spring. And see, they have rigged it to constantly fill and empty. They did leave some soap." She held up an ancient bar of soap, its surface covered with dust. She smelled the odor of roses when she held the soap to her nose.

Takra stepped down into the tub, sighing as she sat down in the steamy water. "Oh Goddess, but this feels good." She leaned her fair head back against the smoothed oak tub planks and closed her eyes in contentment.

Corri slipped into the water beside her, a smile of delight curving her mouth. She rubbed the soap between her hands, working up a lather, then scrubbed her face and body. Last, she lathered her hair and rinsed it in the swirling water. The women took turns washing each other's backs. The soapy bubbles drifted across the tub to disappear in the outlet on the far side. She handed the soap to the Wind-Rider, then leaned back against the oak planking.

"Farblood, are you with child?" Takra's soft words broke through Corri's thoughts like the edge of a knife.

"I, I do not know for certain," Corri stammered. She felt as if her heart was caught in her throat. *Am I? It would be Gadavar's child!* She reluctantly pushed aside her joy. *I will not buy his love with a child. I love him too much for that. And I may not live through the battle.*

"I have watched you since the Trial of the Mask," Takra said as she loosed her long braids. "We are closer than sisters, Corri, close enough that I know your moon flow has stopped." Her amber eyes met Corri's across the steamy water. "If you do not wish this child, I know which herbs the shakkas use to end pregnancy."

Corri shrugged. "The signs may be false because of the tension under which we now live. I heard the pleasure-women of Grimmel's household speak of such a thing."

"I do not believe that, nor do you." Takra's eyes held hers.

"Besides, if I am with child, I will not end the pregnancy nor will I buy the father's love with that responsibility. If I live through the coming battle, this child may be all I have of someone I love." The picture of the tangled life-threads holding Gadavar's death rose in Corri's mind. *Not Gadavar! Please, Lady!*

"It would be Gadavar's child, would it not?"

"Yes." Corri felt a rush of blood to her cheeks.

Takra cupped her own breasts with her hands. "Are your breasts tender?"

"I have not been sick," Corri protested. *But my breasts have become tender,* she thought.

"Some women do not experience sickness." Takra's amber eyes held hers until Corri looked away. "You will show little by the time of the battle. There is no shame in being with child, Sister-Friend. Among the Tuonela, a woman may choose to have children but take no heart-oath with a man. As for the Kirisani and Asur . . ." Takra gave a gesture of contempt for the customs of the other Peoples. "You are my Sister-Friend and the Dream Warrior. Do not bind yourself by their narrow laws. Imandoff and I will stand by you, whatever you decide."

"My heart says you may be right, Takra," Corri finally admitted. "But no one must know until after the battle! Not Gadavar, not Imandoff, no one! Do you understand?"

"I understand that you have things to do for the Goddess, things so important that without you the Peoples may fall." Takra lathered her head, then ducked and rinsed it. She pushed her streaming hair out of her face and looked at Corri. "I will say nothing, I give you my word. Just as your presence is vital to the outcome of battle, so may my presence be. That is why I will stand at your back, no matter how pregnant I am."

"I would wish you safely out of the fighting, as does Imandoff. But I also want you at my side when I face Kayth. Is that selfish, Takra?"

"Only a stupid captain leaves her best warriors behind." Takra grinned. "Just think, Farblood, when we are old women, we can tell our children they went into battle with us."

They climbed out of the tub, laughing and joking. As they rubbed themselves dry with the coarse towels, Takra raised her hand for silence and reached for her sword. Corri's sharp ears caught the sound of light footsteps pausing before the closed door. She grabbed up her belt dagger as the door creaked open.

"What a lovely sight!" Imandoff's deep voice filled the bath house as he stepped inside. "I shall be a gentleman and turn my back until you have dressed." He turned around with a grin, then held up a bundle of clothing. "I thought you might like something clean to wear. And a comb to get out the rat's nests."

"Imandoff Silverhair, a gentleman?" Takra smothered a laugh as she plucked the clothing from the sorcerer's hand. "Never!"

"Are you saying our clothes smell less than fresh, old man?" Corri finished drying her hair. "What of you?"

"I too will soak off the travel dust," he answered. He half-turned his head, grinning at Takra's snort of disapproval when she shook out the clothing. "Alas, I could find no Tuonela garb, and we cannot tarry to have your leathers cleaned."

"At least you did not bring those horrid long Kirisani skirts these women wear." Takra pulled on a pair of trousers and a shirt with bloused sleeves. She plucked self-consciously at the tattered ruffles on the cuffs. "No good for sword play. Your opponent could kill you while you were trying to untangle your sword hilt." She slipped into her own laced vest and scuffed boots, then buckled on her sword belt.

"Where did you get these?" Corri asked as she looked down at her slim green trousers and brown shirt. "This looks like the garb of a Green Man." She smiled as her thoughts leaped to Gadavar. She remembered clearly the touch of his lips against hers, the feel of his body under her hands.

"A friend found them for me. But a Green Man's garb, no. Some of the young city men like to imitate the woodland guardians." Imandoff shed his cloak as he turned. "A bath! What a wonderful end to a day." Leaning his staff against the wall, he kicked off his boots and dropped his clothing as he walked to the tub. With a sigh, the sorcerer slipped into the tub and took up the bar of floating soap. As the odor of roses wafted from the suds, he grinned. "I shall smell like a city dandy now." He winked at Takra.

Corri pulled loose his belt with the blue-stone buckle, the long sword, and belt pouch, checked the sorcerer's hidden pockets, then tossed all the clothing into the tub with Imandoff. "At least yours can be washed," she said with a grin.

"Stay and talk with me." Imandoff disappeared briefly as he ducked under the steamy water. "I will tell you what I have learned here at the Cup and Sword."

Corri sat on the step-platform to comb out her dark red hair while Takra rolled up her sleeves and soaped down Imandoff's back. Then the Dream Warrior motioned Takra to sit closer to her while she combed out the Wind-Rider's tangle of long damp hair.

"There is a song-smith here at the Cup and Sword who has all the marks of being a trustworthy friend," Imandoff said as he leaned back against the oak planking, his eyes closed in pleasure. "Taillefer is a mine of information. He says that Malya and Roggkin were seen in Leshy less than two days ago. And he has seen them right here at this inn talking to someone from the Mystery School." He turned his head to look at Corri. "I thought certain Malya would run for Frav, her tail between her legs."

Corri paused, her fingers clenching around the comb. *She may be my half-sister, but Malya is as evil as Kayth. I wish she would disappear into the earth and be gone from my life forever!*

Imandoff reached for his soaking clothes, rubbed them vigorously with the soap, then rinsed them clean. Takra wrung each piece of clothing and shook it out before piling it on the step-platform beside her.

"So we must watch our backs for those two." Takra handed the sorcerer a dry towel as he stepped from the bath. "Did this Taillefer say who they met from the Mystery School?"

"He did not know the woman's name," Imandoff answered as he wiped himself dry. "At least he thinks it was a woman. The initiate was so hidden by the cloak, he could not tell." He slipped into the rest of the clean clothing and tugged on his worn boots before he gathered up his wet garments. "He found hoods for you and Corri. Best no one sees your Tuonela hair or Corri's red-flame curls just now."

"Agreed." Corri pulled on a green hood and fastened it under her chin, then handed the worn brown one to Takra. "We do not know what spies Malya may have bought in Leshy." She took the amulet from her belt pouch and slipped the chain over her head.

"I think we should ride out in the morning." Imandoff checked the slide of his sword in its sheath as they left the bath house. "First, however, we will enjoy a meal, part of the fee for a night's lodging."

"And a good night's rest, hopefully," Corri murmured as she watched the sorcerer climb the stairs to hang his wet garments in his room.

The common room of the Cup and Sword was nearly full as Corri and Takra made their way among the noisy tables to one of the uncurtained high-backed booths against the rear wall. As they slid onto the benches, a stocky young man walked near their table with a lap harp cradled in one arm. At his side hung a sword, its hilt worn from use. Broad muscled shoulders stretched his deep blue tunic and calluses were plain on his hands, all the marks of a true swordsman. His dark blue eyes widened just for an instant when he saw Corri and Takra.

"Greetings, strangers to Leshy," the song-smith said as he paused by the table. One lock of his dark auburn hair, so deep in color as to be mistaken for black, hung rakishly over his brow. "Has my reputation brought you to the Cup and Sword?" A wide grin crossed his sharp face.

"How can I say?" Corri answered. "Who are you?" *This man has a little power, but not strong enough to get him into the Temple.*

"Alas, I had hoped you had heard of Taillefer, the singer of ancient songs." The young man rubbed his bent nose, broken in an old fight, with a long-fingered hand. The crescent scar at the corner of his left eye crinkled as he grinned again. "Ah well, one can always hope. May your evening be a pleasant one, ladies." The song-smith bowed and walked away.

"How could he be certain we are women?" Corri asked as she leaned across the table.

"Either Imandoff told him or it is the soap." Takra sniffed her hand suspiciously, then wrinkled her nose. "What is this scent?"

"Roses." Corri's mind remembered the walled gardens of Grimmel's villa where the pleasure-women strolled among the roses and honeysuckle in the cool summer evenings. She realized Takra was staring at her with a puzzled look. "Roses are sweet-smelling flowers. Grimmel had them in his gardens. The petals are soft, like the finest of cloth, but the bushes are studded with sharp thorns. They are much prized for their scent, which some of the Asuran pleasure-women make into perfumes."

"A pleasant odor," Takra said as she signaled to one of the barmaids. "Nothing to wear if one is trying to sneak up on an enemy, but pleasant for other times." She grinned at Corri.

Silence fell over the noisy room as the song-smith seated himself on a tall stool in one corner of the room. The dark head bent over the harp as he stroked the shining strings, sending a ripple of music through the room.

"Sing us the tale of the Lost Maidens," someone called from the crowd.

Taillefer raised his beautiful tenor voice in song. "The Maidens fled into the hills, into a secret cave."

Imandoff slid onto the bench beside Takra. "It is rare to hear the old, old songs still sung," he said softly, his eyes on Taillefer. "It is not the fashion among song-smiths anymore."

A barmaid set a tankard of ale and two mugs of apple cider on the table. Imandoff caught her by the arm and whispered instructions. She nodded and left, but returned quickly with a large tray containing plates and eating utensils, a crusty loaf of bread, baked tubers, and a plate of juicy roasted meat. Three ripe peaches, golden-red, filled another bowl.

"I could eat it all," Takra said as she slid one of the cider mugs and a plate in front of her, then speared a large tuber with her fork. She heaped the plate with meat and a large piece of the bread.

"We shall have to increase our travel supplies, I think." Imandoff smiled as he put one of the peaches beside Takra's plate.

The song ended, and Taillefer took a drink from his tankard, his eyes scanning the room. Suddenly, he struck a chord and sang, "Keep watch, keep watch, the soldier cried. The enemy is near." He looked straight across the room at Imandoff and barely nodded his head.

"Not that one," shouted one of the audience. "Play us the Harvest Dance!"

Taillefer's slender fingers flashed across the strings, and the crowd began clapping to the beat of the lively tune.

"Who came in behind me?" Imandoff murmured to Corri.

She furtively watched two muffled figures slide into the booth behind the sorcerer. The strangers were quickly followed by a well-cloaked figure, the face hidden in the deep hood. Corri shook her head. "Impossible to see. First, two people whose faces I could not see, but the third who followed I think might be the initiate who met with Malya." Corri grabbed her cider mug and a piece of bread. "I will try to find out."

"Too dangerous!" Imandoff grabbed at her arm, but she evaded him to slide out of the booth. Drawing the illusion of being a different person about her, she slouched away.

All of Corri's instincts screamed "danger!" as she passed the booth. She kept her head down, her shoulders bent, as she shuffled by. Out of the corner of her eye she saw a worn Tuonela boot stretched from the bench near the sorcerer's back. On the floor by the other bench lay the folds of an initiate's blue cloak.

She shuffled on and collapsed into the next booth. Her hands shook as she carefully set the mug on the dirty table and leaned her head back against the partition. Like a cautiously groping tendril, Corri mentally reached out for the mind of the person directly behind the partition.

Malya and Roggkin! And this one has dealt with them before. Corri's hand clenched around the bread, mashing it into a ball. *Yes, there is the mental pattern of the Mystery School in this woman's thoughts, but why does she seek out these two?*

An abrupt break in the strange woman's thought-patterns warned Corri, who bent forward over her cider, carefully looking sideways from the shadows of her hood. The cloaked woman paused beside her to look back at Roggkin and Malya, her face visible for only an instant. Then the tall form of Roggkin joined her.

Another song ended, and Roggkin's husky murmur reached Corri's ears. "Trust her, Morvrana."

"Malya failed in her bid for the School," the woman answered in a flat tone. "She no longer works for the Peoples, but for Frav. Those are not my loyalties." Morvrana turned on her heel and walked away.

Corri sat frozen on the bench as Malya joined the Tuonela outcast. *What is Malya planning now? And why meet with this initiate Morvrana when the woman obviously does not support Malya's cause? What if they see Takra and Imandoff?*

When neither of the conspirators appeared to notice the sorcerer and Tuonela warrior woman, Corri guessed that Imandoff had covered himself and Takra with a "look elsewhere" spell.

She waited until Roggkin and Malya swept past her to the outer door before rejoining her friends.

"It makes no sense," Takra said between mouthfuls of food. "Why would Malya have anything to do with an initiate who is loyal to Kirisan?"

Her brows creased in thought, Corri picked at the food on her plate. "What do we really know of Malya's powers? Perhaps she has planted some deed to be acted upon later, a thought that this Morvrana would think her own."

"I do not like the idea of leaving this question unanswered," Imandoff said, rubbing at his chin. "But we cannot delay finding Varanna's armor. We must continue our journey to Kystan."

Malya has set some mischief at work in this woman Morvrana, Corri thought. *A mischief that will breed deep trouble in the future, I know it!* Corri looked up into Imandoff's storm-gray eyes and nodded. "Yes, time presses. We must go on to the Temple for now. But I do not like having Malya and Roggkin at our backs."

Imandoff turned away to watch the song-smith. "Besides his promise to find out certain things for me, Taillefer also has some plan of his own," he murmured. "I wonder where he fits into this wasp's nest of intrigue."

"We cannot afford the time to watch the weaving of all these webs." Takra bit into the juicy peach. "We will watch our backs and trust in the Goddess."

Corri suddenly frowned as a tendril of thought pushed against her mind. *Malya seeks to know if we are in Leshy!* A quick glance at Imandoff's face revealed the sorcerer's surprise.

The song-smith struck his fingers across the harp, sending a discordant chord ringing through the common room, shattering the probing power of the questing thought-pattern. His face was grave as he stared across the room at Corri and her friends. Then, with a smile at the people about him and a shrug of his muscled shoulders, the song-smith made his way through the noisy crowd to the outer door, harp in hand.

How much does this Taillefer know? she thought, watching the man across the crowded room. *As a singer of ancient songs, does he recognize me as the Dream Warrior? Is he friend or foe?*

"That one is prideful," Malya said, as she and Roggkin stood in the street shadows, watching Morvrana swiftly walk back through the narrow, dark lanes toward the Mystery School. She caressed the pale, translucent red stone strung on a silver chain about her slender neck. "She denies that she will help us, but she will think upon my suggestion. Soon, very soon, she will not be able to resist acting on it. I will have Vikkarr and Nebel keep watch while we are about our business."

"When that woman does as you wish, then all will be as it should. You will be in control." Roggkin reached out to touch the pale oval face, but Malya turned from his caresses and led the way through the deepening night to another small inn.

Taillefer crouched in the black shadows of the alley until the pair was well out of sight. *So this woman of the evil aura lays plans to gain control. But of whom or what?* He leaned back against the rough stone, one hand on his sword hilt, the other thoughtfully pulling a lock of his hair. *The sorcerer Imandoff asked for news of such happenings. But what have I to tell him? That a man and a woman I believe to be enemies whispered in the dark of intrigues? I must wait and watch and listen, for eventually rumors of what those two do will creep through this town.*

He watched the silent street for several more minutes in case the conspirators returned, but he only saw a cautious traveler going toward the inn. *If I can find the truth of what Imandoff seeks, perhaps he will take me with him when he goes to face the evil of Frav. To write of the great battle to come I must be in the thick of the fighting. What better place to be than at the side of Imandoff Silverhair? What an epic song that would make!*

Taillefer smiled to himself and slipped unnoticed back to the Cup and Sword.

Chapter 2

Corri stirred restlessly in her sleep. Her dreams had suddenly changed from a pleasant walk with Gadavar through the forest to disjointed fragments of action, the kind of dreams that would leave her tired the next day. Twice she awoke, lying motionless as she listened to the faint sounds of the inn. Each time she reached out with her mind to Takra and Imandoff in the next room, only to find them deep in slumber. Each time she drifted back into the disjointed dreams.

My powers have grown. I should be able to contact and influence her, yet I cannot. A male voice cut through Corri's dreams.

Corri looked around as Kayth's voice sounded close to her ear. *I am dreaming, not dream-flying,* she thought. The same rush of meaningless activity went on around her as it had all night. *I am dreaming, but how do I know that? And how can I hear Kayth in my dreams?*

She strained to see through the flutter of dreams about her. There was a tiny flash, a spark of light, then another. Corri concentrated on the flashes until they slowed, revealing a different scene within the bubble of light.

I feel her presence, yet I also cannot find her. The Trow priestess Xephena lay back in a chair, a glossy black wall behind her. *It would seem that your daughter's powers have grown even more than we suspected.* A puzzled frown wrinkled Xephena's brow.

Corri instantly willed a protective shield around herself. Xephena's weak psychic probe bumped it, then slid off the shield like water off a stone. *I dare not seek for Kayth,* she thought. *If I try to see him with my mind, he may become aware that I eavesdrop.*

Then I must strengthen my powers even more. Kayth remained out of Corri's sight. *I must have the remains of Minepa's skull! I must take into myself that Volikvi's powers, adding them to my own.*

Corri released her concentration on the bubble of light, and it snapped out of existence. Her dreams still flitted around her but her attention was drawn to a beautiful rainbow-colored bubble that floated toward her. As she reached out to the bubble, she heard a singing music like she had never heard before.

What is it? she thought. *I feel no danger.*

The bubble slowly slid around her, drawing her into its brilliantly lit interior. Corri gasped as a shining serpent reared up before her, flashes of rainbow lights coming from its glistening scales.

Do not fear me, it said. *I will help you in your times of great need.*

Corri felt no dread, only a deep sense of peace and love. *When will I see you again?*

When you need me, came the answer as the lights blinked out.

For a moment Corri drifted in a place of comfortable darkness before sinking down into dreamless slumber. In the morning she only faintly remembered the dream of the serpent and did not think it important enough to share with Imandoff and Takra.

Corri and her companions rode out of Leshy just as the false dawn rimmed the mountains in the east. Hung from Mouse's saddle was the bag carrying Varanna's ancient helmet, the only piece of the ancient warrior woman's armor they had found in the Temple. The sword hilt, its blade long ago melted in the battle in which Varanna lost her life, was still housed in the sacred Cave.

Since a sword hilt is not armor, I cannot see why we should worry about it. Corri shivered as she remembered the dark cave with its burial urns.

Takra and Imandoff dropped back to ride one on each side of Corri as they made their way along the dusty road leading from Leshy to the high city of Kystan.

"Have either of you thought on why Kayth has chosen the Harvest Moon for the attack on the Peoples?" The sorcerer watched each passing traveler, his hand never far from the deadly sword at his side. "There must be an important reason, but I am unable to see what it is."

"I cannot see why one full moon would be any different from another." Takra reined Lightfoot through a herd of cattle being driven across the road to upper pastures. "Harvest Moon is a full moon celebration for the Peoples. Perhaps Kayth thinks the Fravashi army will catch the border guards unaware at that time. If so, he is a fool." Her mouth tightened.

"I do not think Kayth is a fool." Imandoff looked sideways at Corri, his hands gentle on the reins as Sun Dancer pranced in the early sunlight. "I believe Kayth has learned something we have not, something that may well add to his powers."

"One thing I know," Corri answered. "Kayth's power has grown. And now he plans to take in Minepa's power. Can he do that, old man?"

Imandoff looked at her in surprise but she only shrugged and did not answer the unspoken question.

The sorcerer's face was grave. "Ancient legends tell of such things," he said, his gray eyes hard. "But it is a chancy, evil thing to do." He did not question how Corri knew. "I wonder if there is some way to prevent Kayth's doing this."

"I doubt we can." Corri waved a cloud of insects away from her face as the gnats and flies began to rise in the growing heat of the day. "I think I must search for some way to make my own powers stronger. If I cannot find a way, many good men and women will die when Kayth and his armies cross the border into Tuone."

Like Gadavar, Corri thought, her mind rushing back to the Trial of the Mask and her struggle with the knotted lifethreads. Her hands clenched on the reins as she remembered Imandoff sliding the strange helmet-mask over her head, the terrifying flight through the darkness of the Otherworld, and her frantic efforts to untangle the slippery weaving threads that held pictures of the future. *Were my efforts useless? He must not die, not Gadavar! I will not accept his death!* Corri blinked back tears and set her jaw. *There has to be a way to turn that destiny aside. I cannot imagine my life without him.*

A mental picture of the Green Man rose up before her inner sight. She remembered his height as he leaned down to kiss her, his strong arms and gentleness as they lay together in the narrow bed at Leshy, the smell of his pipe around the campfire in Deep Rising.

"Perhaps the strength you need to tap is within your family's bloodline." Takra fumbled into the provisions bag hanging from her saddle and pulled out an apple. "Imandoff tells me that your mother Ryanna was of the same bloodline as Varanna. Is that not true?" She bit into the red fruit.

"So my uncle Geyti says," Corri answered, "although I do not understand how that can be since Varanna died without children. And the legends never mention that Varanna had any brothers or sisters."

"I do not understand either." Imandoff pushed back his hood in the rising heat. "The books of the bloodlines at the

Temple do not show this. But much of the information of that time has been lost or was never recorded, so I do not doubt Geyti's word. However, it will do no harm to seek inner strength as if Varanna were your ancestress, Corri. Perhaps when I search through the Temple records for a clue to the hiding place of the armor, I will discover an answer to this puzzle also."

They rode up the steep walled road into the city of Kystan three days later, just as the sun was setting. The merchants of the great city were closing the shops, and business among the taverns, prostitutes, and petty thieves was just beginning.

Corri looked at Takra, a question clear in her eyes, as Imandoff bypassed the inns and headed straight through the meandering streets toward the Great Temple. The Wind-Rider shrugged her shoulders as she followed the sorcerer through the dimly-lit streets toward the lake-surrounded Mystery School.

The bridge guards closely scrutinized the trio before they were allowed to ride over the slender connection between the stone promenade surrounding the city-side of the lake and the walled and towered Temple.

Imandoff drew rein before the great gates at the end of the bridge and waited patiently, his face turned upward in the torchlight toward the shadowed guard-houses on the wall above. Within minutes, Corri heard the sliding of wooden bars against the heavy planks of the gate. Two armored guards pulled back the great gates, allowing the riders inside, then shut and barred them again.

Imandoff swung down from Sun Dancer and handed the reins to a young initiate who approached at a fast pace from the courtyard beyond. Only a handful of initiates and armor-clad warriors were visible in the wide cobblestone yard.

"Where is the Oracle?" he asked, his deep voice echoing slightly across the stone-paved yard and off the clustered buildings of the School. From somewhere deep in the maze of structures came the ring of a mighty hammer and the bellow of a forge.

Corri and Takra slid down to hand the reins of their mounts to the initiate. Untying the bag containing Varanna's ancient helmet, Corri slung it over her shoulder as she watched the man take the horses off toward the stables.

One of the guards stepped forward and snapped a salute of fist against chest-plate. "The Oracle is at her devotions, sir. We have had word of your coming. The High Priestess and Commander of Her Own will meet with you in the audience hall." The feminine tones were hardened at the edges, the voice of a warrior woman on duty.

Something about the guard's voice drew Corri's attention. She moved closer, searching the browned oval face illuminated in the torchlight. The guard's pale blue eyes widened, the full lips curving in a smile, as her eyes met Corri's.

"Breela?" Corri stepped closer. "It is you. So you made it to the Temple after all and into Her Own, I see."

"We have both come a long way from our lives in Hadliden and the injustices of Asur," the woman answered. Bitter memories hardened the woman's eyes. "Perhaps we can talk when I am not on duty."

"Yes," Corri answered with a lift of her hand. "We might be here for some time." She followed Imandoff and Takra across the worn courtyard stones toward the building that housed the audience hall of the Temple of the Great Mountain.

As they climbed the steps and passed the massive gong in the shadowed alcove by the hall door, Takra flicked the metal disk with her finger, then raised her eyebrows in surprise as a deep rolling sound murmured through the still evening air.

"By the time a warrior made it across the courtyard to ring this, a skilled enemy could be within the walls." Scowling, she flicked it again with her finger.

"It is used by those wishing to become initiates." Imandoff tugged open one of the great doors and stepped into the wavering lantern light of the great audience hall. His voice was muted as he spoke over his shoulder. "And by those seeking an audience with the High Priestess and at one time with the Jabed."

The only light in the great, long room came from the lanterns on either side of the alcove door and two more at the foot of the dais at the far end. Corri saw Takra's hand fall to her sword hilt as the Tuonela stared down the room. Her own hand rested lightly on her dagger as she watched the jumping shadows flickering over the pillars, illuminating for an instance the painted murals on the walls and the stone-latticed windows that ran down one side of the room.

"Come." Imandoff's face was a mask of light and shadow from the overhead lantern. "The Oracle will be here shortly."

Imandoff silently walked across the smooth floor toward the dais, Corri and Takra at his heels. When he reached the steps, he stopped and leaned on his staff, staring up at the single high-backed chair. As the purple draperies covering the wall behind the chair moved gently, Corri's hand tightened on her dagger. She felt Takra's shoulder flinch where it rubbed against hers.

Even Takra worries that we may find unpleasant things here now. Corri glanced at her friend, but Takra's eyes were locked on the curtain. *We found too many initiates in the other Mystery Schools chasing after power over others to fully trust without seeing how things have changed.*

The slender figure of the young Oracle stepped through a break in the draperies. The woman's head and the lower part of her face were covered by a violet veil; its folds swept back over her shoulders.

"Greetings, Dream Warrior." The Oracle's quiet voice carried clearly through the silent room. "And welcome to you and your companions. There are refreshments in my quarters." She reached out one pale hand to draw aside the purple draperies. "The High Priestess and captain of Her Own will join us there."

Corri and her companions climbed the steps and followed the Oracle through a short passageway that opened into the young woman's private quarters.

The Oracle motioned them to a semi-circle of chairs arcing out from each side of a tall-backed seat. The young woman sat down, her dark head resting against the high back. She pulled aside her violet veil, revealing her face. Purple smudges of exhaustion underscored her dark eyes; two pin-scratches of new wrinkles shown plain between her dark eyebrows.

"I see you carry the ancient helmet." The Oracle pointed to the bag in Corri's hand. "I have consulted with all those familiar with the ancient writings. They, in turn, have searched through our oldest books. But we have found no clue as to the resting place of the rest of Varanna's armor." She smiled at Takra. "We swept the Temple clean of all trouble-makers. You need not fear secret plans here."

Takra sank into one of the chairs with a sigh, stretching her long legs before her. Corri sat beside her, the ties of the bag clutched in her hands.

Imandoff took a chair beside the young girl, a puzzled frown creasing his forehead. "There are no oral tales, some among the country people?" He pulled at his beard when the Oracle shook her head. "I thought not, or I would have heard them in my travels. The oldest books . . ." His voice trailed off as he thought.

"Perhaps you will tarry long enough to look at those books yourself," the Oracle said. "Many of the oldest scrolls contain archaic words and phrases that have double meanings. Perhaps a clue lies there. Some of them are so tattered that pieces of the parchment are missing. Only one who has long studied the history of the Peoples could guess what might have once been written there." She turned toward Corri with a faint smile. "And while this scholarly sorcerer seeks through ancient tomes, the blacksmith will have time to complete the reforging of the blade to fit into Varanna's sword hilt."

"If Imandoff does not find what we seek in the ancient books," Corri said, "we dare not stay here. The Harvest Moon is not far off."

"Yes, the Harvest Moon." The tall High Priestess, clad in leather armor, a sword swinging at her side, stood in the doorway. A metal helmet with a silver crescent moon on top covered all but a few strands of her dark hair. "Kantal, the Temple astrologer, has just learned the importance of this coming Harvest Moon."

Corri's surprise at the woman's silent entrance was mirrored in Takra's face.

"The heavens will be the same as when Varanna fought her last battle." Corri's voice was barely audible. "A guess," she said as Imandoff raised his eyebrows in question.

"Not quite the same, but close enough," answered Vairya as she sank into a chair beside the sorcerer. "However, Kantal says that the major stars and planets will be in the same places and making the same conjunctions." She pulled off her helmet and pushed damp strands of hair from her face.

"So the same powerful magickal energies will be affecting Sar Akka at the Harvest Moon." Imandoff rubbed the bluestone buckle on his belt. "If Kantal knows this, you can be certain that Kayth knows it too."

"Yes," said the Oracle, leaning her head back against her chair, deep weariness in her eyes. "This underscores the warnings in my dreams. It is imperative that you find Varanna's body-armor before the battle with Frav."

"And if we do not?" Takra fingered the medallion hanging on her breast.

The Oracle's eyes were black pools of concern as she looked at the Wind-Rider. "Then we may lose our freedom to worship the Goddess, to live our lives as we choose. If the tide of battle turns against us, the Peoples will drown under the tide of Volikvi-driven Fravashi pouring over the land."

"Looks like the room we shared the first time we came to the Temple," Takra said as she sank onto one of the narrow beds. "At least we will not have to worry about vermin in the mattresses."

"We probably will not see much of Imandoff," Corri answered as she pulled off her boots. "Already he is deep in those ancient scrolls. Do you think he will discover the resting place of Varanna's armor?" She slid her boot knife under the flat pillow out of habit.

"If anyone can find that armor, Imandoff can." Takra stripped off her trousers and ruffled shirt. She held up the nightshift with a grimace, then shook her head as she dropped it back onto the stool.

"Takra, the statue we found in the mountain cavern, do you think it plays a part in all this?" Corri asked.

"Willa of High Limna says not," the Wind-Rider answered. "That is why I felt safe in leaving it with her. She promised to bring it when the child is born. I did not want the ancient statue broken in our hard riding."

Wrapping herself in a robe, Takra gathered up the towels left on the bed. "The priestess said there is a bathing room just down the hall. Are you coming?"

Corri's answer was interrupted by a swift knock on the door. Before either woman could move, the door flew open and a little girl burst into the room.

"Dakhma!" Corri held out her arms as the Tuonela child raced toward her. She lifted the thin girl onto her lap, smoothing the light brown hair and smiling down into the gray eyes.

"The priestess said I should wait until morning, but I had to talk with you." Dakhma's face was serious. "They have explained to us the dangers you must face, Dream Warrior. And we had to tell you something." She turned toward the door and called, "Come here, Athdar. I told you they would not be angry."

A very small boy shuffled around the corner of the open door. Corri's breath caught in her throat as the child stepped fully into the lamplight. The dark golden-brown hair was set off by the black lashes and brows above the light hazel, almost lidless eyes.

"He is just a baby," she said softly. She remembered the face of his father Ayron, the Soothsayer, comparing it to this tiny child.

"Come," Takra said, holding out a sun-tanned hand. "We will not harm you."

The strength of the nose, chin, and cheekbones was softened as a smile warmed the little boy's face. He took Takra's hand without hesitation. She sat down on a stool and took him into her lap.

"I like Athdar," Dakhma said. "He is my friend, even if he is littler." She took Corri's face in her hands to make her look at her. "Dream Warrior, I do not have your powers. The priestesses say mine are different, but sometimes I feel things." One hand dropped to touch her abdomen, then lifted to touch the center of her forehead. "Or I know things. Do you understand?"

"Yes." Corri nodded.

"Your strange stone, the owl stone." Dakhma struggled to find the words. "There is more to it than you have discovered. I do not know its full power, just that it is stronger than you know. When you go into battle against Frav, trust the stone."

"Frav!" The little boy's voice changed into a guttural growl, ending in a hiss that raised the hair on Corri's neck.

Takra looked down in shocked surprise at the child in her lap. Athdar's face contorted into the wrinkled muzzle of a strange creature, his hands raised like claws prepared to strike.

"Athdar, there is no danger here." The deep voice from the shadowed doorway caught the boy's attention. His crooked fingers straightened; the overlay of alien characteristics faded from his face. "I thought I might find you two with the Dream Warrior."

A tall slender woman clad in a white robe stepped into the room. Her black hair, streaked with strands of white, was pulled back into a knot at the nape of her neck. From a thick silver chain about her neck hung a crystal pendant.

"How are you adjusting to life in the Temple, Zanitra?" Takra soothed Athdar's tremblings by gently stroking his hair. "If you seek your brother, look to the rooms where they keep the ancient scrolls. You know how he is when he is tracking an old mystery."

"I like the Temple," Zanitra answered as she closed the door behind her. "As for Imandoff, I did not come to speak with him. I came for these errant children and to see you, Takra Wind-Rider." A wide smile lit the long narrow face and high bridged nose with an inner beauty. "I came to welcome the mother of Imandoff's child and one who, I hope, will be my Sister-Friend." She placed her wide strong hands on Takra's shoulders, then bent to kiss her cheek.

"I would welcome you as Sister-Friend," Takra said softly. "But with this battle to come, who knows if the child or I will live. If I should fall, and the child live, will you raise it as your own?" Takra's amber eyes locked with Zanitra's brown ones.

"I give my word, but we must trust in the Lady to bring you through safely." Zanitra gripped the warrior woman's shoulder for an instant, then she turned to smile at Corri. "So has Dakhma delivered her urgent message?"

"Yes, and it is something I must think on," Corri answered. "I know the owl stone amplifies my emotions and power. Beyond that it is a mystery to me."

"In time the Lady will reveal what you need to know. Breela sends word that the Asuran women who came with her are learning the way of the sword. They are going out on patrol in Deep Rising early tomorrow." Zanitra took a stool beside Takra. "The network of women left behind in Asur still get reports out with the merchants who travel to Kystan. When the last battle comes, we cannot look for aid from Asur, no more than from Sadko." Zanitra's mouth twisted in bitterness at the name of the Mystery School she had left. "Word has come from the Green Men that Sadko has shut its doors to all and the government in Asur has tightened its control over the people. No, we need expect no aid from them."

"Are Dakhma and Athdar safe here?" Corri's mind leaped back over the dangers she had faced to get Dakhma to the Temple and the promise she had made to the dying Ayron.

"There are no traitors in this Temple!" Zanitra's voice was confident. "The Oracle swept clean when she threw out the Jabed and his followers."

"Where is this Jabed now?" Takra asked. The little boy leaned his head sleepily against her breast.

"The Green Men and the mountain people drove them from place to place in Deep Rising," Zanitra answered. "Once they showed signs of running for Frav, raiding and terrorizing as they went, but then they retreated once more into the mountains. Lately they have been quiet, hatching some new plot, no doubt." She motioned with her hand to Dakhma. "I know two children who are long past their bedtime."

The Tuonela child smiled at Corri and obediently slid from her lap as Zanitra picked up the sleeping Athdar. Takra held open the door as the healer, followed by Dakhma, disappeared into the lamp-shadowed hallway.

"Is the boy not young to come into such powers as shape-shifting?" Takra asked as she once more gathered up her towels.

"I was his age when I first dream-flew," Corri answered. She tried to smother a yawn and failed. "Go off to your bath, Sister-Friend. I cannot stay awake much longer."

Takra grinned as Corri lay down on the narrow bed. "Sleep well, Corri. Tomorrow we shall seek out the blacksmith and see what magick he works on your sword."

Corri was already slipping into sleep when the Wind-Rider quietly closed the door.

Morvrana laid her plans carefully to coincide with the absence of the High Clua, who had gone with some of the older initiates into the mountains in search of rare healing herbs. She waited for a moonless night when the remaining initiates were sleeping before she silently left her dormitory room and slipped through the central courtyard of the Mystery School at Leshy. The stone paths were shadow-striped by the weak lantern light that fell across the herb beds.

Wrapped and hooded in a dark cloak, the woman paused by the great door to the High Clua's quarters, listening for any sound within. She eased open the door, slipped inside, and closed it without so much as a click of the latch.

Now we shall see how worthy I am of advancement! The old High Clua set a path for this School, and Jehennette is making changes I do not like. This so-called Dream Warrior is not the only one who can master the Mask of Darkness.

Morvrana frowned toward the inner door of the High Clua's empty rooms before taking a flight of stairs down to the deep vaults beneath the building. Down she went and along the eerie, black, rock-hewn corridor, dark shadows reluctantly retreating before her light, until she came to the iron gates. These she opened with the key stolen from the High Clua's rooms that afternoon. The grating of the lock echoed back along the corridor. Morvrana listened, but there was only silence from the floors high above.

Beyond the inner gates hung a heavy blackness that seemed to push against her, denying her entrance to the ancient chamber. Pushing aside a momentary sense of apprehension, she quickly moved along the short corridor that ended in another door of time-hardened wood. This barrier creaked ominously as it yielded to the key from the high shelf by the door.

At last! Morvrana set her lantern on a rock shelf by the door beside a tiny lamp and a miniature goblet, then closed the door. *Jehennette has never undergone this Trial, but I shall. And by passing this ancient test, I shall prove myself worthy of leading Leshy. When I control Leshy, I will sweep it clean of all dissenters! I shall return it to the original path set by the only High Clua I will ever acknowledge.*

She swept the dark chamber with a glance, noting the spring, the light-drinking Mask, and the high-backed silver chair.

Pushing back the hood of her cloak, Morvrana took up the goblet and filled it with water from the tiny spring to one side of the rock-walled room. She hesitated only a second before taking it and the little bottle of herbal tincture with her to the throne-like chair in the center of the chamber.

The Dream Warrior was only able to take two drops, she sneered. *I am able to withstand more.*

She tipped four drops of the dangerous mixture into the water, swirled it twice, and quickly drank it. She set the bottle and goblet on the floor next to the chair, then took up the Mask of Darkness from its nearby pedestal.

I have the courage to go into the other realms and do deeds this so-called Dream Warrior dared not do. Regardless of what Jehennette says, I know I have depths of power within myself that will be released. I do this for the good of Leshy, she told herself.

She stared down at the ancient Mask in her hands. Its dull surface drew in the lamplight, reflecting nothing, while the faceted crystal eye-pieces glittered like the eyes of strange animals. A sense of strangeness began to slip over her as the potion coursed through her body.

I shall conquer this Trial, and when I succeed, the others will gladly make me the High Clua. When Malya lived here in the School, she sought knowledge and power only to sell it to Frav. I undergo this test, not for the benefit of that Fravashi-loving spy, but for the good of Leshy.

Morvrana slipped the Mask of Darkness over her head and stared through the eye-pieces that broke the view of the chamber into a thousand tiny pieces. She leaned back against the chair, watching the lamplight begin to glow with strange colors. The drip and murmur of the little spring intensified, then faded away like sounds echoing down a long tunnel.

She gasped as reality was ripped away. She felt as if she were being sucked into a maelstrom of deepest blackness. Bursting through the choking darkness, Morvrana found herself still gently swaying, but now in the center of blinding, pulsing, colored light. She vaguely felt her fingers clutched on the chair arms, but those fingers seemed to belong to someone else.

The ancient records speak of going through a sea of old memories and future possibilities before you can reach the center of the mind-maze.

Morvrana tried to force her mind to seek the center of possibilities, but she had no control. Nebulous faces came at her from all sides, their mouths working, but she heard no sounds. Some she recognized and impatiently pushed aside; others she did not know. She ignored them all. Finally she passed once more into a place of darkness, her mind exhausted but determined. There, she spied a tiny pinprick of light and willed herself into it.

All around her were strands of brilliant light, some straight, others twisted about each other. These threads pulsed with energy, changing colors as they touched, then danced away. They swept around her and on into the blackness. Within these life-threads, Morvrana saw moving pictures of events, forms and faces of people.

Now I shall change my future. Morvrana moved among the life-threads, searching for the one she wanted. *These are nothing to me,* she thought as she cast aside thread after thread. *I command that my life-thread appear!*

A tangle of several threads moved into her hands. With a cry of triumph, Morvrana grabbed at the knotted threads in which she saw herself. Then she frowned and her anger rose.

No! I do not accept this. I deserve better!

She plucked at the tight knots, then in frustration ripped the threads apart. Loose ends whipped back and forth, trying to reunite, but the woman slapped them aside. As she looked down at the end of the life-thread in her hands, she cried out in anguish. What she held was a shortened life, the picture within the thread changing to show her death during the Trial. She reached out and plucked up a thread whose pictures showed a future Leshy. Determined, Morvrana knotted the threads together, then again looked at the picture within. This time it showed Jehennette, the High Clua, returning to take back control of the School.

No, I will make it otherwise! The woman ripped out that section of pictures and cast the broken thread into the swirling energies about her. She caught at a thread revealing her sitting in the High Clua's chair, a smile of triumph on her face. *This is the one.* Quickly, she knotted it to the others in her hand. *My will has triumphed! I have done what even Jehennette has not dared to do!*

Morvrana released the life-thread into the moving mass of colored ribbons sweeping by her. Her mind clouded with self-importance, she failed to notice the strange movement of the thread as the portions she had ripped away reunited, changing the pictures flowing within it.

Release my hidden powers, she commanded. *I do not ask but demand that you do this. And you powers of this realm must answer my bidding.* She felt a powerful surge of unknown energy pulse through her. Streams of energy poured from her fingertips as she held up her hands.

At the edges of her mind, Morvrana heard the incessant whispering of many voices, the words indistinct yet persistent. She shook her head to clear it but the voices remained. The words became clearer, a babble of sound from disembodied spirits whom she felt but could not see. She concentrated on one voice out of the invisible multitude and found that the others faded away.

You called for aid from this realm. I am here to do your bidding. The masculine voice spoke within her mind, deep with power. *I will aid you in your quest for control of Leshy.*

Who are you? Morvrana demanded. A great dark eye surrounded by swirling blackness sprang into her inner vision. She reached out with her mind to test the spirit within the eye, finding only a sense of power and knowledge overlaid with what appeared to be good will.

I am Azzi, came the answer. *I have long waited for you to reach out for the power that is rightfully yours. I will be your advisor, your friend, even your lover if you wish it.*

Morvrana smiled as she felt the spirit move closer. *Then stay with me, Azzi. Give me control of Leshy.* She felt the spirit slide closer until it was like a second skin around her own nebulous body. *Now back to my body,* Morvrana ordered. *I command that I be returned at once to the physical realm!*

A surge of power shot through her as she felt her mind snap back into her physical body. For several moments she clung to the chair arms, the chamber swirling and dipping around her, the tinkle of the spring like a huge pounding drum in her ears. The lamplight tortured her sight; tears streamed down her cheeks. Every line of carving on the chair felt like a knife against her back.

Breathe! Morvrana heard Azzi order as she fought against a crushing weight on her chest. *Breathe, and go forth to take your rightful place in the High Clua's seat.*

Slowly, the woman began to take deep breaths. She felt the prickle of circulation returning to her arms and legs, her sweat-dampened hair clinging to her cheeks and neck. Removing the Mask, she staggered upright and laughed aloud. She lurched to the spring where she splashed her face and neck with water; then she continued her pacing about the shadow-filled chamber until she felt she could manage the flights of stairs without falling.

Lantern in hand, Morvrana made her way back up the stairs and out into the herb-filled courtyard. The stars in the black sky were sharp points of scintillating light to her drugged mind as she gazed upward. She set down the lantern and thrust her arms skyward.

"Fire, come to my command!" she shouted. "Let all within these walls see my power!"

Bolt after bolt of red flame shot upward from her fingertips as she shouted. Thunderous booms echoed around the courtyard, bouncing off the dormitory walls and shattering the peaceful stillness.

"Morvrana, you have succeeded?" A robed man crept out of the darkness to stand before her. The shadowed figures of other men and women stood behind him.

Show these little followers what you and I can do, Azzi said. *Let them learn to fear what might happen if they disobey.*

"Can Jehennette or her prized Dream Warrior do this?" Morvrana pointed a forefinger at the stones at her feet and smiled as the rock bubbled, melted, and turned into a spring of water flowing across the other stones. "Do not the laws of Leshy say that only the most powerful shall be High Clua? *I* am the most powerful here. *I* shall be High Clua."

Initiates poured from the dormitories, wrapped in blankets or clad only in nightshifts. They huddled behind Morvrana's followers, their frightened voices a low murmur.

"The laws of Leshy are clear," the man said in a disdainful voice as he turned to the crowd behind him. "By law Morvrana is most fit to be the High Clua. And so all must acknowledge from this time onward."

"What is this?" Jehennette pushed her way through the crowd of confused and frightened initiates, still clad in her dust-covered traveling cloak. "I enter the gates of Leshy to find confusion and strange bursts of fire. You." The High Clua faced Morvrana across the flickering lantern. "I see by your eyes, by the very energy field around you, that you have dared the Trial of the Mask. You were not prepared, indeed are not even fit, to try such a thing!"

"The old High Clua thought me fit enough to stand at her side, to hold power," Morvrana said, her eyes narrowed. "Then you took her place, Jehennette, and turned this School from the path she set for it. You set me to distilling herbs and dispensing medicines, a far cry from my deep studies under your predecessor."

Now bind her! whispered Azzi. *Let her and these others see your power. Let them fear!*

Morvrana pointed a finger at the High Clua. A bright line of projected energy splashed over Jehennette, preventing her from moving or speaking. "Take her, and any who come to her aid, and cast them into the chamber of the Mask. See if she has the courage to undergo the Trial of the Mask."

Jehennette's face turned red with her efforts to break the spell, but she was held fast. Morvrana's followers surrounded the High Clua and hustled her into the building toward her prison. None of the shocked initiates moved, their frightened whispers barely audible over Morvrana's laughter. Her shrieks of triumph were echoed by Azzi's laughter in her mind.

At the back of the crowd, two young girls edged farther into the shadows, then turned and hurried away. As part of the High Clua's herb-seeking party, they were still dressed in their trail-dusty clothing. They gathered up their travel bags and crept unseen out the great gates.

"Here!" a male voice called softly from a side street as they passed.

The startled girls hesitated, then darted into the shadowed alley as they heard raised the voices of pursuers behind them in the School compound.

"Quickly! This way." The light pouring from a high window briefly illuminated the face of Taillefer the song-smith. He led the girls down the alley to another street, where they paused before darting across to the blackness of another alley.

"How did you know to come?" one of the girls asked.

"I have power enough to sense what happened inside those walls," Taillefer answered. "Come. Renaga will hide you until the caravans leave for Kystan in the morning," he whispered as he scratched on one of the doors opening into the dark alley. "I know a pleasure house is not a place for sheltered girls from the Mystery School, but it is the only place I can be certain you will be safe."

"We know Renaga," the girl with black curls said softly. "We have helped her and her women before."

The door opened, revealing a scantily clad woman. The girls hurried inside while Taillefer disappeared down the alley toward the Cup and Sword.

"We must find the Dream Warrior, Sallin. It is the only chance to free Mother," the fair-haired girl said to her sister as they followed the pleasure woman up a back stairs to Renaga's private quarters.

"Yes, Merra," answered Sallin, pushing back black curls from her face. "But first we must go to Kystan to warn the High Priestess at the Temple. We must take care, though, for Morvrana will send her followers after us. Tomorrow we must be very careful to lose ourselves among the other travelers."

"If all else fails, we will flee into Deep Rising," Merra whispered. "The feya women will take us in. Morvrana will not dare set foot in any of the mountain villages."

"I thought I felt someone else behind Morvrana." Sallin frowned in thought. "But when I tried to touch that presence with my mind, I found only a repulsive blank place."

"Could she be possessed?" Merra asked.

Sallin shrugged. "Possession is rare."

"But dangerous to us all if she has allowed it. Something is very wrong at Leshy. I feel our only hope is to find the Dream Warrior."

A week passed, with Takra daily practicing with the warrior women of Her Own in their swordplay in the Temple courtyard and Imandoff buried until late hours in the vast library. Corri became increasingly bored and nervous. At first she was drawn to the bellowing forges of the Temple blacksmith, but once the gleaming blade of the sword was finished and attached to the ancient hilt, she lost interest. When Gadavar appeared at the Temple early one morning, Corri could scarcely contain her joy. After the Green Man delivered his messages to the Oracle, he came to Corri's room, slipping in quietly and unannounced.

"Gadavar! I thought I might miss you." Corri leaned her cheek against his broad chest, her previous discontent forgotten in the circle of his arms.

"I would never leave without seeing you." His breath gently ruffled her hair as he spoke. "The Oracle herself showed me the way here and set a guard. We are to have a little time together, undisturbed." He laughed softly. "I thought there were strict rules here against such intimate meetings, but the Oracle told me she would make an exception for us."

Corri raised her head to look into Gadavar's eyes. "Why?"

But Gadavar laughed and kissed her into silence. "Accept the gift without questions," he finally said. "This time is ours to do as we will with her blessing."

"Then I want to spend this time in loving, in feeling your arms around me," Corri whispered. *If I cannot change the future, I can at least store up memories.*

Gadavar lifted her into his arms and carried her to the narrow bed. His hands quivered as he slowly removed her clothing and then his. Corri sank back on the bed and reached her arms to him. Without a word, they lay together, losing themselves in loving and being loved.

As they lay in each other's arms, Corri sighed as she ran her fingers over Gadavar's muscled body, memorizing every part of him. "How soon must you return to Deep Rising?" she finally asked.

"Before nightfall." He kissed both her eyes, then her mouth. "Many troubling things are happening in the mountains and along the border with Asur. Come with me."

"I cannot. The Oracle told us we must seek Varanna's armor in preparation for the final battle." Corri bit her lip and pushed back the tears she felt burning her eyes. "Why must we be kept apart like this?"

"It will not always be this way, my love." Gadavar hugged her to him. "When this war is over, I will take you with me to Deep Rising. I have a cabin there. I will show you all the beautiful sunsets over the Valley of Whispers, the secret waterfalls and the hidden places the deer go with their little ones in the spring."

The Green Man spoke on of the wonders seldom seen by any except the mountain guardians, and Corri soaked up his words and love, storing them in her heart and soul. She resented the little time she had with Gadavar, yet was thankful she had what little she did. When he left an hour before sunset, Corri went with him to the gate.

"I will think of you often," he whispered as he held her close. "As I know you think of me. I will always love you, Corri, never forget that. I will protect you with all my heart, my strength, my very soul."

"I love you," she whispered back. "I will never love anyone but you." *Shall I tell him of the child?* But the words stuck in her throat, and she said nothing.

Corri watched until Gadavar and his horse Nuisance were lost from sight in the city streets beyond the moated island of the Temple. Then she wandered back to her empty room.

Takra must be with Imandoff, she thought as she straightened the blankets on her bed. *I feel as if I am waiting for something to happen,* she thought as she paced up and down the room she and Takra shared, the unfamiliar weight of the sword swinging against her hip. *I have had no definite dream-warnings but still I feel something is wrong.*

Her thoughts leapt back to the bellowing forge and the blacksmith standing before the glowing fire. In his muscled hands he held out to her the reforged blade of Varanna set in the ancient hilt.

"I have put what magick I can into the blade," the man had said. "But I dared not use any on the hilt. Yet the blade and hilt went together as if they had always belonged so." He shook his head as he placed the sword into Corri's hands. "When I joined blade and hilt, there was a rush of power beyond what I could have imparted to this weapon. May it guard you, Dream Warrior, wherever you go and whatever you do." He hesitated, then went on. "Follow the way you are led and do what you must do. Do not let the fears or desires of others rule your actions." The man turned quickly back to his forge.

Corri was alerted by the blacksmith's words and for the first time consciously noted the extra guards in the corridor leading to her room. She knew she had been too caught up in thinking of Gadavar and the child she carried, but still she chided herself for not being more alert.

You have been lazy and careless, Farblood. You would not last a night as a thief now.

She carefully checked the room itself and found what she should have noticed the first time she entered. There was no way to escape through the windows, not so much as the tiniest of ledges on the outside of the building, even if she could have broken out the thick lattices. At least one guard was on duty at all times somewhere in the corridor, removing any opportunity to leave that way unseen. Even when she casually walked about the Temple courtyard, there was always someone loitering along behind, watching her.

By the hell fires of Frav, she thought as she continued pacing the room. *Once more I am a prisoner of a Mystery School, although this time I cannot see why. The Oracle knows I am willing to help. But something, or someone, here interferes, not only with my freedom and the strengthening of my powers, but also with my dream-flying.*

She shuddered as she thought of the strange dream-events that had come to haunt her while in this Temple. Each time she tried to dream-fly, she came up against a heavy veil of darkness. In its center was a swirling mass lit deep within by a strange red glow. Each time she faced that curtain and kept herself from being sucked into it, she would see a great Eye staring at her out of the whirling blackness. Then across this black veil would flash an image of the great serpent, rainbow colors glinting from its scales as it struck at the Eye. Instantly, Corri would find herself back in her physical body.

An Eye of Darkness, she thought. *I know it is evil, yet I feel no earthly intelligence directing it. It is as if something within the abyss of the Otherworlds has waked and become aware of me for the first time. And what does the serpent mean? But what does any of this have to do with my being guarded, a prisoner of the Temple?* She paused in her pacing, her brows pulled together in thought. *It is the power of this place that hinders me! The Oracle draws upon the power here to protect us, not realizing that this power has made evil entities in the Otherworlds aware of my presence. The very power that is a strength to the Oracle is a weakness to me. I must get out of here!*

Be strong, Dream Warrior. The voice of the Goddess was as clear as if She stood at Corri's side. *I will guide your steps on the right path. It is time for you to leave this place, to go into the mountains again.*

Corri paced back to the latticed window and gripped the sill with both hands as she watched the warriors dancing in swordplay in the courtyard below. *Lady, should we leave tonight?* There was no answer to Corri's question, merely an intense feeling that she must go at once. *If I try to warn Imandoff and Takra, the Oracle and High Priestess will find some way to convince them otherwise. And all of them will truly believe that here I am safe. But I am not!*

"Dream Warrior?" A soft voice interrupted her thoughts.

Corri turned to find one of the Temple priestesses standing in the doorway.

"The Oracle sends a message," the young woman said. "She has noticed your discontent and suggests a ride about the countryside for a day or so. One of the warriors will wait for you in the audience hall. Whatever supplies you need you may take from the kitchens." The priestess smiled when Corri nodded agreement, then disappeared into the corridor.

I have no need of a keeper, she thought as she hastily packed her saddle bags. She pushed her Tuonela leather clothing deep in the bags, slung the saddlebags over her shoulder, and grabbed the bag containing the ancient helmet in the other hand. *Nor do I need a guard to bring me back here if I decide otherwise. This place is beginning to feel like a trap.* She thought of her captivity at Leshy under the old High Clua. *I need to talk with someone who has no connection with the Mystery Schools, but one who has a strong sense of the land, the people themselves, and the Lady. I need to talk with Uzza of Springwell and I need to do it by myself,* she suddenly decided as she strode out of the room and down the long corridor toward the outer doors.

"Tell Imandoff and Takra Wind-Rider that I ride out to see the countryside," she told the guard in the courtyard. "I will be back within a day or so."

Her thoughts jumped back to the voice in her dream while on the journey to Kirisan. *The key to the hiding place of Varanna's armor lies in Deep Rising,* the dream-voice said. *I will go there after I speak with Uzza. I should have asked Gadavar if he knew the riddle of the key.*

Quickly, Corri gathered supplies at the kitchen, then hurried to the stable, where she saddled Mouse. She paused long enough to send out a tendril of thought to Gadavar, but she abruptly cut it off when she felt a curious probing from somewhere in the Temple. Determined to be gone before the warrior appointed as her escort could find her, Corri Farblood was quickly out of Kystan and riding toward the mountains of Deep Rising.

Chapter 3

Kayth Farblood sat in thought, his blunt fingers steepled against his lips, as he stared down at the black cloth bag on the dark table before him. A faint odor of old rotted flesh rose from the bag; the noxious odor subtly blended with the powerful fumes of harsh incense curling up from a burning brazier set against one of the slick black walls of the chamber. Two thick yellowish candles burned brightly at each end of the table; they cast their wavering light over the man's face, outlining his cruel mouth and reflecting in his ice-water blue eyes. The candle-light flickered across the furnishings, gilt-edged and gem-trimmed. Rolled scrolls, their edges tattered with age, and rare bound books filled a shelf by the thick door.

"So you will dare this thing?" A woman clad only in a diaphanous robe and a gold decorated girdle moved closer to the table, her black eyes intent on the strange bag. "By doing this you can gain great power?" Her gold-painted nipples rose and fell with her excited breathing.

"Do you think to secretly try it, Xephena?" Kayth raised his eyes, cold and forbidding, to meet hers. His mouth curved in a cruel smile as she drew back, shaking her head. "So there is wisdom in you, Trow, besides your fascinating sexual skills. To answer you, yes, I will do this thing, and yes, I will gain great power."

"Minepa was a devious man, one who lived for power and the flow of blood on Jevotan's altar." Xephena pursed her lips as she sank back onto a cushioned bench. "Unlike you, Kayth, he was not a man of vision beyond the power he had within his grasp." Her pointed tongue brushed across her scarlet lips as she pushed back a lock of raven hair. The candle flame caught the red tints in her long curls, creating a halo of dark flame about her face.

"Minepa was also easily misled, Xephena. Do not make that mistake with me." Kayth's cold eyes continued to stare at her without blinking. "Have you forgotten so soon that I ordered all to call me Jinniyah and not by my Otherworld name?"

"Forgive me, Jinniyah." The Trow priestess nervously fingered the three earrings in her left ear. "The power I see within you is intoxicating, exciting to me. But I would never underestimate your power. Only you are able to read the Books of Darkness, the Books of the ancient Jinniyah. Only your knowledge of those old powers can restore the worship of Jevotan to all the Peoples, even to our enemies, the Goddess-loving Clans. It is right that you should take his place, his rooms." She waved a hand to the chamber around them.

"Leave me, Xephena." Kayth stared down once more at the black bag on the table.

Enjoy your power while you can, Kayth, Xephena thought as she walked to the door, her wide hips swaying below her narrow waist. *As soon as you win this battle for Frav, you will die under my claw blades, and Zalmoxis will take your place.* She glanced back at Kayth, who still stared fixedly at the bag.

"Xephena, do not ever come into my presence wearing your claw blades. The day you do, you die." Kayth did not even look up as the Trow hesitated briefly, a flicker of fear in her eyes. The Trow priestess closed the door softly as she left the High Priest's chamber.

"Now to perform the ancient spells from Jinniyah's book," Kayth said in a voice barely above a whisper. He scrubbed one blunt hand through his bright red hair. "You and I shall join spirits, Minepa. I shall absorb and control your power and knowledge. Then the people of Sar Akka will see such a powerful leader as they have never seen before."

And you, my daughter, will come willingly into my hands when I call. Your powers may conceal and protect you now, but when I have taken in Minepa's spirit, I shall once more be the stronger. Kayth smiled as he pictured Corri kneeling before him. *Now where is the best place to perform these rituals unobserved by spying eyes and listening ears? No, not here,* he thought as he tossed a handful of incense onto the smoldering coals of the brazier. *My private chamber is more secure.*

He took up the black bag from the table, smiling to himself as he opened the heavy door and strode down the hall toward the stairs. Down one level he went, then along a torch-lit hallway until he came to a door carved with the leering faces of demons. Kayth inserted his forefinger into the open mouth of the central demon until a hidden lock clicked. The door swung open silently.

Barring the heavy door behind him, Kayth's ice-cold blue eyes raked the room. Flickering black candles burned at the four corners of a waist-high stone block in the center of the room. Iron chains and shackles set in the block's sides cast crooked, twisting shadows across the deep red stone floor. The room smelled of throat-choking incense and old tortures. He went to the block, laid the black bag onto the bloodstained stone, and carefully pulled a skull from its depths.

Part of one side of the hideous skull was patched back in place with clay, where Tirkul's horse Hellstorm had danced his rage upon the fallen Volikvi priest. Turning the skull until the empty eye sockets faced him, the man stared down at the hole pierced through the top. One cheekbone bore a crescent indentation from a horse's hoof, the bone cracked and driven back into the socket. The skull was bare, picked clean of flesh and brains by insects and small animals, but a musty odor of rot still rose in the air of the room.

"My daughter was too strong for you, Minepa," Kayth said to the grinning skull, his own mouth twisted in a satisfied smirk. "Her powers slew you with one stroke of lightning through your head. Be glad it was her, not me, Minepa, for I would not have killed you so quickly." He stroked the shattered cheek with his blunt fingers. "I would have kept your body alive, your mind alert, while I practiced every known torture. You would have died only when I tired of hearing you whine and plead. You were weak, Minepa, and I shall prove it by taking in your spirit and binding you to do my will now."

Kayth turned, kicking off his low boots and stripping off his robe as he went to a wall cabinet. From it he pulled out another robe, gem-encrusted and stinking with strange incenses and old blood. Dressed in this robe he took out an ancient scroll from a chest and spread it beside the skull, anchoring the fragile corners with four small statues from a nearby shelf. He opened another chest and pulled out a sword, a small dagger, and a strange jar carved to resemble a hideous demon's head.

Laying the ritual tools on the stone block according to instruction in the scroll, Kayth then stood for a moment, exalting in the excitement building within him.

"At last," he said. "I will take the power that is rightfully mine. I planned for this day, worked for it, and it shall be done!" His shout echoed in the high ceilinged room. "I, Kayth Farblood, exile from another world, shall establish a kingdom so powerful that no one can destroy it or go against my will!"

Moving counterclockwise around the room, Kayth carefully drew two semi-circles with a piece of crumbling white stone, one crescent at each end of the chamber. He then connected their curved ends with zigzag lines that led to the corners of the central block upon which the skull rested. Stepping carefully to avoid smudging the lines, Kayth moved back to the altar. He then sketched a triangle to enclose the skull.

The chants written on the old scroll were in a language unknown to the present Volikvi priests of the Fire Temple, but Kayth had practiced reading them until they now rolled off his tongue like a second language.

Once he paused to cast incense from the demon-jar onto the burner, another time to open a small vein in his wrist with the dagger and let the blood drip onto the smoking coals.

In a commanding voice Kayth chanted in the forgotten tongue until his body was dripping with perspiration, his bright red hair wet and clinging to his cheeks. He lost all sense of time; the ritual was the only thing real to him as he meticulously followed the scroll's instructions.

The shadows cast by the candlelight began to thicken and creep toward the altar. What had been ordinary darkness became a mass of blackness that no light could dispel or penetrate. Within this unnatural darkness were far-off flickers of dark blood red, like the glow of the fires deep within the crack in the lower levels of the Fire Temple. A hint of volcanic sulfur tinged the air, an undercurrent to the stinking incense smoke that coiled through the chamber, finally drawn out through the air vents set high in the walls.

Kayth took up the sword and tapped the broken skull, first on one side, then on the other, while he chanted. Perspiration dripped from his nose and chin and ran in streams down his body beneath the heavy robe. With a feeling of triumph, he shouted the last words on the scroll, then stared at the skull in expectation.

Deep within the empty sockets a red glow began to pulse like a slow, rhythmic heartbeat. Kayth's eyes narrowed as the cracked jawbone moved slightly. The glow within the sockets pulsed faster. A sudden swirl of wind and a long groan of agony burst through the room.

Who calls me? Minepa's cold tones of contempt were plain in the disembodied voice. *You! Now I shall live again!*

The incense smoke and the thick shadows roiled together over the skull, forming a tall thin shape that reached clawed hands toward Kayth. It shrank back as the man quickly sketched a symbol in the air before it.

How did you learn this? The shadowy form tried to pull free from the skull that anchored it. The triangle about the skull began to smoke; rising streams of energy from the chalked lines glistened black and red in the candlelight. *No! I will not be a slave to you, Kayth Farblood!* Minepa's spirit fought against the power rising from the triangle, but was unable to leave.

Kayth shouted the last words of the ritual again and smiled cruelly as the spirit changed to a wisp of coiling vapor. He motioned toward his chest with one hand; the vapor reluctantly curled closer and was absorbed into his body. A wailing cry shattered the silence of the chamber, then faded away.

Kayth sank to his knees, the sword still gripped in his hand. His lips drew back in a snarl of defiance as he struggled for control over the absorbed spirit of Minepa. His facial features twisted and writhed, changing back and forth between his own appearance and that of Minepa, until at last he gained control once more. With a sneer of triumph, he pulled himself to his feet, his eyes colder and crueler than ever.

"So you did not tell me everything you knew," Kayth whispered. His voice was cracked and strained from the ritual and his struggle. "There are other ancient books and powers within the Fire Temple to be explored and used." He saw within his mind the way to these hidden places, the secret of which only Minepa had known.

Free me! Minepa struggled against Kayth's control, locked within his mind and soul like an insect caught in amber. *You do not realize the great danger if you rouse the hidden ancient powers! He is not to be trusted!*

"You do not control me. I control you." Kayth closed his eyes as he mentally pushed the remnants of the Volkvi priest's personality and thought-patterns into the background. He lifted his lip in a sneer of contempt as Minepa's cries faded to a distant whine.

Carefully, Kayth followed the scroll's instructions for breaking the connection to the evil Otherworld realm. The dark doorways opened by the strange circle closed as he brushed away the last line. He shoved the skull back into the black bag, then locked it inside a chest covered with twisting symbols.

"As long as your skull remains in my possession, Minepa, you cannot escape from me." Kayth rolled up the scroll and put it and the ritual tools into a chest. "No one among the Volikvis will guess what I have done until it is too late to stop me."

Still clad in the gem-encrusted robe, Kayth left the chamber. He tapped the central demon face on the door's outer surface and heard the click of the hidden lock before he turned away to follow Minepa's thoughts of more power-places within the Temple.

Kayth descended one staircase after another until he was deep within the bowels of the Fravashi Fire Temple. A faint sulphurous odor hung in the air as he finally reached the level floor of a black-walled tunnel. Its glass-like walls reflected in shattered sparks the guttering flames of widely spaced torches. He followed the tunnel for some time until it opened onto a platform high above the floor of a great natural cavern.

Below the stone platform on which he stood, Kayth saw the huge crack that cut the cavern into two sections. A sulphurous smelling cloud, tinted by the glow of a far-away subterranean fire, puffed from the gouge in the earth, drifting upward until it disappeared into a natural vent leading to the surface. The ends of this crack were close together, while the middle was very wide. Across the narrow ends were two wooden bridges leading to the dark holes of more tunnels. Near the crack stood a great dark-stained altar.

The flames of thousands of candles glittered off the glass-like black walls as Kayth descended the narrow stairs to the cavern floor. His soft footsteps echoed faintly as he crossed rapidly to the altar. Laying both hands upon the blood-soaked stone, he inhaled deeply, drinking in the vibrational remains of the emotions generated by the victims raped and sacrificed there. With each breath, his vitality grew stronger, his domination and integration of Minepa's spirit more complete.

Kayth swung to his left, then toward one of the bridges, led by the memories of Minepa as if pulled by an invisible chain. He hurried across the bridge and into the black maw of a tunnel lit only by a torch far down its inky shaft. He felt within his mind Minepa's fear of a thing called the Footed Serpent that lived in a bottomless lake at the end of that tunnel, but he shoved aside that fear as his mind grasped the dead Volikvi's knowledge of a hidden room half-way down the tunnel. As if he had always known how, Kayth's hand grasped a knob on the metal bracket holding a torch. A quick twist to the left opened the concealed entrance; he slipped through, pushing the door shut behind him.

Kayth instinctively reached for the fire striker on the shelf by the door, using its spark to light the tall candles nearby. As the candles burst into flame, he looked in surprise and triumph around the rock-hewn chamber.

Shelves of very ancient scrolls lined two of the walls; deeply carved chests and elaborate cabinets were fitted into the remaining spaces. A black and gold altar with a throne-like chair set before it filled the rear wall. On this altar sat a chalice, a rock crystal bottle filled with a dark liquid, and a rare bound book. The whole wall above the altar was carved with scenes from ancient Fravashi history. Around the edges were hung twisted ribbon-ropes from which swung great faceted jewels.

These things belonged to Jinniyah himself! I know it! I feel it! Kayth walked about the room, trailing his fingers over the edges of the scrolls, the deep gilded carvings on the altar, the rare gems and wood of the throne. *I feel some great hidden power here also, some power Minepa never discovered how to use,* he thought as he paused before the altar. He shook his head in irritation as Minepa's protests continued to whisper at the edges of his thoughts.

He picked up the heavy chalice, turning it in his blunt hands as he studied the ancient engraving. As if led by an inner impulse, he uncorked the crystal bottle and poured a swallow of its contents into the chalice.

There is more than Minepa speaking to my mind in this place. Kayth stared down into the dark liquid. *Who speaks to me?*

A faint whisper just outside his hearing came to his mind, overriding the continual buzzing protests of Minepa. Kayth set aside the chalice and opened the book to a marker placed in it. He bent close to the faded page until he could read the spidery writing.

Written by Jinniyah's own hand! Kayth felt the spirit of Minepa within him cringe. *You were afraid of him, Minepa, even though he is long dead. Yet you sought to learn what he had written here.* Kayth closed his eyes and laid his hand on the book. *Yes, I feel the power in these words, but the power comes from the spirit that was the man, not the book.* He pivoted on his heel as his icy eyes searched the chamber. *That can only mean one thing: the spirit of Jinniyah exists here somewhere. You misread, Minepa. The power is not in the book, but in the remains of the man! Somewhere within this chamber is the secret hidden burial place of Jinniyah.*

Kayth sat on the throne facing the altar. For a long time he stared at the strangely decorated wall as if by willpower he could see through the black rock. Then he rose to read again the marked page in the ancient book. His hand trembled slightly as he raised the chalice and drank the strange liquid.

The new faintly buzzing voice in his mind grew clearer, overriding Minepa's frantic warnings. Kayth felt the strange liquid working through his body as he staggered back and sank down onto the throne. A deep male voice rang in his ears, and a man's face sprang clear in his inner vision.

Greetings, Kayth Farblood. I have long waited for one with your courage and determination. Your cleverness in learning the ancient tongue and performing the ancient ritual has made it possible for us to speak together. Minepa was nothing beside you.

In his inner sight, Kayth saw a heavy black curtain; in the center of this curtain was a blacker swirling, shot through with sparks of blood red, which revealed a great eye. Kayth watched in fascination as the blackness surrounding this eye drew back to reveal the long-dead face of the ancient Volikvi priest Jinniyah. The tipped, light blue eyes were piercing in their stare, the face thin with jutting cheekbones and a sharp chin and nose. Long curls of bright red hair hung on each side of the shaven skull.

Yes, we look somewhat alike, you and I. Minepa's yammering voice was suddenly silenced as if a hand were clapped over his mouth. *There is nothing to fear, Kayth Farblood, for I am only a spirit and you are a man with a body and powerful magick at your command. I will share my knowledge with you so that you can fulfill your destiny as ruler of Sar Akka.*

What do you offer? Kayth's voice fell into its old pattern of superiority.

There are things of the last battle, the one with Varanna, Jinniyah's voice was filled with contempt, *that are not known. Although she destroyed my body, my essence was not destroyed as the Peoples thought.* The mouth on the cruel face curved with amusement. *Knowing there was a chance I would die, I made certain preparations. As I felt the power surge back into me from Varanna's sword, I sent my essence into a charged stone hidden deep within this altar. The altar cannot be opened without a key, a key lost long ago to the Kirisani.*

And why should I open the altar and set you free? Kayth asked.

Because only I know of the existence and whereabouts of a stone that will turn the tide of battle in your favor, a piece of a very unusual sky-stone. This sky-stone can cause a plague to ravage the Peoples and leave the Fravashi untouched, if used by one with the proper knowledge.

The land of Kirisan is wide. How could I find such a stone and this mysterious key? Kayth felt Minepa feeding his doubts. He gathered his willpower and shoved the dead priest deeper into his subconscious mind.

The key lies in the treasure room of Rising Fort, the mountain fortress-home of your dead wife's people. To them it only has value because of a story that says it opens the vault containing Varanna's armor. They do not know that it was also made for a lock within this chamber.

And the sky-stone? Is it as impossible to get? Kayth's lip lifted in a sneer.

Only with my aid can you gain both the key and stone.

Jinniyah smiled as he felt Kayth's cunning thoughts sorting out how to get the power and still control him.

I will agree to this. Kayth did not recognize the first tendrils of control the evil Jinniyah wrapped around his mind and spirit.

Send a disguised Volikvi to the Fort, entering in this manner. Jinniyah sent a series of clear pictures to Kayth's mind of a secret way into Rising Fort. *As for the sky-stone, this is what you must seek and this is where it now lies.*

In his mind Kayth saw a jet-black disk decorated with angry red symbols. It hung before his inner sight long enough for him to memorize its details. Then the scene changed, showing a mound in a Kirisani mountain valley.

This is an old burial site, Jinniyah told him. *A Kirisani warrior took the disk from the body of a Volikvi priest during battle, and himself died of the plague. His family buried the disk with him, but all those who touched it died soon after. Thus began the legend of the curse against opening the ancient burial mounds. This disk communicates with the plague-stone that is hidden even now within this altar.*

If I touch this disk or the plague-stone, will I not also die? Kayth said scornfully. *I am no foolish Volikvi, Jinniyah. Do not make the mistake of thinking me such.*

But you know the great ancient magicks, Kayth Farblood. You cannot die. The spirit face of Jinniyah smiled again. *The disk fits thus into this very altar.* A bony hand pointed to a depression at the base of the altar near Kayth's feet. *The disk will open the altar, but the key is necessary to reach the very inner vaults. The key fits into the center of the disk and the two together release hidden magickal locks.*

Kayth stared at the apparition. *Why do all that when the lock can be forced open?*

But revealing the plague-stone is not all the key and disk can do. When fitted into their proper places, other secret portions will also open. Hidden within these secret panels are devices that will aid you in strengthening your magick powers through domination of Otherworld spirits. And when you free my spirit from the bonds of this Otherworld realm, I will willingly merge with you and help you defeat the Peoples. All I ask is to see through your eyes and experience through your bodily senses.

Kayth sat unmoving, listening to the persuasive voice of the dead Jinniyah, as the spirit told him which priest and men to send for the disk and the key and exactly where the men should go to get them.

"It cannot be!" Imandoff slammed his fist down on the table hard enough to slosh his goblet of wine.

"What cannot be?" came Takra's voice from the doorway.

"All this time I have carried that plaque from the Valley of Whispers, and I never once suspected its use." Imandoff pushed out a chair for Takra with one foot as he bent back over the tattered scroll spread before him.

The Tuonela warrior woman sat down beside him, her long legs stretched to one side. She sighed as she eased the belt at her thickening waist.

"There is a vague reference here to the plaque being able to counteract the Volikvi-caused plague." The sorcerer absently scratched his beard. "So that is how they finally stopped the spread of that killing disease. And this record," he pulled another scroll to him, tracing its faded writing with one finger, "tells a tale I have never heard. A huge sky-stone fell during the times of the Forgotten Ones into the Fire Mountain now in Frav. The Volikvis used dust from this stone to cause the plague."

"How did the writer know that?" Takra questioned, one eyebrow raised. "The Forgotten Ones left no records, and the Peoples came long after they had vanished."

"There must be ancient records of the Forgotten Ones inside Frav that we know nothing about. The writer of this scroll was an old man named Munichad, a Kirisani, who says he was able to cross the spellbound border into Frav many times. There he discovered many Volikvi secrets before he had to flee for his life." Imandoff took a swallow from his goblet. "He told his tales to a priestess here at the Temple as he lay dying. This was one generation after the plague." He sat back in his chair, rubbing his chin in thought.

"Then who made the plaque you found, old man?" Takra shook her fair head as Imandoff offered the pitcher of wine, instead reaching for a goblet of fruit juice.

"Why, Munichad, of course." Imandoff looked at her in surprise. "After he used the plaque to stop the plague, he placed it in the Valley of Whispers in case it should ever again be needed by the Peoples. But he writes nothing else of those ancient records he found in Frav."

"If the Volikvis have these records, then they could know how to use the dust of the sky-stone to once more kill the Peoples with the deadly plague." Takra's amber eyes met the sorcerer's gray ones. "And what of Varanna's armor? Have you found a clue to its hiding place?"

"Nothing very plain," Imandoff answered. "However, there is one brief mention of some of Varanna's things being sent to a child at Rising Fort."

"What child?" Takra leaned forward and rested her elbows on the table. "I thought Varanna had no family. The old tales say nothing about a child of hers."

Imandoff shrugged. "Remember, Corri's family is supposedly descended from Varanna in some way. We must go to Rising Fort and look through Geyti's records." He looked up sharply at Takra. "Where is Corri? I have not seen her all day."

"The Dream Warrior has vanished." The High Priestess Vairya stood in the doorway, still clad in her dusty fighting kilts, her hair braided and bound tight around her head. "The Oracle gave her permission to ride about the countryside with an escort, but she disappeared before the warrior could join her."

"Damn!" Imandoff rolled up the scroll and reached down for his staff lying on the floor beside his chair.

"Why should Corri leave without telling us?" Takra's brows pulled together in suspicion. "Unless she felt threatened in this place."

"Special guards have had her under surveillance these past days," answered the High Priestess. "But we never thought she would deliberately creep away on her own."

Takra rose to face Vairya, one hand dropping to the long dagger at her waist. "And why would you have her guarded?"

"The Dream Warrior is vital to the outcome of battle." The High Priestess' mouth set in a firm line. "We could not chance that one such as Druk would enter here to harm her."

"Nonetheless, guards would make her feel like a prisoner." Imandoff strode through the door, Takra at his heels.

"Where do you go?" Vairya called.

Takra whirled to face the High Priestess, her mouth curled in anger. "That is no affair of yours, woman. See that you send no one after us unless you wish them returned to you across their mounts." *Will they never leave her alone?* Takra thought as she hurried after Imandoff.

Within a short time, Takra and Imandoff were mounted on their horses, riding through the city of Kystan with provisions and saddlebags hung across their mounts.

"Where would Corri go?" Takra asked as they rode down the inclined causeway connecting the mountain city to the main road below. "Surely she would not return to Rising Fort, not with the unwelcome that aunt of hers would give."

"I would guess to the mountain feya women, Uzza or Thalassa." Imandoff glanced over his shoulder as he guided Sun Dancer onto the dusty road. "We can ask at Rising Fort, for during these unsettled times Geyti's watchmen will note all travelers passing near the Fort."

"She could slip by unseen. She was the best thief in Hadliden, remember?"

"Then we will push on and ask among the mountain villagers and the Green Men." Imandoff turned a grim face to Takra, who urged Lightfoot forward to ride beside him. "One thing the High Priestess did not say, but which I know to be true, is that none of the seers at the Temple will be able to find Corri through their crystals. Like the Oracle and me, she will not appear to seers. According to the Temple records, neither did Varanna nor Ryanna, Corri's mother."

"Then you cannot find her that way, either." Takra nudged Lightfoot with her heels. "We can only hope that human eyes have noticed her passage, sorcerer, since neither you nor I are much good at animal-talk. We may not find her unless she wishes it."

Corri turned Mouse off the main road that went into Leshy, heading instead along the trail leading up into the mountains of Deep Rising. She found her troubled thoughts too often on the barrier that seemed to keep her from contacting the Lady.

What has happened? Lady, where are you? Speak to me! All Corri felt was a sense of rightness in the choice she had made. A sudden warmth flowed around her, like loving arms.

The Oracle meant well. The comforting voice of the Goddess was clear in Corri's mind. *But there are things you must do, and these cannot be done behind the safely guarded walls of the Temple.*

Watch and listen, my Dream Warrior, for your powers will soon be needed.

Corri sighed at the cryptic message, but was pleased that her contact with the Lady was once more open. She glanced back briefly at the travelers moving on toward Leshy, but no one followed her. As the trail led up into the thick forests, away from the lower open slopes, she no longer felt the urge to watch her back constantly.

At least I know I am traveling in the right direction. Unless some surprise happens along the trail, I will journey on to Uzza or Thalassa and stay until time to march to the border, she thought as she straightened the green hood that hid her dark red hair from sight. *Perhaps I should stop at Rising Fort. Uncle Geyti may know something about this "key" the dream-voice spoke of. Do I look for a real key, or did the voice mean only something written down?*

A flicker of movement in the brush ahead caught Corri's attention. The girl halted Mouse while she reached out with her thoughts for any sign of danger. She jerked back in the saddle in surprise, for first a sense of fear, then a determination to know who sought, reached her mind. She snapped off her seeking and waited, one hand dropping to the dagger at her belt.

Slowly, two young women rose from their hiding place in the thick undergrowth. Side by side, the girls edged carefully back onto the trail facing Corri. Except for walking staffs, they appeared to be unarmed.

Corri held up her hand. "I am no threat to you," she said. "I only travel into the mountains."

"Do you hail from Leshy?" asked one of the girls, the hood on her cloak falling back to reveal black curly hair. Her green eyes were wary.

The other girl stepped closer, looking at Corri with intent dark eyes. "She is no initiate, Sallin, but the one we seek. It is the Dream Warrior!"

Corri kept her hand on the dagger hilt. "Who are you and what do you want of me?"

"Quickly!" The girl Sallin motioned with her hand as they headed back into the undergrowth beside the trail. "We must not talk in the open, for there is danger on our trail."

Corri dismounted and led Mouse off the trail after the girls. Once under the trees, the brush thinned, opening into a pocket clearing.

"We are the daughters of Jehennette, the High Clua of Leshy," said the dark-haired girl. "I am Sallin, and this is Merra. The initiate Morvrana has taken our mother prisoner, and we flee for our lives. We had thought to go to Kystan, but we saw some of Morvrana's followers loitering along the trail ahead. So we decided to disappear among the feya women, hoping the Green Men could get our message to you."

Corri felt a thrill of fear shoot through her as she remembered both the Lady's words and Morvrana's meeting with Malya. *My instincts tell me Malya is behind this rebellion. So she did manage to influence Morvrana, even though the woman declared she wanted no part of Malya and her plans. Does Malya herself plan to take control of Leshy? Wherever Malya plots and plans, Kayth's power is never far away.*

Corri looped Mouse's reins over a bush, then squatted beside the girls. "Was there a woman called Malya who helped her?"

The girls shrugged, and Merra answered. "We know of Malya, but she has not been seen since the old High Clua died."

"What of the other initiates?" Corri asked. "The High Clua's rule is inviolate. Did no one try to stop this Morvrana?"

"Morvrana underwent the Trial of the Mask," Merra answered. "It did something to her, gave her strange but mighty powers. No one dared stand against her. When she took over the Mystery School at Leshy, she called forth great blasts of fire and placed invisible bonds on our mother. Now she rules there with an iron fist."

"Whatever happened during the Trial that gave her those strange powers also did something to her mind." Sallin twisted her fingers together as she thought. "I could feel something wrong within her, but I dared not push into her thoughts lest I be caught by whatever evil Otherworld powers now aid her."

"Morvrana was forbidden to undergo the Trial, yet she did so while our mother and we were on a journey." Merra glanced at Sallin, then back to Corri. "Our mother is imprisoned in the underground chamber with the Mask. Morvrana is insane enough with her new power to cost the Peoples the war with Frav."

A deep sense of uneasiness prickled Corri's skin. *Evil Otherworld entities! For certain Kayth and Malya are using this way to strike at the Peoples and at me, knowing I will not turn aside from this challenge.* "The healing powers of the High Clua and the others at Leshy will be greatly needed during the coming battle. Besides, we cannot leave a pocket of tainted power behind us when we march. I see no way open except to rescue Jehennette," she finally said. "But while we wait for soldiers to come from the Temple, Morvrana will have more time to grow in power. I must go now, and I must go alone."

"Not so." Sallin's mouth set. "We do not have your powers, Dream Warrior, but we know which initiates to trust and which ones follow Morvrana. We can warn the faithful initiates and give you time to free our mother. Besides, we will be allowed entrance with little resistance. We can get you inside with us as one come for a healing. I know of certain herbs that can simulate the red blisters of cow-pox." She smiled at Corri's look of disgust. "Such a contagious disease will keep others away and allow you the privacy of a room. I see no other way."

"Then we must return to Leshy, arriving just before the gates close for the night," Corri said. "Once inside the walls of the School, I must go alone to the underground chamber where your mother lies imprisoned."

"We understand," Merra answered. "We know how to make our way unseen through the School to warn those who do not follow Morvrana. If necessary, we can create a diversion to draw away those Morvrana will have guarding the door to the underground hall. We willingly follow you into battle, Dream Warrior."

Corri saw the glint of battle-fever in the girl's eyes. "Are you certain you are not Tuonela?" she asked with a grin.

"As it happens, my father was." Merra smiled back, her slender hand falling to a belt dagger half-hidden beneath her cloak. "I am a healer by training, but I do not hesitate in battle against those who would drown the Peoples in a flood of Fravashi fanaticism."

"Why am I not surprised?" Corri murmured to herself. She leaned back against a tree and closed her eyes. "We rest until late day," she said to the girls. "Then we go back to Leshy with the last of the crowds. Among so many people, we have a better chance of not being noticed."

So this is where You led me, Lady. Corri heard the small rustling sounds of the two young women as they settled down to rest. *I have changed so much since You gave me this responsibility. But knowing what I do now, I would not change anything.*

Yes, you have changed, like a butterfly emerging from its cocoon. There was a delighted laugh tingeing the voice in Corri's mind. *Where once you cared only for your position as the best thief in Hadliden, now you fight for the freedom of all the Peoples.*

Yes, I now know the hopes and desires of the other people around me, and I want to see them free to live their lives as they feel right. Is this what love does to you, Lady?

It opens your eyes to the love around you, My daughter. You see all things with new eyes. The voice faded away.

As Corri moved Varanna's sword into a more comfortable position, she felt a vibration running through the weapon and heard a faint humming within her mind. *What powers now lie within this ancient weapon since hilt has been joined with blade?*

she thought. *Can I learn to use these powers in time to help the Peoples?* She pulled her hand away from the sword and willed herself to fall into a light sleep.

Chapter 4

"How can my own people do this?" The Tuonela warrior Tirkul paced back and forth across the interior of Halka's tent-wagon, his jaw set, his big hands clenched. "We exchanged heart-oath, and by Tuonela law Balqama is now a member of the Clan of the Asperel. How can they now meet to decide if she is to be cast out? The Baba himself has sent his blessing to our heart-oath."

The light from the drawn-back leather covering at the door outlined his sharp cheekbones and square jaw as he stood looking out across the tent-wagons to the waving grasslands. His pale braids glowed from a stray sunbeam. He turned on his booted heel and strode back to stand beside his heart-wife Balqama. Gently he laid his right hand on her shoulder, the Clan tattoo of the winged globe plain on its back.

"She has brought nothing but good to the Clans. That is more than can be said of Roggkin, a Clansman and a traitor."

His mouth tightened and his dark eyes grew hard as his fingers touched the scar on his neck.

"These are dangerous times, and there is much unrest among the Tuonela people." The shakka Halka reached out to Balqama, taking the girl's hands in her long, wrinkled fingers. "As shakka, I have already given my thoughts, and by Clan law it should be enough. But this gathering is held outside the law, without me or the chief of the Asperels. The Clans, like the other Peoples, fear what they do not understand, what is different. They are afraid because you come from Frav." Halka's brown eyes held Balqama's darker ones.

"I know," the girl murmured. "Every time they look at me they see only one from Frav, and they fear more." She raised her face to look at Tirkul, her long dark-red braid sliding back over her shoulder. "Is there no way I can convince the Clans that I am not here to spy for Frav? I think as they do about that land. My own father has declared me dead because I heal with my hands."

Halka shook her head and sighed. "Fear makes narrow minds. There are even those who speak out against Takra Wind-Rider, saying that she has no place here. As if the blood of her Kirisani mother was all that runs in her veins. Silverhair also has Clan blood, gotten from a Tuonela grandmother. The two are strengthened from the blood-mixing."

"If the Clans drive Balqama out, I will go also." Tirkul sat on one of the carved chests, his long legs stretched before him. "All my life I have believed in Clan law. Now I find those who would twist it to serve a dark purpose. Do they not realize what they give up in Balqama? She is a good healer."

"You cannot stop the wind." Balqama smiled at the tall warrior. "Is that not what your people say when you cannot change something or someone?"

Halka gave a little chuckle as she got to her feet. Stoop-shouldered, the tall old woman moved to the rear of her wagon, where she paused before her altar. "There are always

ways to win a battle, ways in which the loser will not realize he is loser at first." She caressed the roughly carved statue on the altar, a figure of the Goddess and a colt. "If you were to leave before these nathlings stir up their courage, the victory would be yours, not theirs."

Halka turned to look at Tirkul, her bird-bright eyes challenging him to understand. The warrior stood and frowned for a moment, then his mouth drew up into a cold smile.

"The old tradition of shaking off the dust." Tirkul fingered the long dagger at his narrow waist. "Yes, that would be a sour victory for them."

Halka took a leather bag from the altar, shaking it gently between her wrinkled hands as she came back to sit beside Balqama. "Now we will ask the Mother of Mares to show us the path you should take."

Tirkul sat once more on the chest while the shakka murmured her invocation, then spilled the little bones onto the wagon's wooden floor. Tirkul and Balqama leaned forward to look at the tumble of oracle bones as they waited for Halka to speak. Finally, the old woman sat back with a smile of satisfaction.

"It is clear," she said. "You are to go to Kystan. The Oracle must hear from you, Balqama, all that you know of the roads and cities within Frav. What you can tell her may save many lives. And you, Tirkul," she stared at the warrior, "will need to keep a sharp sword and much courage. Your path will lead into Kystan for a time, but then it will take you into an eye of Darkness." She held up her hand as Balqama began to speak. "A place you cannot go, girl." The shakka looked up at the tall warrior beside her. "Can you do this? Leave this Clan without regrets or looking back?"

"I can and I will. My parents understand my love for Balqama and why I do this. And we will see them again."

"Yes, there will come a day when the fears die down and you can return. But life will never be the same for any of us, I think." The old woman sighed and shook her head. "If you go, go quickly before hotter heads and less clear minds cause more trouble."

"The horses are packed and ready." Tirkul held out his hand to Balqama. "We thought to go to another Clan, but the Mother of Mares has chosen otherwise."

"I have no fear of the future if I am with you." The girl smiled at him, her dark eyes trusting. "I need no family, no Clan, to be happy. But this Clan has been your life. Stay, Tirkul, and I will go to the Oracle in Kystan."

"Never! If you go, I go with you! You are my life."

Halka stared at the bones again, then returned them to the leather bag, tying its strings to her belt. "Do not let others tear apart your joy," she said. "The past has been hurtful, but it is gone. Build the future you want. The bones say that one day you both may again come among the Clans and be greeted with friendship." *If you survive this eye of Darkness,* she thought, *there will come a time when you will be the voice between the Clans and the other Peoples.* She sat, her eyes half-closed as if she listened to an inner voice. "They still meet and argue. Now is the time to ride out. You remember the words to say when you reach the edge of the camp?"

"I remember," Tirkul answered.

Halka watched from the door of her tent-wagon as the two mounted their horses. Tirkul rode out on Hellstorm and Balqama behind him on her horse Cloud-Shadow, leading a packhorse.

This warrior must go through great danger before his journey is finished, the shakka thought. *Protect him, Mother of Mares. I think he knows well the evil that waits for him, but he will go to meet it with the war cry of a Tuonela warrior on his lips.*

When Tirkul and Balqama reached the edge of the clustered Tuonela Clan wagons, he held up his hand. "Dismount and do exactly as I do," he told the girl. "I will say what needs saying. When we ride out, do not look back."

For the last time Tirkul and Balqama looked back upon the camp. Those who had gathered against Halka's wishes stood watching the pair. With a derisive smile on his face, Tirkul brushed the dust from his tunic, his leather trousers, and then his boots, and Balqama repeated his actions.

"I shake off the dust of this Clan." Tirkul's deep voice echoed through the quiet camp. "I cast off these people. May the Mother of Mares and Her consort visit upon them their own evil." He gave a rude Clan gesture to the staring people, but Balqama only turned her back on the hard stares.

Tirkul turned without a backward glance and mounted Hellstorm. Balqama hurriedly mounted Cloud-Shadow and touched her heels to the mare's flanks. The pair rode on into the grasslands.

The chief of the Clan of the Feathered Spear sat in counsel with the Clan's elders. He was uncomfortable with the old men and women gathered in the circle. Each one in turn had voiced their opinion on Burrak's failure to obey the shakka Norya, who had then left them to join Frayma's Mare.

"Your place as Clan chief is now questioned." The oldest woman in the circle stared at Burrak, her voice hard and her eyes cold. "Because of your actions, the Baba himself has decreed punishment upon us. The shakkas will gather soon to decide what that will be. And because of Melaina's lies and treachery, we have no shakka to speak kind words for the Clan of the Feathered Spear."

"Melaina will go for us." Burrak nervously played with the hilt of his dagger.

"Hah! She is no shakka, Burrak, nor will that one ever be. The true shakkas will never let her into their circle." One of the old men puckered his mouth in distaste. "By Melaina's lies, the Dream Warrior was whipped, and you did nothing. The chief must hold to what is true; he must know what happens in his Clan, so he can judge fairly. You chose to believe the lying prattle of a jealous woman because it suited you. Now we are outcast from the other Clans until you take action and remove Melaina from our camp."

"And that you do not do." Another member of the circle glared at the chief.

"If I cast out Melaina, who will treat our sick?" Burrak looked around the circle, seeking but not finding a sympathetic face among the group.

"Better to be without a shakka than to have one filled with deceit and bitterness," answered the first old woman. "I call for a Clan gathering to decide on a new chief."

Burrak sat silently as a murmur of agreement rose from the elders. *It will split the Clan forever,* he thought, *and they all say I am to blame. I should have heard the lies in Melaina's words. I should have cast her out as Norya demanded. But I was too proud to admit I made a mistake. Even now I should speak the words and step aside.* But he could not speak the words.

"Better to die in battle, Burrak, than to answer to the Mother of Mares for splitting this Clan." The old woman waited for Burrak to speak the proper words, but the chief sat, stone-faced, his pride holding him back.

The elders rose and stood in a circle, loudly chanting the call for Clan assembly. The people, who had been listening quietly in the shadows of the surrounding tent-wagons, moved forward like a flow of water until they surrounded the circle of elders and chief.

"A new chief of the Clan of the Feathered Spear must be chosen," said one of the elder men. "We speak for the outcasting of the woman Melaina. All those of the Clan who follow Burrak, gather about him. All those who would have a new chief, gather with us."

The elders all moved away to stand facing Burrak. There was movement among the Clan as people chose for or against their chief. Finally, there were two groups facing each other, with only a handful of people behind Burrak.

"The Clan has spoken, Burrak." The old man stood like a warrior, his white head up, one hand resting on his long dagger. "A new chief will be chosen. Yield to the Clan will, or take your followers and ride out."

"We will ride out, and may the hell-fires of Frav burn your souls!" Melaina stepped up beside Burrak, her light brown eyes burning with fury. "The woman you call the Dream Warrior stirred this trouble within the Clan. She is an Out-Clanner, and you believed her over one of your own!" The young woman's golden hair glowed like flame in the sunlight. Her lips were drawn back in a grimace of hate, her hands raised to begin a curse.

"Silence, woman!" A warrior pushed forward, his sword drawn. "The grief you made has taught you nothing! And you, Burrak, may you reap what you deserve from this false shakka with her evil tongue."

The people behind the elders began to mutter; the sounds of mountain steel leaving sheaths were sharp in the air.

Burrak shook his head. "I will not draw sword against my own people," he said, "nor shall anyone who follows me. Gather your wagons, for we ride at once." He turned on his heel and walked away.

Within the hour, six tent-wagons pulled away from the camp, a small herd of silky-haired goats behind them. Burrak rode before the caravan, head up, back straight, but his heart was heavy. *I should not have allowed the division,* he thought. *I should have willingly stepped aside. I should have cast out Melaina.* But he rode on without a word or a backward glance.

The warriors of the remaining camp stood with drawn swords until the wagons were only a vague, distant blot in the summer heat. They had kept peace when the flocks were sorted out and the wagons readied for the journey. They had backed those women who chose to stay behind, making certain that the departing men did not try to separate mother and children. But if one of the followers tried to return now, they would drive that person out onto the grasslands with no remorse.

"Melaina will be the death of Burrak," said one of the warriors as he watched the distant wagons. "His foolish pride will keep her at his side. Sooner or late, she will bring him deeper trouble, trouble he cannot escape."

The warriors beside him nodded in agreement.

Balqama stirred the coals beneath the roasting prairie hens as Tirkul unsaddled the horses and picketed them for grazing. A week alone with the tall warrior, crossing the Tuonela grasslands, had been difficult. At first he had ridden without a word to her for hours. Then she had coaxed him into a few short words in reply to questions.

Enough of this, Balqama thought. *I weary of this childish game. He will speak with me as before, or we will part trails.*

"What trail do we take to get to Kystan?" she asked as Tirkul sat on his heels across from her. He muttered and shrugged his shoulders. "Enough!" Balqama stood straight, hands on hips, eyes flashing, her Fravashi skirts swirling about her boots. "I took heart-oath with a man, a warrior of the Tuonela. When did he turn back into a child? What night-wraith stole his spirit and left an idiot changeling in his place? This pouting male," she pointed one shaking finger at the surprised Tirkul, "is not my husband. I do not ride with strangers. If I cannot find my husband, I will ride on alone."

"Woman!" Tirkul roared as he surged to his feet.

"Do not speak to me, stranger." Balqama rushed around the fire until she stood toe to toe with the tall warrior. She tilted back her head to look up into his face. "I will be an equal in my husband's eyes, or I will not be wife. I will be about the business the Mother of Mares gives me to do, and no man will stop me. But I say again, I will not live with a stranger." Her dark eyes burned with anger.

"I did not know you were so much like a Tuonela woman on the inside." Tirkul grinned lopsidedly as he took a step backward. "I think I have much to learn about you, Balqama."

"And I about you, Tirkul." Her face softened. "But I cannot live with you if you shut me out of your problems or try to control me."

"I thought I had learned that lesson." Tirkul thought of how his attitude had broken the budding love he shared once with Corri. "I do not wish to part from you. You are my life, Balqama." He held out his muscled arms, and she stepped inside them. In a low voice, he said, "I am afraid of what the future holds. My blood still burns at what my Clan said to you. I do not know if we will both be alive when this great battle is finished."

"I learned the value of patience long ago in my father's house in Frav. I learned that plans always change, that if you do not flow with the water you will drown. But still there came a time when I stood up for my beliefs, risking all to be myself. I was alone, Tirkul. How much stronger I am when another shares the burdens of life!"

"I have wronged you." Tirkul pressed his lips against her hair. "We will share all the fears and joys, my love. But when I go into battle, let me see no tears or hear your cries, for I could not be warrior-strong if I knew you feared."

"I promise, no tears," she answered. *I shall not tell you that I plan to be among the healers at the border,* she thought, *for you can only be strong if you think I am safe, and I can only be strong if I am using my healing.*

The next morning Tirkul chose a little-used trail up into the mountains of Deep Rising. They met only few travelers, most of them after they took the trail-branch to the east, and each of whom exchanged news and greetings from a safe distance.

As they passed near Rising Fort, Balqama's head jerked up, and her eyes widened for a moment. "Stop," she said softly to

Tirkul who rode close to her side. "Something of Frav has been or will soon come this way."

"How do you know?" he asked as he scrutinized the brush and trees along both sides of the trail, one hand ready on his sword.

"I cannot put it into words," she answered. "I only know what I feel." She shook her head in bewilderment. "There is a danger, something I have never encountered before, but it comes from no living man. I feel it here." She touched the pit of her abdomen.

She has some of Corri's talent, Tirkul thought. *I will not make the same mistake again. I will accept what she is without fear.* "The danger may only be a fear-trap set by one who favors Frav and has a little of the sorcerer's talent. But we will be cautious. Let us ride on, and leave the trap unsprung."

The pair rode on down the trail toward Leshy, where they would join the road leading into Kystan. They were ever watchful of their backs and what might come before, but they found nothing else to threaten them.

Chapter 5

Corri felt her dream-self pull free from her body and rise in the sultry afternoon air. As she hung just over the tops of the tall trees that concealed the sleeping girls, she turned to view the city of Leshy, hazy with dust and the smoke of cooking fires. Behind the aura of seeming innocence, she felt the prickle of strange powers centered behind the high wall of the distant School. *Morvrana and whatever spirits help her do not seem aware of me yet,* she thought. *I will not warn them by going there now.*

She turned to the west, scanning the horizon where the mountains separated Kirisan from the coastal cities of Asur. Black thunderclouds were building there, bumping and pushing against the worn peaks of the Barren Mountains, slowly grinding their way over the barrier toward the inland valleys. *It will be a wet and noisy night, all the better to slip past human guards.*

She reached out with her mind, testing for travelers along all the trails and roads centering on Leshy. A pattern of familiar thoughts snagged at her, drawing her attention to the narrow trail leading up into Deep Rising. *Tirkul? Why should Tirkul be here?* Corri swiftly dropped lower and followed the trail, around one bend, then another, seeking the source of those thoughts.

Two riders were cautiously coming down the trail to the junction where they could either go to Leshy or turn to follow the road to Kystan. The straight-backed form of Tirkul, clad in his leather Tuonela trousers and tunic, led the pair, one hand resting on his sword hilt, the other gripping the reins of the buckskin Hellstorm. Behind him on a white mare spotted with dark gray rode the girl Balqama, leading a packhorse.

Why do Tirkul and Balqama come into Kirisan? Corri reached out gently, then recoiled at the anger she felt radiating from Tirkul. *What has happened among the Clans to send Tirkul away with hatred in his heart?* She glanced again at the packhorse, this time noting the carefully packed bundles lashed to the animal. *The Clans have refused to accept the Fravashi girl! And Tirkul has given up his place among his people to be with her.*

Corri quickly retreated to her physical body asleep deep in the bushes, floating downward until she settled inside herself. Moving cautiously, she sat up and looked around. Merra and Sallin were still asleep, huddled in their cloaks. Quietly, she stood up and inched back among the trees until she could move more freely toward the dusty trail. There, sitting on her heels and chewing a blade of grass, she waited for Tirkul.

Hellstorm scented her first, shaking his head and blowing softly at the remembered smell of a friend. Tirkul's dark eyes narrowed and his hand tightened on his sword until he spotted Corri in the late afternoon shade under the trees. His white-blonde braids glowed against his browned skin as he turned his head to speak softly to Balqama. Then he turned Hellstorm onto the grassy edge of the trail and dismounted, his hand out in welcome.

Corri rose and stepped forward to be drawn into a bear hug against Tirkul's muscled chest. Slightly breathless when he released her, she looked up at his broad shoulders, then up to his square jaw, her heart leaping. *A part of me still loves him,* she thought as she turned to greet his Fravashi companion. *Not as I love Gadavar, but still a kind of love.*

"Greetings, Balqama. May the trail before you be smooth." Corri took in the girl's appearance in a quick glance: long red hair braided Tuonela-style, but with a scarf knotted around her head to protect her from the heat. The young healer still wore the feminine skirts and blouse of Frav; beneath the swishing hem peeked the toes of stout Tuonela boots as she dismounted.

"Smoother than the trail behind us," Tirkul said. His jaw set in anger as his eyes met Corri's. "Although Halka and the other shakkas greeted Balqama with friendship and joy for her healing powers, there were many among the Clans who spoke ill words against her."

"Somehow that does not surprise me." Corri sighed. "Trouble was brewing, even against me, before I last left the Tuonela."

"They are afraid." Balqama stepped close to Tirkul and placed one browned hand on his arm. "I understand their fears. If I had not spent my life journeying among your Clans and the other Peoples, I, too, would be afraid of any stranger now that war looms so close."

"You have suffered enough. Can they not see that?" Tirkul smoothed her hair gently. "Your own father cast you out when he learned of your healing powers."

He truly loves her. Corri smiled to herself, happiness for Tirkul welling up in her heart but followed by a sadness. *But he still does not completely understand what his decisions will mean to him.*

"It does not matter. My life is now with you." The girl smiled up at the Tuonela warrior. "Do you regret leaving the Clans?"

"Never! I took heart-oath with you. By law the Clans must accept you." Tirkul's hand tightened on his sword hilt.

"They never will." Corri's soft voice broke the tension as the tall warrior and the Fravashi girl turned to look at her. "No more than they will ever accept me, even though the Baba himself declared me part of the Clans. Times are changing. I feel things will never again be the same as we once knew them, Tirkul. Where will you go and what will you do now?"

"We go to Kystan," answered Balqama. "The shakka Halka told us that we must be intermediaries for the Baba with the other Peoples. So we go to the Temple of the Great Mountain to speak with the Oracle."

"We must also speak with Imandoff and Takra." Tirkul looked around for Corri's companions.

"They are not here." Corri motioned toward the bushes and trees behind her. "I think we should move off the trail where we will not be seen."

Although Tirkul raised his brows in question, he and Balqama followed Corri back toward the hidden resting-place. Corri was not surprised to see that Sallin and Merra were gone.

"These are friends," she called softly. "You need not fear them."

The bushes rustled, then the two girls stepped from the shadows in which they had taken refuge. Balqama flinched as the girls seemed to materialize out of nothing, but Tirkul only smiled.

"Healers from Leshy," he said softly to the Fravashi girl at his side. "But why are they hiding?" he asked Corri.

"First, tell me all the news from the Clans and the border." Corri sat cross-legged on the grass. "Then I will give you news to carry to the Oracle."

Balqama looped the horses' reins over bushes at the edge of the small clearing, then sat beside Tirkul and the girls.

"The name of Out-Clanner is now given to all who are not of full Clan blood." Tirkul plucked a blade of grass and twisted it in his fingers. "Although the shakkas all speak against these thoughts, even Imandoff and Takra will no longer find welcome among most of the Clans."

"Halka and the Baba both say that any blood mixed with Clan blood only makes the person stronger." Balqama sighed as she pleated her skirt between her slender fingers. "But the Clans fear me because of my Fravashi blood and my knowledge of how to cross the spellbound border. I tried to tell them that I would go to Kystan to give information to the Oracle about the roads and cities of Frav."

"The nathlings called her a liar!" Tirkul's fair brows pulled down, his mouth set in a hard line. "I should have called on Clan-right and defended your honor."

"It would have changed nothing." Balqama's face was calm. "I made my choice, Tirkul. Perhaps with time and the end of this inevitable war, we can once again go among your people."

"Perhaps. But I tell you now, I will never again live among them." Tirkul dropped the shredded piece of grass, then looked at Corri. "Now tell me, Dream Warrior, why do you and these Leshy healers hide in the forests of Deep Rising? And where are Imandoff and Takra?"

Cutting her story to the bare bones, Corri outlined the troubles at Leshy and their plans to free Jehennette. "Have you seen Imandoff and Takra along the trail?"

Tirkul shook his head. "After one skirmish with bandits, we avoided all travelers. It is dangerous to travel unarmed and alone in Deep Rising these days."

"Perhaps they did not receive my message yet. You will probably meet Imandoff and Takra on the road to Kystan. Tell them to meet me at Springwell."

"You must not go alone into such danger as lies in Leshy," Tirkul protested.

"Think," Balqama said, one hand on his arm. "Corri has the right of it. As when she went into the Fravashi temple alone to rescue you, so must she go alone into the deep places of Leshy to rescue the High Clua. Her powers are not ours, Tirkul. We would only hinder her."

"We will aid the Dream Warrior by rousing the faithful of the School," Merra said. "And those who would try to stop us will regret their actions." She pushed aside her cloak to touch the dagger hidden beneath it. Her freckled nose wrinkled as she frowned. "Your words of the Clans touches me as well as others of half-Clan blood. My father was Tuonela. Our mother's freedom may be one of many keys to help the Peoples win the war and recover their senses afterward."

Sallin pushed back her black curls and regarded Balqama with curious green eyes. "And my father was a trader from Frav. So not all the Peoples are hostile toward your lady, Tirkul." She took her sister's hand. "But the Dream Warrior does have the right of it. No one at Leshy will suspect us, and only we can get the Dream Warrior into the School. If others come with us, Morvrana will know at once what we have come to do."

"Besides, Tirkul, your skills are greatly needed at the Temple." Corri raised her hand when Tirkul started to interrupt. "The High Priestess tries to train the warrior women of Her Own. The Lady blesses her for her efforts, but she has never fought in battle. Without your help, Her Own will be destroyed in the first skirmish."

"And what shall we tell Imandoff when we meet him?" Tirkul stood up, hands on hips, looking down at Corri. "You know he will want the truth."

Corri sighed as she stood. "Tell him to seek for Varanna's key at Rising Fort, then meet me at Springwell. And tell him to beware Malya and Roggkin."

"Kayth's daughter?" Balqama's hand tightened as she gathered up her horse's reins. "We traders know of her," she explained at Corri's questioning look. "But this Roggkin . . ."

"A traitor from the Clans who follows Malya like a dog follows a bitch in heat," Tirkul growled. "I should have killed him long ago."

"Forget him," Balqama said as she turned to lead the horses back to the trail. "Word is that no companion of this Malya lasts long. He is already a dead man, though he knows it not."

Corri and the girls watched Tirkul and Balqama disappear down the trail before they, too, started back toward Leshy.

Malya sat silent, her pendant cupped in her hands. Her pale blue eyes were nearly shut, her gaze upon nothing in the room, as she listened to a voice her Tuonela-renegade companion could not hear. She was aware that Roggkin stared at her, his lustful and plotting emotions plain as she reached out a tentacle of thought to him.

He will be easily entangled in my spells, she thought as she lifted the strange pendant-stone so that it was outlined by a stray sunbeam coming through a crack in the inn's shutters. *Relax, my warrior. Sink down and sleep, forgetting what I do and what I say.* The tiny mole at the left corner of her mouth moved as she smiled to herself. The Tuonela slumped back onto the bed.

Again, Malya cupped the pale, translucent red stone in both hands, gazing at the web-thin black lines in its depths. The sunbeam moved slowly, lighting the stone to the color of watery blood in her slender fingers.

I am here, daughter. Kayth's powerful voice startled her. She frowned for a moment, picking up the subtle changes she heard. *It is truly I, Kayth, your father.* The words were etched with amusement. *My power has grown much since I last spoke with you, so much that I am now called by the ancient name of Jinniyah. I have great work for you, Malya. When you have done it, I want you to come to me in Frav.*

What am I to do? Malya's breath quickened as she thought of the power and position waiting for her by Kayth's side.

First, have your contacts with the Mystery School in Leshy borne fruit? In her mind Malya could see Kayth's arrogant face.

Yes, she answered. *Rumors are buzzing through the town about Morvrana taking control of the School. It is said that the initiates are divided in their support, but those opposing Morvrana cannot overcome her. There is talk that she has gained strange new powers. It is even said that she is possessed by an Otherworld entity.*

Kayth laughed. *Well done. With Morvrana controlled by her delusions, the School will not take part in the coming battles. You no longer need to stay in Leshy. I want you to seek out Imandoff the sorcerer and Corri and destroy them.*

Malya sucked in her breath. *You no longer want Corri to bear your child?*

She is far too dangerous now to bring to Frav. I have decided to set you by my side instead.

Where are the sorcerer and my sister? I would do your task quickly and be on my journey to you.

I cannot see either of them, Kayth said, his mouth twisting with distaste at revealing a weakness. *Just find them and kill them. Can you not do that?* His ice-blue eyes stared at her, reaching deep into her mind. *And do it before the Harvest Moon.*

Yes, I can do that. Malya snapped back her reply. *I will be in Frav well before the rise of the Harvest Moon.*

Kayth's face faded from her mind as Malya slowly lowered the red pendant. *Now, Roggkin, I will see if my time has been wasted with you.* She stood and stared down at the sleeping Tuonela, her sensual mouth pursed in thought.

"Awake, Roggkin," she demanded as she shook the warrior. She stepped back from the reaching hands, contempt in her heart as she saw the lust clear on his face. "We have one last task to perform. Then I will fulfill our bargain."

"You have promised long and delivered nothing," Roggkin complained, a whine creeping into his voice.

"Did I not tell you in the beginning that I would reward you when my tasks were finished? The end is now in sight."

Malya casually rested her hand on the dagger at her side when the tall man reached for her again. Roggkin scowled, the scar stretching from his lobeless ear across his face writhing with the grimace, but he quickly dropped his outstretched hand.

"When we have found the sorcerer Imandoff and my sister Corri and killed them, then our bargain will be fulfilled." Malya's mouth smiled, but her pale eyes were calculating. *And if you believe that, Roggkin, you are a fool. Never will you lay hands on my body.*

"Where are they?" Roggkin scrubbed his hands across his broken nose and down the stubble on his chin.

"Surely you can ask among your drinking companions. Some traveler will have heard of them." Malya went back to her seat by the shuttered window, watching the big man intently as he rose from the bed and walked to the door.

"The courier from the Temple should arrive today." Roggkin paused with his hand on the door. "Kystan will not have heard of the takeover at Leshy yet, so the courier should arrive as always." His dark eyes slid over her curves, his tongue licking across his lips. "Do not think to break our agreement, Malya, or I will take my reward by force." He stepped out into the inn hall, closing the door behind him.

You will never have me, by force or otherwise, Tuonela scum. A derisive smile curved the woman's mouth as her hand caressed the poison-dipped dagger at her side. *You will receive the payment I promised from the start: death.* She leaned back in the hard chair, her thoughts on Frav.

It was not long before quick footsteps in the hall brought her out of her reverie. Roggkin burst through the door, excitement in his eyes.

"Imandoff and Takra Wind-Rider have been seen this day, riding up the trail into Deep Rising. The man who told me could not say for certain if Corri Farblood was with them."

"She must be!" Malya rose from the chair. "Those three always ride together. Find Vikkarr and Nebel. Hurry, for we must be on the trail at once!"

"I have already sent Vikkarr and Nebel for the horses." Roggkin grinned as he paced the room, one callused hand on his sword. "Farblood is mine, to do with as I wish before I kill her. You promised." His narrowed eyes dared Malya to say otherwise. "She spurned me, called my courage and manhood into question before others. For that I want her to pay."

Malya shrugged. "As I promised," she said, pointing to the saddle bags. "I care not what you do with her. Come." Without another word, she left the room, Roggkin at her heels with the saddlebags.

Before the sun touched the western mountains, the four riders were well up the trail into Deep Rising, near Geyti's fort. A chance encounter with a cattle herder from the Fort and the payment of a small gold piece gave them the information that the sorcerer had been seen, probably on his way deeper into the mountains.

"Where does he go?" Roggkin asked as they pushed on.

"The Valley of Whispers," Malya answered. "He has long been fascinated by that place."

"Talk in Leshy says they seek Varanna's armor." The man Nebel pushed back his stringy black hair from his narrow pointed face. His beady black eyes furtively eyed the money pouch at Malya's belt, his thin claw-like hands twitching at the thought of stealing it. "Is this armor valuable?"

"You have no idea how valuable, thief." Malya's voice dripped contempt.

"There be fighting?" Vikkarr's vicious little eyes brightened at Roggkin's nod. His thick, stubby fingers curled and uncurled at the thought of violence. He bit his thick lower lip, his flat face suddenly filled with concern as his horse stumbled. "Here now," he called. "Ta horses got to rest. Ands too dark for them to see good."

Malya raised a hand as Roggkin started to protest. "He is right," she said. "Find us a camping site, Nebel."

"Do we need those men?" Roggkin said softly, his mouth twisted in dislike, as they followed the two men off the road and under cover of the forest.

Malya turned her head slightly, her eyes narrowed. "They have their uses besides fighting. Think, Tuonela. I will make a sacrifice before I cross the border into Frav. Would you rather I sacrificed you instead of these gutter-rats?"

Roggkin made a swift Tuonela gesture against evil. "Sacrifice of a person is forbidden. It is wrong, Malya."

"You kill men in battle or one of your petty fights. What is the difference?" Her piercing stare silenced the warrior's outburst. "And what you plan to do to Corri, that is not a fight with a warrior. Roggkin, you are a hypocrite."

She urged her horse ahead of him, bending down as the heavy, needled branches brushed over her. Roggkin followed, his eyes narrowing as he watched her back.

What else is on your mind, woman, besides capturing Corri and killing the sorcerer? I do not trust you, Malya.

The warrior could hear protests from the men as he unsaddled the horses. Their voices were rough with fear and uncertainty.

"We done heard of the Valley of Whispers," Vikkarr said. "That place full of wicked spirits what kill people."

"I will protect you." Malya stood, hands on hips, frowning at the two men before her. "The money I pay you should be more than enough for such an adventure."

"What if we just take your money now and ride back to Leshy?" Nebel grinned and reached for his belt knife.

"Nathling!" Malya's words were a low, dangerous hiss. "You dare to threaten me?"

Her hands wove a strange hypnotic pattern before Nebel's eyes as she whispered strange words. Nebel's beady eyes widened as he clawed at his throat, spittle forming at the corners of his mouth.

"What you do?" Vikkarr stared at his friend, whose face was slowly turning purple.

"He threatened me!" Malya stood watching the struggling man with a gloating smile on her face. "No one threatens me. Do you?" Vikkarr stepped quickly back as she turned her gaze on him.

"Not me." Vikkarr's little eyes shut in fear as he covered his head with his arms. "Nebel not hurt you. I promise."

"Is this true, Nebel?" Malya stepped closer. The gasping man frantically nodded his head. "Then I release you." She made a grabbing motion before the man's darkened face, and he drew in air with a loud sob as he sank to the ground.

"Do what I ask, and I will reward you. Deal treacherously with me, and you die, and not easily." Malya smiled down at Vikkarr kneeling beside his friend. "We will follow the sorcerer, not attacking until he enters the Valley of Whispers. The Green Men do not go there, so we need not worry about their interfering." She turned away and imperiously motioned for Roggkin to spread her blankets.

You are good at lying, Malya, Roggkin thought as he smoothed the blankets to suit her. *I do not trust you at all. After you bind the sorcerer and finish with Corri, I will kill you. You gloat too much to be a warrior. Gloating over your foe always leaves an opening for a sword thrust.*

"Thoughts of killing excite you, do they not?" Malya's soft voice was close to the warrior's ear. He turned slowly to face her, only his eyes giving away his fear that she read his thoughts.

"Hunt and capture give the thrill, Malya," Roggkin answered. "The kill itself is merely an ending for a warrior."

At least you cannot read all my thoughts, or I would die here, he thought as he watched Malya lie back on the blankets. He sat down with his back against a tree and stared across the darkening campsite at Nebel and Vikkarr huddled together near the horses. *Know fear, little men,* he sneered. *Know it well, for this woman will not let you live, whatever she says. While she dallies with your sacrifices, I will put my sword in her back. Then I will ride hard back to Kystan with the money she carries. No one will find me there.*

Malya stared at Roggkin's profile. *I do not need to read minds to know what you plan, Roggkin.* She laughed silently to herself. *Little you know, for I will never leave you alive at my back. You also will die, Tuonela scum.* Her thoughts turned to Frav and Kayth as the men about her slept.

Chapter 6

"Are you certain Corri came this way?" Takra asked as they rested their horses on the hilltop above Rising Fort. "Perhaps she rode elsewhere."

"Her instincts would draw her to the deepest and safest cover she could find, these mountains. She is not running away this time, but seeking a place to think and plan." The sorcerer pulled at his gray-streaked black beard as his gray eyes scanned the fields of corn and grain below them. "I felt her faint presence once on the trail as we rode. But since her powers have grown, she is impossible to trace if she does not want to be found." He paused and frowned.

Rising Fort lay deceptively quiet below them, its forbidding walls turning dark as the long shadows cast by the approaching storm leached all color from the great stones. The red roofs of the towers could be seen above the walls, their tiles still bright in the few rays of the sun that pierced the edges of the gathering storm. Imandoff silently pointed out the small figures of guards making their way from one post to another atop the walls.

"A rider comes from the Fort." Takra gestured toward the open gates and a horseman galloping fast toward the bend in the trail leading up to them. "Why should a swift horseman leave the Fort on a journey with this storm breaking soon?"

"Only something very important would cause Geyti to send out a messenger during such weather." Imandoff touched Sun Dancer with his knees, and the big roan pranced down the trail with Takra on Lightfoot behind him.

The young man on the galloping horse pulled up sharply as he rounded the bend to face the sorcerer. "Give over!" he cried as Takra blocked his way. "Urgent message for the Temple!"

"Do you seek Imandoff Silverhair?" The sorcerer held up his long-fingered hand in a gesture of friendship. "If so, I am he."

The man frowned as he looked from Imandoff to Takra and back again. "How do I know you are Silverhair?"

Imandoff snapped his fingers, catching the created ball of blue light on the palm of his outstretched hand. "Does this not say I am a sorcerer? And Imandoff Silverhair rides with a Tuonela war lady, does he not?"

The young man nervously patted the neck of his prancing horse. "I had to be certain, sir. Many wicked people now roam these mountains." He fumbled in the pouch at his waist, finally pulling out a folded paper and a key on a red cord. "The master said to give these to Imandoff Silverhair who rides with a Tuonela warrior woman and the Dream Warrior."

"Have you seen the Dream Warrior?" Takra asked as Imandoff carefully unfolded the paper. "She came this way ahead of us."

"No, war lady. If she came this way, though, she could have passed by unseen." The boy eyed the growing shadows under the trees with obvious nervousness. "We have had troubles with the Jabed and his men again. Any solitary travelers would have avoided the conflicts. This storm may well give those trouble-makers cover to attack us again."

"I think we should talk with Geyti," Imandoff said as he tucked the paper and key into his belt pouch, and Takra nodded agreement. "Perhaps we can be of help to him if the Jabed and his followers attack tonight. Corri is skilled enough to avoid any trouble. Let us go, lad, before the shadows grow deeper."

"I will go ahead and send for master Geyti," the boy said. "No one is allowed inside except by the master's orders." He wheeled the horse and galloped back down toward the Fort.

"What is it?" Takra asked as she edged Lightfoot forward till she rode boot to boot with Imandoff.

"It seems Geyti may have found what we sought so fruitlessly at the Temple." The sorcerer's gaze raked across the brushy slopes of the trail as he urged Sun Dancer down the road to Rising Fort. "The clues I found that spoke of a key, well, it seems they meant an actual key. In his note Geyti says this key," Imandoff tapped the pouch at his waist, "has been long in the family, passed down to each new generation with a certain ritual." His hand fell instinctively to his sword hilt as the trail grew darker, the trees pressing closer to the road.

"A key to what?" Takra's jaw set in exasperation at Imandoff's tacit reply. *I think he enjoys speaking in riddles.* She sighed and half-smiled to herself.

"That is what we must discover," the sorcerer answered as he glanced up at the fast-approaching storm. Rumbles of thunder rolled down the slopes of Deep Rising, echoing through the valley. "Geyti was hesitant to put into writing all he knows. With trouble-makers such as the Jabed and his men about, this was wise."

"If he tried to send the key to you, this Geyti must have thought that Rising Fort might fall into evil hands." Takra felt the first drops of rain and urged Lightfoot into a trot. "Better hurry, sorcerer, or we will be soaked."

They were met at the great gates by Geyti himself, backed by a group of armored men. Two servants with lanterns stood behind him. One leaf of the gates was opened just wide enough to allow Imandoff and Takra to ride through, then quickly closed behind them.

"You are a welcome sight!" Geyti said, as Imandoff dismounted. "This is the one time all day that we have not been defending ourselves against the Jabed."

"We saw no sign of him when we rode this way. Has he grown so powerful?" Imandoff took his staff and gave Sun Dancer's reins to Takra, who followed a boy across the cobbled courtyard to the stables. "I was told the men he took with him from the Temple were not fighting men, but priests. And he has never had any talents, other than that of causing trouble of the ordinary kind."

"It seems he has gathered to him outlaws and renegade fighting men." Geyti's blue-green eyes were hard in his sharp face as he headed through the rain to the door of the great hall, Imandoff at his side. "We have been hard put to repel his attacks."

As the two men entered the candle-lit hall, Takra dashed out of the pounding rain and through the door behind them. The great hall was set up with trestle tables for eating, with stout benches along the sides of each table, but only servants moved about the room. Platters of roast meat, tubers, and thick-sliced bread covered the table nearest the door. Wooden trenchers and mugs sat side by side with large pitchers of ale and cider.

"Food for your men to be eaten when they can." Takra nodded her approval.

"Needa," Geyti called to one of the bustling women. "Bring three plates of food to my study." The stout, older woman nodded, then snapped her fingers at two of the lesser servants to help her.

Geyti led the way around the tables and into a short hall at the far side of the room. At the rear of the building, he opened another door, and they entered Geyti's private quarters. Two hanging lanterns lit the room, casting dim shadows in the corners. The master of Rising Fort cleared off a side table and motioned to two chairs beside it.

"A little more cluttered than when you last were here, Silverhair," he said as he sank into a chair behind a carved desk. He stretched his legs and frowned down at his dust-covered black boots.

Imandoff scooted the chairs closer to the side table and motioned Takra to sit while he went to stand at the corner of Geyti's desk.

"Now, why would the Jabed continue to harass you here at Rising Fort?" Imandoff scratched at his beard, his eyes intent on Geyti. "There are a number of smaller holds, all easier to capture."

"My thoughts exactly." Geyti meet the sorcerer's stare with a steady glance. "Unless someone within the Fort, one who has certain information, traded it for gain."

"The key?" Imandoff asked.

"And what goes with the key," Geyti answered. "But why would the Jabed want information of the whereabouts of Varanna's armor?"

"So your family had the responsibility of the armor. It explains much. As to why the Jabed attacks you, he desires power over the Temple once more. But what did Cabiria hope to gain?" Imandoff's smoke-gray eyes turned thoughtful.

"So you guessed Cabiria was the traitor." Geyti sighed and shook his dark head. "It took little thought to reach that conclusion, Silverhair. I learned of the planned deception from one of my servants. I have imprisoned my sister in her room."

"Your own sister?" Takra frowned as she leaned back in her chair. "She left no doubt that she hated Corri, but to do this."

"Hatred can excuse itself of any action," Geyti said. "Cabiria planned to give the key and the secret to the Jabed for just one reason—to see Corri fail."

"Have you seen Corri?" Imandoff's question took Geyti by surprise.

"I thought she was with you at the Temple." Geyti pushed aside scrolls on the desk as Needa and the servants entered with plates of food and pitchers of ale. "We must eat while we talk," he added as the door closed behind the servants. "Always before, the Jabed has attacked by day. But my scouts say that they prepare for battle now, just as night comes. We must be ready for such an attack at any time after dark."

Imandoff and Takra sat at the side table to eat while Geyti used the desk. "Is my niece in danger?" the master of Rising Fort finally asked.

"We have no reason to think so." Imandoff dipped a piece of bread into the meat juices. "I think she came into these mountains for solitude until the war with Frav begins."

"This key you sent to Imandoff, what is the tale behind it?" Takra watched Geyti with intent amber eyes.

Geyti sighed. "What I now tell you, no one outside my family has ever been permitted to know. It has been a closely guarded secret for generations, ever since my forebears came to this Fort." He poured another mug of ale, then continued. "This secret was only passed down through a special ritual to the oldest child in each generation when he or she came of age. As you know, Silverhair, in my house either man or woman may inherit. When my father Hakran passed the secret to me, he allowed Cabiria to take part. Perhaps he thought that doing so would sweeten her somewhat."

"Not that one!" Takra said as she forked another piece of meat. "She has the temperament of a tujyk."

"A poisonous grasslands snake," Imandoff said in answer to Geyti's puzzled expression.

"An apt description." Geyti sopped up the juices on his empty plate with bread. "As descendants of Varanna, my family has always had the responsibility of guarding the armor's secret resting place."

"Now that puzzles me," Imandoff said. He looked over the rim of his mug at Geyti. "How could your family be descended from Varanna when she had no brothers or sisters or children?"

"But she did have a child, a son born little more than a year before the first great battle." Geyti turned his mug round and round in his hands. "That son is the ancestor of this house. It was a closely guarded secret, and as far as I know never written into the history of the Peoples. That is part of the secret passed down in this family."

"So that explains the old writing I found at the Temple." Imandoff stared across the room, deep in thought. "Does your family know for certain where the armor lies?"

"I have never gone to see if the stories were true," Geyti answered, "but there is no reason to doubt the records. However, I suspect that once there were more details given during the family ritual, details that have now been forgotten. The ritual spoke of the resting place of Varanna's armor being guarded by the Whisperers and only the key opening its hiding place."

"The Valley of Whispers!" Takra shivered as she thought of their last journey through that place. "Perhaps the ritual means another place."

"There is no other place close by with Whisperers," Imandoff said.

"You are looking forward to going to that place again, are you not?" Takra grumbled.

"But of course. Think what we might find this time, besides the armor." Imandoff smiled. "Do not fret about Corri," he said to Geyti. "We will likely find her with Uzza at Springwell. Then we all can go down the back way into the Valley."

"Here are the secret family records." Geyti shuffled through the scrolls on his desk, then held out two of them to Imandoff. "Read them while I go to check on the walls."

"I do not think I can outrun a barsark this time, old man," Takra said as Geyti left the room. "And the Whisperers, will they harm our child?"

"I will protect you, Wind-Rider." Imandoff sat down in Geyti's chair and spread open one of the scrolls. "You and the child you carry are the most important things in my life. But we must go there, you know that, for the outcome of the battle with Frav surely depends upon Corri wearing Varanna's armor. And if Corri fails in the battle, you and I will have to ride for our lives. Kayth will hunt us down like animals."

"I know," Takra whispered, "but my heart tells me this will be no simple finding of that armor."

"Listen to this." Imandoff motioned Takra to move her chair closer. "This was written by a priestess, one called Hyanthus, daughter of Gyran, son of Varanna." He looked up at Takra, excitement plain in his eyes. "This record has come down from the early years of the Peoples in this land."

"Perhaps this will help us recover the armor. The Mother of Mares knows we have had no luck at the Temple." Takra leaned her elbows on the desk.

He bent back over the scroll, tracing the words with one finger as he read aloud. " 'The resting place of the ancient dead lies beneath the earth, covered by a grove of stone trees. There I placed the armor of my foremother Varanna, to guard it against the greed and misuse of the High Priestess Kinla. When Kinla declared she would wear the armor during Temple ceremonies to celebrate the Peoples' victory over Frav, Varanna herself came to me in a dream and warned me against this. She showed me the way to the ancient burial ground and bade me hide the armor there. With the help of the older priestesses, I took Varanna's armor from the cave by night and fled into Deep Rising. By dreams I was led to a strange valley where I was safely guided through many dangers. At last I found the entrance to the under-earth chamber, and there I left the armor according to the dream-instructions.' " Imandoff paused. "The rest of the scroll is too damaged to read."

"That priestess was a brave woman," Takra said. "To go alone into the Valley of Whispers is not something I would do willingly."

"But what has a key to do with the Valley?" Imandoff fumbled in his belt pouch and took out the key on its red cord.

"I understand that keys go with locks," answered Takra. "The Tuonela have no need of locks, since word of our punishment usually keeps thieves away."

Imandoff folded his long-fingered hand around the key and opened the second scroll. "Ah, it seems someone of the house of Gyran did go to the Valley years later to check on the armor." He continued to trace the lines on the scroll with his finger as he read. " 'After much searching, I found the cave mentioned in the family records. With much thought I deciphered the plaque there. Its information led me through the grove of stone trees where I fitted the key into the altar and descended into the earth. There, as told by Hyanthus, lay Varanna's armor, as fresh and clean as the day that great warrior woman wore it into battle. I told no one of my journey or what I found, but my wife worries about the dreams I have sometimes. I dream of the voices. I will never go there again.' "

"A man with sense." Takra frowned and pursed her mouth in thought. "He spoke of a cave and a plaque, perhaps the cave we entered and the plaque you took from the wall, Silverhair?"

Imandoff never had the opportunity to answer, for the sudden tolling of the Fort bell sounded a warning. Imandoff and Takra raced down the hall, through the great hall, and into the courtyard, all thoughts of Varanna's armor forgotten for a time.

The long night was filled with attacks by the outlaws and renegade priests who followed the deposed Jabed. From time to time Imandoff sent balls of light floating above the enemy to reveal their attacking position, but he conserved his strength for what he feared might be a greater attack later. Until midnight the storm continued to rumble and flash about the hills; the rain poured steadily down. Not until the storm clouds began to break apart and the moon come through did the Jabed's men try for more than attacking the great gates. As watery moonlight flickered across chain mail and helmet, stinging swarms of arrows flew from the high walls down into the groups of men trying to batter in the gates or scale the walls. But to expose oneself long enough to aim put the Fort's bowmen in peril.

"This must stop!" Imandoff said as he looked down from his position on the wall at the Fort's wounded and dead being carried inside the great hall.

"Shield yourself!" Takra yanked him back into the shelter of a wall tower as several arrows sang by. "Being a sorcerer does not make you deathless."

Imandoff closed his eyes and began to create a ball of swirling bluish light between his hands. When it was larger than a man's head, he cast it up and over the wall, where it hung motionless above the gates. The invaders cried out against the light that revealed the position of every man skulking about the base of the Fort's walls. The sorcerer continued to create balls of light, casting them up to hang at intervals along the wall, illuminating every possible line of attack. The Jabed's men began a hurried retreat to the cheers and catcalls of Geyti's people.

"Not any too soon," Imandoff said as he steadied himself against the wall tower.

Takra saw streams of perspiration running down his face, glistening in his beard like drops of dew. The light from the magickal balls overhead revealed the weariness in his gray eyes. He drew himself up tall as he walked to the very edge of the Fort's wall, clearly visible to the hidden attackers in the dark beyond.

"I would speak with the Jabed." Imandoff's deep voice echoed up the hill in the night suddenly grown quiet. "Come forth, you who call yourself the Jabed, and speak with me. Do not hide behind your outlaws like a coward."

There was the faint rustle of bushes, and a tall man stepped just to the edge of the magickal light. He ventured no more than one step away from the concealing darkness.

"It took no great intelligence to see that Geyti has a tame sorcerer at hand," the Jabed called back. He kept his face shadowed in his hooded cloak. "What do you want, Imandoff Silverhair? Did you not receive enough acclaim that you must now sell your services to common bidders?"

Imandoff stiffened at the insolence in the man's voice. His eyes narrowed as he leaned perilously over the barricade. "You have no place among the Peoples." His deep voice sliced through the growls from the men about him. "Your expulsion from the Temple should have been warning enough. This land rejects you. Go to Frav, where your tendencies will be admired. For I tell you, Jabed, every man's hand in this land is now lifted against you. We cast you out! You are as nothing to the Peoples!" The last words were spoken with such power that the Jabed rocked backward. "Go to Frav, and lick Kayth's feet for the power you crave."

A ball of power had been growing in Imandoff's right hand as he spoke, not one of bluish color, but tinged with dark red. "Be gone!" he cried as he threw the ball at the Jabed.

The Jabed whirled and ran back into the darkness, the red ball exploding at his heels. "I will go to Frav," the priest screamed at Imandoff. "At least in Frav I will be honored for what I am and what I believe. I spit upon the Peoples and will rejoice when Frav grinds them into the dust!"

There were muffled clinks of armor and bridles in the darkness, but no more arrows flew toward Rising Fort. The men at the Fort watched and waited well past dawn before they truly believed the siege had been lifted.

Imandoff and Takra slept until noon, when one of the servants came with the message that Geyti wished to speak with them. The servant took them back to the study at the rear of the great hall, where they found Geyti pacing the floor with news.

"I sent two of my best men to track the Jabed and his men," Geyti said. "He truly is heading straight for Frav! They also found several dead men along the Jabed's trail."

"Wounded in the battle?" Takra asked as she settled into a chair.

"No, killed by sword or dagger in the back." Geyti continued his pacing.

"So he weeds out all who will not follow him unquestioningly." Imandoff shook his head. "What have the Peoples become that they allow such men into positions of authority?"

"I am sending messages to all the towns along their line of march. My riders know where to find the Green Men. They will carry word where they can, freeing my men to prepare for the final battle." He looked at Imandoff, his eyes weary and sad.

"And that too soon, Geyti of Rising Fort," the sorcerer answered. "The Peoples will be on the march to the border within a few weeks. The Fravashi will surely strike at Harvest Moon."

"We must send word to the seamen of Asur," Takra reminded him.

"The Asur will not fight with us, as all know." Geyti slammed his fist on the desk. "Those puling cowards will hang back to see which way the wind blows, hoping to pick up the pieces after for power and profit."

"The seamen will fight," Imandoff reassured him. "They have given me their word."

"The way Corri told it, they desire this fight." Takra grinned.

"I have a way to send such a message." Geyti pulled out parchment and pen and slid them across the desk to Imandoff. "The Forts of Deep Rising have long kept men posted in secret along the Barren Mountains. They use a system of flashing shields by day and torches by night to send messages to sympathetic men inside Asur. Write down your message, Silverhair, and the seamen of Asur will have it within four days."

Imandoff pushed his chair to the desk and took up the pen. On the parchment he wrote a single sentence in bold strokes: *The Dream Warrior arises at the Harvest Moon.*

"Now we must reclaim Varanna's armor," he said as he rose and handed the paper to Geyti. "It may take us some time to discover a way into its resting place, but the Dream Warrior must wear it during the final battle."

Takra and Imandoff rode out of Rising Fort, with Geyti's blessings, at dawn the next morning.

The Volikvi, disguised in a dingy white robe, and his small band of Fravashi warriors dressed as Kirisani traders waited until the deep night before they crept across the border between Tuone and Frav. The priest carefully wrapped the small black box that had opened a hole in the spells for them and placed it in the saddlebag slung across his horse.

"I still do not understand how we can ride all the way into Deep Rising without being challenged." The captain of the soldiers looked at the sharp-faced priest with distrust.

"I will explain again." The Volikvi mounted his horse and reined it close to the man. "Each of you wears a special belt buckle that distorts your true appearance. Do not speak to anyone, for this device will not change your voice. Only I will answer questions, for only I know how to sound like our enemy. Our mission is of great importance: to bring back a certain key and a piece of sky-stone stolen from us by the Kirisani." He leaned closer to the captain, staring at him with glittering eyes. "Or must I send you back so that Jinniyah can explain, perhaps before the altar of Jevotan?"

"I understand, Lukalus." The captain's eyes filled with fear. "I understand and obey."

"Good." The Volikvi turned his horse toward the Tuonela grasslands, and the small band of warriors followed silently.

By morning they had worked their way around the Tuonela patrols strung out along the border and were in the fringes of the vast land of waving grasses. They rode throughout the day, undetected. At night they camped without a fire. By pausing only for food and sleep, they reached the foothills of Deep

Rising within ten days, and still no one within Tuone or Kirisan was aware that their defenses had been breached.

"Hell-fire, how are we to find what the Volikvi seeks in those mountains?" one of the soldiers said quietly to the captain.

The captain looked around at the rugged, tree-covered slopes. "Do not ask questions," he murmured. "That way we may all get back home alive."

Oblivious to the warriors, Lukalus cupped the watery red pendant-stone in his hand as he listened to Kayth's instructions.

"This way," he said as he dropped the pendant inside his robe. "Jinniyah says the burial mounds lie to the west along this trail. When we have recovered the sky-stone, we will go to a certain fort here in Deep Rising. I will slip into that place and steal an ancient key. Then we will return to Frav."

The Fravashi soldiers followed the priest up the mountain path without question, their eyes and ears alert for danger. But the Volikvi Lukalus rode with a smile on his thick lips, confident in the protection promised to him by Jinniyah.

They met no one on their way up the mountain toward the isolated village of Springwell. Although the soldiers grew nervous at not seeing people, Lukalus rode on, unconcerned, unerringly finding his way into the burial valley hidden deep in a fold of hills. There, the Volikvi ordered the soldiers to stand guard while he and two of the men dug into one of the mounds.

"I do not like disturbing the dead, even if they are Kirisani." One of the guards glanced nervously over his shoulder at the opened grave.

"Quiet, Juak! That Volikvi has ears like a fox." The other man glared at his companion. "Just be glad you were not ordered to dig." He wiped at his nose with his hand. "I have a feeling that Tedri and Warro, " he jerked his thumb toward the two diggers, "will not live to return to Frav."

None of the soldiers, except the two who dug into the grave mound, saw the jet-black disk decorated with glaring red symbols that Lukalus placed in a special sack and stowed in his saddlebag.

The Fravashi priest and warriors quickly left the burial valley, retracing their path down the mountains until they came to a branching of the trail. There, Lukalus turned away from the path leading to the grasslands and headed east, the alert men behind him.

"There is a storm brewing," the captain said as he edged his mount up beside the priest. "Should we not find shelter for the night?"

"Jinniyah sends the storm." The Volikvi turned cold eyes toward the warrior. "It will cover my entrance to this fort, which has the key I seek." He looked straight ahead as the captain fell back among his men.

Just before sunset they reached the hill above Rising Fort. Below them all appeared quiet, although the Fort gates were shut and guards manned the walls.

"Stop!" The captain's hissed whisper and hand on his arm brought the Volikvi alert. "Below us, along the treeline. There are armed men hiding among the trees. This place will soon be under attack."

"Jinniyah provides." The Volikvi smiled coldly. "We will lead the horses downhill to the rear of the Fort. I will enter a secret tunnel there while you wait. When I have what I seek, we will return to Frav."

The first drops of rain from the storm struck them as they made their way through the trees to the northern Fort walls. They reached the place the Volikvi sought just as darkness and the storm fell over the mountains. Quickly, the priest searched along the base of the wall until he found a small ring set in one of the stones. With an imperious wave of his hand, he motioned one of the soldiers to tug open the hidden door. Behind it lay blackness, but the Volikvi did not hesitate. He entered the Fort, leaving the men to stand in the pouring rain and wait.

"Listen!" The captain's voice was nearly lost in the grumbling thunder. "Sounds of battle at the gates."

"Sorcerer's lights!" One of the warriors pointed. High over the Fort they saw bluish-colored balls of light hanging steady in the storm.

"Stand ready," the captain ordered, but even his hand gripped the hilt of sword.

Within a few moments, the Volikvi stood again at the secret door, his sudden appearance startling the uneasy warriors.

"We ride," he said as he mounted his horse. A flash of lightning illuminated his cold face. "There is nothing more to be done here."

The priest and the Fravashi soldiers made their way back to the trail into Tuone, avoiding the battle-area. Without a word, the Volikvi pushed the pace of their travel. By midnight the storm was gone as quickly as it had come.

How can I tell Jinniyah that I failed? the priest thought. *The key was not there.* He felt a vibration from the pendant under his robe and reluctantly took it out.

Did you do as I ordered? Kayth's face was clear in the priest's mind.

The disk was just where you directed me, the priest answered, then hesitated. *But the key was not there.*

The priest's body shuddered as Kayth roughly invaded his mind, searching for lies and evasions. *So,* Kayth said, *someone has taken it before you arrived. Return to Frav at once. And remember what I told you. If any of the men fall ill, leave them behind and ride on. The soldiers are expendable. The protection I placed upon you will keep you free of the plague. I need one man to bring me what I need, and that man is you.*

I obey. Lukalus shivered as Kayth's face faded away.

"Captain, Tedri is ill." One of the warriors rode close to the commander and whispered his words, his eyes on the Volikvi ahead of them. "You know the legends about opening old graves."

The captain urged his mount forward. "Lukalus, one of the men ails."

The Volikvi turned toward him, his face plain in the watery moonlight. "Stay away from him. When he can no longer ride, leave him behind and take his horse." The priest faced the moon-dappled trail and rode on. *Thanks be to Jevotan, Jinniyah's ritual protects me thus far.*

As the invaders hurried farther down the trail toward the grasslands, Tedri began to rave with a high fever. When he reached the stage of vomiting and no longer could sit on his horse, the warriors refused to go anywhere near him. Finally, the Volikvi himself dumped him in the bushes along the trail and ordered the rest to move on. The deserted man was too ill to resist or follow.

Four days onto the grasslands, Warro, the second man who had opened the grave, fell from his horse, unable to rise. Again, the Volikvi coldly ordered them to ride on, leaving the plague-stricken man behind to die alone.

Chapter 7

"Are you certain this will deceive the gatekeeper?" Corri fidgeted beneath the cover of her cloak. The blistery rash from the herbs Sallin had rubbed on her face and arms itched horribly. It took all her willpower not to scratch. She raised her head enough to stare at the closed gates of the Leshy Mystery School.

The storm rumbled overhead, blocking out the moonlight. The first drops of rain began to splatter on the street around them.

"Yes," Sallin answered, her mouth dimpling at the corners. She pushed one of her black curls away from her face. "Now keep quiet. We must be quick, for the effect of the herbs will not last long."

"Open the gates," Merra called out to the gatekeeper. "We have with us one ill with cow-pox."

A man opened the shutter in the gate and peered out. "You two! Where have you been?"

"Where is old Riman?" asked Sallin.

"I am the new gatekeeper," the man answered roughly. "Now, hurry inside. The High Clua wishes to see you at once. And get that sick one into a safe place. Cow-pox is catching."

I wager Morvrana wants to see them all right, Corri thought as they dismounted and made their way through the gate.

The two girls quietly handed over the horses to the gatekeeper, then hurried Corri off in the direction of the infirmary. Once out of the gatekeeper's sight, they turned aside to huddle in the shadows of the dormitories.

"What now?" Merra whispered. "Morvrana will have taken over Mother's rooms."

"The gatekeeper thinks we do not know what happened," Sallin murmured. "He does not suspect, or he would have sent someone to warn Morvrana. The courtyard is empty. No one comes from Mother's rooms." She pointed at the candle-lit windows across the herb-planted court.

"Can you create a diversion?" Corri gauged the distance across the court, into the building, and down the stairs to the room of the Mask. Within her mind, the path to the rooms far below within the earth remained clear, as if she had walked it just yesterday. The storm was expending itself in full force now and rain pounded all around them.

"First, we must get help from those initiates who did not follow Morvrana." Merra twined a lock of her red-blonde hair about her finger as she thought.

"Tell the elders, and the word will spread," Sallin whispered. "We can gather in groups about the courtyard, not all in one place. That way, Morvrana will have great difficulty controlling us."

These are healers? Corri grinned to herself. *If I am ever in battle, Goddess, I hope I am on their side and not their enemy.*

"Yes, but first we must lock in those who follow Morvrana. Can you get the keys while I keep watch?" Merra's voice held the same battle-eagerness Corri had heard in Takra. Sallin nodded and slipped away into the darkness. "We go now." Merra patted Corri's arm as she slipped away into the dormitories behind her sister.

Help me, Goddess, Corri thought as she ran light-footed through the pouring rain toward the High Clua's building. She darted into the deepest shadows near the door and waited. Crouched there, the rain dripping down on her, she reached out with her thoughts to find the building's occupants.

Morvrana feels secure. There are only two people in the room with her, she thought as she delicately probed into the High Clua's room. *The girls spoke true. Something strange and evil is close to her.* Corri reached out farther. *One guard at the top of the stairs, another at the door of the Mask chamber below.*

Corri gently tried the door and was surprised to find it unlocked. She eased inside, her senses alert for traps. Silently, she made her way down the hall, listening to the murmur of voices from the High Clua's rooms. She squeezed into a dark corner between a cabinet and the wall.

Help me, Lady. I need those guards below to come up into the courtyard, or I see little chance of freeing Jehennette.

Corri leaned against the wall and relaxed. Within seconds, her dream-self was free of her physical body and flying down the torch-lit stairs to the secret underground chambers of Leshy.

The first guard was a man, idly leaning against the wall, a dagger slung on his hip. He showed no awareness of Corri's presence as she hovered over him.

You must leave your post and go to the courtyard. Corri carefully fed the thoughts into his bored mind. *There is a disturbance at the gate, people from the city trying to get inside.*

The man suddenly looked agitated. He turned as if he heard an order called from the top of the stairway, then dashed up the steps. Corri followed his progress into the courtyard where the faithful initiates were gathering. There was a brief scuffle as two of the men disarmed the guard, bound, and gagged him.

Now for the other one, Corri thought as she swiftly found her way to the door of the Mask chamber. This time a young woman stood guard, already uneasy from the thoughts Corri had fed into the first sentinel. *The High Clua needs you at the chapel. The initiates who do not follow her have barricaded themselves there.*

With a shout of anger, the woman pounded up the stairs and out into the night, to be met with the same fate as the man.

This is too easy, Corri thought as she flew back to her body. She blinked to orient herself and carefully eased herself out of her hiding place. Then she slipped down the stairs, keeping careful watch as she made her way quickly to the Mask chamber. She fumbled the key from its ledge and unlocked the heavy door.

"Jehennette! Come quickly! Your daughters are even now outside creating a diversion." The chamber appeared to be empty as she peered hesitantly inside.

"It is the Dream Warrior!" The healer Gertha stepped from of the shadows and motioned the others to follow.

"Hurry! We may not have much time, and I do not wish to be trapped down here." Corri urged the prisoners up the stairs ahead of her.

The outer door stood open to the storm and darkness. They heard shouts from the courtyard and the faint sounds of scuffles over the rain.

Stay! The Lady's voice was clear in Corri's mind as she stood on the last step, one hand on the frame of the upper door. *Your battle against the one of Darkness must be here, not out among the others. Quickly, let your dream-self fly free!*

Corri sank down onto the step and leaned back against the wall, already willing her dream-self to break free of her physical body. As she floated above herself, she saw what her physical eyes had missed: a growing blot of Darkness with flashes of red within it in the hall before her.

So this is the evil that I felt before! Corri steeled herself against the insidious pull directed toward her from the Darkness. *This is what I felt but could not see around Morvrana when I touched her thoughts. What is this creature, and how do I fight it?*

The center of the Darkness suddenly began to swirl faster. The swirling solidified into an eye staring back at her.

Stand firm! A woman's voice sounded in Corri's ear, as if the speaker stood just behind her shoulder. *This is not the time for battle with the eye of Jinniyah. He cannot see you, Dream Warrior, although he seeks. The creature you must battle hides behind the influence of the eye of Darkness. Wait for the eye to leave, then press forward to the woman Morvrana. There you will see clearly the creature out of the abyss who now rules her.*

You are not the Lady, Corri thought, not a doubt in her mind that her assessment was true.

I am Varanna, came the answer. *My time has come to be at your side, to finish what I could not do before. Even though you are now in the land of shadows, none of the evil ones can see you unless you will it so. Stand firm, daughter of my blood, and wait.*

The eye continued to stare toward the stairway where Corri's physical body leaned against the wall, as if it felt her presence in some manner but could not find her. Then, as quickly as it had appeared, the eye in the swirling blot of Darkness vanished.

Corri dream-flew down the short hall, through the closed doors of the High Clua's building, and out into the rain-splattered courtyard. The faithful initiates were scattered in little groups, just as Merra and Sallin had suggested, while Morvrana's personal guards ran from place to place in a vain attempt to put them in bonds. Every time Morvrana had to focus her attention on another group, she lost control over the ones she had just frozen into inaction.

"Seize them, I tell you!" Morvrana screamed in rage. The woman stood near the door, her face distorted with the overlaid image of some being who had never walked the soil of Sar

Akka or any other world. "I command you to be unable to move!" She pointed her hand at Jehennette and a group of initiates who rushed toward her.

Corri saw hair-thin filaments of dark red energy issue from Morvrana's fingers and wrap themselves about the initiates, holding them immobile. Morvrana seemed to be completely unaware of Corri's spirit-body that now hovered close behind her.

The sword of Varanna. Corri thought of the strange sword slung on the belt about her physical body now resting at the top of the stairs. Instantly, a phantom copy of the sword was in her hand. *If it feels real, it is,* she told herself as she clutched the ancient hilt. She willed herself up and forward, soaring over Morvrana, who still screamed with rage. *I do not understand why you linked yourself with Kayth and Malya when you swore you would have no dealings with them, but this will stop now!* Corri brought the sword up, then slashed it down across the red filaments. They shattered into tiny sparkling particles that quickly faded into nothingness.

"I cannot see you, but I know you are here!" Morvrana stopped her attacks on the initiates, turning her attention upward, her narrowed eyes frantically searching for her unseen enemy. "I will blast your soul into the abyss, Dream Warrior." She raised crooked fingers toward the heavy storm clouds, her mouth pulled into a grimace against her set teeth. Her clawing fingers moved in twisting, grabbing motions as she pulled hidden lightning out of the night sky. "You cannot defeat me, Dream Warrior. No one can defeat me!"

Corri felt the lightning strike from the thick clouds. *Enough! You are companying with evil, Morvrana. May you bring down upon your head what you deserve for meddling with creatures out of the abyss.*

She threw up her sword arm, deflecting the lightning. It struck the phantom sword blade and ricocheted into one of the tiny courtyard fountains, sending splintered pieces of rock flying. The second strike was sucked into the sword itself, appearing to Morvrana and the initiates as if the powerful energy disappeared into thin air.

Morvrana staggered back, caught her heel against a step, and fell backward. Instantly, Corri hung before the gesturing woman, blocking the malicious energy she projected from reaching any of the astonished initiates. Morvrana babbled strange words as she struck out with her hands; specks of foam gathered in the corners of her twisted mouth.

Seal the energy within her, Varanna ordered. *Then you can deal with this creature from the abyss without danger to the others.*

Seal it? How do I do that? Corri felt a hand fit over hers on the sword hilt. She felt the sword gently pushed down until its tip touched the center of Morvrana's forehead, just above the wild eyes.

The possessed woman screamed in agony at the light touch and scrambled away on her hands and knees. The guards stood in shock, their mouths open. They did not realize their vulnerability until the initiates swarmed on them, taking their weapons and binding them with their own ropes.

Return to your body, Dream Warrior. Varanna's voice grew fainter. *You can easily drive this possessing entity back into the abyss now. Call it by its name and order it to leave in the name of the Goddess. It will have no choice but to go.*

Corri swung around, hoping to see the ancient warrior woman, but there was no one with her. Quickly, she thought of her physical body, swooping back to the stairs and settling herself inside it.

Every muscle aches, she thought as she stretched her cramped legs and arms. *I feel as if I have been run over by a horse.* She forced her stiff fingers to release the sword hilt and saw clearly the indentation of the hilt's design imprinted on her hand. *These dream battles are getting more real all the time.* She looked at her hands in astonishment; the red rash from the herbs was gone. *The dream-flying must have scoured the effect of the herbs out of my body.*

Morvrana's ranting voice broke into her thoughts. The hysterical voice rose and fell as the woman fought against the hands that forced her back into the building.

"By the hell-fires of Frav!" Corri swore as she stood, bracing herself against the wall with one hand until she regained her balance. "You will not defeat me, Kayth, neither you nor this Jinniyah. I will end your part in this trouble at Leshy once and for all."

Several initiates were trying to hold Morvrana against the wall when Corri reached the hallway. All of them bore scratch marks on their faces and arms from the struggle.

I must show no fear, she told herself. *Varanna said I could send whatever possesses Morvrana back into the abyss, and that I will do!*

Corri stopped before the wildly struggling woman and stared deep into her eyes. What she saw looking back at her was not human or even sane. Morvrana lunged suddenly, scattering her captors like chaff in the wind. She stepped close to Corri, spittle dripping like venom from her mouth, her hair hanging in dark swaths about her face.

"You cannot defeat me! I am all-powerful!" Morvrana's lips were flattened against her teeth. She threatened with her sharp-nailed fingers, but Corri stood firm.

"How could you, an initiate of this Mystery School, allow some dark creature from the abyss to enter within you, Morvrana?" Corri asked. "Surely you knew it would take control."

"Nothing and no one controls me." Morvrana looked around her, a sneer curling her lips.

She really believes she is not controlled by this creature, but has power over it! Corri thought.

"Be gone from this woman!" Corri ordered, willing herself not to step back from the promise of violence in Morvrana's dilated eyes. "In the name of the Goddess, I command you to be gone!"

"Who are you to issue orders to me, girl!" The voice that came from Morvrana's mouth held the deep tones of a man's voice. "The name of the Goddess is nothing to me."

The initiates stood in shock, their eyes wide. They drew back from Morvrana as if the fabled abyss had opened at their feet and spewed out the legendary creatures they had long thought to be only fantasy.

Morvrana suddenly seemed to be two people: one the woman who had done the forbidden in her grasping for power, a woman now filled with horror at what she found within herself; the other an entity of evil who had no intention of relinquishing its hold of a physical body. Emotions changed on Morvrana's face as quickly as ripples spread across a pool of water, first the woman's wide-eyed terror, then the smug satisfaction of the entity. At last, only the overlaid visage of the entity remained.

Corri drew her sword and held the hilt up before Morvrana's eyes. "I order you to leave this woman and return to the dark abyss."

The entity laughed, its evil, mocking tones sending the initiates scurrying to put more distance between them and the possessed body of Morvrana. Only Corri and Jehennette remained where they were.

"Can you bind its strength in this world?" Jehennette murmured as she stepped closer to Corri.

Corri kept the sword hilt steady between her and Morvrana. "I do not know," she answered, never taking her eyes from Morvrana's face. "The sword hilt seems to keep it from harming anyone, but the name of the Goddess did nothing."

Jehennette chewed her lower lip in thought. "Drive Morvrana before you into my study. We can at least bind her, thus keeping her in one place."

Corri stepped slowly forward, the sword hilt held steadily in front of Morvrana. The entity moved the woman's body backward with each step Corri took forward. In this slow, silent dance Corri maneuvered the possessed initiate down the hall and into the open door of the High Clua's study.

Corri faintly heard Jehennette's whispered orders and heard the sounds of running footsteps in the hall. She ignored the murmurs and shuffling feet just outside the door as she continued to maneuver Morvrana toward Jehennette's high-backed chair. The woman bumped into the chair, then collapsed into it as Corri advanced, the sword hilt now only inches from Morvrana's face. Within moments, two male initiates appeared with heavy ropes.

"Bind her to the chair," Jehennette ordered.

The entity began to scream profanities at its captors, but it was held fast to the chair by the power of the ancient sword hilt. Fear plain in their eyes, the men wrapped the rope tightly around Morvrana's body, immobilizing her.

"Now what?" Corri asked, as she continued to hold the sword between her and Morvrana. Morvrana screamed and called down curses as she struggled against the power of the ancient sword. "You dare not loose her."

"Cast it out by ordering it by its name." Jehennette looked at Corri in surprise when the young woman said nothing. "What is its name?"

"I do not know," Corri answered, shrugging her shoulders. "Nor do I know how we can discover it." She looked at Morvrana, and the entity glared back.

"Can you fly between worlds, into the place of shadows?" Jehennette asked. "There you may be able to discover the name of this creature."

Why always me? Corri thought, then sighed as she answered her own question. *Because I am the chosen Dream Warrior.*

Jehennette motioned with her hands for the other initiates to leave the room. Corri gave the sword to Jehennette, who kept the weapon before Morvrana's eyes, and walked to the narrow couch near the window. As she lay down, Corri saw

Sallin and Merra standing with their mother beside the bound Morvrana, their prayer beads rattling through their fingers. Corri closed her eyes and shut out Morvrana's wild raving.

On her third breath, she found herself free of her body. She thought of the sword and found it in her hand. *At least this time I will go armed. Varanna, what is the creature's name?*

The legendary warrior woman's voice was faint as she answered. *In the shadow world.*

When Corri called again to Varanna, there was no answer at all. *Now how do I find this shadow world? If it is a different place than the one I visit in my dream-flying, it is a place I do not know.*

As she centered her thoughts on Varanna's words, Corri found herself whirled away through a blazing light that coiled away at the far side of her vision to form a tunnel. Corri aimed her thoughts at the tunnel and rushed down it until she came up against a scintillating barrier that yielded slightly at her touch but would not allow her to go through.

There has to be a gate, an entrance of some kind, she thought as she scrutinized the wall before her. *There seems to be no end to it, up, down, or sideways.* She considered all she had learned in her past dream-travels. In exasperation, she aimed her thoughts at the barrier. *I want a gate, an opening I can pass through, and I want it right here!*

A dark crack began to run up the wall, the sparkling substance drawing back slowly, as if a curtain had been carefully pulled aside. Corri pushed through the crack and found herself falling, tumbling down into a place with no sense of direction.

I can dream-fly. There is no need to fall. Her descent stopped, but she hung suspended in a formless darkness. *Enough! I seek the land of shadows, and I will go there. And when I arrive, I demand to see where I am.*

The darkness around her rolled away like a sea fog to reveal a strange, alien countryside. She settled gently onto a rocky, ashen landscape; there was no color except shades of gray. A few wind-twisted trees clung to the ash-colored slopes, their leafless branches clawing at a leaden sky. Ten paces from where she stood, the ground ended in a sharp drop. In the far distance to her left, she saw the faint smears of more mountains. Brittle dead grass crunched under her boots as she turned to look around her.

This looks like a shadow land. A fine cloud of dust rose about her as she walked to the edge of the cliff to look down. A weird rolling light, rising and falling against the dead-gray sky, drew her attention. *The sea? What is this shadow land?* She caught her breath as an idea formed in her mind. *It is the shadow of our world!*

Corri shielded her eyes against harsh streamers of light that flashed across the landscape like lightning, yet ran horizontally a few feet above the ground. A hundred feet below, she saw the charcoal image of a walled fortress and towers crouching near the banks of a pearly-gray sea.

Wherever this place is, there appear to be people living here. She corrected herself. *Probably creatures of some kind. Now how do I find someone to tell me the name of the entity?*

Corri stepped back from the rocky cliff and sat down on a dusty boulder. She drew out her belt knife and idly tossed it back and forth as she thought. As she pondered what action to take, she leaned forward and began to draw in the dust at her feet with the tip of the blade. Over and over, the blade carved one symbol into the dust. At last, her mind jerked back to what she was doing, and she stared down at the symbol.

The star of Friama! Why did that come into my mind? I never wore such a sign when I thieved in Hadliden, nor have ever I worn such, but the Asuran women do. Light! The star of Friama symbolizes light!

Corri rose, sheathed her dagger, and felt for her fire striker. *By the Goddess, I do not carry one since I learned to call fire.* She smiled and held up her hand. *One thing this place could use is light.* She snapped her fingers, creating a spark of fire. But instead of fading quickly, the fire became a steady pure blue flame on the tips of her fingers. The flame appeared to feed on nothing, causing neither pain nor harm to her hand.

A streamer of the harsh light she had noticed earlier suddenly flashed over the side of the cliff from the ocean shore below and swirled around her. Corri stood still as the strange glow circled closer, then darted back over the cliff.

For good or ill, I feel certain someone knows I am here, she thought. *I have only to wait. That someone will soon come seeking me.*

Corri closed her fingers inside her hand and the blue flames disappeared. She stood with one hand on her dagger hilt out of old habit and waited.

It was not long before Corri heard the clatter and roll of small stones to her right. Soon she saw the head, then the rest of a man as he climbed some hidden path to her high perch. Unlike the rest of the landscape, he was bright with color. His slightly tilted eyes were a warm brown in a sharp-chinned, fair face. His silvery hair hung down over his cloak, which was the color of deep forest trees and trimmed with silver. At his side swung a bright sword with flashing red stones set in the hilt.

"You seek me?" the man asked as he gained the cliff-top and moved quickly to Corri's side. "I heard your call as I sat in the castle below." One long-fingered hand pointed toward the cliff.

"I seek one who can give me a name, a name that will aid me in casting out a possessing entity." Corri flushed as the man looked at her hand on the dagger and smiled.

"You are one from the mirror-world," he said. As he tipped his head, his hair fell back to reveal ears pierced with silver rings. "A dream-traveler. It has been long since one of your kind found the key to enter our world, except while sleeping. And then you either do not remember or choose not to believe."

"I do not know what this world is or where it lies, but my seeking brought me." Corri dropped her hand from the dagger, but watched the man closely. "Who are you?" She eyed the gilded leaf-green tunic, the slim reddish-brown trousers, the tasseled boots on his slender feet. "And why are your clothes bright when all about is gray and dull?"

"I had forgotten how impatient those of the mirror-world are, and how much their preconceived thoughts distort everything here." The corners of the man's eyes crinkled with suppressed laughter at Corri's frown. "It has been long since a trained initiate has come seeking our aid. My name is not important to you. And as to the colors, you see what you expect to see."

"I do not mean to be rude," Corri said, "but I must hurry back. There is great urgency."

"Time has no meaning here." The man stepped closer, his eyes scrutinizing the space immediately around Corri's body. "Yes, I see the urgency. We did not know that your world was in such danger." He cupped his hands together, then opened them to reveal a small crystal ball in one palm. "Name your world."

"Sar Akka," Corri answered. "I came from Leshy . . ."

The man held up his hand for silence as he looked deep into the crystal. "As always, an entity from the abyss was called by one who thought to gain power. She allowed, even desired, his possession." His mouth puckered in distaste as he cupped his hands again and the ball disappeared. "Such is it always with your kind. You meddle where you have no business." He turned on his heel and headed back for the hidden path.

"No!" Corri drew her dagger as she grabbed at his sleeve. "There is no time to beg you for what I need. If I must force you to give me the name I need, then I will." She raised the tip of the dagger under his chin as he turned.

"You would threaten me?" The man's eyes were piercing in their stare. "You would chance your soul and the life of the son you carry, just for a name?"

"Yes," Corri said, and set her jaw. *My son! A boy to walk at Gadavar's side.* Her blue-green eyes stared back at him, her determination clear. "For if I do not get this name, if I lose the coming battle, then my son and I are as good as dead anyway." *I would rather my child and I die than fall into Kayth's hands. I love you too much for that, little one,* she thought as she projected her love to the small life she knew lay within her belly.

"You are one of courage, even though you fear. Your world is fortunate to have such a warrior who is concerned for their freedom." The man gently pushed aside the dagger. "The entity is called Azzi, a wicked one from the black abyss. But there is another seeking full entrance into your world, one more evil and dangerous than Azzi could ever be. When the time comes, you must fight him here, in the shadow world, not where he chooses."

Corri reached out with her thoughts to test the man's words for truth. *There is no evil in him,* she thought and her cheeks blazed with color as the man smiled at her. *He knows what I do, yet he does not dislike it. He is testing me!*

The man pulled a silver chain from under the neck of his tunic and held up its dangling pendant before Corri's eyes. "I like your spirit, warrior. When your hour of greatest need comes, and it will soon, look for this charm. It will come to your hand in the shadow world when things look blackest for your people." He dropped the pendant to hang on its chain as he stretched one finger to stroke a strand of hair that lay on her cheek. "My mark to show you I speak true and that what we shared is real. Warrior of Shadows, go with my blessing and know that I will aid you when and where I can," he said as he turned away.

That pendant, there is great hidden power in it! Corri felt her fingers move as if to gather the strange stone to her.

The strange man walked rapidly to the cliff and disappeared down the path. Corri stood for a moment, frowning at the landscape around her, deep in thought. Then she turned to seek her way back. There was no scintillating wall, no tunnel of light, nothing but dusty, gray rocks and barren trees.

I will return now! she commanded, but nothing happened. Fear shot through her. *Relax,* she told herself. *The man said that we see what we expect to see. So leaving the shadow world must be like breaking into some guarded building—there is always a way. Look at everything. Find the way out this time, instead of in.*

Her mind clicked back to the strange man's words about the landscape appearing as she expected it to be. *I expected the shadow world to be gray, so it was. But shadow world does not mean the color of shadows, it means it is like a shadow to our world! Shadow world, mirror world! It exists as my world exists; yet somehow they are connected.*

Corri smiled, and with her understanding the landscape around her became bright with colors. Although the rocky cliff and the barren trees still existed, now they were shades of tan and brown and dull moss green instead of only gray. Before her, hanging like a gauzy drapery in mid-air, was the black crack through which she had passed. She thought of her physical body, and her dream-self flashed through the barrier and into the light. She came out in the High Clua's room and settled into her body.

"Dream Warrior, how do you fare?" Merra sat beside her, a cup of water in one hand.

"I am well." Corri sat up and drank the water. "I am ready to cast out the entity." She glanced at Morvrana and saw she was still bound tight in the chair. The woman's eyes were filled with hatred and evil.

Corri walked over to stand before Morvrana and took the sword from Jehennette. The entity within the woman tried to overturn the chair, but Sallin and Merra held it upright. It screamed and cursed, turning Morvrana's head to avoid looking at Corri, but she stood where she was, as if the entity's acknowledgment was of no importance.

"I call your name," Corri said quietly, her voice barely audible over the entity's loud curses. "You are called Azzi, and you belong in the black abyss, not here. Look at me, demon!"

Azzi turned to glare at Corri. She felt the magnetism, the power in its glance, but shoved the attempt at control aside. "I will not leave," it said. "You are powerless over the abyss and its creatures."

"I think not." Corri held the sword hilt up as she stepped closer. "You are Azzi, and I command you to return to the abyss!" With her last words, Corri struck Morvrana's forehead with the hilt. "With light I blind you! With fire I drive you! Be gone through the gate of Darkness, Azzi of the abyss! You may not answer to the Lady's name, but I am Her warrior and know yours."

Morvrana's body writhed as the entity struggled against Corri's command. Its foul curses filled the room, making Sallin and Merra cower against the far wall, hands over their ears.

"Be gone, Azzi!" Corri struck Morvrana's forehead again with the sword hilt. The entity howled and screamed. "Be gone, foul Azzi!" She touched the woman again with the hilt. *Three is the charm,* she thought.

The entity gave one last scream that spiraled upward in pitch until it suddenly ended, leaving Corri's ears ringing. Morvrana's head fell forward as she slumped unconscious in the ropes that bound her to the chair.

"Thanks to the Goddess, the entity is gone." Jehennette leaned against one of the chairs, her face pale. "Now the hard work begins. I doubt Morvrana will return to us sane."

"I do not understand," Corri said as she sheathed the sword. "The entity has gone back to the abyss. That is the end of it."

Jehennette shook her head. "I have never dealt with such possession. I know only what I was taught by the old healers, all of them now gone Between Worlds. Possession by minor entities, they told me, always left the person in a weakened condition, unfit to be an initiate, but the stronger entities destroyed the essence of the possessed. I do not know what we will have when Morvrana awakes." She motioned to her frightened daughters to fetch mugs of cider. "But of this I am certain, Dream Warrior. It will not be the Morvrana any of us knew before. We will send her to the locked chambers we use for the mentally ill until we can determine what damage she has suffered. She may well live there the rest of her life."

Corri accepted the cider Sallin gave her. "You and this School are free. Will you take your healers to the borders for the battle at Harvest Moon? The Peoples will have need of you and your healing wisdom."

"My daughters and I, and all the healers who are able, will travel behind the armies when they go to the border." Jehennette's eyes narrowed. "All those who still feel that initiates should stand apart from troubles will be given leave to journey to Sadko, where they will have like companions."

"Mother, have you not heard?" Merra laid her hand on Jehennette's arm. "We first heard the news when we escaped into the city. Sadko is also divided. Even this night a band of their initiates came to the gate, asking admittance just after the gatekeeper was captured. They joined us in the battle."

"So much like your father." Jehennette sighed as she stroked Merra's hair. "When we reach the border, fight with your healing powers, not that hidden dagger you carry." She smiled at Merra's surprise. "Call the Mind Keepers to fetch Morvrana and lock her safely away so she cannot hurt herself or others when she awakes. Sallin, announce an assembly in the chapel in one hour. We must work night and day on medicines. And send word to the new gatekeeper that all initiates from Sadko who seek admittance are to be brought directly to me."

"There is no more need for me here," Corri said as she watched the girls leave. "Is there a place I can sleep this night? By first light I will continue my journey into the mountains."

"The feya women would be good company. They will give you the solitude you need before you ride into the great battle." Jehennette stared at Corri, then raised a hand to touch

Corri's hair. "What is this? Look in the mirror." She pointed to a small oval hung on the wall facing the door.

Puzzled, Corri went to stand before the mirror. One lock of her red hair was completely silvery-white. She gently pulled the hair through her fingers as she stared into the mirror. "Only a sign from one who helped me in the shadow world," she answered. She turned back to Jehennette, a slight smile lifting the corners of her mouth. "A sign to prove a promise for later. I must sleep now, and you have plans to set in motion. I remember my way to the sleeping quarters." She quickly walked out into the hall, across the courtyard, and to the dormitories to find an empty bed.

The sky above was free of storm and wind and wild rain. The moon poured its light onto the drenched herbs and the stone buildings. A thin stream of water from the destroyed fountain flowed across the stones and flooded the herb beds.

If the shadow-man left this sign to be seen in my world, then the pendant must also come. But what will it do? Will I know how to use it? Corri yawned as she opened the door to the women's sleeping quarters.

Chapter 8

Corri rode out of the city of Leshy as soon as the sky lightened enough for her to see her way. She guided Mouse past the sleepy-eyed merchants sweeping the streets before their shops, the last of the all-night revelers staggering home from the taverns, and the travelers coming in through the just-opened gates. Only one person spared a second glance at the hooded figure on the mousy-colored horse. The man stood near the entrance to the Cup and Sword inn, a harp case slung over his back, a sword with a worn hilt at his side.

The young friend of Imandoff! I wonder what business she had in Leshy and where she now goes by herself? Taillefer stared after her, his dark blue eyes thoughtful. *Could she have helped Sallin and Merra? And during that storm last night, I am certain lightning struck inside the School.* He shrugged the harp case farther up on his broad, muscled shoulders. One callused hand dropped to rest on his sword hilt as he set off toward the gates of the Mystery School.

"I would speak with the High Clua," Taillefer said to the keeper who peered through the grille in the gate. "If she is busy, then send for her daughters, Sallin or Merra."

"Are you ill, harper?" The gatekeeper pulled the rope that ran the bell above the gate.

"No, I have news that may affect the coming battle." Taillefer brushed a lock of his dark hair off his cheek, the early sun picking up its auburn tints. "Only the High Clua can judge its worth." *At least you are one Jehennette can trust,* he thought. *What happened to the other woman's chosen trouble-makers? Did the storm last night cover the sounds of conflict when the usurper was thrown down, for she has surely been replaced? Did Imandoff's young friend have a hand in all this before she rode out?*

Taillefer paced back and forth before the gate until it finally opened. Sallin smiled at him and motioned him to enter.

"I am glad to see you escaped retribution for helping us." Sallin's black hair hung in disarrayed curls about her face. "Last night was wild with storm and action within these walls."

"Your mother is back as the High Clua?" Taillefer matched her hurried steps across the courtyard.

"Yes, and Morvrana is in the care of the Mind Keepers," Sallin answered as she pulled open the door to the High Clua's building. "Merra and I found the Dream Warrior. Only she could have conquered Morvrana and the evil entity within her. Now we prepare for the long journey to the border."

"So the Dream Warrior was here and truly is the one who travels with Imandoff. I saw several other people in robes pass through the streets to the School late last night." Taillefer followed the girl along the hall to Jehennette's rooms. "They were not from this School, but I thought them to be initiates."

"They came from Sadko. Some at that Mystery School are unhappy with the changes forced upon them and have come to join us." Sallin opened her mother's door and stood aside for Taillefer to enter. "Soon you will see initiates of Leshy, those who choose to follow Morvrana, leaving these walls. Some will make the journey to Sadko; I do not know what the others will do."

"Enter, song-smith." Jehennette sat in a high-backed chair near one of the windows. "My daughters told me of your aid. You have my thanks for helping them."

Taillefer crossed the room to sit in a chair beside Jehennette. He looked at the High Clua, not regal and forbidding as the old one had been, but with a wide laughing mouth, a sprinkling of freckles across her nose, and sparkling green eyes.

"What brings you here?" Jehennette asked. "Surely there is no trouble in the city."

"No, something far different." Taillefer slipped his harp case off his shoulder and set it beside the chair. "You know that long ago I trained at the Temple in Kystan, but did not have enough talent to earn a position as a priest." Jehennette nodded. "So I earn my living as a song-smith."

"And a good one, I am told. You sing the old songs that most have forgotten." She took his broad hand in her dimpled ones. "But you keep your sword-skill, I see." She ran her fingers over the calluses.

"I want to go with you when you journey to the borders." Taillefer waited for her answer, afraid of refusal. "I have only my song and sword-skills to offer, but those I give gladly."

"Strange, is it not, how we are led to do certain things? I thought to send for you later," Jehennette said. "Not for the journey, but rather to ask if you knew the oldest of our Peoples' songs, the ones which may give clues to the coming battle." She held up her hand when he started to speak. "And yes, you may go with us. How could I deny you the opportunity to sing of this battle when it is finished?"

"You knew what I desired most." One corner of Taillefer's mouth raised in a grin, then he turned solemn. "Surely, you are not going—not the High Clua?"

"I will not send my healers where I would not go myself." Jehennette frowned and turned her head to stare through the window at the initiates harvesting herbs in the courtyard. "Some of my people will not return, song-smith, as you may not. Think carefully how much you are willing to wager to go on this terrible journey."

"I would wager all I am," Taillefer said softly.

The High Clua's green eyes locked with his, assessing his motives. "I believe you," she answered with a smile.

"As to the songs you asked about, I have remembered one that I think may be of value. That is why I came."

Jehennette leaned forward, her attention full upon him. "Tell me."

"A very few of the song-smiths and the initiates in the Temple are aware of the Lay of Destruction, a very old song, but I think they do not realize its importance."

"I have heard it." Jehennette's probing eyes watched his expression with interest. "Its meanings are cloaked with strange word choices. My teacher did not know how to interpret it."

"It speaks of the black disk of Frav, something that can bring about the defeat of the Peoples, unless . . ."

"Unless a mighty warrior destroys it with a plaque of Light. Have you discovered what this means?" Jehennette rose to twitch the curtain across the window to keep the sun out of their eyes.

Taillefer shook his head. "We have no knowledge of what Frav has, nor do we know of this plaque. However, I may have unraveled the secret of how the plaque can destroy this disk." He closed his eyes and began to sing, his clear voice filling the room.

"From the secret cave the treasure came, carried by one of great fame. The warrior crossed the bridge with one, who fought with five and carried one. He dared the flames and Footed Snake to reach the altar, melt and break. The black disk shone there, key to the door of evilness, corruption, more. Yet forth he strode and slammed it down, the plaque into the evil crown. It melts and boils, the two are one, And she who dreams the battle done, shall risk her life for victory and in her flight shall set us free."

"I had forgotten that part, if I ever knew it." Jehennette's voice was quiet.

"I have found no song-smith who does know it," Taillefer replied. "I learned it from an old initiate who died shortly after I entered the Temple." He leaned forward, elbows on knees, chin in hand. "I think Imandoff Silverhair may well be the warrior who crosses the bridge into Frav, and if he can find this plaque and put it over the black disk there, I think the plaque will melt the disk. But as to the woman who dreams and the one fighting with five and carrying one, that I cannot interpret."

"The one who dreams must be the Dream Warrior." Jehennette smiled at Taillefer's raised brows. "She is a young woman who rides with Silverhair and Takra Wind-Rider. She will do battle for us with her powers."

"The one with red hair? I saw her ride out this morning and have heard the whispers of her powers." Taillefer shook his head in disbelief. "But she is too slight to be a warrior."

"She is truly a warrior, song-smith, a warrior who can do battle in places you and I will never see—the shadow world."

There was a knock on the door and an initiate stepped inside. "Pardon for interrupting you, High Clua," the young woman said, "but Lydon has cleansed the speaking crystal and reached the Watcher priestess at Kystan. All is well there. They prepare to march to the border in three weeks."

"Good. Send word that the healers of Leshy will join them."

The woman nodded and left the room. Jehennette walked to her desk, her plump hands behind her back as she thought. She turned to face Taillefer.

"If you would go with us, song-smith, bring your possessions to the School at once. I will have a room made ready for you. Three weeks will give you time to prepare your soul for this battle, for none of us knows if we shall return when the fighting is done."

Taillefer nodded agreement, then rested his hand on his sword hilt. "I would sharpen my sword skills as well as prepare my soul," he said. "The School is a place of healing, not fighting."

"We will make allowances," Jehennette answered. "Whether our healers live or die may well rest on your fighting abilities, for we do not fight. I choose you to be our protector. The other warriors will be battling at the border and may not have time to think of the healers behind the lines. I lay that burden on you. Do what needs doing to sharpen those fighting skills, song-smith."

Taillefer walked back across the busy courtyard to the gates, deep in thought. *I am going! The opportunity will be mine to write and sing of the great battle! If I live,* he thought, then grinned. *If I die, I may become part of another song-smith's epic. Either way, the adventure is worth living.*

Jehennette opened the deep chest that sat beside her bed. She lifted out parcels wrapped in yellowing paper and tied with faded ribbons until she found what she sought. The little wooden casket was richly carved with twining flowers and leaping animals, a sample of ancient art. When she opened the lid, the faint scent of roses reached her nose. Gently, she pushed aside the parra-seed fluff inside and lifted out a pendant strung on a silver chain.

"What a shame that the High Cluas of Leshy did not continue wearing this," she murmured. "Now we no longer know if this has power or is merely a symbol of the office of High Clua. Still, I feel I should wear it when I face the armies of Frav."

Jehennette slipped the chain over her neck and let the pendant fall on her breast. She cupped the golden globe with the silver wings in one hand as she opened her senses to any flow of power.

"No strange powers, only the feeling of all those who wore it long ago." She let the pendant fall back on her breast. "I shall wear it as a symbol of all the High Cluas who stood against the Fravashi evil over the centuries." A warm feeling wrapped around her as she left for the assembly with her people in the chapel.

"All is now well at Leshy." The tall young priestess stood very still as she reported to the Oracle. Her dark blue eyes were nearly purple in the shadows of the room. "One initiate called Morvrana temporarily took control of the School with aid from troublemakers there." The woman's rose-bud mouth tightened in displeasure. "Jehennette has been restored as High Clua."

"I am not surprised that such a thing happened." The young Oracle rubbed her fatigue-smudged eyes with her thin hands. The delicate black brows and sooty lashes were stark against her pale skin. *I am so tired,* she thought, *but I must keep watching with all my powers through as many hours of each night as I can. No one else's powers are as strong to see the future as mine are. I must watch for any signs of danger that we have overlooked. I must always be prepared.*

"The Watcher at Leshy says that this Morvrana did the forbidden. She secretly underwent the Trial of the Mask and opened herself to an entity from the abyss."

The Oracle sighed and looked at the priestess. "Yes, I know. The Dream Warrior sent the entity back into the abyss. Jehennette will care for Morvrana."

Lirna plucked nervously at the braided blue belt at her waist. "They say Morvrana must always stay in the care of the Mind Keepers."

"Yes, she would now be insane." The Oracle rose and walked to the window. Her violet robe and head-veil glowed in the early morning light. *I remember the terrors of the Trial,* she thought and shivered. "Is the Dream Warrior still at Leshy?" *It frightens me that I cannot see her in my visions.*

"No, the Watcher said she rode out for Deep Rising at first light."

"Alone?" The Oracle whirled to face the girl, whose face went scarlet under the scrutiny.

"No one knew that you wished it otherwise." The young priestess fidgeted, her white robe sending reflecting flashes of light around the chamber.

"You are not at fault, Lirna," the Oracle said gently. "Go rest for a time before you go back to the crystal. But first, send someone to bring Zanitra to me. The Dream Warrior should not be alone during these dangerous times, and I know not where Imandoff Silverhair is." *I cannot see him either,* she thought. *Even Takra is hidden from me when she rides with Imandoff.*

Lirna inclined her head and hurried off to deliver the message to Zanitra herself. It was not long before the initiate, once of Sadko, knocked lightly on the door to the Oracle's chamber. The tall woman entered at the Oracle's call.

"I understand that the Dream Warrior rides alone in Deep Rising." Zanitra did not wait for the Oracle to speak. "The Green Men keep good watch there."

"These are dangerous times, Zanitra." The young Oracle motioned the tall, slender woman to sit in the chair beside her. "Reports come in each day of new attacks by the Jabed and his followers, roving bands of brigands, and even dangerous animals come down from the isolated areas. We do not even know where Corri goes in Deep Rising." She paused. "You know no one can see either her or Imandoff in visions?"

"I discovered that when I sought my brother. Little sister," the older woman said gently, "you must not worry so much. You take all upon your shoulders instead of asking the help of others." The crystal pendant on her breast caught the light as she patted the Oracle's thin arm. "I will go after the Dream Warrior and see she is kept safe. I think I know where she might go."

"Take Odran with you." The Oracle sighed as she leaned back in her chair. "Whatever you need, you have only to ask." *When this battle is finally done, perhaps I can sleep completely through a night without waking and wondering.*

"I will ride out within the hour." Zanitra looked in pity at the girl's face, the cheekbones stark under the pale skin, the blue marks of fatigue under the dark eyes. "Rest now, little sister."

"There will be time enough to rest when the battle with Frav is done," came the soft reply. "If the victory is ours, I shall rest easy, knowing the Peoples are safe once more. If Frav should win, I shall rest in the arms of the Goddess. Never will I let the Volikvis take me into their evil power." The Oracle's eyes closed in weariness.

Zanitra said nothing as she left the chamber, but at once made preparations for horse and supplies. Dressed in her traveling cloak, the tall woman rode out of Kystan before the sun was an hour older. It was not discovered until nightfall that with her she took one of the mystical sejda balls, a shining globe of crystal purity, or that she rode alone.

"Do not bother the Oracle with this," Vairya ordered, as she paced her chamber still clad in her fighting kilts. "I did not expect such willful disobedience from Zanitra. Imandoff, yes. He has always gone his own way."

"They were born of one birth," Odran answered, looking down at the tall High Priestess, who stood more than a head shorter than he did. He held his helmet, shaped like a snarling Rissa head, in the crook of his arm, the thin scars of sword practice clear on his hands and forearms. "I will ride after her, and I ride fastest alone." His words stopped Vairya's protests, and she nodded in reluctant agreement.

"Zanitra said she knew where Corri might go." Vairya stared up into Odran's green-flecked light brown eyes. "You and Hindjall followed her into Deep Rising once before. Can you guess where she means?"

"She knows the way to Springwell, but I think she may go beyond that place." The warrior rubbed his narrow jaw with his hand. "If I cannot find her, I know a Green Man who will surely know, for he was with her before."

"Go then, and the Goddess go with you."

Vairya watched the giant of a man stride out the door; his broad shoulders held straight, his dark blonde hair in its knot atop his head gleaming in the lamplight. *Find the girl and keep her safe, Odran, for she is our only hope,* the High Priestess thought as she sat on the couch by the window and lowered her head into her hands. *Without her special powers, how can the Peoples hope to overcome the Fravashi armies that will soon pour across the borders?*

The farmer who brought the message sent by shield and torch from over the Barren Mountains into Asur shifted nervously from one foot to the other as he waited in the courtyard of the Red Horse Inn in Hadliden. He did not know or quite trust Rympa, the innkeeper, but then he did not really trust any city man. He had given Rympa the proper words, learned against just such a need, and now must wait until someone arrived from the wharves to take the secret message on to the fishermen and sailor-merchants.

A young man, his rolling gait marking him as a seaman, sauntered through the open gates and looked around. His eyes fell on the farmer, standing near the inn's door and twisting his broad-brimmed hat in his hands. Without hesitation, the young man went straight to the farmer, linking arms with him and leading him inside the dim inn.

"Two mugs of ale," the seaman called to the barmaid as he led the farmer to a table. "Now, tell me what you have for us," he said as they sat down.

The farmer looked down his nose at the young man's long braid hanging over his shoulder, the curved gutting knife stuck through his belt. "The signal came over-mountain early this morning," he said. " 'The Dream Warrior rises at the Harvest Moon.' " He fell silent as the barmaid set the ale on the table, took the coin offered by the seaman, and walked back to the far side of the room.

"Are you against the Peoples winning this war?" The seaman stared at him with narrowed eyes as he quickly drank down his ale.

"We farm on the slopes near the Limna forests," the farmer answered, turning the mug of ale between his broad hands. "The Magni have always been a thorn in our side. We have no love for them and their narrow ways. But we are not stupid." He sipped at the ale and found it to his liking. "Whoever wins this coming battle, those who live in and around the Limna forests will stand apart. The Fravashi will make slaves of us all, but are those of Asur any different? If the Peoples win, the temple Magni of Asur will tighten their fist even more."

"Think on this," the young seaman said as he rose. "If the Fravashi win, we all will sooner or late be slain on their filthy altars. If the Peoples win, you can petition Kirisan for protection."

"Would they cross the border to drive the Magni away?" The farmer looked skeptical.

"By that time, man, the Kirisani will be heartily sick of persecution by any religion. Stiff-necked religions always bring strife and battles, for they always want to prove they are right and others wrong, by the sword if necessary. You think the Kirisani and Tuonela will allow that?"

"I will take your words back to the farmers and the Limna workers," the farmer said. "We will do what we can to rankle the Magni and their spies." He stood up and carefully placed his hat on his head. "We have no war-skills to offer, just our stubbornness against control."

The seaman slapped him on the shoulder. "That is more than enough. Safe journey."

The seaman hurried off to deliver his message, while the farmer claimed his horse and rode out of Hadliden.

I still dislike cities, he thought as he urged his mount into a trot. *But that seaman had wise words. There will be no problems urging that course of action on the farmers and Limna workers. The Magni are in for a time of trouble they never expected to see from us.* He grinned to himself as he left the city of Hadliden behind.

Chapter 9

"Someone is on the trail ahead," Imandoff said to Takra, who rode close beside him. "If it is one of the mountain people, perhaps they will have news of Corri."

"You have felt no more sign of her?" Takra's eyes narrowed when Imandoff shook his head. "Perhaps she did not come this way. There was no news at Tree-Home, when we passed there."

"I have no doubt she is headed for these mountains." Imandoff held up his hand in greeting as the lone traveler stopped and eyed them with suspicion. The man was dressed in the rough clothing of the mountain villagers, a broad-brimmed hat on his head. "We are friends," the sorcerer called. "I am Imandoff Silverhair, and I seek news of one Corri Farblood, known to Uzza of Springwell and Thalassa of Tree-Home."

The man walked closer, his hand never far from the dagger at his belt. In the other hand he held a thick walking staff. "I come from Springwell. No strangers have been in our village. But a rider could have passed by without our knowing."

"The Green Men, have they spoken of a visitor?" Imandoff slid down to stand beside the man.

The villager pushed up his hat and scratched his head in thought. He squinted against the bright sunlight, the fans of wrinkles deepening at the corners of his eyes. "They have spoken of no one, except outlaws. We have seen little of the Green Men for days now, what with the Jabed's men causing trouble."

"I think you need not worry any longer about the Jabed," Imandoff said, the corners of his mouth turning up in a half-smile. "He and his men attacked Rising Fort during the storm and were driven off toward the Fravashi border, tails between their legs."

"That is good news, something to tell those of Tree-Home when I get there." The man closely watched Takra, his blue eyes taking in the sword at her side, the spear in the holder by her leg. "Tuonela," he said shortly. "Any news from the border?"

"We have come from Kystan," Takra answered. "Do the villages send men to fight at the Harvest Moon?"

"We are no trained warriors." The man ground the end of his staff in the damp earth. "But we have fighting skills that will hold these mountains at your back. Some of the Green Men prepare to march north. Village men will take their place, guarding against roving outlaws who hope to take advantage when the soldiers are gone."

"We need brave men to hold the land while the armies face the Fravashi warriors." Imandoff remounted Sun Dancer. "Fair journey," he said as the man saluted and went on down the trail.

"Do we wait or go on?" Takra nudged Lightfoot to follow Sun Dancer. "That they have not seen Corri means nothing. She is wise enough to take to hiding rather than chance a meeting with strangers who might be hostile."

"Corri is not in danger or we would feel it," Imandoff answered. Takra nodded. "We have no time to wait. We must find Varanna's armor," he continued, "before time to march to the border. And we have little time to do that."

"So now we go to the Valley of Whispers." Takra's voice was very quiet.

"Geyti's records say the armor is there. We have no choice but to see if we can discover its hiding place."

"We had better find it, sorcerer. If we do not, the battle may be lost before it begins."

"Whether the armor has powers may not matter." Imandoff looked over his shoulder at her. "Seeing Corri dressed in Varanna's armor, the ancient sword in her hand, may well inspire the Peoples in a way no magick can." He looked sharply at a small cairn of rocks along the edge of the trail. "A signal from the Green Men. They know of us." He pointed at the cairn. "We will turn aside and see what news they have."

Takra followed him as he turned Sun Dancer off the main trail and onto a deer slot that ran back among the trees. *Armor inspiring the warriors is well and good,* she thought as she looked at Imandoff's broad shoulders, *but I am not against a little magick turning the tide of battle.*

"We have seen no lone woman riding through the trails of Deep Rising," the Green Man said, as he and Imandoff sat smoking their pipes in the evening dusk. Takra sat leaning against a tree, trying to keep the clouds of insects away from her face with one waving hand.

"You would not have known she was a woman," Takra said. "She can move unseen if she wishes."

"You speak of the Dream Warrior." The man blew another cloud of smoke, and the cloud of insects moved away from his face. "Still, she would leave trail-sign."

"If your men do see her, Tuman, send word to us. We will ride on to the Valley of Whispers on a search for something that may turn the tide of battle in our favor." Imandoff tossed his bag of smoke-leaf to Takra. "Rub some of that on your face and arms," he said. "The spring-gnats hate its odor."

Takra rubbed a piece of smoke-leaf on her arm and sniffed, wrinkling her nose. "How can you smoke this?"

"It has a pleasant taste but a repelling odor when unburned." Imandoff grinned at her.

Takra grumbled, but rubbed the leaf over her face and exposed arms. The annoying gnats moved away.

Tuman carefully knocked out his pipe on a bare spot of ground and covered the burned leaf with dirt. "I must ride on. There is news of another band of men coming over the mountains from Asur. Since they come in secret and are armed, we must expect the worst."

"My thanks for bringing word that my message reached the seamen of Hadliden," Imandoff said as Tuman mounted his horse. "Attack from the sea will draw off some of the Fravashi soldiers."

"If I do not see you again before the border, Silverhair, I will surely see you there. Many of the Green Men prepare to march with the Kirisani army, and I go with them." Tuman raised his hand in farewell, then rode off through the shadowed trees.

Imandoff and Takra slept soundly that night in the little woodland clearing. When the first faint marks of dawn touched the sky, they rode on toward the cliff tops above the Valley of Whispers.

"We can reach the Valley from here. Finding Corri must wait a little longer." Imandoff pointed to a narrow canyon leading from the cliffs, winding to the valley floor. "We will have to lead the horses, for there is much loose rock. Watch your footing, Takra."

"We climbed such a canyon when we left the Valley before," Takra said as she dismounted. "But that one is farther west."

She started after Imandoff, Lightfoot following her. "I have seen no hoof prints."

"That does not mean Corri has gone elsewhere. My instincts still tell me that she will come this way. And we have the task of following the few clues we have to the hiding place of the armor."

Imandoff threw Sun Dancer's reins over the horse's back and stood aside as the roan sat nearly on his haunches, sliding and half hopping down the pebble-strewn canyon. Takra pressed herself against the rocky wall and let Lightfoot follow the big roan.

"If she came up this far, she is headed for Ayron's cabin," Imandoff said as he slid after the horses, one arm out to help Takra. "I will cast a fire-ball when it gets dark. Corri will recognize the signal, if it is truly her up there."

At the bottom of the canyon, they remounted and rode toward the center of the Valley of Whispers. An unnatural quiet drifted through the Valley. No birds called from the sparse groves of trees; no animals fled through the tall, dry grass at their approach. Without a word, Imandoff turned Sun Dancer toward the distant misty center, where the wavering forms of dark trees and tall stones could be seen.

"Will we have to face the Whisperers again?" Takra spoke quietly as she nudged Lightfoot alongside Imandoff.

"I truly do not know." The sorcerer's storm gray eyes held hers for a moment before he turned back to stare at the stones where he and Takra had fought the Volikvi priest. "Perhaps this time they will let us pass without challenge."

You do not believe that, Silverhair, nor do I, she thought, but she said nothing as they rode on.

They were within a quarter of a mile of the standing stones and the ancient altar when thick mists suddenly dropped around them. It was impossible to see more than ten paces before or behind. The faint buzz of disembodied voices began to whisper in their ears, growing stronger and clearer as they pushed farther into the Valley.

Takra kept her place at Imandoff's side, unwilling to voice her fears, yet not wanting to lose him in the mists. She set her teeth, dreading the illusions she knew would soon plague her. The horses plodded on, carefully picking their way through the dense mists and completely undisturbed by the strange Whisperers. She saw Imandoff fumble at his saddlebag, finally drawing out the plaque of the Forgotten Ones he had taken from the cave. He pressed it against his forehead, then reached out to grab her hand.

"This helps, though by the Goddess I do not understand how." Imandoff gripped her hand tightly with one hand, while the other held the plaque to his forehead. "Does contact with me lessen the pull of the Whisperers?"

Takra realized that as soon as Imandoff had touched her, the Whisperers faded to an incoherent buzz. "Yes," she answered. "Why should this work? You carried the plaque last we were here, and it gave no such protection."

"I do not know, but bless the Goddess it does."

Takra watched the swirlings of the mist around them, forming and dissolving, half-revealing images of dead companions and enemies. *Mother of Mares, protect the child I carry.* Trembling with fear, she glared at the illusions, willing them away.

An hour of riding finally brought them to the edge of the ruins in the center of the Valley. The mists coiled back a little, revealing the moist-streaked, moss-covered stones, some strewn across the ground, others still upright. The illusions and voices disappeared.

"It must be near sunset," Imandoff said as he dismounted and led Sun Dancer through the ruins of the Forgotten Ones. He slipped the plaque back into the saddlebag. "What sun we see is far to the west now." He pointed up at the glowing mists above them. "First thing in the morning we will begin our search."

"I could wish for a different place to camp." Takra dismounted and followed him.

"The mark of a barsark, and the bones picked clean." Imandoff stopped near the ancient altar, touching the bones of the Volikvi priest with his staff. "This is the safest place to camp in these mountains," he said as he led Sun Dancer a few yards beyond, where there was a grassy spot clear of stones. "The rogue outlaws who roam these hills and harry travelers will never come here."

"Frayma help us," Takra mumbled. "Even though they are vicious outlaws, they are smarter than we are."

Imandoff unsaddled Sun Dancer, turning him loose to graze among the ruins. "The horses will not go far," he said when Takra raised her eyebrows. "Neither will anyone try to steal them. And they will warn us if a barsark comes hunting." He knelt to clear a small circle of ground from the dry grass as Takra unsaddled Lightfoot.

The Tuonela warrior woman stood with the water-bags in her hands as she looked at the mist-slicked ruins. Then her nostrils flared as she scented water. "Is it safe to move from here?" she asked.

"Do not go more than twenty paces from this spot without me," Imandoff answered. "I will seek dead wood from among the grove."

Takra slipped off into the swirls of mist, following the scent of water until she found a tiny spring under the very edge of the dark, forbidding trees of the grove. She could hear Imandoff's footsteps, amplified by the clinging fog, as he gathered dead branches. Quickly, she filled the water-bags and hurried back to the campsite. Imandoff was nearly on her heels with an armload of firewood.

"I still do not like this place," she grumbled as she watched him stack the wood, then snap fire from his fingers.

"Nor do I," the sorcerer answered. "Yet the only clues to Varanna's armor point to this ancient place, and here we must search."

"And Corri?" Takra dug out journey bread and dried meat.

"Tonight I will send up the fire-signal." He glanced upward at the mists that blocked the rays of the setting sun, allowing only a diluted glow to reach the ruins. "I only hope Corri will see it."

"If she is near." Takra shook her head as she looked at the mists that seemed to be growing thicker.

"She is near," Imandoff answered. "Somewhere."

Corri reined in Mouse under the trees on the hill above Rising Fort. The day promised to be hot, even in the mountains of Deep Rising. She watched the guards on the walls, the armed men who stood watch while the hay was brought in from the fields surrounding the Fort. Everywhere she felt a sense of alertness, a cloud of unease.

Something has happened here recently, she thought. *I wonder if Uncle Geyti will welcome a visit, or if he will even let me look for this key the voice in my dream said is here?*

She started to nudge Mouse with her heels, then hesitated. She turned her head to look back at the trail that led farther into the forested mountains that went to Springwell and beyond.

Go on into the mountains! The Lady's voice demanded. *The key will come to you, but first there are greater things to be done.*

Startled at the voice in her mind, Corri involuntarily twitched at the reins. Mouse danced nervously at the sudden jerk.

Halka said to trust the Lady and my feelings. Corri looked with regret at the Fort, then turned Mouse back to the trail. *Perhaps Uzza will have had word of Imandoff and Takra. Perhaps they have even discovered the rest of Varanna's armor and all this running about the countryside can cease.*

Although she had not pushed Mouse on the journey to Rising Fort, Corri now began to feel a compulsion to hurry, a sense that something needed to be done and soon. Still, she kept a wary eye and ear for other travelers, taking to the trees whenever she sensed or heard someone on the trail. Once it was an armed party of merchants, their guards riding with drawn swords; other times it was only solitary travelers, mountain people by their dress, going from one village to another.

She paused where the trail branched into Springwell, but felt an overwhelming urge to go higher into the mountains.

Ride on, a woman's voice said.

Are you Varanna? Corri asked. *You are not the Lady.*

Yes, I am Varanna. I have long awaited for the Prophecy to bring forth one of my blood so that I may complete what I left unfinished.

Corri reached out with her senses to test the unseen speaker. *I feel the same energy I felt in that other voice, when I fought Azzi in Leshy. There is no evil, just a strength and firmness of purpose.*

The urge to ride on became stronger. She thought of Uzza with regret, but let her feelings guide her on. As she rode past Springwell, the sun began to slip over the tops of the Barren Mountains to the east. Although she had ridden that way before, once hampered by the pain of a broken arm, the second time in fear for Dakhma, Corri unerringly found the narrow path that led along the cliff tops above the Valley of Whispers. The hoof prints of two horses marked the trail for a time, then turned aside and disappeared down a narrow canyon that led to the valley below.

If the riders are Green Men, they are about their business, she thought. *If they are outlaws, they will find things in that valley best left alone.* She rode on up the trail, eyes and ears alert, one hand never far from her dagger.

Why am I led this way? she wondered as Mouse continued to follow the valley's rim to the west. *Will I eventually be led down into that haunted valley alone?* She felt no urge to turn Mouse aside into any of the pebble-strewn cuts that led downward. *Or am I to go up to Ayron's cabin of death?* She shivered and hunched her shoulders.

Ride on! Varanna's voice was stronger this time. *I will be with you until your task is finished. I will do all I can to protect you and your child.*

Lady, why does this Varanna speak to me? A prickle of unease ran through Corri as she remembered the possessed Morvrana.

She is My messenger, even though only her spirit remains.

Calm flowed through Corri's mind. *Then I will go.*

It was deep-shadowed under the thick trees. By the time Corri reached the clifftops, the Valley of Whispers below was sunk in deep shadows with a dense misty cloud in its center. It was too dark to ride on. She dismounted and cared for Mouse before she built a tiny fire, more to keep her company than for warmth.

The summer heat had been building all day. Usually the night brought cooling, but instead the heat hung heavy over the mountains, muggy and uncomfortable. Corri splashed water from a little spring over her head and face, then settled beside the fire to eat a meager supper of journey bread and apples. Mouse drowsed on her tether, showing no signs of uneasiness.

How strange my life has been since I chose to follow the Lady's will and be Her Dream Warrior, she thought as she lay on her blanket, hands behind her head. *Not only do I have true friends in Imandoff and Takra, but I have Gadavar to love me. And soon I will have a child!*

As drowsiness began to slip over her, she reached out with her inner senses for any sign of evil, but found nothing except calm and peacefulness. With a sigh, she fell asleep and never saw the fire-ball glimmer for a few moments above the dense fog in the valley below.

Dream Warrior, do you hear me? The voice cut through the meaningless dream in which Corri had floated. *I have been sent to help you, as a way of paying penance for my wrongs.* The face of the soothsayer Ayron hung before her.

I am not dream-flying, Corri thought, looking at the formless place around her. *Ayron is dead and buried, so he must speak to me from Between Worlds.*

The Goddess has granted me this time to guide you. Ayron's almost lidless eyes were filled with sadness. *You did well by Dakhma and my son. I thank you for that. Goddess knows, you had no reason to be kind after the way I treated you.*

I made a promise to take Dakhma to safety. Corri concentrated, and Ayron's robed figure came into focus. *And your son has nothing to do with what you did.* Ayron hung his head. She reached out with her senses, but no taint of evil clung to the figure.

What help I can now give you, I will. Go to my cabin, Ayron continued. *There, in a hidden place under the far left hearth-stone, is an ancient neck-piece. I found it in the Valley of Whispers but never knew of its use, although I surmised it had ritual power. I never dared try to determine its use. You must go there, take it from its hiding place, and wear it.*

You want me to trust you, after what you did to me? Corri was still suspicious of anything Ayron suggested. She remembered clearly his use of the addicting fenlix spores to heighten his powers and how he had abused the child Dakhma's powers. *Why should I wear this necklace?*

I can see only a little way into the future now and know that the necklace in some manner will increase your powers for the final battle. I truly do not know why, just that it must be. The figure began to fade. *Ask the Goddess if I speak true, for I swear I do not lie. When the woman Zanitra comes for you, go with her where she leads.* Ayron's voice and form faded completely from the dream.

Wait! Why will Zanitra come for me?

There was no answer. Corri floated for a few more minutes in the formless place of her dream as a beautiful singing rose around her, accompanied by the flash of colored lights. The lights clustered into a long sinuous form that wrapped itself around her, filling her with peace and confidence. As she reached out to touch the light, she suddenly surfaced into wakefulness with a deep breath.

The first faint streaks of dawn colored the sky and tumbled into the valley below, sparkling off the strange swirls of mist. The heat from the day before still clung, sticky and stale; already the summer sun threatened to add to the discomfort.

Corri sat for a few moments, thinking about the beautiful lights and Ayron's strange words. *Lady, tell me what I must do.* But no answer came from the Goddess.

Ride on, Varanna said. *Follow your intuition. I shall be with you.*

Corri chewed her lower lip as she pondered the things she had seen and heard. *My senses for detecting evil have sharpened,* she thought, *and I felt no evil in Ayron, the lights, or this Varanna who now speaks to me.*

The urge to move on still pressed against her. Corri splashed her face again with water from the spring and rolled up her blanket, then saddled and mounted Mouse.

"If I am wrong in following Ayron's words," she said to Mouse, "then we may be in deep trouble. However, I would know if this path led to evil, so I will listen with my inner senses and travel the path pointed out to me."

Mouse snorted and pushed ahead. A faint breeze rolled through the trees from the west, providing a temporary surcease from the morning heat as Corri headed toward the deserted cabin.

There was a rustle of leaves in the bushes behind them, near Corri's camping place. A catlike creature, almost as tall as Corri's waist, watched her leave. The breeze blowing from the woman to the big Rissa kept the horse from scenting it. The Rissa's lip curled in a soundless growl until it recognized the scent of the woman. The Rissa reached out with its thoughts and gently touched Corri's mind. Yes, it was the same woman it had helped before, the one who aided the child the Rissa had rescued from the evil ones. Unaware of the Rissa's mind-touch, the woman continued in the direction she needed to go.

The huge cat narrowed its silver-gray eyes as it slipped silently through the trees and bushes behind the woman and horse. It passed through the mottled patterns of light and shadow, almost invisible, its golden-brown sides and dark brown-tipped fur on its back blending with the trunks of the trees and the earth.

Corri rode on to Ayron's isolated cabin, completely unaware that the Rissa followed her.

Corri reached the deserted cabin on the high mountain side late in the afternoon. It crouched in the center of a mountain meadow, a low building made of stone blocks and a timber roof. Close beside it, on the downhill side, were a pole corral and a lean-to shelter for horses. Beyond the cabin, the slope faded into thick groves of fir and yellow-bark pine, the last forests of Deep Rising. The stark teeth of the Barren Mountains rose in the distance, a reminder of how close Corri was to the border between Kirisan and Asur. Owl-light slipped gray and shadowy down the mountain.

"Plenty of owl-clover for you," Corri said as she unsaddled Mouse, rubbed her down, and turned her into the corral. "It may be dry in the lowlands, but up here the rains have been kind."

Shouldering her blankets and saddlebags, she walked to the cabin, remembering the tragedy of her last visit when she and her friends had found Ayron dying of tujyk poison. *This had better not be a place of ghosts,* she thought. *If I find it is, I shall walk back down the mountain in the dark. I have no need of moaning ghosts.*

Corri lifted the latch and the door swung open to reveal an empty room, cold ashes on the hearth and a dark stain on the floor. Two beds along the far wall were piled with musty blankets; a small table sat in the center of the room, with overturned chairs beside it.

She dropped her equipment by the door and walked hesitantly to the fireplace. The iron hanger still held a kettle with a ladle stuck in a hard gray mass inside it.

The last meal Ayron was cooking for Dakhma when Malya and Roggkin found them. Corri lifted the kettle by the bale and set it to one side of the hearth. *I am here,* she thought, looking around the room. *Now what? First, I do the needful things, bring in water, find wood, build a fire. Then, after I wash off the trail dust, I will eat and go to bed. Ayron's cache of Forgotten Ones' treasure can wait until tomorrow.*

There was still a plentiful supply of firewood stacked along the cabin wall outside under the protection of the eaves. Corri brought in an armload and soon had a fire going that took off the chill of the mountain air. When she pulled the musty blankets off the bed, she jumped back as a family of field mice scampered out. They disappeared through a crack under the door, like a line of fat, little retreating soldiers. Laughing, she dumped the blankets outside by the door.

"You might as well continue to sleep in them," she said to the vanished mice. "I brought my own."

By the time it was dark, Corri had cleaned out the nest of one wood-rat and several colonies of common spiders, washed at the little spring behind the cabin, and brought in two buckets of water. She found a rough lean-to behind the cabin that obviously served as an outhouse. Only after checking on Mouse and reassuring herself that she was alone on the mountain did she feel content to eat a light meal and spread her blankets on the straw ticks.

There had better be nothing crawling about in these, she thought as she gave the ticks a vigorous shaking before she spread the blankets. Nothing fell out on the fire-lit floor.

Before she settled on her make-shift bed for the night, she laid the ancient sword and the bag containing Varanna's helmet on the floor beside the bed. Quickly, she stripped off her boots and clothes, then crawled between the blankets with a sigh. It was not long before she drifted off to sleep.

The Rissa crept cautiously to the cabin, taking care to stay downwind from the horse grazing in the pole corral. It blended into the shadows as it chose a resting place where it could clearly see the cabin door. The bright moon hung unobstructed overhead.

The Rissa reached out with its mind to the woman and found her sleeping. Laying its great head on its outstretched paws, it waited, keeping the slender thread of communication open. It was not long before the cat-like creature jerked awake, its tufted ears pricked forward, an almost inaudible growl rumbling in its throat. The Rissa lay its head back on its paws and prepared to follow the woman in her dream-flying.

Chapter 10

Corri found herself hanging in the night air above the mountain cabin, the Valley of Whispers below her to the east. She looked up at the moon, noting the tiny sliver of darkness that covered one edge.

The time is short now, she thought. *Soon we must leave for the border, armor or no armor.*

Dream Warrior, you must seek my armor. The figure of a woman wearing a misty white robe, her head covered by Varanna's damaged helmet, appeared at Corri's side.

Corri recognized the woman's voice she had heard during the battle with the evil entity at Leshy and later on the trail into Deep Rising. *You are Varanna.* Corri knew with certainty she was corrected in the naming. *I have many questions to ask you. Why is your armor so important to the battle, and why have I, a thief from Hadliden, been chosen to be the Dream Warrior?*

You are of my blood, thus the choice was made. The armor is a symbol to the Peoples and to an ancient foe who will be at the battle, Varanna answered. *Your friends are even now near the place where it is hidden. Its real importance is the protection it can give the child you carry. He must not die, as my child did.*

Your child? There was no answer from Varanna. Corri tried to see the woman's eyes through the openings of the helmet, but only darkness lay within. *But why am I the Dream Warrior instead of a true warrior?*

The woman shook her head. *I only know you were chosen by the Lady. Do Her will, Dream Warrior, and look for me in this battle. I will be at your side. But remember, you are more than the Dream Warrior now, for a great adept has named you Warrior of Shadows.*

Wait! Corri reached out a hand, but the woman disappeared, fading quickly away. *Now what?* There was no answer. Corri tried to return to her body, but instead her dream-self turned to face north toward Frav. *Perhaps I should see what Kayth and the Fravashi are planning. It has been a long time since I spied to see what they plan.*

With the thought, she found herself speeding swiftly through the night sky, straight toward the Fravashi temple-city of Vu-Zai. The great Fire Mountain cast its long shadow over the buildings clustered about its base. The Kratula Gorge was a deep, black chasm in the moonlight.

Corri lingered only a moment before diving downward. The stone walls of the Temple were no barrier, and she stopped only when she hung near the ceiling of Minepa's old room.

The Trow priestess Xephena stood at the door, her head tipped as she listened. She was covered with a dark cloak; her pale legs a flash of lightness as she moved. Satisfied that she was alone, the priestess moved farther into the room, her dark eyes reflecting glints of light from the thick yellowish candles on the table. She pushed back the cloak from her head and arms, revealing her sensuous body clad only in a golden girdle that hung down over the front of her diaphanous skirt.

Where would Minepa hide such a powerful stone? Xephena's thoughts were clear to Corri, although the Trow seemed unaware this time that the girl's dream-self was in the room with her. *I know Kayth did not find it.* She hesitated, looking around the room at the shelves of scrolls, the slick black walls, the furnishings rich with gilt and rare woods and gems. *Minepa was a crafty one. He knew Zalmoxis would take it if he could.*

Why am I here with her? Corri thought, then held her breath in fear that Xephena may have heard her. The Trow gave no sign that she knew of Corri's presence, but continued her slow circling of the room, touching each piece of furniture with her long-nailed fingers. *She cannot detect me in any way! What stone does she seek?*

The Trow returned to the dark table in the center of the room. She leaned her scantily-clad body against it as she thought. *Minepa always used this table to do his magick. The stone must be close by.*

Xephena suddenly knelt beside the table, her sensitive fingers searching the edges for a hidden drawer. She frowned when she found nothing. She reached farther under the table, then smiled as her fingers touched leather. Concentrating, she quickly unfastened the leather straps and gently lifted out a black slab of rough stone as large as both her hands.

The power-sink stone! And now it is mine! Xephena stood up and pulled her cloak around her, the stone hidden in the bend of one arm. *Now we shall see, Kayth who calls himself Jinniyah, if you have as much control over this Temple as you think. This power-sink stone will greatly amplify my talents and those of Zalmoxis. Together, we shall destroy you during the battle and take control of the Temple. Then let the unbelievers of Tuone and Kirisan beware!*

A triumphant smile lifted the corners of the Trow's mouth as she quietly opened the door and escaped down the dark hall to her own chambers.

So she would use a stone contaminated with Minepa's evil to kill Kayth. If this assassination would end the battle, this theft would count for something, but it will not. Corri drifted closer to the floor as she thought. *Besides, I do not think this Trow and the priest Zalmoxis have any chance of slaying Kayth, not from what I have seen and felt of his growing power.*

Corri flinched as she felt a cold tendril of thought flick around the room. She rose to the ceiling again and concentrated with her inner senses. Below her was a swirling mass of darkness, a tainted roiling of power straight out of the abyss. In its center she saw the great eye and shivered.

The Eye of Darkness! she thought. *Does it search for Xephena or for me?* She tried to flee the Temple but could not.

I feel her close, but I cannot see her. The impatient tones of Kayth's voice were clear to Corri's mind. *Are you certain my daughter has invaded the Temple, Jinniyah, or are you merely edgy with every sound in the night?*

I felt an invader. A strange male voice cut across Kayth's words, full of anger and arrogance. *The Trow Xephena has been in this room.*

Xephena often visits Zalmoxis. Kayth sneered at the disembodied voice with him. *She practices her sex magick to keep control of him.*

Take the final step, Kayth, the arrogant voice continued. *Merge with me completely. Let me sense life more intensely through you, and I can make your conquest of Sar Akka total and unassailable.*

Yes, now is the time. Corri could read Kayth's confident thoughts of domination of the spirit of this evil and long-dead priest. *The Harvest Moon is not far off. I must have all the power necessary to defeat and destroy the armies that come against me.*

Jinniyah said nothing, but Corri could feel his smugness at Kayth's greed and self-deception. Like a whisper of wind, the thoughts of the two men left the room, leaving it silent.

Corri became aware of a soft rumbling sound close by her side, a sound which had begun, she realized, as soon as Kayth and the spirit of Jinniyah had entered the area. She turned her head and caught her breath in surprise. A great Rissa floated beside her, its lips drawn back in a snarl, an almost inaudible growl coming from between its bared fangs.

Awed by the huge cat, yet fascinated by it, Corri pushed back her fear. The cat's anger was centered on the others, not her. *Why have you come with me to this place?* Corri's spirit fingers gently touched the fur, and the Rissa looked up at her with silver-gray eyes. It butted its head against her hand. *If you are real to me, and I to you, then why did Kayth not see either of us? Are we stronger together than apart?* She smiled at the Rissa. *Now what are we to do? Show me where I need to go, for you must have been sent to guide me. I feel the Lady's power and goodness around you as I did when Gadavar and I came to your den for Dakhma.*

The Rissa growled once more at the door, then changed to a rumbling purr as Corri fastened her fingers in its fur at the back of its neck. She felt herself streak out of the Fire Temple, the Rissa at her side, across the Gorge, and then to the east. Soon the pair hung over forested mountains where the Takto Range joined the Mootmas. Two pin-dots of fire glowed below.

Too far from the border to be Tuonela warriors, Corri thought as she and the Rissa came closer. Soon she clearly heard the voices of men, quarrelsome and discontent.

"We have proved that we do not want worship of the Goddess to continue. Women should be subject to the rules of men." The Jabed stood across one of the fires from a Volikvi priest. At his back were clustered the ousted priests who had followed him.

"You are not Fravashi," answered the priest Lukalus, his thin face sharp in the firelight. The soldiers at his back stirred nervously, their hands never far from their swords.

"You mean you have no way to cross the border," the Jabed sneered. "Your black box was broken in that last race to escape the Tuonela. We all saw it, even your own men."

The Volikvi glared at the Jabed and his men. "If you had not followed us, we would never have been seen."

"It was not my men the Tuonela saw, but your black robes. And I did not drop your precious box, you did."

"It does not matter now." The captain of the Fravashi soldiers took a step forward. "Those of the Fire Temple will be seeking us. We have only to wait here until they come."

Both groups of men muttered as they drew apart to their separate fires.

So, the ousted Jabed has done more than cause trouble at the Temple in Kystan, Corri thought. *Now he and his followers turn traitor to the Peoples as well. Imandoff must know of this.*

The Rissa took her spirit-hand in its mouth and tugged gently. A mental picture of Ayron's hearth formed in her mind.

You think I should return now. The picture of the hearth came to her mind again. *You want me to seek out the treasure Ayron spoke of. I can at least look at it, even though I may not use it.* Without resistance, Corri let the animal lead her on the swift flight back to the mountain cabin.

As they passed over Deep Rising, Corri picked up a coil of thought she recognized as Zanitra. *What is she doing alone in these mountains?* The Rissa urged the woman on. Near the Valley of Whispers, she sensed the presence of Imandoff and Takra and would have turned aside, but the Rissa firmly drew her away.

Nothing out of place here, Corri thought as the Rissa released its hold and dropped down to settle into its hidden form. The moon had scarcely moved in its path since her start of the night's dream-flying. She watched the Rissa's descent, noting where its body lay, then returned to her own body.

"What is happening?" Corri murmured as she sat up in the dark cabin. "Zanitra on the trail into these mountains, Imandoff and Takra in the Valley of Whispers." Varanna's words came back to her. "Have they found the armor? But why is Zanitra coming?"

Mouse snorted uneasily in the corral, bringing Corri instantly to her feet. Then she heard the faint scratch of claws on the cabin door. Quickly, she crossed the room and eased open the door to find the Rissa pressed against it. The big cat shouldered its way past her and walked purposefully to the hearth as she closed the door.

"So you have been guarding me in more than spirit-form." When she reached out to the big cat with her senses, she felt only the presence of Light; no trace of evil clung to the cat's aura.

In the light of the glowing coals in the fireplace, Corri saw the Rissa's head turn toward her, as one huge paw pressed on the far left stone. She stared back at the silvery eyes, knowing what the animal wanted her to do but wondering how it knew about the words of the dead Ayron.

"I can at least see what the Soothsayer hid there," she said with a shrug of her shoulders. "Perhaps the treasure will be of interest to Imandoff." She knelt and felt around the large stone at the left corner of the hearth, but found it tightly wedged. "I will have to find something to pry it up."

The Rissa reached past her with one paw and hooked its sharp claws under the edge of the stone. With one quick jerk, it tipped back the flat rock, revealing a deep, dark cavity. Then it sat on its haunches, the breath of its low purr ruffling Corri's hair.

Corri peered into the dark hole, cautious about putting her bare hand into a place she knew nothing about. She got a thin limb from the pile of wood near the hearth and probed into the hole. Nothing hissed or came running out. The Rissa lowered its head and sniffed at the cavity.

"Nothing for it but to reach in." Corri sighed and lowered her hand into the darkness. She felt around nervously until her fingers found what appeared to be a circle of metal, then a leather bag beneath it. Gingerly, she pulled out the metal circle and laid it on the hearth. Without investigating her find, she again probed the dark hole until she managed to drag forth the heavy leather bag. It landed with a thud on the plank floor.

"What is in this, rocks?" Corri said as she loosened the leather ties on the bag. The Rissa sniffed the bag, but gave no warning growl. "A book!" she said in surprise as she dragged out a very thick, rare bound volume, the leather cover scuffed, the parchment edges tattered with age. Gently, she opened the book to stare at the strange markings. "No language I know."

She carefully emptied the rest of the contents of the bag: a tiny metal and gem wand, no longer than her hand; a pair of what appeared to be oval-shaped bracelets; three rings with strange gems; several pieces of torn parchment covered with more of the strange language.

"This jewelry reminds me of the circlet holding the owl stone," she said to the Rissa. She dug the circlet, a possession that never left her side, out of her saddlebag and held it alongside the rings. "Yes, the artwork is very similar, although not carved with flowers. Rings for a man, perhaps?" She laid the owl stone by her side, then put everything else back into the leather bag and set it beside the bed. "I will take those to Imandoff. If they truly belonged to the Forgotten Ones, he will be wild with excitement."

The Rissa hooked its claws into the metal circle and dragged it toward Corri. Its unblinking silver eyes held hers, and she saw a mental picture of her putting the old circlet about her neck. "I know I promised, but I fear what it may do. There is my child to consider." She thought of what she had endured during the Trial of the Mask. The Rissa purred as it lay down beside her.

Do not be afraid. I will see that no harm comes to the child. Varanna's voice, full of promise, comforted Corri. *This circlet will strengthen you. Perhaps if I had undergone its changing power and met its Otherworld guardian the Peoples would not have suffered so much.*

How can I know my child will be safe?

I say the child will be safe. The Lady's voice came from a glowing light at the edge of Corri's inner vision.

Corri straightened her shoulders as she gathered her courage, then looked at the Rissa by her side. "Will you guard me as you did when you followed me into Frav this night?" The animal's rough tongue swished across her arm in comfort. "Well, if I must, I must."

Corri held up the neckpiece to the low firelight. The engraving around the band was deep, a mixture of what appeared to be leaping Rissa, swooping birds, and dancing women. It took her several minutes to master the intricacy of the strange catch on one side. The Rissa gave her another reassuring lick as Corri fitted the metal around her neck and snapped the catch. There was a momentary prick from a piece of rough metal along the edges, then nothing. Corri ignored it.

"I will wear the owl stone also," she said as she fitted the band in place across her forehead. "I know its power. If this necklet proves troublesome, I can call upon the owl stone to help free me of its power."

She sat cross-legged, her body tense as she waited for something to happen. "I do not think it has any strange powers," she started to say and realized that she had formed no words with her mouth. Instantly, she became aware of a prickly feeling at certain points on her neck. Her hands fumbled feebly in her lap, as she thought of releasing the catch and throwing the necklet from her.

Its power is subtle, she thought in panic. *Somehow it is forcing me out of my body, just as with the Trial of the Mask. Those pricks I felt, did this thing put some drug into my body? I do not want this!* Only a faint moan crossed her lips.

The Rissa watched the woman with unblinking eyes as her body twitched. It laid its great head on its paws and began to purr loudly.

Corri no longer knew where her physical body was, nor did she know what realm her spirit-body had entered. All around her were flashing colored lights playing across a silver lake, the crystal shores reflecting their brilliance. As she watched the bursting lights from where she stood on the crystal sands, she became aware of a strange, haunting melody coming from somewhere on the lake.

How beautiful, she said to herself. *It sounds so familiar, as if I have heard this song before. This is not the abyss, nor is it the gray place I saw when I went to the shadow world.*

The silvery waters before her suddenly erupted as a great slender serpent reared up from the depths of the lake. Rainbow colors played across its scales and the fin-like protrusions along its backbone. Corri drew back, her heart pounding, her hands reaching for her sword, but the weapon would not come to her hand. The serpent lowered its long, thin head until its red eyes were only inches from hers. Corri found she had no control over the movement of her spirit-body.

Welcome, honored warrior woman. I bless your coming. The serpent's words sang in Corri's ears. *Long have I waited for my deliverer, the woman who will make me whole once again.*

I do not understand. Corri felt the serpent's tongue flick gently across her cheek. *I have never heard of you. Who are you?* In her mind, Corri understood that this was not just an animal, but an Otherworld creature with a distinct personality and powers. *Are you the guardian of whom Varanna spoke?*

The Old Ones knew me as the Singing Serpent, came the answer, all in song. *I was with Varanna at the last battle, although she did not know it, and was split in twain from the death-blow she took. I have waited long for you, Dream Warrior, for only you can reunite what has been made two. The other part of me, created by contamination with the evil of Jinniyah, lives in your world.*

Where? I have never heard of you. Corri tried to remember if she had ever heard such legends, but all that came to mind were the rumors of the fabled Fravashi Footed Serpent.

Alas, my other half is trapped in your world, within the Fire Temple. The evil ones there call it the Footed Serpent and feed its confusion with their own corrupted thoughts. The song of the serpent was sad. *When you go into that place, reunite me, I beg of you. As long as I am divided, I cannot come to help the special ones of your world as I once did.*

Tears slid down Corri's cheeks as she felt the serpent's sadness wash over her. *The Footed Serpent is real, then? I do not understand how a creature of the Otherworlds could be trapped in the physical.*

The singing serpent coiled the upper part of its shining body about Corri, its tongue constantly caressing her skin. *Know only that it is so,* the serpent sang. *To return to me, the one you know as the Footed Serpent must die in your world. If you fail, then I will fade away and nothing will be left except the perverted form of what I once was. My time is short, warrior woman. Save me, for in saving me, you save your people.*

How do I know you are not evil in a beautiful form? Corri clung desperately to common sense, as the serpent's music threatened to sweep her into realms of ecstatic non-caring.

Evil cannot do this without great harm. The serpent raised its head and touched its nose against the owl stone on Corri's forehead. There was a feeling of gentle warmth as like powers met and mingled.

How are you tied to the saving of the Peoples? No prophecy mentions you.

The prophecy about me has been lost. I can tell you only this: By reuniting my two forms, you unite within yourself all the pieces of personality and the powers necessary if you would survive the greatest evil Sar Akka has ever known. The serpent bent its head, looking into Corri's eyes.

You are truly beautiful! Corri raised her hands cautiously and stroked the skin of the great serpent still wrapped around her. The serpent's song rose in ecstasy, and Corri's heart and soul became one with the song.

As the notes of the song gradually ended, Corri felt as if she had been purified and strengthened, had passed some important step in her spiritual growth. *I will do what I can to reunite you and the Footed Serpent,* she promised, and meant it.

Blessings upon you and those brave ones who walk beside you. Protection will I give, and strength of spirit. Love to the child you bear. Walk bravely the path of the Goddess, warrior woman. The serpent loosed its coils, reared up with the lights playing about it, then slipped silently back into its silver lake.

Come. It is time to return. Varanna stood beside her, this time the ancient helmet tucked into the curve of her arm, her radiant face plain. Long black hair tied with a leather thong hung down her back; her blue-green eyes were bright in her pointed face. High, strong cheekbones were flushed with happiness as she put one hand on Corri's shoulder. *I will walk with you each step of your journey, my blood daughter, until together we have seen the end of your geis, whatever the end may be.*

The lake and its dancing colored lights disappeared, and Corri felt herself slipping back into the space occupied by her world. She hung above the Valley of Whispers, her spirit-body motionless under the windless, moon-bright sky. Far below, deep within the mists at the center of the valley, winked a tiny campfire. Instantly, she felt compelled to go there. In the blink of an eye, she hovered beside the fire.

"If Corri had seen your signal," Takra said as she sat, arms crossed on her knees, "she would have surely come to us by now."

"Perhaps I was wrong about her being in these mountains." Imandoff sighed, his forgotten pipe drooping in one hand. "Have I become so sure of my powers, Takra, that I no longer listen to the truth of my instincts?" His face was lined with worry.

No, you are right! I am here! Corri tried to get Imandoff's attention, but he neither heard nor felt her.

They do not sense you. Varanna stood at Corri's side. She smiled. *They are tired, Dream Warrior. Trust the sorcerer to be his old confident self by morning.*

"We should sleep, Silverhair." Takra pushed more wood onto the glowing coals of the fire. "Tomorrow we must search for this underground hiding place, retrieve Varanna's armor, find Corri, and prepare to march to the border."

Imandoff picked up the old plaque from the cave and turned it round and round in his hands. "This must have great importance, besides helping to stop the ancient plague, but I cannot determine what!"

"It kept away the Whisperers. Is that not enough?" Takra lay down and rolled up in her blankets.

"No." The sorcerer frowned at the plaque as if by will alone he could discover its secret powers. "My instincts tell me there is more, much more."

Come. You need rest. Varanna took Corri's arm and pulled her away from the fire.

Corri sped back to the cabin, slipped into her physical body, and opened her eyes. The Rissa still kept guard beside her. Her numb fingers fumbled with the catch as she hurriedly removed the strange necklet. She stared at it in wonder, then put it in the leather bag with the rest of Ayron's treasures.

Do not go far, Varanna, she thought as she crawled to the bed. *I must be ready for action at a moment's notice.* She pulled on her clothes and climbed inside her blankets. *I feel things will move swiftly now, and I need your presence, Varanna, to keep up my courage.*

Corri's thoughts went to her unborn son. For the first time she felt the aura of the child she carried and was surprised when she sensed her love being returned. *So I have changed. The Singing Serpent was right. Now I will have to learn just what all the changes are and how I can use them.* She sought for Gadavar's presence in the mountains and found only a jumble of thoughts, as if the Green Man's attention was busy with many decisions. Reaching out with her mind to test the safety of the surrounding area, she found nothing to cause alarm. Only the peacefulness of the mountain night hung over the cabin.

She closed her eyes, a calmness and serenity wrapped around her, and drifted back into sleep.

Xephena smiled to herself as she took the stolen power-sink stone from the locked chest she kept in her room. *My powers have reached new dimensions,* she thought as she set the black stone on a small table in one shadowy corner. *How simple it was to strengthen my control over Zalmoxis. Now he will be open to anything I say.* She flexed her fingers over the stone, her long gold-painted nails flashing in the candlelight. *Now to see if the stone will help me to spy on Kayth. Since this stone is a link with Minepa's spirit, and that is now a part of Kayth, it should be child's play to listen to his thoughts and plans.*

The Trow priestess laid her hands flat on the stone and bent her head forward as she concentrated. Her long black hair, with its red glints, fell around her face. She closed her eyes, a smile lifting only the corners of her sensuous mouth as she heard Kayth's conversation with the spirit of Jinniyah.

The Harvest Moon with its eclipse will soon be upon us. Jinniyah's deep tones sounded in Xephena's mind. *The Volikvi you sent is trapped just beyond the border. Send Zalmoxis to help them cross through the spells. By the time Zalmoxis reaches the priest with the disk, your daughter Malya will have also arrived at the border. He can bring them both to Vu-Zai.*

And Corri, has Malya killed her yet? Kayth asked. *In some manner she is shielded. I cannot find her thoughts, nor can I enter her dream-state. It is as if she does not exist.*

Malya will surely find her, Jinniyah answered. *Trust her. However, Corri is not the only threat against which you must protect yourself. The sorcerer Imandoff is more than he seems. He also is shielded from detection, and for a reason I had not considered. He is Varanna's Tirkul reincarnated.*

How long have you known this? Why did you not tell me sooner? Xephena flinched at the anger in Kayth's words. *If he, like*

Corri, is shielded from all seers and cannot be corrupted, he too must die before the battle begins.

Patience, Kayth. We must choose the time and place for this sorcerer's defeat. In that way the defeat of all non-Fravashi will be that much greater. A slyness entered Jinniyah's voice as he continued. *You have yet to completely merge your spirit with mine, to allow me to fully savor all things through your senses. As long as you withhold even a portion of yourself, your power cannot be complete. As joined spirits, think of the offspring we could create with your daughter Malya! No one would dare oppose you!*

Then pour all of your spirit into me! Make me the most powerful priest on the face of Sar Akka!

Xephena jerked her hands away from the power-sink stone as she felt Jinniyah leap into Kayth's spirit.

Fool! she thought. *You have willingly given control to one long dead, one who has been a long time without the pleasures of the flesh. With my new powers, it will be simple to seduce such a one through sex magick.* She placed the stone back into the chest and turned the lock. *Once Malya is within this Temple, how easy it will be to kill her. Then I will bide my time, waiting until the heat of battle occupies your thoughts, Kayth. My poisoned claw-blades will end your life, and Zalmoxis will be head of this Temple.* She smiled at her reflection in the mirror, running her hands over her narrow waist and flared hips. *But the real control will be mine, for I shall rule the Fravashi as the true power behind Zalmoxis.*

Xephena took a tiny vial filled with a greenish-black liquid from a cabinet beside the mirror. Taking it to the table, she opened the small box containing her claw-blades, the deadly, thin, sharp knives that fitted over the ends of her fingers. Carefully, she dipped each blade into the vial and set them aside to dry.

Tujyk poison is the most deadly of venoms, she thought as she looked down at the glistening claw-blades, *but the magick I have learned makes it even more powerful. I will try it first on*

Malya. Then I will savor your death, Kayth, when I mark you during the heat of battle.

The Trow opened the door to her chamber and signaled to the priestess who waited in the hall outside. "Prepare that woman caught trying to escape Frav by ship. Take her to the great cavern and chain her to the altar. I will make a sacrifice to Croyna."

And I will savor every moment of it, she thought, licking her lips in anticipation.

Chapter 11

The city of Hadliden was alive with its usual night noises of rowdy tavern singing and busy inns as shadowy figures, in small groups or singly, walked confidently down the wharf-side streets to the warehouse used by Kanlath, leader of the Asuran fishermen. A weak light and the muffled sound of voices poured out briefly each time the small side door was opened, but only fishermen and sailor-merchants dared to enter the building.

Inside, the great, dark-raftered room was nearly empty of boxes and bales, its vacant center full of men.

"I tell you, there is something not right about Korud," one of the fishermen said, his thumbs hooked in his belt. "Ever since Farblood warned us, we have watched him. He never goes near this Yanni Clow, who took Grimmel's place, but somehow he communicates with him."

Kanlath stood in the center of the crowd of sailors, a thin man with sinewy hands from a lifetime of fishing. A frown dipped his brows as he considered the men about him. "How did this Yanni Clow manage to get control of the master thief's domain, I wonder? I have never heard of the man before."

"Dare we leave him alive?" one of the men asked. "Word is out on the streets among the unmastered thieves that this Clow asks many questions about us. And with word come from the sorcerer to be in the waters off Frav at the Harvest Moon, will he be a danger when he learns we have sailed? Even now he gets bolder with each day."

Kanlath shook his head. "I do not know. It would be a simple matter to overcome our locks while we are gone, loot and perhaps torch the warehouse. But how would he know about our plans to fight?" His hand dropped to the fish knife at his belt as the door to the alley opened and closed quickly.

"We are here." The bass tones of Gran, leader of the sailor-merchants, rumbled through the tense silence. He stood just at the outer edges of the light, a tall heavyset man with one eye covered by a patch. The shadowy figures of other men clustered behind him.

Gran walked forward to join Kanlath while his men mingled with the other seamen. "Our ships are ready to sail at dawn. My men on the waters have contacted the Fravashi seamen. They await us in the Zivitua Sea, just across the narrow strait." He looked at Kanlath, a gold tooth flashing in the subdued light as he gave a half-smile. "Why so serious, Kanlath? Surely you have no second thoughts about this venture?"

"About the venture, no," Kanlath answered. "About Yanni Clow, yes."

"I too have wondered about that one. One Magni greedy for power was enough to make me cautious." Gran touched the eye-patch with one callused finger. "Cleeman was filth, a man who liked to wallow in the miseries of others, especially if he created the misery. But we bring someone who may have the answers we seek about this Yanni Clow." He turned his head and motioned to one of his men beside the alley door.

Kanlath's men all faced the door, hands on gutting knives, as Gran's man ushered in a slight figure, a young boy who looked about him with wide eyes.

"Who is this?" Kanlath growled, frowning up at Gran.

"One who has had enough of Yanni Clow." Gran watched with intent eyes as the boy hesitantly moved into the circle of light. "Charri came to us at the boats, seeking sanctuary in return for the information he has. Now, young thief, tell us again what you know of Clow."

"Those who must work for him know for certain he is one of the temple Magni, in fact, one with great influence," came the quiet answer. The seamen gasped, and an angry mutter filled the warehouse. "Grimmel was a hard master of the thieves in Hadliden, but he never reveled in unnecessary punishment or subjected his pleasure-women to cruelty. Yanni Clow, under the influence of the drugs I have seen him take, has already maimed three of the women and whipped two thieves nearly to death for minor offences. And afterward he stood and smiled, licking their blood off his hands!" The boy's young face was white with the memory.

"In their temples on worship-day, the Magni always preach against theft and murder, and many more things they call sins," said one of the fishermen. "You would think they would follow their own preachings."

"They like torture and murder in the prisons they have," murmured another man. "We all saw the results from their loving touch when we rescued the sorcerer." There was a swell of confirming voices from the seamen.

"And I can vouch for the truth behind the lie of their worship-day speeches," said Gran, one hand touching the patch over his empty eye-socket. "I lost an eye to Cleeman, one of their most influential Magni."

"I beg of you, do not send me back to Yanni Clow!" Charri stood straight, fear of rejection plain on his face, but also determination not to show it. "I would rather die at your hands than be sent back. By now Korud will have told Yanni Clow I sought you out. There are those loyal to Clow who take as much pleasure in torture as he does."

"What is this you say about Korud?" Kanlath stepped close to the boy. "Can you say for true, lad, that Korud spies for this Magni? We knew he once spied for Grimmel, but since then we have seen nothing in Korud to arouse our suspicions."

"Yes, he spies for the Magni! Even now you can find him outside the Golden Woman, where he waits for Clow's messenger." The boy's hands shook, but he looked Kanlath in the eyes. "I have learned that you sail tonight, that you go to war against Frav. Take me with you, for if I remain here I am dead."

"What can a stripling like you do with a gutting knife?" One of the fishermen shook his head. "You would be dead in the first battle, boy."

"I am in training as an assassin," Charri replied. "Even though Gran's men searched me well, I still have surprises hidden on me. Not to attack any of you, but to prove I have value." He slowly pulled a thin strand of garrote wire out of the cuff of one sleeve, then produced two hiltless needle-knives out of the lining of his boots.

Gran frowned for a moment as he took the boy's weapons, then threw back his head in a great laugh. "We can always use a clever lad like you. I say we let the boy sail with us," he said as he clapped the boy on the shoulder. "And if we ever return to Hadliden, he may be of great value to us in getting rid of such men as Yanni Clow."

"You cannot reach Clow this night," the boy said, "but you can take Korud if you wish. From what I have learned, Korud has been traitor to you for years."

"Your thoughts march with mine, lad." Kanlath pointed to several of the fishermen. "See that Korud gains the reward he deserves and meet us at the docks when you are finished." The men quietly slipped out the back door and into the dark city.

"Your families are all safe in Zoc?" Gran asked Kanlath, after he had sent all but his bodyguards back to the ships.

"The last of them secretly left Hadliden just before the moon turned," answered Kanlath. "They will be safe in Zoc. The last word we had from there, the Keffin of that city had expelled all Magni and driven them south to Hadliden." He smiled, showing a gap where several teeth were missing. "Zoc will never allow the strict control of the Magni to rule them as these sheep do in Hadliden. The people of Zoc believe that religion and government should never mix."

"And they have the right of it." Gran flexed his big hands, then looked around at the bales and boxes. "You would leave all this merchandise?" he asked Kanlath.

"All this is a gift for the Magni and their soldiers when they come looking for Korud's executioners," Kanlath answered with a wide grin. "A very special surprise."

Gran and Kanlath led their men out of the warehouse and through the dark alleys to the docks. The ships pushed off into the current of the Adag River and turned their prows toward the Taunith Sea, all except one that lowered a sea-anchor to hold its place in the center of the river. Not even a lantern showed to mark the passage of the ships or the one that waited.

"There!" the lookout said softly after a tense hour of waiting.

The sound of muffled oars could just be heard as a small boat headed toward the ship. The rope ladder was quickly lowered and several fishermen scrambled aboard.

"Let the boat drift!" whispered one of the men to Kanlath. "The Magni were on our heels all the way to the docks."

The chain of the sea-anchor grated as it was raised and the great sails creaked under the night wind as the ship headed for the Taunith Sea to join the others.

"Watch." Kanlath and his men faced the area of the wharves where their warehouse made a black blot among the city light.

Suddenly, an enormous ball of fire billowed up in the night, the sound of the explosion reaching their ears seconds afterward.

"They found our surprise." Kanlath's teeth gleamed in the light of the fierce fire. He spit over the rail. "A surprise the Magni deserved," he said, his mouth pinched in anger. "Now let us sail on and give the same to the Volikvi filth they harbor in Frav."

The ships sailed through the waters of the Taunith Sea and ran the gap by the Krake's Nest without incident. By dawn they were headed across the Zuartoc Sea toward the thin division of mountains to the north, where their Fravashi allies waited.

Zanitra stared into the sejda ball just as dawn penetrated the forest where she had camped for the night. "Where is she?" Zanitra said quietly. "And where is Imandoff? I should have guessed that neither can be scryed." She tucked the fist-sized ball of flawless crystal back into its pouch.

She saddled her dark gray horse and mounted. The trail along the rim of the Valley of Whispers was quiet; not a bird sang in the heavy summer air. At the far side of the Valley, where the trail left the rim, Zanitra dismounted and studied the ground for a time.

One horse and rider came this way recently, she thought, then caught her breath. *The mark of a Rissa overlays the horse's trail! But the Rissa do not hunt us. What does this mean?*

She remounted, then took out the sejda ball once again, cupping it in both her hands. Instead of gazing into the ball, she closed her eyes, touching the ancient crystal only with her mind.

Where is the Rissa whose mark is on the trail? she asked. A clear picture of a solitary mountain cabin came into her mind. There, the Rissa lay on the cabin floor next to a space where, try as she might, Zanitra could see nothing. *This must be the place where the Dream Warrior is. Now, show me the horse of Takra Wind-Rider.* The distinct form of Lightfoot appeared. As Zanitra poured more power into the ball, she at last forced Takra to appear also. The warrior woman was standing beside what appeared to be an ancient altar surrounded by ancient monolithic stones, some upright, others tumbled upon the flat ground. At her side was another blank place.

"Well, my wandering brother, you appear to be safe enough. I will ride on until I find the Dream Warrior. Then the two of us shall join you in your search for the armor."

Zanitra put the sejda ball back into its bag and urged her horse on. Within the hour she came out in the mountain meadow. The cabin was silent until Mouse neighed a greeting from the pole corral. Then the door opened slightly, and a voice called out, "Zanitra? It took you long enough."

As Corri threw open the door, the great Rissa appeared by her side, its muzzle wrinkled in a silent growl. Zanitra's mount danced at the smell of the cat-like creature, and Mouse shrilled a cry of mingled fear and anger in return. The Rissa darted out and was quickly gone in the brush and trees on the hill above the cabin.

"I see you have talents I knew nothing of," Zanitra said, after she finally had her mount under control. "If I had known the Rissa watched over you, Corri, I would never have worried about your safety." She stared at the white curl by Corri's face but said nothing when Corri shrugged and smiled.

"Imandoff and Takra are below, in the Valley of Whispers." Corri had her saddlebags, the bag with Varanna's helmet, and a heavily-laden leather bag in her hands as she shut the cabin door. "I think we should go to them."

"You knew?" Zanitra raised an eyebrow. "Then surely you knew that the Green Men have found traces of Fravashi in these mountains."

"Fravashi here?" Corri paused as she saddled Mouse. "No, I did not know."

"I talked with the women of the Green Men at one of their villages before I came here." Zanitra kept a wary eye on the trees along her back-trail. "They did not know what stirred up the men, only that traces of a Fravashi band had been found."

"Then we had best get down into that haunted Valley and find Imandoff and Takra." Corri mounted, then turned and raised a hand in farewell to the hidden Rissa. "Did the Oracle send you after me?" she asked, a frown of suspicion on her face.

"I slipped away, just as you and Imandoff did," Zanitra answered with a chuckle. "By this time, Vairya has probably sent one of her best warriors after me."

Corri grinned and turned Mouse toward the Valley. "Let us see how brave this warrior is then," she answered. "I saw a steep, downward slope on this side of the Valley rim. If we take care, we can get in that way, but it will take a steady head."

"I never cared for heights." Zanitra urged her horse to follow Mouse. "Unlike my brother, I have never found heights or deep holes attractive."

"I do not care for heights either," Corri answered, "but when you are pursued, never make the trail easy."

Corri and Zanitra reached the Valley floor by mid-morning. They were both shaking and dust-covered, their horses snorting with displeasure over the rough, steep trail.

"Smoke did better on that steep slope than I thought she would." Zanitra patted her horse's neck as she led her out onto the Valley floor. "Where do we go now?"

"I would guess there." Corri pointed toward the center of the Valley, where the faint images of tumbled ruins and the tall standing stones could just be seen in the wisps of mist. "Imandoff took us there when we were here before."

Zanitra lifted the sejda ball from its bag and cupped it in her hands. She closed her eyes and stretched out her senses. "Yes, I find Takra Wind-Rider and the blank space beside her. They are standing in the midst of ruins, near what I think is an ancient altar stone."

"Now all we must do is avoid the Whisperers." Corri shivered.

"What are the Whisperers?" Zanitra asked as she returned the ball to the bag hanging on Smoke.

"Some kind of defenders that the Forgotten Ones set in place. They work through your mind somehow, by bringing up illusions of people long dead out of your past." Corri set her jaw as she mounted Mouse and turned toward the center of the Valley. "But they seem to have no effect on animals."

"Illusions." Zanitra mounted her horse and followed Corri. "I wonder if an illusion can be turned aside by an illusion."

"I cannot create an illusion," Corri said as they rode on. "Neither have I seen Imandoff create one."

"But I can." Zanitra smiled at Corri. "That talent was forbidden at Sadko, but I practiced it in secret. Now I will see how adept at illusion I have become."

"When we reach the outer edges of that mist, we will find out quickly enough." Corri eyed the wispy mist with foreboding.

They rode steadily on, the sharp cliffs at their backs, the morning sun growing hot upon their faces. Both Corri and Zanitra silently watched the mists thicken over the ruins, hiding them from sight. The closer they rode, the more opaque the mists became, until after an hour they halted the horses at the very edge of the dense, clinging fog.

"Now we have to face the Whisperers," Corri said softly. "Sounds echo strangely in this place, so you cannot tell where the noise originates."

Zanitra dropped the reins on Smoke's neck and stretched out her hands. Her long fingers wove intricate designs in the air before her as she whispered words Corri could not hear.

Then she picked up the reins and touched her heels to Smoke's flanks. Without a word, Corri rode after the initiate into the mist-cloud.

"They come!" Corri's tense whisper broke the uneasy silence in the fog. The faint whispery sound of voices began to be heard all around them.

Zanitra gave a flick of her fingers to first one side, then the other, and duplicate forms of riders suddenly appeared to be riding along with them through the mist. At the same time, Corri and Zanitra seemed to be encased in a wavering wall of twisted light.

"It works!" Corri's face was pale as she watched the phantom riders move along with them, unconcerned about the voices now buzzing about them like angry bees. "It would seem we are invisible to them," she added as she guided Mouse around the first of the great fallen blocks of stone.

"Part of the illusion I wove. Do these Whisperers plague you all the time you are within these ruins?" Zanitra asked, her eyes bright with interest as she listened to the strange voices.

"They did not pursue us after we reached the center of this place, nor when we left." Corri dropped one hand to the dagger at her belt. *I should practice using Varanna's sword,* she thought, *but this is not the time or the place to prove how clumsy I am with it.*

"Imandoff Silverhair!" Zanitra raised her voice to call loudly through the mists. Echoes bounced back from all directions.

"No!" Corri's urgent whisper had its own echo. "We do not know who else might be here."

"Zanitra?" The sorcerer's deep voice sounded almost at their side. "This way, sister."

Corri drew her dagger and held it ready as she and Zanitra wove their way among the standing stones and fallen blocks toward the center of the old ruins. *What if this is not Silverhair, but someone who can impersonate his voice?* she thought. *We could be going into a trap.*

As Zanitra came in sight of the ancient altar, the mists thinned enough to see who stood there. Takra Wind-Rider stood with drawn sword, a frown on her face. Imandoff strode forward to greet Corri and Zanitra as they dismounted.

"You took a great chance," Takra said. "Enemies could have awaited you in this place." She frowned at Imandoff. "Or enemies could be following you."

"So I tried to tell Zanitra," Corri said, as she stuck the dagger back into its sheath.

"Come quickly." Imandoff hurried back to the altar stone. "I think we have found the underground chamber."

"What chamber?" Corri turned Mouse to graze with Lightfoot, Sun Dancer, and now Smoke. She raised her eyebrows at the horses, saddled and laden with bags and ready to ride.

"In case we come back out of that hole and find enemies waiting," Takra said. "A good warrior always must be prepared."

"What is this chamber Imandoff spoke of?" Corri followed her to the altar stone where the sorcerer and Zanitra stood beside a dark hole in the ground, its covering stone laid back against the altar.

"Silverhair found more clues at Rising Fort." Takra sheathed her sword, but kept an uneasy eye on the mists around them. "Varanna's armor is said to be down there."

"Come. There are stairs that lead downward," Zanitra said as she followed Imandoff into the blackness. A faint blue light filtered upward from one of Imandoff's light-balls. Takra sighed and shook her head, then scrambled after them.

Corri stood for a moment, listening intently to the silence within the mist-shrouded grove of stones. *I feel that itch between my shoulders,* she thought. *It always used to come when someone followed or spied on me.* But she saw and heard nothing, even when she reached out with her inner senses. With a resigned shrug of her shoulders, Corri eased herself down the steps and into the underground darkness. Behind her, the mist thinned rapidly.

"We have them all!" Roggkin boasted, as he pointed across the Valley. "Not only have we traced the sorcerer and Wind-Rider to this place, but that is the Dream Warrior! I wonder who rides with her?"

"It does not matter." Malya urged her horse on, Roggkin and the two hired men close behind her. "We will kill them and be gone before the Green Men know of us." She lifted the watery red pendant from beneath her gown and cupped it in her left hand. "Stay within the light of the stone when we enter the mists," she ordered. "My father says that this stone will protect us from the influence of the Whisperers."

"What are these Whisperers?" Nebel asked, his little rodent eyes darting nervously from side to side.

"Nothing you need concern yourself with, if you do as I say," came Malya's abrupt answer as they entered the edge of the bank of coiling mist.

"It is fortunate that we met along the way," Odran said as he and Gadavar rode up the trail toward the Valley of Whispers. "Perhaps you can talk some sense into the Dream Warrior and the initiate Zanitra. The Peoples cannot take the chance that some misfortune will befall the woman before the battle at the border."

"Corri is stubborn." Gadavar's dark eyes constantly swept the bushes along the trail. "And if this Zanitra is sister to Imandoff Silverhair, then she is even more so." *Not that I would have Corri be any other way,* he thought. *She follows where the Lady leads and that I can understand and respect.*

Odran grinned down at the Green Man. "Perhaps we will be fortunate and find these Fravashi you said were sneaking about Deep Rising."

"I do not think so," Gadavar answered. "We did not know a party of Fravashi entered these mountains until after they were gone. Now we have discovered one of the forbidden graves disturbed, but no sign of the Fravashi. I think they took with them something of importance. You know the legends of what lies in the forbidden graves. However, the signs all said they went back toward Frav."

Odran's face held a momentary overlay of Rissa features before he got his shape-shifting under control. "Fravashi soldiers only?" he snarled.

"No, for I caught the scent of great evil. A Volikvi rode with them, but not up into these mountains." Gadavar reined in Nuisance, then slipped down to study the trail. "Those we follow up here were not of that party. The first two horses turned off into the Valley farther down," he said as he studied the ground. "Two horses, one later than the other, went on up the mountain toward Ayron's cabin."

"That might be where the Dream Warrior has gone," Odran said as he rubbed his chin in thought. "We know she rode out alone and that Zanitra followed her, also alone. And she followed Ayron to the cabin before."

"But now, four more horses left the trail for the Valley." Gadavar stood up and dusted his hands on his dark green trousers. "I do not like this, Odran. Although this party does not hold the evil scent of Frav, still there is an odor I do not like."

"We must protect the Dream Warrior at all costs." Odran's horse pranced nervously as the man struggled to retain his hold over his shape-shifting.

"The cabin is farther up the mountains," Gadavar said as he remounted. "It will take us at least another four hours to get there. But you are right, Odran. We must protect Corri and get her to safety. The other Green Men will soon know who else rides these high places."

Protect yourself, Corri! Gadavar directed his warning at the cabin, but met with no answer. *I feel certain she went to the cabin, yet it is unlike her not to respond to my thoughts. Corri!* He felt a faint trace of Corri's presence, but heard no reply.

The two men rode up the forest-edged trail, their eyes and ears intent on everything around them. By the time they reached the clear places along the rim of the Valley of Whispers, Corri and Zanitra were out of sight in the concealing mist, as were Malya, Roggkin, and the men who rode with them.

Chapter 12

The Tuonela warrior women of Frayma's Mare were uneasy. They had patrolled the border between Tuone and Frav steadily for the past year, but skirmished only with the Fravashi who managed infrequent forays through the weakening spells. Now they were faced with an invisible enemy, one who invaded their dreams each night, bringing choked cries of terror from even the toughest of them.

"Who sends these nightmares upon us?" asked Charissa, her big-boned figure dim in the pre-dawn light. "Battle against an armed warrior, that I can face without flinching. But this!" She shivered and looked down at her boots. "And now the warriors tell of strange half-seen forms coming and going in the air before them."

"There is no shame in the fear that has come over our camp," Norya answered. She turned her head to look at the border, her long gray braids falling about her face. "I only know the sender of these nightmares is in Frav. In time, the evil dreams may well be the least of our troubles, for those with this power can also plague us with worse things."

A scream broke the stillness of the air in the mountain camp, bringing all the women to their feet, swords in hand. One of the perimeter guards staggered into the clearing, clutching one arm, blood dripping through her fingers. Two warrior women leaped to her side, while others fanned out to take defensive positions around the camp.

"Attack by sharrock?" Charissa asked the woman as she was half-carried to Norya's shakka wagon.

"Not sharrock," the woman gasped as Norya lifted her wounded arm and studied the bleeding mark. "The border was quiet. Nothing moved on either side. Then out of the air before me came the fore-part of a strange beast with the stink of the abyss about it." She gritted her teeth as Norya poured mountain water over the gash and began to stitch it closed.

"Is this what you foresaw, shakka?" Charissa tightened her grip on her sword hilt.

"Someone, most likely this Kayth, has learned how to call up the old terrors," the shakka answered, her eyes never leaving her careful stitching. "Tuonela legends tell of a great Footed Serpent that was sent in the night to terrorize and kill those who watched the border. Yet this has not happened since the Peoples first came to this land."

"It was like a serpent," the injured warrior said through her teeth. "A great serpent, almost as tall as the trees, yet it had two taloned feet to the fore. It lashed out at me when I raised my sword." She bent her head in shame. "Then I screamed and ran, like a weak Kirisani woman."

"Gather the warrior women," Norya said as she laid aside her sinew and needle and bandaged the woman's wound. "I would speak with them all at once."

"Call in the border guards?" Charissa shook her head at Norya's nod, then dashed off to do the shakka's will.

Within the hour, the camp of Frayma's Mare was full of silent, armed women standing before the door of Norya's tent-wagon, their subdued voices like the faint murmur of ocean waves. At last Norya raised her hand for silence.

"We have all been plagued by evil nightmares," she said, watching the sea of faces below her. "Even I have fought with these vile dreams of terror. I have seen a great eye amidst the swirling darkness of the abyss, watching for a way to open those gates and spew forth its terrors into our world. Warriors of steady head have reported strange, half-formed entities coming and going, as if they fought to enter our world from the black abyss."

There was a faint clink of sword against buckle and the squeak of leather armor as the women moved uneasily.

"Let none of you bear shame for your fear at these things you see and hear. A wise person fears such evil, for it is attack straight out of the heart of the Volikvi Fire Temple. This attack I cannot fight alone. I need the help of other shakkas. Someone must carry my words to the Clans."

"We will carry your message to the shakkas and the Baba." Two women stepped forward.

Norya nodded. "Go with the blessing and protection of the Goddess," she said. "And have the Baba send word to Kirisan. Their armies must march at once, bringing the Dream Warrior with them. They must delay no longer."

Within five days, the Tuonela Clans had sent their elders, pregnant and nursing mothers, and children by tent-wagons, followed by their herds, to Neeba and the protection of the Baba. The able-bodied men and women, sharp swords by their sides, armor and helmets covering their bodies, rode toward the Fravashi border.

Messengers from the Baba streaked across the dry grasslands into Kirisan with a plea to march at once. The lands of Kirisan came alive with plans for battle, like a stirred hive of bees. The Oracle and the High Priestess in Kystan fretted that they could not find Corri and waited impatiently for her to hear word of the march to the border.

The Mystery School at Leshy was now filled to overflowing with those initiates who had left Sadko in discontent. The healers worked night and day, brewing medicines and gathering herbs, packing their supplies, and waiting to join the Kirisani army as it marched from Kystan.

The younger Tuonela shakkas, and the older ones who could be spared from their Clans, rode to join Norya and Frayma's Mare in their fight against the night-terrors and half-formed entities who now terrorized all the border camps.

But Burrak, Melaina, and their tiny group were shunned and forbidden to take their place with the other Clans. Burrak turned the tent-wagons aside and into the forested foothills of the Takto Range, hoping that during the battle he could redeem himself and the few malcontents who had followed him.

The second day at their new camp, Melaina discovered a body, half-hidden in the sparse grass and rocks on the slope above the camp. When she raced back to Burrak with the news of the dead Fravashi soldier, he stared at her in horror.

"Did you touch this body?" he asked as Melaina excitedly described her find.

"Of course." The young woman stood, hands on hips, the sun casting a halo about her golden hair. "I have no fear of the dead, Burrak. It was a Fravashi, and I needed to know how he died." She pursed her mouth in thought. "I have never seen disease-markings as were on the man, strange fiery marks like boils, but when I cut them with my knife, there was nothing within. He appeared to have been dead only a short time, for this body was still hot from a fever."

"Frayma help us!" Burrak's face paled under its sun-browned tan. "You stupid woman! Did you touch or speak face to face with anyone before you reached me?"

"No," Melaina answered, her mouth tight with anger. "You said you wanted to do deeds that would bring us back into the Clans, so I came straight to you. If you and the men follow this band at once, you can catch them before they get to the border. Who cares what the man died of?"

"You should fear the death he carried. Did you not listen when you were taught about the ancient plague? What you describe are signs of the plague that nearly wiped us out long ago!" Burrak backed away from her, his drawn sword in his hand. "Drive your wagon apart, Melaina, and stay there until we are certain you do not carry the seed of death." He pointed the sword at Melaina, his eyes hard. "Drive apart from us, or I will kill you where you stand."

The small group listening to Burrak drew back as Melaina stamped to her tent-wagon. No one came near as she harnessed the horses and drove out of the Tuonela camp.

On the third day of her exile, Melaina felt the first signs of fever. She dosed herself with goose grass, but it did not help. The next morning she lay in a sweat-drenched coma, her body covered with the strange fiery marks. She died as the sun set far over the grasslands.

Burrak drove his wagon next to Melaina's just as night fell. A safe distance behind him rode two of the men who had come with him into exile. Burrak shook with fever as he stumbled down from the wagon, unhitched the horses, and drove them away with a slap on the flanks. He pulled himself up the steps of Melaina's wagon and peered in.

The woman lay rigid, her body contorted in death. The Clan chief rested his head against the door for a moment, then stumbled back to his wagon, where he brought out skins of oil. He threw the oil over the sides of both wagons before climbing once more into his own tent-home. He paused briefly at the door to raise a fist in salute to the waiting men, then went inside.

Burrak's hands shook as he drew his sword for the last time, carefully positioned it against a chest in the wagon and shoved himself quickly onto the sharp blade. The sword slipped easily between his ribs and pierced his heart.

Burrak's men built a small fire and waited until the moon broke over the hills to the east. They burst into the death wail as the moon's light splashed over the two isolated wagons. Then each man drew his bow, fitted it with an arrow whose point was bound with cloth, touched the point to the fire, and shot it at the wagons. The night silence was broken by a roar as flames shot up into the night, the funeral pyre for Burrak and Melaina.

"Melaina was arrogant," said one of the men. "Only a fool would cast aside the Tuonela teachings about the plague. Now I see why Norya condemned her."

"We were all fools," said another man, as he hung his bow on his saddle and mounted. "We believed her."

"Now we can join the Clans at the border." The first man mounted and looked back at the fiercely burning flames.

"No," answered his companion, "for we do not know if we also carry the plague. We must do as Burrak commanded and wait."

"And if we die, one by one, with this Fravashi plague, what then?"

"Those who live burn the bodies of the dead. The last to die must die in the flames of his own wagon, a sword through his heart, as Burrak did. I was a fool to side with Melaina, and for that foolishness I may die. But I will not carry such death to the rest of the Clans."

Malya looked into her red pendant and smiled. *They are all there, below us,* she thought in triumph. *One blow will end Corri, Imandoff, and the others. You are a fool, Roggkin, to believe I would let Corri live and perhaps escape again. When I have finished with them, I will kill you and be off to the border.*

Roggkin arrogantly stood, hands on hips, only a step behind Malya. "Remember, you promised Farblood is mine to do with as I please."

"How many times must I tell you what I will do?" Malya said. *You are getting far too bold in questioning me, Roggkin.*

"Want us to go after their horses?" Nebel asked. "They cannot have gone far."

"That Tuonela horse would kill you before you knew of it," Roggkin sneered at the man.

Malya raised her eyes from the pendant and glared at the men. "Move back," she ordered. "I will close this hole with magick, trapping the ones we hunt underground forever."

Vikkarr's little eyes went wide as he scuttled back behind one of the huge fallen stones. Nebel quickly joined him.

"You are certain Corri Farblood did not go below with the others, but is hidden among these ruins?" Roggkin asked as he stood, hands on hips, only a step behind Malya. "Remember, you promised she is to be mine."

"I told you so, did I not?" Malya answered. She knelt beside the open door in the ground, carefully setting in place four small medallions. Quickly, she rose and moved back to the safety of a stone, Roggkin at her heels. She raised the pendant to her forehead as she concentrated. There was an ear-splitting roar and pieces of rock and earth ricocheted through the mist-shrouded air.

"We have triumphed," Malya said as she tucked the pendant back into the neck of her gown. "Now we will go to the border as quickly as we can."

"You promised us a reward." Nebel frowned at her.

"You shall have your reward when I am within sight of the border." Malya noted the suspicion on the man's weasel-face. *The reward you deserve, you greedy Kirisani thief.*

"Now, tell me where to find Corri Farblood." Roggkin moved close to her, his eyes threatening. "You said you would tell after we trapped the others. Do not think to play with me as you did with Shilluk and Menec when you sent them to their deaths at the hands of the shape-shifting warriors."

Malya looked up at him without fear as she drew her poison-tipped dagger under the cover of her cloak. "I promised you should be with her, Roggkin, and so you shall. Corri Farblood is underground with the others."

With a cry of frustrated rage, the Tuonela warrior reached for her throat. Malya was waiting for just such a move and leapt aside, digging the point of her dagger into his throat as she went. Roggkin clamped his bleeding neck with one hand, then went after her again, death in his eyes.

"You reached too high when you bargained for me, Roggkin." Malya's eyes narrowed as she kept out of his faltering reach. "Now you have the reward I promised: death."

Roggkin stumbled and fell to his knees, still trying to reach the retreating figure. *How could I have misjudged my control over her? I thought she needed me.*

"Get our horses," Malya snapped at the two cowering men behind the stones. "If you follow my orders, your reward will be of greater value than this nathling received."

Nebel and Vikkarr untied the horses from the trees at the edge of the ruins and helped Malya mount. They looked at each other with fear-filled eyes but said nothing as the three of them rode out of the Valley of Whispers.

Roggkin crawled after them, the tujyk poison already working through his entire system.

Amandoff stood at the bottom of the stairs in the black underground tunnel, the ball of blue light floating above his head. Behind him, Corri, Takra, and Zanitra watched as the sorcerer's left hand brushed over the door shutting off the stairs from whatever else lay within the ancient underground place. In his right hand he held his staff, the stone he had taken a year before from the altar fitted into the end. The gem caught the blue light and broke it into a thousand reflections against the stone blocks of the walls.

"There must be a way in," he murmured. "If Geyti's ancestor got in, then so can we."

"What of that plaque you carry?" Takra kept a close watch on the opening at the top of the stairs, one hand never far from her sword. "Be quick about it, Silverhair. I hate creeping about underground."

"I have seen no sign of black jumpers here," Imandoff said, a slight smile turning up the corners of his mouth. Takra shivered at the thought of the huge, venomous spiders in the hidden cave they had explored near here. "I see no place that would hold the plaque or even allow it to be used as a key."

"Move the light to one side," Corri said as she looked up at the top of the tall, stone frame surrounding the door. Imandoff's magick light slid to one side. "There, at the top. Is that a place for some kind of key?"

Imandoff raised his staff to touch the small depression in the frame with the top of his staff. "It appears to be such," he began.

The magick light shone through the stone in his staff and into the depression, creating a blazing spot of brilliance. There was a groaning sound from the door as it slowly began to open. At the halfway point, the door creaked to a stop against a dusting of fallen dirt and broken stone.

"Mother of Mares," Takra whispered, "who would have thought that old stone was a key!"

Corri dropped one hand onto her dagger as they cautiously slipped past the half-open door into the black corridor beyond. A musty smell of earth and stale air filled their noses.

"A temple!" Zanitra ran her hand over a tall, carved pillar, the first of two long lines of columns that stretched off into the darkness. "I can feel the power that built here from long years of worship."

"Yes." Imandoff's voice echoed back to them from unseen walls. "The carvings of vine and flowers and leaf are the same as in the secret cave." He moved out into the darkness, the ball of blue light floating with him. Corri, Takra, and Zanitra followed closely at his heels. "According to Geyti's old records, Varanna's armor should not be far from here."

Takra glanced at Corri and her eyes widened. "In all the excitement and mist, I did not see that. What happened, Corri?" Takra touched one finger to the white curl along her face.

"A long story for a night about a campfire," Corri answered. She felt a binding on her speech, as she had after the Trial of the Mask. *Why does all this happen, but I can never share it?* she thought.

Imandoff moved on down the line of columns, Zanitra confidently at his side, while Takra and Corri kept a wary eye on their surroundings. Corri judged that they had not gone more than thirty paces when the sorcerer came to a sudden halt.

"Here it is!" Imandoff said, his voice full of excitement. He called the light closer as he peered into a wide niche in one wall. A latticed stone door covered the niche. Pulling Geyti's key from his pouch, Imandoff twisted it in the lock, then eased back the door. "Varanna's armor! I never thought to hold this in my hands."

"I never thought we would find it." Corri felt excitement, followed by a rush of adrenaline, shoot through her. "Now all events will speed toward the great battle. Nothing can stop this clash between good and evil until I kill Kayth." She clenched her hands at her sides, feeling that once she touched the ancient armor the last unbreakable link with her destiny as the Dream Warrior would be forged. *I know this must happen but I want to wait just a little longer.*

Imandoff brushed aside a thick layer of dirt and dust, then pulled out a shimmering breast-plate. Zanitra took it while he pulled out the back-plate, then guards for the arms and legs.

"It is not metal," she said, rubbing her fingers over the armor. "What is it?"

"It appears to be fashioned from the tough shell of the giant sea krynap," Imandoff answered. "But the fishermen do not catch them, they are too dangerous. And I do not know of any smith skilled enough to make this into armor."

"Did you hear a horse nicker?" Takra turned back toward the door, its shape hidden now by blackness.

"Listen!" Corri held up her hand. "There is something strange happening above."

"Back! Get back quickly!" Imandoff's orders brought them scurrying to his side just as a roar, followed by a cloud of choking dust, rolled down from the far opening.

Gadavar and Odran reached Ayron's deserted cabin in late afternoon, the shadows growing long as the sun rested with its edge beyond the Barren Mountains. They searched the cabin and the meadow around it carefully for signs of Corri.

"She was here." Gadavar closed the cabin door tight behind him.

"As was another rider," Odran added. "Both horses went straight back toward that steep incline we saw that leads down into the Valley of Whispers."

A bird call floated across the mountain meadow as they prepared to mount and ride out.

"This place is too high for giddies." Odran dropped one hand to his sword.

"Rather a Green Man." Gadavar whistled the call back to the hidden observer.

The Green Man stepped from among the trees. He raised a hand in greeting. "Plague has come to Deep Rising," he said.

"When and where?" Gadavar's face was stern.

"We found one body near Rising Fort, a Fravashi by the dress," the Green Man answered. "We allowed no one to touch the body, but burned it where it lay. The plague signs were plain. At least we need only fear the men involved. Our ancient records say animals do not carry the disease."

"A fitting end for one of those who robbed the ancient grave." Odran nodded his head at the justice. "Surely they would have run for Frav by now. There may be other bodies out on the grasslands that no one has yet found."

"We sent word to the Clans, but our messenger met one of theirs. Word was sent from the Baba that the shakkas call for Kirisan to march to the border. The Green Men even now gather to meet the Kirisani armies at Leshy."

"We must find the Dream Warrior!" Odran scowled and stared at the Valley to the east of them.

"The Harvest Moon is little more than two weeks away." Gadavar rubbed his chin as he thought. "The armies need that time to march to the border, but a small party could move faster." He nodded to his fellow Green Man. "I am more certain now than ever that Corri has gone down into the Valley of Whispers in her search for Varanna's armor. We will go there and bring her back with us," he said. "And my instincts say that Imandoff Silverhair, and likely his sister, will be with her."

"That is not all," the Green Man added. "One of our men saw four strangers headed for the Valley earlier this day. One was a Tuonela warrior and the woman the daughter of Uzza the feya woman. Will you need aid, brother?"

Gadavar's mouth tightened. "No, I know that Tuonela, and he is a coward."

"Ride with the Goddess," the Green Man said as he turned and disappeared back into the forest.

"We must find them quickly," Odran said as they mounted and rode back toward the cliff-tops. "If this Tuonela is Roggkin, then the evil Malya rides with him."

"That was the strange but different presence I sensed near the Valley! I should have recognized Malya's aura and mindscent." Gadavar slammed his fist on his knee. "I saw her inclinations toward evil when she was at Sadko."

They turned their horses toward the Valley cliffs and urged them into a gallop.

"She does not have the odor of the Volikvis, although she works for Kayth." A half-snarl crossed Odran's face for an instant. "Silverhair will not let her get near the Dream Warrior."

"*If* he senses they are stalked." Gadavar held up a hand as they halted their horses at the cliff-top. "Listen!"

A roar of blasted earth came from the Valley below. The mist coiling in the center blew out streamers of fog, then once more pulled in upon itself. Odran and Gadavar watched in bewilderment for several minutes.

"What was it?" Odran shielded his eyes with one hand as he stared at the Valley floor.

"Evil," answered Gadavar as he dismounted and began leading Nuisance down the steep slope. "Corri is down there, I know it. I pray that the evil did not find her or her friends." *What will I do if I lose her? How could I face life without her?* Gadavar's mind shied from the thought as he set his mouth in a grim line and focused on the slope before him.

Chapter 13

Roggkin collapsed among the ancient ruins, unable to crawl farther. He watched through blurred eyes as Malya and the men rode away, leaving him to die.

You evil Fravashi-loving nathling! he thought. *I curse you to die as you have left me to die: alone and in great pain.* He felt the poison working through his veins, smelled its nose-clogging sweetness as it burst the blood vessels in his nose.

Only one such as you, Malya, would use tujyk poison to keep from paying a debt. Roggkin writhed with pain as the snake poison reached his organs and began eating at them. *May you burn forever in the hell fires of Frav!*

First a froth of blood, then a red stream, poured from between his lips as the tujyk poison burst his organs. His eyes glazed; his breath faltered, then stopped.

A huge black and white form lumbered out of the mist. The barsark sniffed the tainted air, shaking its great head when the smell of the poison reached it. Its lips curled back to expose the wicked fangs, but it backed away from the dead Tuonela warrior, a low rumbling growl in its throat. It would have ripped apart and partially devoured any other man it could catch, but its instincts warned it away from this one. It raised its head to sniff the air. Horses had been here. It would track them a short way and see if they could be caught.

"Blessed Goddess, what was that?" Zanitra wiped the dust away from her eyes and nose.

"Someone using great magick to trap us here. Stronger magick than I can do." Imandoff knelt beside Takra. "Are you hurt?"

The Wind-Rider shook her head, coughing in the dust that floated through the dark corridor. "Give us some light, Silverhair, so we can see the damage." She struggled to her feet, Corri at her side. "Are you hurt, Sister?"

Corri coughed and shook her head. "But what of you and the baby?"

"I feel well enough." Takra sneezed, then tried to wave away the dust with her hand.

Imandoff created a ball of light and sent it sweeping back down the corridor to hang near the door. "By the Nine Words of Natira! The explosion blocked the door!"

They scrambled over pieces of fallen blocks, under tilted columns and through a drifting fog of dust until they reached the door where they had entered the underground chamber.

"We are trapped," Zanitra said as she eyed the heavy door. She felt along its edge; a tiny stream of dirt and debris fell through the crack along one side. "The stairs are blocked."

Takra gave a strangled sound that brought Imandoff whirling around to gather her in his arms. "I will get us out," he said as he stroked her hair. "We will not die in this place, that I promise."

Corri patted Takra's shoulder soothingly, then smiled as she heard the faint singing of the mystical serpent in her mind. "We will find a way out of this place, Takra. I know we will."

Takra slowly calmed; her shaking and strangled sobs stopped as she gained control of her fears. "I hate underground places," she finally whispered.

"So do I." Zanitra clutched at one of the fallen pillars, her knuckles white. "They always make me feel as if I am suffocating." The two women looked at each other in sympathy.

"Stand back." Imandoff stepped away from Takra and drew the long sword at his side. His jaw set, his face determined, the sorcerer set the sword blade into the crack around the door and began to pry at the wedged stone.

"It will never work," Corri said in a soft whisper to Zanitra. "We must find another way." *The map I once saw, it had a picture of a maze-like drawing in the center of this Valley.* She watched Imandoff futilely put his full weight on the sword.

"Blessed Goddess!" Imandoff cried as the blade snapped with a retort that echoed down the corridor. He held up the sword, the blade broken off two hands above the tip. Casting the sword aside, he raised his hands to blast the door with magickal fire.

"Imandoff, there may be another way out." Corri smiled at the sorcerer's questioning look. "I remember the map and the maze drawn over the center of this Valley."

"The map?" For a few moments Imandoff stood still, the magick sparking fiercely around his clenched hands, his brows bent down with thought. "Yes, your memory and the map," he said at last. The anger raised by his fear died away, but his jaw remained set and his mouth tight with tension. "Corri once stole an ancient map from me," he explained to Zanitra. "Although it was destroyed, she has an exceptional memory."

"One part of the maze appeared to coil off from the rest and headed for what I took to be cliffs. There was a marking there that must be a door." Corri linked arms with Takra and gave her an encouraging smile. "We have a mission to do for the Lady. She would not leave us here and that mission dead."

"I am pleased that you are so confident." Takra's hand trembled against Corri. "You would think by now I would be used to scurrying around in underground holes."

Corri laughed and gave Takra's arm a light squeeze. "We must go straight ahead," she said to Imandoff. "When the tunnels become more tangled than they are now, I will need to stop and think my way through the map in my head."

"Fair enough. Come then." Imandoff created a ball of light and sent it ahead of them down the black corridor. He slid his broken sword into its sheath and strode back to Varanna's armor, now scattered about the debris-covered floor. "By the hell fires of Frav, I will not sit down to die and let Kayth win the battle before it is started."

Each of them carried part of the armor as they set off down the ancient corridor, with its web-like intersecting halls and temple rooms. Their progress was slow and tiring as Corri painstakingly thought through the map as they reached each new hub of mazes.

"Horses!" Gadavar pointed to the bottom of the natural ramp as four saddled and packed mounts began their scramble up the steep incline. "I recognize Mouse and Silverhair's Sun Dancer."

"The one in the lead is Smoke, Zanitra's horse. The one forcing them on is a Tuonela mount," said Odran as he eyed the climbing horses. "See, there is a spear set in its holder on one side."

Gadavar looked back over the Valley, then gave a shout of warning. "Barsark!" He pointed out the huge black and white monster loping steadily along some distance behind the horses.

Odran's sword sang as he drew it and took his stand at the top of the incline. Gadavar grabbed his bow, whipped one of his arrows out of its case, and fitted it to the string.

The four horses, scenting the barsark on the wind, plunged past the two warriors. Lightfoot herded them back from the cliff-edge with nips at their flanks, but kept them from racing wildly away.

"It moves fast." Odran prepared to loose his shape-shifting powers, his face already taking on aspects of the Rissa. He gave a coughing grunt of the hunting cat-like creature as the barsark started up the incline.

"Wait." Gadavar drew the bow-string along his tanned cheek. "If I can put an arrow in the right place, it may well fall down the cliffs and be killed."

"And if it does not fall?" Odran snarled.

"Then we fight side by side with swords. A barsark on a trail never gives up." Gadavar's fingers trembled as he waited for the animal to reach a boulder where the ramp made a slight turn. "Goddess, help us," he whispered as the barsark paused by the boulder and lifted its huge head, its great fangs bared. Its howling challenge echoed across the Valley.

"Aim true, Green Man." Odran answered the barsark's challenge with the warning scream of the Rissa.

Guide my hand, Gadavar prayed. *I know how difficult these creatures are to kill, and I have seen what they do to men who hunt them and fail to kill.*

Gadavar's arrow whined through the air and struck the beast in the left eye. The barsark reared up on its hind legs, its front claws ripping at the air, howling in pain and fury. It took three more steps up the ramp, then slowly tilted to one side and fell, bouncing and howling down the cliff. As it struck the cliff, part of the ground gave way. Boulders and a cascade of earth plummeted with the animal, burying it completely as it hit the Valley floor.

"The incline is destroyed." Odran's voice was still rough with Rissa-power as he walked to the cliff-edge and peered over. "A good shot, Green Man. There is no movement from that pile of earth below." His narrowed eyes still sparked with hunting fire.

"We must go back along the trail to find another way down," Gadavar answered, his bow clutched in his still-shaking hands.

"It is too dark to ride now." Odran sheathed his sword as he gained control over his powers once more. "If the barsark had found the Dream Warrior and her friends, it would not have trailed the horses." He turned to face Gadavar. "She is in no danger from that animal."

"What of those who followed her?" Gadavar stared off across the dark Valley.

"If they found her, we are already too late."

Corri, where are you? Gadavar sent his thoughts winging toward the woman he loved, her face clear in his mind. *I will come for you. I will come.*

A sense of peace settled over the troubled Green Man, then a vision of Corri's face, smudged with dirt, rose before his eyes. *We are safe,* came the faint reply. *Watch for us.*

"We wait here," Gadavar said as he walked to the horses and began soothing them.

Odran raised one eyebrow, but said nothing as he helped Gadavar with the horses.

It feels as if we have walked miles, Corri thought as she trudged with Takra and Zanitra behind Imandoff. They had passed down countless corridors, through painted rooms full of strange altars and dusty stone benches, the magick light casting flashes over the carvings and frescoes of the Forgotten Ones. For once, the sorcerer had no interest in exploring. Now they stood before another closed door.

"Imandoff, we must rest." Zanitra caught her brother's arm as he raised his staff to touch the stone to the lintel of the door. "We are all tired and do not know what we may face ahead. It must be near nightfall."

Imandoff sighed. "After we pass through this door, we will rest," he promised. "I understand how working our way through this maze is wearing on the nerves and draining to the energy. I feel it myself."

Corri sighed with relief. She glanced at Takra's weary face and knew that the same tiredness must show on hers.

The barrier grated in the dust underfoot as he touched the stone against the carved depression at the top of the lintel. A faint puff of air, fresh but dry and warm, struck them as they crowded through.

"A burial place?" Zanitra ran her hands slowly over the walls. "See, niches have been cut into the rock and sealed with stone slabs. Each place is man-length and carved with strange characters."

"The language of the Forgotten Ones." Imandoff spread his cloak on the floor and insisted Takra lie down before he went to stand beside his sister. "Do you realize, Zanitra, these are the first burial chambers we have ever found? Undisturbed for thousands of years." His voice went soft as the enormity of the discovery soaked in.

"Eat." Corri emptied her belt pouch and handed out several small pieces of jerked meat. "I saved it against just such a time," she said with a wink at Imandoff's surprise. "Old habit. As a thief, you never know how long you must wait somewhere."

Imandoff and Zanitra sat down beside Takra, their backs against the wall, and took the meat. No one talked as they chewed at the tough journey food. No one spoke of their dry mouths or of water. Finally, they fell into an exhausted sleep.

Corri woke from a bewildering dream she could not recall, knowing only that someone had called her name. There was no way to tell the time of night. The others slept on, unaware of her restlessness.

Who called me in my sleep? She opened her mind, listening with her inner senses. *Who knows my name in this place?*

Child of the skies, arise. A woman's voice sounded in her mind, the accent one she could not recognize. *Warrior of Shadows, I freely give you what was once mine. Use it to save Sar Akka.*

Who are you? How do you know the name given to me by the shadow man, for I told no one? Corri asked, but no more messages came. Quietly, she got to her feet and looked around. The ball of magick light was dimmed, casting long shadows along the burial chamber, highlighting the names and designs carved into the stone enclosures.

Goddess, help me find a way out, she thought as she snapped her fingers. Blue fire sprang up on her fingertips. Holding her hand before her, Corri started off down the corridor.

Soon the ball of light over her friends was hidden by a turn in the long chamber. Off to her right, she saw a tiny open chamber rough-cut into the stone, different from the others as it was uncovered on the front. She stepped closer to shine the light onto the contents, then caught her breath in surprise. The well-preserved body of a woman lay there, a woman who in life would not have reached Corri's shoulder. On a shelf above the woman's head were two boxes and in her hands lay a sword, its blade broken in two.

Is this a woman of the Forgotten Ones? No, she is buried differently, and this place in the wall was made not many years ago. Corri edged closer, her fear forgotten. She stared at the two boxes, each only slighter longer than her hand. *Who were you?* she thought as she gazed down at the smooth unlined face, its long brown hair spread across a woven covering.

Nimuanni gives freely to the Warrior of Shadows, came the reply. Corri staggered backward at the strength of the sending. *The sword I send by you to the young warrior of shapes, to keep for the day he becomes a man. The rest are yours for the great battle.* The voice died away with a long sigh.

"You have to make this fire into a traveling ball of light," Corri said to herself, then started as the echo of her soft voice rolled about the corridor. She concentrated on the fire on her fingertips, her face determined, until the fire broke free and hung in the air. It was only a seed-fire, much smaller than what Imandoff created, but enough to light her way if she went carefully.

Once I would not have hesitated to take grave-goods. I could never be a thief again. I have changed too much. Corri slowly reached out to take the boxes from the shelf. She set them on the floor, then gently eased the broken sword from under the dead woman's hands. The body appeared to be as supple as the day it was buried. Corri tucked the sword through her belt, picked up the boxes, and turned to go back to her friends.

A tiny tinkle of metal against stone caught her attention. She turned back and caught the glint of metal on the floor beside the burial chamber. She knelt and carefully scooped up an earring. The sudden voice within her mind made her nearly lose her balance with surprise.

Corri, where are you? I will come for you.

Gadavar! Corri's breath quickened and she started to answer aloud, then realized the words were in her mind. *We are safe. Watch for us,* she replied, and was filled with a peace she had not felt since she had entered this place.

"Corri Farblood! Where are you?" Imandoff's deep voice echoed down the corridor.

"Here." Corri tucked the earring into her belt pouch and turned to face Imandoff, Takra, and Zanitra as they rounded the bend in the corridor. The free-floating ball of light picked up the concern on their faces and the relief when they saw her.

"I was brought here," Corri said, holding up the boxes. "A woman named Nimuanni called me as I slept and gave these."

Imandoff made no effort to take the boxes, only strode close to the open burial niche and peered in at the body.

"Wella?" he asked Zanitra, who nodded. "And an Oracle woman by her dress."

"By chance, did she tell you the way out of this hole?" Takra looked about nervously.

Corri closed her eyes in thought, then smiled. "No, but the door that leads outside is not far from here." She turned and pointed on up the black corridor. "We go that way. After a time, the corridor will end. Then we climb stairs from one chamber to another until we are up high." She shrugged her shoulders and smiled at Takra's look of skepticism. "From there we will come to a door and a way out to where Gadavar awaits. It is daylight outside, and we shall be in the sunshine soon."

"If Gadavar waits for us," Imandoff said, "then events have moved swiftly since we left Kystan. I think we must hurry now." He touched Corri's seed-light with one finger and smiled. "A good attempt, but you still need more practice."

Corri reached out and enclosed the light in her hand, snuffing it, as Imandoff's ball of light floated off down the corridor ahead of them.

Except for two short rest periods, the group moved steadily along the corridor, following Corri's directions for each new turning, until they came to the first flight of stairs. They climbed these and entered a massive round chamber, its walls covered with ancient scenes. At the far side of the room, they discovered another flight of steps that led upward to another chamber, this time with cleverly carved slits of windows in one wall.

"You can see the whole Valley," Takra said as she peered through a slit, Imandoff at her side.

"From below, you could not tell anything was hidden within the cliff." Zanitra glanced out a slit, then prowled about the chamber. "Here," she called. "I have found another door."

"Finally, a way out," Takra said as she crowded behind Imandoff. "Your stolen stone had better work once more, Silverhair."

"This one has no need of a key," Imandoff answered and set his shoulder against the barrier.

The door groaned open, and they pushed through into another corridor, then stopped short. The stairway ended in open air a dozen paces from where they stood. Fresh grooves in the dirt and an occasional rattle of still-loose soil marked a newly-made slide that had torn away the ancient exit from the secret underground chambers. The faint rays of dawn turned the stone around them to rose and gold.

"Someone comes." Odran's soft voice broke through Gadavar's sleep at the same time his mind registered the tread of feet on the grassy slope above them.

The Green Man scrambled to his feet, one hand already drawing his sword, before his mind cleared enough to see the strangers were not enemies.

"The Wella," he murmured to Odran and placed a restraining hand on the warrior's arm. "I wonder what brings them out of their mountains and the Metal Mines?"

"I have long heard of the Wella," Odran said in wonder, "but I never thought to see one. It is said they never leave their mountain's caves and tunnels."

The twenty men and two women stopped before the warriors and looked up at them with solemn faces. The tallest of the men only reached up to the tall Odran's waist. The men were broad-shouldered, the thick muscles of their arms and thighs visible through their tunics and trousers. They were dressed uniformly in earth-toned clothing; their hair was brown and their eyes black as night. Swords, as well as long daggers, swung at the belts of even the diminutive women.

The tallest of the Wella took one step forward and raised his hand, palm forward, his eyes on Gadavar. "Greetings, defender of the mountains," he said in a bass voice. "We follow our Oracle woman, who has been led by Otherworld messages."

"I am Odran, warrior from the Temple of the Great Mountain. Who . . ."

Gadavar interrupted the shape-shifter with a hand clamped tight over his muscled arm. "The Wella rarely share their names," he told the warrior. "It would be insult to demand it of them."

The shape-shifter nodded and bowed to the Wella.

The smallest of the women, very young and with an unlined face, balanced a Qishua Tear on her open hand, first sighting it on Odran, then on Gadavar. Satisfied with what the Tear revealed to her, the young Oracle woman moved to Gadavar's side and looked up into his face.

"The Warrior of Shadows is safe," she said in a soft, whispery voice. "Word came from Nimuanni from her place in the Otherworld that you needed our assistance in finding her."

"You speak of the Dream Warrior?" Odran noted the thick coils of rope slung over two of the men's shoulders, the long slender hide-wrapped bundle that they laid on the grass along with their backpacks.

"We speak of the Warrior for the Goddess. The Wella Oracles heard the red-haired woman as she struggled to pass the last test two nights ago, the test that would open doors to greater powers and free her of the last of her father's taint." The young woman slid the Tear into a pouch hanging about her neck, then motioned to the men with the ropes. "She is the Dream Warrior no longer, but now the Warrior of Shadows."

Corri, what have you done? Why did you not wait until I was with you? "We seek the Warrior now. Do you know where she is?" Gadavar asked as he watched the men uncoil the ropes along the edge of the cliff.

"Below," answered the Oracle woman. "You are forbidden to go down, for you may not see our secret, sacred places."

The Wella men proceeded to tie one end of the ropes to the saddles of Sun Dancer and Odran's mount. Lightfoot looked on with interest, once nuzzling against the Oracle woman but never once baring her teeth at the strangers.

"Go." The Oracle woman motioned to four of the men who slid down the anchored ropes, dropping out of sight along the cliff.

It was not long before one of the men scrambled back up the rope, followed by Zanitra, her gown tucked up into her belt to free her legs, her string of prayer beads clacking against the rocks. At the sight of the Wella Oracle woman, Zanitra held out both hands, palms up, and bowed. The Oracle woman returned the acknowledgment. Takra pulled herself over the lip of the cliff-top next, nearly on the initiate's heels, her tanned face pale with suppressed fear. Behind her came Imandoff, then Corri.

As soon as Corri scrambled to the top of the rope, Gadavar pulled her to her feet and into his arms. "You are safe now," he whispered. "And what is this about another test, one you passed through alone, Warrior of Shadows?"

"How did you know?" Corri turned her head and noticed the little Wella Oracle as the woman moved closer and smiled. "She is like the one buried below, one who was an Oracle. She has power."

"She said they heard you during the test. I should have been with you." He kissed her gently and, with an arm still around her shoulders, walked with her to Imandoff's side.

"You cannot always be with me, Gadavar. But our love is strong enough to see me through anything, even though you are far from my side." Corri leaned her head into the curve of his shoulder, content just to be near him again.

The Wella men scrambled up the ropes, Varanna's armor divided among them. Imandoff repeated Zanitra's gesture to the Oracle woman before turning to Gadavar and Odran.

"A welcome sight," Imandoff said to the two men. "We could not retreat the way we came, neither could we climb the cliff without aid. I began to fear we would miss the great battle." He bowed his head to the Wella Oracle. "We are honored that the Wella come to aid us," he said simply.

"I almost forgot." Corri loosened the ties on her tunic and pulled out the two boxes.

At the sight of these, there was a gasp and rapid words in a strange language from the Wella. Apprehension clear on her face, Corri looked around at the strange men and women.

"I did not steal them," she said. "Nimuanni freely gave them to me." She held them out to the Oracle woman, who smiled and refused with a shake of her head.

"I knew of Nimuanni's gift," the young woman said. "She called to me in my dreams, telling us to aid you."

Why does it always surprise me when others hear dream-voices? Corri thought and shook her head. "What are they?" she asked the little woman, "and what is their importance?"

"That you must discover. I can tell you only that we will reforge the dragon-sword and send it to the boy who shall one day bear it. Even now he resides at the Temple in Kystan."

"She must speak of Athdar," Zanitra murmured.

Imandoff stepped forward and held out the ancient broken sword on his hands. Odran drew in a quick breath when he saw the coiled form that made the hilt.

"Never has there been a shape-shifter of such a fabled beast," he whispered.

The Oracle woman took the broken sword, then motioned to one of the men, who carried forward the long hide-wrapped bundle they had brought with them.

"It has been long since we forged your sword of mountain steel, Imandoff Silverhair," the woman said. "I saw you break your sword in your struggles underground. We brought another to replace your broken weapon, one forged with our strongest magick. It has been blessed by the Lady and Her Lord, something not to be taken lightly in this coming battle."

Imandoff took his broken sword from its sheath, exchanging it for the shimmering blade that the Wella handed him.

"My thanks," he said. "May this sword shatter and free the magick before the Fravashi take me alive." There was a murmur of approval from the Wella.

Several of the Wella men sat cross-legged on the ground, the ancient armor close by, and began to thread leather ties through a series of holes along the sides of chest and back plates, lacing them together.

"Come, let us rest and eat before we part." The Oracle and the other Wella woman walked to the packs, where they brought out fruit and bread spread with savory nut-paste. The men coiled the ropes, then joined the others as they sat on the grass to eat. Soon flasks of fiery mountain liquor or plain water were making the rounds to wet the dry throats.

The Oracle woman dipped into her pack again, this time pulling out a chain mail shirt with double-thick links covering the front. "To protect the child," she said as she laid it in Takra's hand. Takra's eye brightened at the intricate forging of the mountain steel into links.

The other Wella woman smiled as she patted Takra's belly. "Daughter," she said. "Beautiful daughter." When Takra tried to talk with her, the woman just smiled and shook her head.

"She does not speak much of your language," the Oracle woman said. "Only a very few of the Wella do."

The tallest of the Wella men stood, one hand resting on the hilt of his sword. He looked at Corri and her companions, his face serious. "We will guard the way to the sea," he said in his deep voice. "Long ago we laid a ban upon our people. We cannot leave these mountains, but we can hold the passes that lead down to the great waters. This much we can do." He gestured to the Oracle woman.

"The elders of our people have charged me with telling you of our ancient prophecies we feel tell of this coming battle," the young woman said. " 'When the moon races through the storm to stand once more at the place of battle and her light is extinguished, the Warrior of Shadows must face the Eye of

Darkness. To defeat the Eye, the Warrior must reunite what was separated. Five souls bound together, five shining swords for the Lady, five shadows on the Bridge of Death and Fire, five battle-cries sound, but only one enters the realm of Shadows. The child cries his defiance to the Evil Ones.' "

Imandoff's face was grim. "How do your elders interpret these words?"

"We have no clear interpretation." The Oracle woman smiled at Corri. "I think the Shadow Warrior has guessed at some of the meaning, but the rest, that I do not know."

The leader of the Wella band eased Varanna's armor over Corri's head and tightened the leather thongs at the sides. He laid the leg and arm guards beside her, fresh leather straps fastened to them.

"Word has reached us from the Oracle that you have the helmet." The Oracle woman smiled as Corri looked down at the rounded chest plate that dipped low beneath her belly. When a puzzled expression crossed Corri's face, the young Wella woman looked surprised. "Did you not know that Varanna was with child during that final battle?"

I did, for Varanna told me, but this is news to the others. Corri fingered the armor. *By the Blessed Lady, I will change this coiling path of fate laid out before me. I will not fail and die, as did Varanna. I have a son who needs my help when he in turn has to face the future prophesied for him.*

Imandoff looked sharply at Corri, who kept her eyes on the Oracle woman. Zanitra slipped her prayer beads rapidly through her fingers, her lips moving in silent prayer. Takra and Corri exchanged quick glances, sudden understanding passing between them. Gadavar shook his head, puzzled by the cryptic exchange.

"Our prophecies have no mention of this." Odran, who had sat silent throughout the conversations, now wrinkled his forehead in deep thought. "Silverhair, do you know who the five will be? For surely the Wella's prophecies speak of five of our people going into Frav."

Imandoff sighed. "I am certain of three," he answered. "Corri, Takra, and myself."

"I will go." Gadavar looked at Corri, determination and love plain in his eyes. "I want to be with you," he said softly. "Do not take this from me."

If I could only know whether Gadvar's going or staying behind is the key to averting the tragedy I saw. Corri reluctantly nodded.

"And I!" Odran looked fiercely around the circle.

"No, Odran, you and I have another duty." Zanitra's calm voice cut through the shape-shifter's battle fervor. "I know the meaning of the Bridge of Death and Fire. It is an ancient name for the land-bridge that crosses the Kratula Gorge into the city of Vu-Zai. Who better to guard their backs but a weaver of illusion and a shape-shifting warrior?"

Odran grunted acknowledgment and nodded his head.

The leader of the Wella group glanced up at the climbing sun and gave an order in his language. The taciturn little people gathered up their things and prepared to return to their mountain retreat.

"Wait!" Corri put one hand on the Oracle woman's arm. "Do you not have more words of wisdom to help me?"

"Warrior of Shadows, trust your heart." The woman smiled at her and raised one hand to gently touch the lock of white hair along her cheek. "You know the way. You have walked it before." Then she turned and followed the other Wella up the meadow and into the thick trees on the slope above.

Corri gathered up the leg and arm guards and tied them to Mouse's saddle. Takra held out the boxes, curiosity plain in her eyes.

"We might as well see what was given to me," Corri said with a grin and opened one of the boxes. "I know you are as curious as I am, Takra. Qishua Tears!" she exclaimed.

Imandoff looked over her shoulder as the rest crowded close. The box held three perfect purple-blue Tears packed in a fluff of fibers. Corri closed the box and hurriedly opened the other one. A number of little carved figures lay in the same kind of fluff, each intricately detailed in face and dress.

"I have never seen their like before," Imandoff said with a shake of his head. "Perhaps we should send them to the Temple Oracle."

"Yes, I feel these things belong with her," Corri answered.

"We can send them with a messenger when we reach Leshy." Odran eyed the sun, then mounted his horse. "The Kirisani armies already march for the border. The Dream Warrior must be there to lead them when the Fravashi attack."

"No," Corri said, her eyes focused for a moment on the distant rim of the Valley of Whispers. "I am the Dream Warrior no longer, but the Warrior of Shadows." *Lady, help me. I am afraid of failing You and all Sar Akka in the battle to come. And I would not walk the same path as Varanna did. Help me to change it!*

Chapter 14

The Kirisani armies marched through the city of Leshy at dusk. The faces of foot-soldiers and horsemen were grave beneath the helmet-visors. The city streets were lined with silent townspeople who watched with worried faces as the healers of Leshy joined the soldiers. Word had leaked out about the plague-dead Fravashi near Rising Fort; war and possible defeat were not the only things worrying those left behind.

The only sounds were the jingle of bridles, the clack of sword against armor, the snap of banners in the light breeze, and a rumble of wagon wheels as the long tail of fighting men and women wound their way through Leshy to the northern gates. Just beyond the gates lay the Crystal Sands and the vast grasslands of Tuone and, farther beyond, the spellbound border with Frav.

Breela rode behind Tirkul and the High Priestess Vairya, the pole of the banner of Her Own with its double-axe tucked into a holder by her left boot. *I never thought to know such freedom,* Breela thought as she glanced at the fighting kilts of the Priestess, the bright armor covering her own body. *By the Goddess, I will never give that freedom into any man's hand again! I would rather die in battle.* She felt a swell of pride at the determined women who rode behind her, the warriors of the group known as Her Own.

At the end of the long line of soldiers came the wagons and horses of the Mystery School of Leshy. Jehennette sat on a wagon-seat beside her driver, mentally reviewing the list of medical supplies they brought with them.

"Greetings, High Clua." Taillefer rode up beside her. The crescent-shaped scar by his eye crinkled as he smiled down at Jehennette. "I am here to guard the healers as I promised."

"The Goddess bless you, song-smith." Jehennette turned to look back at the rumbling wagons bearing the healers. "May She bless us all. We have been most fortunate that so many healers came from Sadko to swell our ranks. The Lady knows we will have need of them all too soon."

"Still no word of heart-change from Asur?" Taillefer asked.

"None." Jehennette shook her head. "Many of the women who spied for Kirisan have fled over the border. They say the temple Magni have become more intolerant. They tighten their religious control over the people, particularly the women. Even the Keffin of the towns will not challenge them. And the Magni have decreed that no Asuran can take part in this battle."

"They still believe they can bargain with the Fravashi if those nathlings win?" Taillefer raised his brows in disbelief.

"As do those who now hold Sadko." Jehennette looked up sharply at the song-smith, new leather armor squeaking, his worn sword at his side. "Where is your harp, Taillefer? I do not see you forgetting to compose the great saga of this battle."

"Nor shall I. The harp is safe in one of the wagons." Taillefer nodded to her, then turned his horse to ride back down the line of healers.

When he reached the wagon driven by Merra and Balqama, he leaped from horse to seat, carefully holding his horse's reins in one hand. The horse ambled obediently alongside as Taillefer settled beside Balqama.

"Does Tirkul still not know you go with us?" he asked.

"Nor shall you tell him," Balqama answered, her eyes fierce, her mouth set firmly. "Every healer is needed at the border."

"I shall not tell him." Taillefer raised his hand in promise. "But do you not fear being seen by your people?"

"They are not my people!" Balqama stared straight ahead. "I thought once to become Tuonela. Now even that is barred to me."

"Healer lady, do not try to be other than yourself. If blood or Clan be rotten, cast them aside. That is an old Tuonela saying." Taillefer laid a compassionate hand on her arm and was rewarded with a smile. "You and your warrior can be a Clan unto yourselves."

"For a song-smith, you are a strange one," Merra said across Balqama. "Almost as wild and unpredictable as Imandoff Silverhair and the Dream Warrior."

"The very reason I was not accepted at the Temple. Where is the Dream Warrior? I have not seen her or the sorcerer."

"News came from the Green Men who march with us," Merra answered. "Silverhair and the others are in Deep Rising. Soon they will follow." *I pray they will,* the girl thought. *And Blessed Lady, may they bring the ancient armor with them.*

Malya and her two hired men rode along the narrow trails of the Takto Range. She had pushed the horses hard, lengthening the distance between her and the Kirisani armies daily. Now, she guessed, she and her men were at least five days' ride in front of the armies and nearing the border with Frav. Nebel and Vikkarr rode before her, nervous eyes darting around the unfamiliar forest, their hands jerking at each sound.

"We will camp tonight near the border," she called softly.

"That be dangerous." Vikkarr turned and glared at her with vicious little eyes. But his hands trembled on the reins with fear. *If we try to leave, I know we die. But if we stay, what happens at the end of this journey?*

"I will protect you," she said in a soothing voice. "Your journey will end at the border, and I will give you your reward." *Your reward will be your blood poured out to Jevotan,* she thought, smiling to herself.

"Mayhap we should sneak off without the reward," Nebel muttered to Vikkarr. "That one is slippery with words. I do not trust her."

"If we try to leave, we will die like that Tuonela did," Vikkarr said softly. "Use your head, Nebel. We dare not double-cross this one." His eyes widened as he scented smoke. "A camp ahead!" he softly called to Malya as he reined in his horse.

"Ride on," Malya ordered. "They await us."

The two men nervously proceeded her into the camp. At the sight of the Volikvi priest who waited, arms crossed, a smug smile on his lips, they tried to turn and flee.

"Take them!" Malya ordered.

Before either man could draw dagger, they were pulled from their horses, disarmed, and tied by the Fravashi soldiers.

"Greetings, daughter of Jinniyah." The Volikvi gestured Malya to a log laid near a cold fire. "Your father has sent his people to help us cross the border. They will be here by moon-rise."

"And I have brought you a sacrifice." Malya pointed at Nebel and Vikkarr. "Do with them as you will." She stiffened as she noticed the Jabed and his priests at the far side of the clearing. "Why are Kirisani here?"

The Volikvi moved close, his voice soft. "The Jabed and his men followed us, thinking to gain the support of Frav for their cause. As if overthrowing the priestesses of their Goddess will mean anything when Frav rules. Your father sends the priest Zalmoxis and the Trow Xephena to open the borders for us. I am ordered to bring the Jabed and his men to the Fire Temple for sacrifice, although they know it not."

"But of course." Malya dismissed the Kirisani men with one disdainful glance.

Nebel and Vikkarr shouted at the Jabed to free them, but the priest only turned away, his mouth puckered with distaste.

Malya sat down on the log and watched the Volikvi as he strode to the captives and smiled down at them. She ignored the screams and pleading voices of the two Kirisani men as the soldiers bent back their heads. She only turned away briefly when the Volikvi drew his curved dagger, chanted the call to his god, and slashed their throats.

When the moon rose over the tall mountains, a heavy fog settled over the Taktos. Malya, the Fravashi, and the Jabed and his men used the magickal fog to creep to the spellbound border where Xephena and an escort of Fravashi warriors waited. The Tuonela warriors, fighting to repel invaders at a break in the border-spells, never knew of their passing.

Kayth stood before the altar in the hidden temple room, his face slick with perspiration from the ritual he performed. As the last words of the unholy spell died away in the silence, he carefully leaned forward to rest his forehead on the altar.

Although there was a final and full joining between us, Jinniyah, he said, *know this. I control you, whatever you may think. Just as I control Minepa.* Kayth felt Minepa struggle deep within his mind and heard the priest's feeble protests. *Silence! You are nothing. I allowed your entrance, Minepa, only to have your powers.*

Jinniyah laughed at the struggling priest as Kayth forced Minepa into silence.

Together we shall be invincible, Kayth Farblood. Together we shall rule Sar Akka. Jinniyah's triumphant tones rang through Kayth's mind. *When the black moon appears at the Harvest Moon, and when you use the ancient disk to open the hidden places of this altar, then all shall cower before us! The demons from the abyss will rise at my command during that dark moon and reap a great harvest of blood on the grasslands of Tuone.*

Kayth felt the full power of the dead Jinniyah seep through his body and mind and spirit. He shook with its force, but smiled in triumph. *This is true power! This is what I sought!* He released all restraints against Jinniyah.

Too late, Kayth felt the trap close around him, entangling his mind and spirit in an Otherworldly web of restraint. He opened his eyes, flailing out with his hands, but the web Jinniyah had cast held him prisoner. The light from the candles stabbed into his eyes, piercing into his brain like daggers.

Greedy little man, your body is now mine. Jinniyah's deep voice hissed in Kayth's ear. *In time I will cast your spirit into the abyss, but your body shall remain mine! You thought to bargain with and outwit Jinniyah, the most powerful of the Volikvis to ever live. I shall let your spirit see through my eyes until I rend your precious daughter limb from limb. Then you shall follow her spirit into the Otherworlds, where you will pay—and pay dearly—for your attempt to use me.*

Kayth's screams of anger were silenced. Jinniyah reached out with his mind and snuffed the candles to dim sparks in the room. *I had hoped to no longer feel the pain caused by the light of fire or sun or moon,* he said, *but no matter. I am alive again!*

The spirit of Kayth Farblood groaned and struggled feebly, locked within his own mind and helpless to free his body from Jinniyah's control. With him somewhere in the darkness, he heard the groans of Minepa.

Charissa wiped the blood from her sword blade on the grass before sheathing it and turning once more to face the shakka Norya. The campfires to drive away the darkness and provide light for the shakkas glinted in her dark eyes.

"Word has come from Kulkar," she said. "The spells along two other places on the border have weakened enough to open for the Fravashi to spill into Tuone."

"And the Fravashi who escaped into Tuone on the other raid?" Norya rubbed at her weary eyes.

"All killed by riders as they sought to flee into the forests of the Taktos or on to Kirisan." Charissa looked about the camp at the weary warrior women. "They found a great evil thing there also," she said in a quiet voice. "Burrak and those of the Feathered Spear who were driven out, all but three of their company have died of the plague. Those who remain warned off the riders."

"Plague!" Norya stared at the tall woman. "Word came of a plague victim in Kirisan, but I never thought it to be here."

"Whether this plague is Fravashi-caused or out of some Kirisani's greed for treasure from an old grave does not matter." Charissa leaned her big-boned body against a tree and crossed her arms. "For years after this battle we shall have to look askance at any bones or bodies we find."

"I have never understood this striving of the Fravashi for control over others," Norya said as she sat cross-legged by the wheel of her tent-wagon. "Once tasted, there is no sating this thirst for power over what others think, how they worship, or how they live their lives. It is a disease the shakkas cannot cure. This control is only a pleasant word to disguise what evil people really do: make slaves of others."

"Think you this lust will come to the Clans?"

"The shakkas have spoken of this." Norya closed her eyes and leaned back against the wheel. "The day this lust for control corrupts the Clans, we will all withdraw. On that day, pray that the Mother of Mares wipes the Tuonela from the face of Sar Akka."

The air suddenly felt heavy in Charissa's lungs and her mind clouded. "What happens?" She drew her sword as she leaped away from the tree, half-crouched in the shadows of the wagon.

Norya slowly got to her feet and looked through the trees at the strange fog coiling and crawling toward them. "Fravashi magick," she said, as she cupped her pendant in one hand. "Why do they use it? I feel no attackers lurking in its depths."

Charissa trembled as the first tendrils of the fog brushed her bare arms. Norya threw up both arms and began an ancient chant, the Tuonela language filling the warriors' campsite with lilting tones of challenge. The shakkas working among the wounded took up the chant until the mountain camp rang, the thick stands of trees echoing it back. The fog pulled back from the wall of sound and passed around them.

"The battle begins soon," Norya said as she traced the patterns on her pendant over and over with her rough fingers. "Mother of Mares, bring the Dream Warrior to us soon, or our fight for freedom is lost."

"Will she hold true to what she says she believes?" Charissa's dark eyes were solemn. "The blood in her veins is tainted by that of this evil Kayth."

"Talent is not evil, warrior. There must always be a seed for the gifts to flourish. What is drawn out of that seed can be evil or good. The responsibility of choice is what all of us with talent must bear. The Dream Warrior will cleave to her mother's blood."

"I pray the Mother of Mares holds her on that path," Charissa murmured as she walked off to join her companions.

"What are they?" Dakhma bent over the box of figurines delivered by the messenger from Leshy. "They are not toys, Oracle. What are we to do with them?"

"I do not know." The Oracle's thin fingers hesitated over the tiny images; a few of them were larger than the others, and they were in two colors, white and red, like chessmen. Finally, she set each of the larger white figures out on the table so Dakhma and the boy Athdar could see them more clearly. "Imandoff Silverhair's message said we must discover their purpose."

Dakhma carefully picked up one of the figures to look at it closer. "Oracle, this is my friend the Dream Warrior, the one the message now calls Warrior of Shadows." She hurriedly set it aside to pick up others. "This is the mighty sorcerer, and this the Tuonela warrior woman. Truly it is. Look."

The young Oracle peered closer at the figure in Dakhma's hand and took a quick sip of breath. "Out of the mouths of children comes wisdom," she whispered. "We will think on this tonight, little ones," she said as she motioned to the priestess who stood near the door waiting to take the children to their room. "Perhaps by tomorrow the Lady will reveal to us what use they may be." She peered at the remaining figures in the box but touched none of them.

The children went quietly to their room, but as soon as the priestess left, Dakhma padded on bare feet to Athdar's bed and crawled in beside him.

"You know what the Lady wants, do you not?" she whispered. "I saw your eyes, Athdar."

"I will draw a picture for you tomorrow," the little boy whispered back. "The Lady said She will guide my hand."

At dawn, while the priestesses were in the chapel, Dakhma and Athdar crept back to the Oracle's room. There they cleaned off the long dark-colored table and, with a piece of chalk they used in their schooling, Athdar climbed onto the table and began to draw.

"What is it?" Dakhma asked when Athdar climbed off the table. The strange lines seemed familiar. "A map!" she cried.

Athdar hunted for the box of figurines and carefully began to take out the white ones, one by one. He made no effort to do more than set the larger white figurines onto the edge of the table. The children watched wide-eyed as the figures began a slow slide across the chalked map, as if invisible hands moved them to and fro to assigned positions. Dakhma brushed one hand against her head as she felt a pulling sensation there each time the figurines moved. Athdar reached back into the box and gathered up the other white forms; the children watched as these settled themselves into groups behind the larger figures.

"There are some left," Dakhma said as she peered into the box, but she made no move to touch the remaining images, nor did Athdar.

"What are you doing?" The stern voice of their teacher-priestess broke through their intentness. "You should not be in the Oracle's rooms. Come away at once." She moved toward the table, raising her hand to wipe off the chalk marks.

Athdar snarled, then threw back his head and gave a roar that sent the priestess scurrying back against the door. "Touch not the sacred guides!" His child's voice held a shadow of the power he would use as he grew older.

"Athdar, Dakhma, what is this?" The Oracle pushed around the frightened priestess, her dark eyes quickly taking in the half-shifted little boy and the Tuonela girl who stood with open mouth beside a chalked table. *What is this creature on Athdar's face? It reminds me of ancient drawings.*

"Leave us," she ordered the teacher-priestess and closed the door behind her. "It is safe now, Athdar." She sat in her chair and held out her arms. "Come, tell me about all this."

"Athdar said the Lady told him how to use the figures," Dakhma said, her eyes full of fascination at her companion's abilities. "They moved, Oracle, truly they did, all by themselves."

"We will not touch the others." Athdar struggled with the shape-shifting powers flooding through him. "Strong evil," he forced between his curled lips.

The Oracle bent to pick up the box by her chair. Inside were several dark red figurines, the color of old blood. Although she felt repelled by them, she took each from the box and set it on the table, then wiped her fingers on her white robe, fully expecting to see streaks of blood there.

The larger dark figures began a slow slide until they stood on the opposite side of the table from the others, groups of smaller figures behind them. The Oracle drew down her black brows in thought as she looked at Athdar's chalked marks.

"It is a map of the Peoples' lands," she finally said. "Athdar, you were truly led by the Lady. In some manner, these figures represent those who hold the keys to victory or defeat in this battle. But how they move, that I do not understand." She looked at Dakhma. "Do you move them?"

"No, Oracle, but when they move, I feel it here." The little girl touched her forehead.

Blessed Goddess, the child has grown beyond the power to move objects on command and has walked, untaught, into the greater paths of spirit-commands from the Lady! The Oracle smiled at the two children, who stood nervously waiting for a reprimand. "You have done no wrong. To work the Lady's will, now we must name the figures."

She pointed to the white figurines and spoke in confident tones. "The Dream Warrior Corri, Imandoff Silverhair, Takra Wind-Rider, Gadavar the Green Man, Tirkul of the Asperel." Her finger moved to the smaller grouped statues. "These must represent the armies who march with them."

Dakhma moved closer to the table and pointed at other figures. "Zanitra from Sadko, Odran the shape-shifter, the High Priestess who leads Her Own."

Athdar stood on his tiptoes to see clearly. The shape-shifting still showed in his voice when he spoke. "Jinniyah, who now rules the mind of Kayth," he said as he pointed to the blood-red images. "A Trow priestess, the daughter of Kayth." His small finger hesitated above the smaller statues. "Their armies."

"How do you know this, Athdar, for you have never seen the ones you name?" the Oracle asked in a soft voice. *So young to shape-shift,* she thought. *He must have more training at once.*

"As you named those fighting against the Fravashi, I heard the Lady tell me names of the others," the boy answered. He stood on tiptoe to peer over the edge of the table. "What is a dragon?" he asked, his eyes firmly on the figurines.

"It is a fabled beast, one that does not exist in our world." The Oracle leaned forward slightly, her dark eyes intent on the child. *That is what I saw on his face!*

"When I get angry, I see what I know is a dragon, yet I have never seen one, not even in pictures." Athdar turned to meet the Oracle's gaze. "Is this wrong?"

"No, little one. Come, and I will show you very old drawings of dragons." The Oracle stood and headed for the door, the children behind her. "It seems that Silverhair has sent us the means to see how the battle goes and how the Fravashi may deploy their men. I, and you with me, shall watch it every day. We can send word to the High Priestess by scrying crystal whenever we see new moves from Frav."

"If the battle goes against us," Dakhma whispered to Athdar, "mayhap you and I can make the figures move so we can win."

"Mayhap." The boy's whisper was a low growl as they walked behind the Oracle toward the temple library. "We can try."

The Oracle walked on, her head held high, pretending she had not heard the whispered words of the children at her heels. *There are depths to both your powers I have yet to see,* she thought. *I would not have you break your hearts and spirits against a tide of evil that might overwhelm you. Children should not know the terrors of war and oppression, yet here the Lady has placed you. I wish you to be sheltered, yet who am I to try to cast aside the will of the Goddess?*

The Oracle opened the library door and smiled at Dakhma and Athdar. "Now I shall show you pictures of dragons and read you ancient tales of their wisdom and cunning."

You think to distract us, Dakhma thought as she followed the Oracle into the temple library. *The Mother of Mares has called us to do something for Her, and that I will do.* Her thoughts turned to Corri. *Hurry, Dream Warrior! Very soon the border will be red with blood. The Peoples need you there!*

Chapter 15

Xephena rode beside the Jabed at the head of the little group. Her voluptuous body was concealed within a closely-drawn cloak, but she rode with the hood of her cloak thrown back to reveal her haughty face. She was looking forward to a soft bed in Vum after two nights of rough camping.

So this is Kayth's other daughter, Xephena thought. She turned in the saddle to look at Malya. A slight smile curved her lips as she turned back to the road ahead. *I have her thought-pattern now. She is no match for me. I dare not challenge Kayth outright, but I can easily influence his daughter, and through her Kayth himself, if necessary. And I have the black power-sink stone to help me. The only problem remains the Volikvi who carries the ancient black disk.*

As if summoned, the Volikvi rode alongside Xephena and leaned over to speak, his guttural voice in the Fravashi temple tongue barely audible above the sound of the horses' hooves, the jingle of bridles, and the clank of swords as they swayed against armor.

"What do you plan for the Jabed and his followers? Surely, Kayth will not let them walk free within the Fire Temple, no matter what promises they make."

"The man Kayth has changed," Xephena answered. "He is more powerful than before and now orders that all must call him Jinniyah. Zalmoxis thinks he has translated the last of the Books of Darkness and is working with the spirit of the ancient Jinniyah." Xephena watched the Volikvi's face from the corner of her eye. "The Jabed will be sacrificed."

"Praise be to Jevotan." The priest smiled and his hand stole to the heavy pouch hanging from his belt. "Now Frav will be supreme once more. Volikvis will wash all the lands clean with the blood of sacrifices."

"This night, when we rest at the temple in Vum, you are to receive part of your reward. Jinniyah is pleased with you." Xephena smiled at the priest.

"You?" The Volikvi licked his lips when the Trow priestess nodded. "A reward indeed! Tonight in Vum then."

The Jabed scowled as the Volikvi dropped back to ride with his soldiers. "I thought Fravashi priestesses did not have power as do those in Kystan. He looks to you as one of power and influence."

Xephena smiled at him, schooling her voice into meek tones and speaking in the trade language the Jabed could understand. "We do not, Jabed. Our sexual skills are used to reward those our leader favors. But, as for true power, that lies within the hands of the Volikvis and Jinniyah."

She watched the Jabed's smug smile with inner contempt. *Like the Volikvis, you will learn quickly where the true power lies if I bed you, Kirisani filth. Your mind may not accept this truth, but your body will. You will be pliable to whatever I suggest, just as are Zalmoxis and the others I have seduced.*

They rode on, each wrapped in their own thoughts, until they entered the city of Vum just as the sun went down over the eastern mountains. Xephena surreptitiously watched the Jabed's expression as the townspeople quickly stepped aside and bowed as they passed. *So you have a deep greed for power,* she thought. *I guessed that, but I never thought it would be so all-controlling of your actions.* She smiled to herself as the Jabed looked down his nose at the cowering people, the corners of his mouth lifted in arrogance.

Once within the temple grounds, Xephena turned her attention to Malya, playing upon the fact that she and the young woman were the only two females in the group traveling to the Fire Temple. At first Malya was suspicious, then flattered as Xephena talked to her of the minor sexual practices of the Trow. Fascinated, Malya did not see the Trow tip a few drops into her goblet from a tiny vial the priestess concealed in her hand.

"Think upon what I say," Xephena said softly to Malya when she showed the woman the richly decorated room where she would sleep. "Your father will be pleasantly surprised if you learn these things."

Two more days of the potion and you will be completely under my control, the Trow thought as she hurried to her own room to prepare for the messenger Volikvi. *Now to bend this priest's mind in the pattern I wish.*

She took a second tiny vial from her saddlebag and slid it under her pillow. Its strange green contents glittered briefly in the candlelight as she concealed it. At the sound of her door latch rising, Xephena arranged herself seductively on the bed.

The Volikvi's eyes were bright with lust as he shut the door and slipped out of his robe. "A few hours of your love-play will ease the aches of my journey," he whispered as he slid onto the bed and ran his long-nailed hands over her body. "Give me my reward, Trow."

Through the next two hours Xephena used all of her sexual skills until the Volikvi lay back on the bed in exhaustion. She stroked his temples until the priest's eyes closed, and he drifted down into sleep.

You will never give that disk to Kayth, she thought as she carefully slid the vial from under the pillow. She held her breath as she dribbled three drops of the greenish liquid into the Volikvi's slightly open mouth. *Once Kayth destroys the armies of the Peoples, Frav will once more rule Sar Akka. Zalmoxis shall have the disk, and I shall rule through Zalmoxis.*

"In two days," she whispered to the sleeping man, "just after we enter the Fire Temple, you will show signs of having the plague. You will retire to your chambers with the disk and not give it to anyone but me."

The Trow lay back on the pillows and her thoughts jumped to Malya. Her eyes narrowed with hate. *And for you, daughter of Kayth, I have plans that will destroy you before any child-seed is planted by your father. By the time we reach Vu-Zai, your mind will be completely under my domination. You will see what I want you to see and do what I want you to do.*

Xephena hid the vial, then roused the sleeping Volikvi. "Time to return to your room," she said with a smile. "I must rest if we are to reach Vu-Zai in two days."

Soon you will think you have the plague, the Trow thought, a smile on her face as the drowsy priest left her room. *Your will belongs to me. Neither Kayth nor any outsider will rule Frav for any longer than it takes to win this coming battle. If I cannot take my rightful place at Kayth's side, if I cannot control him, he will die under my claw-blades.*

The group bound for the Fire Temple was on the road at dawn. For two more days they journeyed across Fravashi countryside. Xephena carefully administered doses of the mind-controlling liquid to both Malya and the Volikvi to whom she had given her favors, watching their compliant reactions to her suggestions with a sense of triumph.

The Jabed and his followers, even Malya, watched the farms and large herds of white cattle with vague interest, their attention mostly on the tall, rugged mountain peak gradually drawing closer as the miles went by. When the city of Vu-Zai and the looming mountain containing the Fire Temple filled the eastern view before them, the Kirisani traitors were awed. Nothing had prepared them for the grandeur of the sacred city or the massive sense of power that seemed to emanate from the mountain. They were silent as the group rode through the narrow lanes of the city crouched around the lower slopes of the mountain.

As they dismounted and left the horses in the Temple stables, Xephena, one hand tight around Malya's wrist, drew close to the messenger Volikvi. "You have carried the ancient disk for many days," she said softly. "Are you not afraid of contracting the plague?"

As the Trow spoke the word plague, the Volikvi's skin suddenly flushed with faint red patches and he began to sweat as if with a fever.

"No," the priest said firmly, but his eyes held a glint of fear.

"Perhaps you should stay apart a few days in your chamber," Xephena suggested, "until you can be certain. With the battle so close, the plague could ruin Frav's chance to regain control."

"Wise words," the Volikvi answered. He walked off toward the Fire Temple and his chambers, his shoulders hunched forward and one hand clutching at the belt pouch holding the ancient disk.

"Come with me," Xephena said to Malya. "You can stay in my rooms until your father calls for you."

"I hope that will be soon." Malya frowned at the retreating Volikvi. But her thoughts vanished under Xephena's soft words and deceptive smile. She willingly followed the Trow into the tunnels of the Fire Temple, the sacred precinct within an ancient sleeping volcano.

Xephena gave a sigh of relief when word came that Kayth-Jinniyah was too occupied to see his daughter until after the war with the Peoples. Malya, at first, was upset, but Xephena turned her attention to other things, dressing the young woman in the sheer Trow garments and teaching her how to move seductively, both while walking and while lying on the bed. Xephena's thoughts visualized Malya's body writhing on Croyna's altar as she watched the woman swaying back and forth across the room.

That night, as Malya lay naked in a drugged sleep, the Trow priestess took out Minepa's black power-sink stone and set it on her altar. Using the stone to augment her powers, the Trow strengthened the drugs clouding Malya's mind. *Now that you are secure,* Xephena thought, *there is one other bit of magick I must do.*

The priestess sprinkled more incense on the burning coals, its scent swirling about the room. She murmured strange words as she stood with both hands on the stone, her head bent forward in concentration. The incense smoke above the altar began to curdle, then roll itself into a hazy form. The form flickered in and out of sight, as if it existed in two worlds.

Shadow-seeker, seek out Corri Farblood, the one called the Dream Warrior, and report to me what she does and plans.

The shadow-seeker vanished back into the coiling smoke as Xephena raised her hands and finished the ritual. With a smile of satisfaction, the Trow went to stand beside the bed, looking down at the sleeping Malya with contempt.

Now I will bring you to your knees, daughter of Kayth, she thought. "You will see only what I tell you to see," she said softly as she projected Kayth's face overlaid with that of Zalmoxis to the sleeping woman. "This is your father, and he will come to you soon. You will open your body to him with joy and the skills I have taught you. You cannot resist him. Your body is on fire for him. Any time he calls you, you will go to him with the same heat." She paused, then added, "When you meet him any time other than in this chamber, you will not recognize this man as your father."

The chamber door opened, and Zalmoxis stepped inside. He pushed the door closed and quickly walked to the bed, his eyes glittering in his flat, cruel face.

"Will you stay to watch?" he asked as he began to fondle Malya.

"I go to petition Croyna for an increase in my powers." Xephena glanced down at Malya, who began to twist and moan under the Volikvi's hands. "When you finish here, go to Minepa's ritual chamber. I will leave the door unlocked. There you will find the spells and tools you need to suck away the Jabed's power."

"And Kayth?" The Volikvi began to disrobe.

A sneer lifted Xephena's mouth. "He is far too involved in translating the Books of Darkness in his secret place to notice what happens in the rest of the Temple. When Kayth is consumed with the battle I will kill her, so enjoy her while you can."

"And the Jabed and his accursed followers, where are they?" Zalmoxis paused, his cruel eyes hard.

"Safely in the dungeons, as I ordered." Xephena pursed her mouth as she watched the Volikvi's face. "See that you use the spells I stole from Kayth, or you cannot hope to rule here when he is dead."

"First I will take in the Jabed's power when I sacrifice him," Zalmoxis said, his mouth lifting in an evil smile. "Then, one by one, I will take in the powers of his followers. Kayth does not know they came with you?"

"I told you, he is too caught up in searching through the Books of Darkness to be bothered with such as me." Xephena smiled back.

"Then I will kill the Jabed tonight. Will you watch?"

"Perhaps." The Trow priestess turned her back and left the room.

So much for your worth, daughter of Kayth, she thought as she made her way along the hall to the stairway leading downward to the ritual cavern. *When Kayth discovers your lust for Zalmoxis, he will cast you aside and take me instead. Your dreams of ruling beside your father are done, Malya. You will answer any call from Zalmoxis like a bitch in heat. I shall soon be more powerful than Varanna ever thought to be. I shall be the supreme Trow in the Fire Temple. And when I have used Kayth to gain the victory, I will kill him.*

Corri's spirit-body hung high over the Kirisani camp in the Tuonela grasslands, the sky above showing the moon near its fullness. Below, the sparks of the fires were plain, as were the Mootma Mountains a day's ride away. She and her companions had caught up with the main Kirisani armies two days before.

Something calls to me, she thought as she surveyed the land and sky around her. *It does not have the feel of Varanna, nor is it a summons for help.*

Corri turned toward the border with Frav, a sense of wariness filling her. Through the dark sky, she saw a nebulous form moving swiftly toward the camp. A stench of evil ran before it, as if the night winds of the grasslands carried the very vibrations of the Fravashi Fire Temple into Tuone.

As the form neared, Corri sucked in her breath in surprise and shock. Its form was that of a cross between a gigantic bird and malevolent-faced human. Its hands and feet were armed with long, curved claws, and its drawn-back lips exposed sharp fangs. The wing-feathers were black as a starless night, but the body glowed a deep, dark red, the color of old blood.

What is it? Corri felt fear wash over her. In defiance, she reached out with her senses, testing the rapidly approaching half-seen form. She recoiled in disgust and anger. *A shadow-seeker with that Trow priestess's print on it! I thought she would have learned better when it rebounded on her before.*

Corri held her position as the entity raced closer, then hung over the campsite. A wave of bafflement and frustration rolled out from the entity as it twisted and turned in the air, seeking its prey. Although Corri hung before the seeker, it could not find her spirit form. Back and forth it moved, the frustration rapidly becoming deep and violent anger. Down it swooped at the silent camp, the aura of its wrath causing many of the sleeping warriors to cry out in terror and the horses to scream and rear at the picket lines.

At a thought, Corri felt the spirit-form of Varanna's sword in her hand, the strange helmet on her head. *Enough! Return to your mistress and take your vengeance there,* she ordered as she struck at the shadow-seeker with the sword. *Back to the one who made you, evil spawn of the abyss! Wreak your havoc in the Fire Temple!*

As she struck a flurry of blows against the entity, it screamed in fear and fled back toward the distant Fire Temple. Corri flew in its wake, over the grasslands and the rugged, forested mountains, until she saw it disappear inside the dark form of the looming mountain that held the Fire Temple itself.

Too long have I held back, she thought as she stared down at the mountain. She hung motionless in the night air, searching with her senses for any trap in the Temple below. *I should have taken the chance, gone into the Fire Temple and caused confusion there as soon as I knew Kayth could no longer find me during my dream-flying. Now I will do just that! But first I must stop Xephena from sending any more seekers on our trail.*

Down she swooped, straight at and then into the great mountain, her thoughts centered on Xephena. Her flight stopped within the Trow's chambers. On the bed, she saw the bodies of Zalmoxis and Malya twined together. The stink of Fravashi incense filled her nose and made her gag. But the priestess was nowhere in sight.

You have caused me nothing but trouble, Corri thought as she hovered over Malya's naked, sweat-covered body on the bed. *But you are part-sister and blind to the truth. I would not willingly leave you or anyone so ignorant to the powers of Zalmoxis and Xephena. I know what they do to such as you.*

She tried, unsuccessfully, to wake Malya. As she drifted above the bed, wondering how to break through the drugs and Xephena's spells, a voice sounded near her ear.

Leave her, my Shadow Warrior. She has chosen her own destiny. The Lady's voice was firm. *I have other tasks for you. The shadow-seeker still flies through this Temple. If you would not have it returning to plague the warriors in your camp, you must harry it until it returns to the abyss from which it sprang.*

Corri spared one last look at Malya, then centered her thoughts on the shadow-seeker. Its emotions of anger and frustration reached her clearly from the cave several levels below, deep within the bowels of the mountain.

She thought of the great smoking crack in the cave's floor and the altar stone soaked with blood and was instantly there. A crowd of Volikvis and Trows were gathered in the cavern, their eyes intent on the dying man chained to the altar, blood flowing bright from the wound in his chest. A Volikvi stood over him, curved bloody knife in one hand. Above the altar hung the shadow-seeker, feeding off the emotions of lust and fanaticism that rose from the worshippers.

Corri spied Xephena standing near the altar, a look of excitement in her dark eyes. She dropped lower, the sword still ready in her hand. Xephena looked around suddenly, suspicion on her face, but she was unable to find the source of her unease. With a shrug of her bare shoulders, she dismissed the feeling that had raised the hair on her arms and rippled cold across her skin.

The shadow-seeker hovered inches above the dying man's chest as it sucked up the life-energy. Corri heard its thoughts as clearly as if the entity had a physical voice. *I will return to the armies on the grasslands and cause great havoc until my prey shows itself.*

With a battle-cry of challenge, Corri darted forward and stabbed at the seeker. The spectral sword sliced through one wing; the severed part folded in on itself, the energy that made it curling off in great streamers like flowing blood. The entity screamed out in anger and fear of its unseen foe. Its energy bleeding away and its balance upset, it dropped to the floor where it half-floated, half-flopped around the cave. In its wake, it spread confusion and disruption among the assembled worshippers. They mindlessly began to run, shoving and falling over one another in their haste, trampling on those who lost their footing.

In her peripheral awareness, Corri instantly knew what occurred in other parts of the Fire Temple as the spectral entity's mindless pain and rage boiled out in waves.

Everywhere there is fear and confusion, she thought with satisfaction. *The longer I can frustrate the shadow-seeker, the less likely it will attack the Peoples.* She drove the entity from one wall of the vast chamber to another, her sword slashing, her will blinding it to her presence.

The Volikvi at the altar hurriedly unchained the dead man and dragged his body to the steaming crack. As he pushed the sacrifice into the dark gouge in the ground, one of the man's pain-crooked hands tangled in the priest's gold neck-chain and pulled the priest, screaming, into the pit with him.

Corri saw the entity's emanations ripple out through the cavern walls and sensed the continued confusion spreading through the entire labyrinthine Fire Temple. Still, the Otherworld being refused to leave the sacrificial chamber from which it drew energy. She continued to harry and attack the entity, her phantom sword bright in her hand, until the entity's spirit-body swelled with pent-up rage. In desperation, it began a hop-flight to put distance between it and its invisible attacker. Its erratic flight sent it low over the heads of the milling Volikvis and Trows who crowded up the narrow steps leading to the tunnels above. Several of the priests were pushed over the steps' edge by the panicky crowd and fell, screaming, to the rocky floor below.

Suddenly, Kayth strode across the cave and the vast array of lighted candles dimmed, nearly guttering out. His pale eyes were hard and glittering, his lips drawn back in a grimace of disgust at the disturbance. He looked up and made a quick drawing motion with one hand, pulling the shadow-seeker to him.

"Be gone back to the abyss!" he shouted. "Do not return unless I call you!"

The entity winked out of existence, leaving dark red streamers of floating energy behind from its wounds. Kayth stared up at the dark ceiling, his eyes narrowed as he sought for any other disturbance in the air. Corri held her position, her sword upraised, the feel of the helmet still on her head.

Can he find me this time? His power is greater than it was. She waited, ready to attack if Kayth showed signs of identifying her.

"Witless slaves," Kayth muttered. "They call up a shadow-seeker to spy on me, thinking I cannot turn aside its powers."

His cold eyes raked around the sacrificial chamber, ignoring the trampled and broken Fravashi victims. Then, without a backward glance, he strode across the bridge toward his secret chamber in the tunnel. Behind him, the candle-flames flared back to life.

What has he become? His powers are truly much greater, yet there is something else about him that is different, something that is not Kayth. Corri drew close to sense the dark bloodshot aura around him, then shivered and pulled back. *Something else shares his soul and body! Something, someone, very old and full of dark evil.*

Corri felt cold from this dangerous game she played with Kayth. *My senses say it is not yet time to attempt to defeat him. But I need to know what he does and where he goes in this maze of rat tunnels. Otherwise, we may not find him in the battle.*

She forced herself to follow Kayth over the bridge and into the dark tunnel beyond. She floated near the tunnel ceiling, watching as he opened the secret door and disappeared into the hidden room.

When I came here before, my powers did not fully work in this place, she thought as she stared at the hidden panel in the tunnel wall. Her mind flitted back over the Trial of the Mask and her encounter with the Singing Serpent. *I have changed as well. I can only pray to the Lady that my change is stronger than Kayth's.*

Corri hovered near the door and started to reach out with her senses to discover what Kayth did inside that place, but her instincts warned her away.

This is his center, the touch-point of the entity who shares his mind, the center from which Kayth draws his new unholy power. I must return to the armies and warn them. We can no longer count on a direct attack of Frav by sheer numbers. We must discover some other way, perhaps by stealth and guile, or we will lose the battle.

She turned her attention to the Fire Temple around her. The labyrinthine passageways were filled with fleeing Volikvis and Trows, their fear as cold and as cutting to Corri's senses as broken glass. They fled to their chambers, convinced that safety lay in hiding there. Then she sensed the presence of Tuonela warriors, their minds full of deep hatred and growing despair.

They are still alive! They are held in the dungeons I saw before. They think about their sacrifice when the moon goes dark and the battle is high.

Her senses briefly flicked across another presence in the dungeon cells. *The Jabed and his followers are held also. How did they get across the border, and why are they here at the Fire Temple?* She shivered at the intensity and hatred of the Jabed's thoughts of betrayal as they struck her like a fierce, hot wind. *So you are still alive. They must be saving you for special attention.* She threw up a mental barrier to shield her from the man's energy.

Back to Imandoff, she thought as she willed herself out of the dark mountain and into the fresh air beyond. *When the armies attack, we must rescue the Tuonela warriors and thwart their sacrifice. Between us, as thief and sorcerer, surely we can find a way to defeat Kayth and whatever now possesses him.*

She centered her thoughts on the distant Kirisani camp and flew back through the night to join her companions.

Chapter 16

"The plans must be changed." Imandoff's deep voice was hard and unrelenting as he argued with the High Priestess and the Tuonela war-leaders gathered in the mountain camp of Frayma's Mare. "Things are not as they were. Tuonela warriors are still alive, deep in the bowels of the Fire Mountain. When the Harvest Moon turns black, which it will in two nights, they will be sacrificed on the altar of Jevotan. I think the Jabed and his men are being saved for the same ceremony. The armies must fight border skirmishes only, while a select band crosses secretly into the Fire Temple."

"Kayth's power has grown beyond killing by sword with a physical hand." Corri stood beside the sorcerer, her thumbs tucked into her belt. "I see no way but for me to challenge him on the spirit level. To do that with any hope of success, I must be within the Fire Temple. Otherwise I will waste strength trying to fight Kayth through the magickal shields he has set around the temple grounds."

"Is it wise to physically go into that place?" Vairya looked around at the grim Tuonela war-leaders and the Kirisani captains. "The prophecy calls the Dream Warrior our only hope. What if she and you, Imandoff, are cut down?"

"No war is wise," Imandoff answered, and sighed. "But to preserve the lives and freedom of the Peoples, Corri and I must do battle in this other way." His smoke-gray eyes touched each of the men and women who stood around him. "The armies will be needed not only to repel the Fravashi soldiers, but also to be a diversion while we cross into Frav."

"You said the Dream Warrior must kill this Kayth in the spirit-realms." Charissa folded her muscled arms. "How will we know if she succeeds? And what of the Tuonela warriors imprisoned there?"

"If we are successful, I have no doubt you will know it soon," Corri answered. "As for the Tuonela warriors trapped within, shadow-hands cannot set them free. We have no choice but to enter Frav."

"Although I have had no foretelling dreams or visions, I will not let her go alone." Imandoff laid a hand on Corri's shoulder. "The battle the armies carry to the Fravashi soldiers will allow us time and space to hunt down and destroy the true controlling power behind the Fravashi."

One of the Tuonela war-leaders rubbed his hand across his broken nose as he frowned in thought. "What controlling power, Silverhair? Does not this power lie in the hands of the Volikvis and the man Kayth?"

"No, Kulkar," Imandoff answered. "From what Corri has told me, the real power now controls through Kayth." His mouth tightened in a grim line. "That power has somehow remained active and aware through the centuries. It is Jinniyah."

There was a sharp intake of breath all around the circle as Imandoff's words sank home.

"And there is another reason for Corri and a small party of warriors to enter the Fire Temple by stealth. Taillefer, the song-smith, has provided the last clue to this tangle. It comes from an ancient song, which says that the plaque I carry must be placed into an ancient altar. There it will lock the door to evilness. What that is I cannot guess, but I must do what I can."

Charissa glanced across the circle of warriors to Taillefer, who stood quietly with one hand on his sword. "Will you go also, song-smith?"

The desire for battle glowed, then died, in the man's eyes. He shook his head. "I cannot. I have sworn to protect the healers."

"Has news of more plague come out of Kirisan or Tuone?" Zanitra's fingers played over her string of prayer beads.

The Tuonela shakka Norya shook her head. "Frayma has blessed us in that way," she answered, her gray braids swinging as she stepped forward. "There has been no word of the plague spreading, but we may well face that danger yet. The Volikvis now hold the ancient source of that disaster, which they stole from the old Kirisani grave, and will use it sooner or late, unless they are stopped."

"It is time I returned to Frav." Thidrick moved up beside the Tuonela shakka. Firelight winked off the worn spots on his dark Fravashi armor and the metal-tipped laces of his knee-boots. "The Dream Warrior and I planted a seed of rebellion within the minds of the Fravashi people. I would see if it has sprouted. If it has, mayhap this battle need not claim so many lives." His black curly hair fell around his golden-skinned face like a cloud. He waited for the protests, his deep-set eyes wary.

"He is to be trusted." Tirkul moved up beside Thidrick. His long braids, nearly colorless in the firelight, framed his square jaw and rugged cheekbones. "When I fell into Volikvi hands and was taken into the filth of a Trow temple, this man helped the Dream Warrior get me back to freedom."

"You would spy against your people for us?" Kulkar's dark eyes were full of skepticism.

"No," Thidrick answered firmly. "That I will not do. But I will rally them against the Volikvis, for a great many of my people have reason to hate them, as do I." Painful memories crossed his face.

Kulkar nodded, then turned back to Imandoff. "What warriors will you take?"

"Only Corri and I will go."

"Not so!" Gadavar pushed through the warriors to stand at Corri's side. "Takra and I go with you." Takra, who stood near Imandoff, nodded firmly.

"And I," Tirkul said, his jaw set in determination.

"You are forgetting the ancient song that repeats the Prophecy," Taillefer said, and Jehennette nodded. "Five must cross together. Are you willing to chance failure by thinking to spare lives you hold dear? It makes sense that five should go, not two. Take care of every choice made, for the tide of battle may turn on a single gesture."

Leave it to a song-smith to cut to the heart of the matter, Corri thought, her mouth pinched against useless protests. *I do not know if I will get out of the Fire Temple alive. If it were my choice alone, I would not take others with me, but Taillefer is right. From now until the battle, every choice I make until the battle is over may decide victory or failure for the Peoples.*

Imandoff sighed and nodded his head. "You are right to speak so. If I knew for certain I could stop this battle alone, no one would go into Frav but me."

"Where will you cross?" Kulkar's eyes were thoughtful as he considered battle tactics.

"At the bridge over the Kratula Gorge, straight into the Fire Temple." Imandoff raised his hand at the loud protests from the warriors. "We must get into the Fire Temple as quickly as possible. The bridge is the only way. Besides, the ancient prophecy of which Taillefer speaks mentions that bridge."

"You will need warriors to hold the bridge for your return." Kulkar and Imandoff locked stares, the sorcerer finally nodding reluctantly. Kulkar pointed at several of the warriors. "I will take Charissa, Rushina, Shayron, and Halman. Their sword-skills are truest in the heat of battle, that I know."

"Think you to leave me behind, brother?" Zanitra lifted her eyes in a piercing, challenging stare at Imandoff. "My talents of illusion may be needed, both when you cross the bridge and when you return. Surely you do not think there are no guards at the bridge."

"And I have promised Zanitra the shelter of my sword." Odran loomed over the tall Tuonela warriors around him.

"Healers must go with you also." The elderly Norya took her place at Zanitra's side. "Do not discount my healing or my battle-skills yet, sorcerer." She reached behind her and pulled forward a reluctant figure from the group. "And this one shall be at my side."

"No!" Corri and Tirkul both cried.

Gadavar grinned ruefully at Balqama, who stared fiercely at Tirkul. "Best to learn when you are beaten, Tirkul." His face grew serious. "Neither you nor I would let the ones we love go into danger if we had a choice, but we have none."

The company needed is complete. Varanna spoke suddenly at Corri's side.

"No more will go with us!" Corri's sharp voice brought all eyes upon her. "Like Imandoff, I would prefer to go into Frav alone, not chancing the lives of others. Those chosen will be enough to guard our backs. All others must protect the borders. Your strength may mean the turning of the Fravashi armies. The company we need is complete." *Perhaps I can persuade Gadavar to stay behind with Zanitra,* she thought. *I still do not know whether his possible death is connected to the Fire Temple or merely to the battle.*

"Do not think to leave me behind with the bridge guard, Corri. You know I will follow." Gadavar's words were pitched low at her side so only she could hear.

We are so close now we hear each other's thoughts, my love. Corri said nothing, but her heart caught in her throat as she pushed back the memories of the Green Man's tangled life-thread, the one whose death she strove to prevent.

"Think like a warrior, Corri Farblood," added Tirkul, his hawk-like gaze bright and determined. "If you fail in your quest, one of us may well wield the sword that brings down Kayth. And if you fall in battle, then we fall at your side."

Imandoff sighed and nodded. "Hopefully, the Lady will not require that of us, Tirkul. However, Taillefer has the right of it, Corri. According to the song he discovered, prophecy says five must cross the bridge into Frav." He smiled down at her. "And you cannot refuse the help of your friends."

"Something still puzzles me," Taillefer said, his frown crinkling the crescent-shaped scar at the corner of one eye. "The song says that five cross the bridge, but one is carried."

Corri tamped down her emotions, keeping her facial expression unreadable. *Nor will I enlighten you,* she thought. *Besides, the Prophecy missed one child.*

Not so, Varanna answered. *It speaks only of the Warrior's child, your child.*

"Not every word in prophecies or old songs come true." Takra drew the warriors' attention away from Corri. "If you seek an answer, song-smith, perhaps the song refers to the child I carry."

Since your child is nearer to birth than mine, I would leave you behind if I could. Corri glanced at Takra, then shrugged, knowing it was useless to press an issue she would not win.

"My warriors and I will see to the supplies." Kulkar cut into the thick, thoughtful silence between Takra and the song-smith. "We must ride out at dawn. It is a day's journey to the land-bridge, if we meet no wandering Fravashi."

"And those who cross the bridge with the Dream Warrior must be rested and prepared for the danger we will find there." Imandoff's long-fingered hand closed about the hilt of his Wella-made sword. "Those who are chosen, be ready to ride at dawn."

The group broke up, returning to their friends to talk, pack what was needed, and to get what sleep they could.

Corri chose a sleeping place away from the others, under the long, drooping branches of an old fir. She felt a pressing need for privacy, a silent time to prepare herself.

Goddess, if someone must die to bring about victory, let it be me. Neither my life nor the life of the child I carry is more important than all the Peoples who have placed their hopes in me. She sat with her chin on her knees, staring out at the darkness and the low-flickering fires. *I do not seek out death, but I would embrace it to save my friends and Sar Akka. I have never sought glory or fame, nor do I now. If Gadavar dies in Frav, what will I do? How will I raise the child I carry? Life will have little meaning without Gadavar.* She sighed and leaned back against the rough trunk.

Trust in Me. The Lady's voice was soft, as if coming from a distance.

Gadavar came slipping through the dark stand of fir and pine, the rustling leaves of the purple meppe trees casting strange patterns on his face. His ability to see clearly in darkness led him straight to Corri. As he pushed his way into her sanctuary, he dropped his gear and sat down beside her, drawing her into the circle of his arms without a word.

So this is love, Corri thought as she relaxed against him. *There is no need for words between us, yet neither strives to dominate the other.* She felt the brush of his kiss against her temple.

"What strange thing has happened since I last was with you?" Gadavar murmured. He reached up to gently touch the white curl in her red hair.

"A mark given as proof by one not of this world who has promised to help in the battle when needed," she answered.

"Is there anything else I should know?" His voice was both a balm to her exhausted spirit and a goad to her conscience.

"No," she said. "Just hold me tonight. Give me courage to face what I must do." *I cannot tell him about the child. That knowledge might place him in even greater danger. I need his thoughts centered only on what will happen soon, not in worrying about me.*

"That I will do." Releasing her, Gadavar spread their blankets over the soft needles under the great tree. "Come," he said simply, and pulled her down beside him.

Corri lay against him, her head in the hollow of his shoulder. After a long time of silence, she whispered softly, "I love you, Gadavar."

"And I love you, Corri Farblood," came the soft reply. "We will go together into this battle for freedom, and if the Lady decrees, we will return across the bridge in victory. We will live to be very old, with many children and grandchildren around us." His hand cupped her cheek. "Seek not death, my love, for death may not be what the Lady decrees."

"I am no Tuonela to seek out death, Gadavar, but I realize how great the task is before me. I have no sword-skills, just powers of the mind I do not fully understand. I began this quest as a thief from Hadliden, a dream-flyer chosen for a task that seemed so fantastic I never thought it would come to pass. Now that the battle is here, I wonder if I can do what must be done."

"But, my little thief from Hadliden, your powers are stronger than you think and you are one guided by the Lady's hand," came the sleepy murmur. "Trust Her."

Corri lay a long time in Gadavar's arms, listening to his soft breathing and watching the stars glitter through the fir branches, before she finally slept.

Imandoff and Kulkar led the group as they left the camp at the first light of dawn the next morning. Behind them came Takra and Tirkul, then the others in a double line, only the sounds of bridle and sword clinking softly in the bird-silent air.

Gadavar rode close beside Corri, his slender face solemn. Often she felt the touch of his brown eyes, those loving eyes ringed with deep blue around the iris. Imandoff called a rest-halt when the sun rode high in the hot sky. Gadavar sat with

Corri, one arm around her shoulders, her head against his broad shoulder. But they spoke little, for they needed no words to know what each felt deep inside.

They all feel the press of their mortality and the closeness of death, Corri thought as she glanced around the group. *Some of those who ride with me: my friends, Gadavar,* her thoughts froze on the Green Man's name, *they may not live to see the sun rise two days from now. Have I done all I can to spare their lives?*

Imandoff bent over Takra with a water bottle, his deep voice only a murmur. Tirkul held both of Balqama's hands in his, love and concern in his dark eyes, as they sat together near the worn trail. The others spoke and moved quietly; even the faces of the guards, who prowled alert and watchful, were contemplative.

I must go into the Fire Temple. We need to know what traps have been set for invaders, she thought as she relaxed her body.

Corri closed her eyes and willed her body to slip away from the physical. She felt the hot currents of air around her and saw the camp below among the sheltering trees. She swung in the brilliant sky, her gaze going to the west, where the Zuartoc Sea touched Frav, and closer, where the land-bridge led straight across the deep chasm of the Kratula Gorge and into the Fire Temple.

Do I dare seek out Kayth? No, I will find Zalmoxis and Xephena. If any within that evil place knows Kayth's plans, it will be them. I must not chance Kayth's powers scenting me just yet.

Swiftly, she flew along the trail to where it paralleled the deep, wide crack in the ground. She followed the black, forbidding ribbon of the Kratula Gorge until the slender bridge of rock across it came into sight.

No one lies in ambush. There are no soldiers waiting to cross the border. Why? She hung above the bridge, puzzled at this lack of defense, her common sense screaming "trap" while her instincts detected no danger. *Surely Kayth cannot think himself and Frav so invincible.*

She settled her thoughts on Xephena and darted downward into the great mountain, into the hidden and labyrinthine Fire Temple.

"Look!" Dakhma's excited voice brought the Oracle and Athdar quickly to the table where the strange figurines of the Forgotten Ones stood on the rough-drawn map. "They are moving!"

The Oracle felt her heart squeeze with dread. "They go west, away from the armies. What do they do?" she said softly, her black brows dipping, her violet eyes full of concern.

"I almost know." Dakhma stamped her foot in frustration. "Why will the knowledge not come into my mind?" She looked up at the Oracle, who only smiled sadly and shook her dark head.

"Use my father's crystal," Athdar said.

Dakhma ran to her pile of belongings and began to dig through them. The Oracle had moved the children into her quarters with her the day the armies left, so that they need never be far from the figurines.

"Here it is!" The Tuonela girl gently cradled the crystal globe in her hands as she walked back to the table. "Mayhap we can see something more in this." She set the crystal on the table in a bowl the Oracle fetched from a cabinet.

"What does the Dream Warrior do?" The Oracle's soft whisper sounded overloud in the chamber as the three watched one of the figurines slowly revolve in its place.

"Does she dream-fly?" Dakhma leaned close to the rotating figurine, careful not to disturb the others that sat so near to it. Athdar climbed up on his stool and bent his head close to hers.

"The dark ones of Frav, look!" The Oracle pointed a thin finger at the figurines clustered tight within the map-area of the Fire Temple. Two of the figurines moved close to a third one, then stopped, facing it.

"What does it mean?" Dakhma's eyes widened in fear.

"We can only wait and see," the Oracle answered with a shake of her head. "We can only wait and pray that the Lady and Her Lord are strong within the Dream Warrior."

Xephena rapped lightly on the locked chamber door. "It is I, Xephena," she said in a soft voice. She glanced back down the half-lit hall to see if anyone lingered in the darkest shadows to spy on her. The corridor was empty.

The lock clicked, and the door edged open. The Volikvi who had retrieved the black disk peered out, his eyes suspicious.

"The red marks are nearly gone," he whispered, "and I have had no fever. It cannot be the plague."

Xephena slid closer to the crack, one hand poised to shove against the door if the priest should decide not to let her enter. "Kayth says this is so. He has sent me to take you to a meeting place," she whispered. "He does not wish the others to know about the disk yet. Bring it quickly and follow me."

The Volikvi left the half-open door for a moment, then returned with the bag that had carried the black disk all the way from the Kirisani grave. He stepped out beside the Trow, his eyes darting repeatedly over every shadow, every door along the corridor, the precious bag clutched tight in his hands.

Xephena led the way without another word, down the corridor, up a flight of stairs, and along a deserted, dusty hallway until she came to a door that was open a crack and lighted by candles inside. The Volikvi nearly trod on her heels in his impatient haste.

"He awaits within," Xephena said, and the Volikvi pushed past her into the candlelit chamber. The Trow went through the door at his heels, one hand flexing her claw-blades as she pushed the door shut with one foot.

"Where is Jinniyah? Why is Zalmoxis here?" The Volikvi whirled to leave, his face white with fear and the knowledge of trickery.

Xephena's claw-blades raked down the priest's neck, along the jugular vein. As he drew back in alarm, she dug the metal claws across his chest, shredding the robe and opening great bleeding tracks. The virulent poison reached his brain in seconds, and paralysis began. His eyes wide and glaring, the Volikvi's face purpled as he began gasping for breath. Xephena noted the telltale symptoms of the swift progression of the poison as the priest clutched his chest and dropped dead at her feet, bright drops of his blood splattering her thin clothing. She stepped quickly back, then watched with calculating eyes as Zalmoxis tore the bag from the dead man's fingers.

"There is a tip-stone in the far corner," she said, as she flicked her claw-blades again to rid them of blood. "The latch is controlled by the wall-candle near the cabinet. Throw the body into the hole beneath the stone and it will never be found." She smiled at the distrustful lift of Zalmoxis' brows. "There will be no smell. I think the passage may end in the Kratula Gorge."

Zalmoxis dragged the body to the far corner, reached up to jerk on the holder, then kicked the dead priest into the hole that opened in the floor. As he pushed the holder back up into place and the stone closed, Zalmoxis watched the Trow intently.

"Do you not trust me?" Xephena said as she swayed to the Volikvi's side. "Hide the disk wherever you wish. Then when Kayth has defeated those who come against Frav, you can bring it forth and use its powers to take control of the Fire Temple." She smiled enticingly at him, but her eyes were cold.

"We do not know what the disk does," Zalmoxis protested.

"You will discover its use. You are powerful, Zalmoxis." She twined her weaponless fingers into his matted hair as she smiled into his glittering eyes. "If Kayth can handle this disk without fear of the plague, can you not learn to do the same? Are you afraid?" She stepped back, a pout on her mouth.

"I will hide the disk," Zalmoxis said, "but who will kill Kayth? I cannot get close to him, and without him dead I have no hope of wrenching control from his hands."

"Leave that to me." Xephena stroked a long-nailed finger along his jaw line. "In two days the moon will go dark. In three days you will rule over the Fire Temple and all of Frav." *How easy it would be to kill you now,* she thought, flexing her other hand, where the poison-tipped claw-blades glittered in the candlelight.

Zalmoxis listened to her breathy words and began to plan.

Xephena shivered suddenly and glanced quickly around the chamber. *I feel as if someone spies on me,* she thought, *but my powers sense no one. If it were Kayth's daughter who dream-flies, I am strong enough to find and trap her.* The Trow's dark eyes darted around the chamber again, then she shrugged her shoulders and followed Zalmoxis out into the hall.

Corri watched from the ceiling of the chamber, the pooled blood near the door sending its coppery stench to her nose.

Can Zalmoxis and Xephena truly defeat Kayth? If they can, should we not wait to invade the Fire Temple? Corri started to follow the Volikvi and Trow, then froze motionless as a thread of thought brushed past her. *Kayth! Does he seek me?*

She saw the threads of thought, like so many black twining vines, touch the blood on the floor, then coil about the chamber. She sensed puzzlement as the threads sucked up the scents of those who had been there. Afraid to retreat, lest she draw attention, Corri cringed as the threads lifted higher, but they did not brush against her spirit-body. Suddenly, the questing threads of thought winked out as they sought elsewhere in the Temple.

Kayth has grown more powerful than Zalmoxis and Xephena realize, Corri thought. *They cannot truly believe they can defeat him.* She turned her thoughts to the camp across the Gorge and flew up through the mountain to the clean, bright air. *There is no retreat for my companions . . . or me,* she thought sadly. *Like Varanna, I must face the geis and the responsibility it carries. I must enter the Fire Temple and kill the man who calls himself my father.*

Corri felt the uncertainty of what would come clench like a fist deep in her chest.

"What does this mean?" Dakhma stared in horror at the toppled figurine that was slowly turning black. Neither she, nor Athdar, who stood beside her, made any move to touch the figure.

"Perhaps the crystal will tell us." The Oracle rested her hand on the globe, only to draw back with a cry of pain. "It is burning hot!"

"It is yours." Athdar turned his head to look at Dakhma, but she put both hands behind her back and shook her head. "But not to use now," he said and turned his attention back to the figure-studded table.

"The Dream Warrior has returned to her body." The Oracle watched the spinning figurine slowly stop turning. "Perhaps Athdar is right in what he feels, Dakhma. The crystal is yours, given to you by Ayron through the hands of the Dream Warrior. When the time comes for it to be used, you will know what to do and when to do it." She smiled at the Tuonela child. "Trust in the Goddess, child."

"I do trust the Goddess, but I did not know it would be so hard. I am afraid." Dakhma threw herself into the Oracle's arms and sobbed.

"I know, little one." The young Oracle gently stroked the girl's braided hair. *It is a fearful time,* she thought as she comforted the girl. *I, too, am afraid, afraid that one misstep will send all the Peoples hurling down into Darkness forever.*

Chapter 17

Corri blinked and sat up. Around her the others were silently getting ready to ride. Gadavar's arm about her shoulders tightened in reassurance as she looked at him.

What has happened to me? Her sight seemed doubled, as if she looked out of both physical and spiritual eyes at the same time. She shut her eyes and tried to settle more firmly into her body, but the feeling of being in two places at once continued.

"We will reach the bridge by nightfall." Imandoff looked down at Corri, a frown pinching his brows. "Are you well?"

You are safe, Dream Warrior. Varanna stood near Imandoff, yet the sorcerer seemed unaware of her spectral presence. *Your soul prepares for the final battle with the Darkness and those who willingly walk the Dark paths. Trust in your feelings. I will be at your side.* The warrior woman's sad eyes looked deep into Corri's blue-green ones. *When this battle is won, I can rest in peace in another time and place. Rest will come for you, also, my blood-daughter.* Varanna's form winked out of sight.

"Corri?" Gadavar's anxious face bent over her.

Does she warn me of my death? Corri thought, pushing down the fear she felt growing inside. "I am well," Corri finally said as she got to her feet. "We will camp out of sight of the bridge for a day, then cross after full dark."

"We do not enter Frav tonight? Is that wise?" Imandoff caught the warrior-tones in her voice, something that had not been there before.

"It is how it must be." Corri looked from the sorcerer to Gadavar. "We cannot change the course of the war, except during the time of the dark moon."

Without further words, the group mounted and rode on toward the land-bridge. Although Gadavar was never far from Corri's side, they seldom spoke. None of the others, except Imandoff, approached them when they finally set up camp among the monolithic rocks and twisted trees near the bridge, and the sorcerer only sat silently by Gadavar's side and smoked his pipe.

After the moon pushed high in the sky, Takra came to sit beside Corri also, knowing she needed to be near her friend, yet disturbed by the inward turn of sight and thoughts she saw on Corri's face. As the hours passed, Takra grew restless.

"Sister-Friend," she whispered. "Do not go so far from us."

"It must be this way," Corri answered as she lay back against Gadavar's shoulder. "If I prepare for death, then fear will not control me. If I survive, then victory will be that much sweeter." *I sound like a Tuonela. I did not realize how much Takra and I had changed each other simply by being who we are.*

Imandoff took Takra's arm and shook his head. They rose and went off to their blankets to catch what sleep they could. Gadavar held Corri close, listening to her soft breathing until he, too, fell into a restless sleep.

The next day Kulkar sent out guards to spy on the border, lest any Fravashi soldiers come upon them unawares. Takra, like most of the other warriors, sat brooding as she sharpened her long sword to an edge that would cut one of her hairs. Tirkul alternatively sat with Balqama and Norya as they sorted again and again through their medicines, or paced with Imandoff along the high, tree-lined paths that gave them glimpses of Vu-Zai across the border.

Corri sat silently staring at the rocks and trees that blocked her view of Vu-Zai. The sun sank toward the western hills, turning the sky blood-red and tipping the mountains in gold.

How is it that I can see through things? she questioned. From the corner of her eye, she saw Varanna's spectral body hovering nearby, as it had all day. *It must be that my bodies are almost parted. Is this in preparation for the battle in the Otherworlds or the final journey?* She felt Gadavar's hand on her arm and turned to find him crouched beside her.

"My love," he said softly, as he brushed back her red curls with one callused hand. "Do not think that sacrificing yourself will win this battle. Whatever comes, you and I shall face it together. You will not be alone, I promise." He put his fingertips to her lips when she started to speak. "You have grown beyond the thief in Hadliden who stole and lied to stay alive and out of danger. Your eyes betray you now when you speak an untruth."

"Gadavar." The words stuck in Corri's throat as she looked up into his eyes. She swallowed hard. "The final battle with Kayth will take me where you cannot follow."

"I will fight beside you wherever you go." The Green Man's jaw set in a stubborn line.

"Do you not understand? I must leave my body to fight in Otherworld realms against him and the evil spirit who possesses him. None of you can go with me."

"Then I will stand guard over your physical body until you return." His gaze was determined; Corri finally looked away and nodded. "Rest while you can," he said softly. "Gather your strength, as do we all, for moon-rise is not many hours away." He settled back against the rock and pulled out his pipe.

Tamping the bowl with smoke-leaf, he lit it, sending the sweet scent of the herb swirling about her.

Even if I go Between Worlds at the last, she thought as she stared at the Fravashi border, *I shall remember the scent of his body, the odor of his pipe in the night, and the touch of his hand against my face.*

As I remember my Tirkul. Varanna moved closer, this time clothed in bright armor. *I thought to return with him when he was born again, but my task was not finished.* A sad note crept into her spirit-voice. *I released our bond so that he could live this life with another and be happy.* Varanna turned her head to watch Imandoff and Takra sitting side by side under one of the twisted trees.

I thought your Tirkul was . . . . Corri stopped, understanding falling together as pieces of a puzzle. *In this life, your Tirkul is Imandoff! But why did he not stay with you until you were free to be together?*

You remember the twisting tangle of the life-threads during the Trial? That is the way all lives are lived. Tirkul and I have grown apart. There is still a love for him in my heart, but not as it was. Varanna started to fade.

What of your son? Did your Tirkul not raise him? Corri felt Varanna's momentary flash of anger.

He chose to leave the boy for others to rear, because he reminded Tirkul of me. Now, as Imandoff Silverhair, Tirkul again has chosen to take a lover and have a child. If the Peoples win this battle, and Takra Wind-Rider and the child she carries lives, I have asked Natira, Lord of Justice, to let my soul enter that child's body. A hint of laughter edged Varanna's thoughts. *A fitting way for both of us to learn lessons. We never escape our lessons, Corri Farblood; we can only delay them through cowardice. I was as much to blame as Tirkul, for I chose to place myself in danger needlessly.*

But the child lives now, Varanna. How can your soul enter its body?

The soul enters when the living child draws its first breath. Now sleep, for the child you carry needs you to rest. The spectral form faded completely from sight. Corri leaned back against Gadavar and slept.

Takra helped Corri tighten and fasten the laces on Varanna's ancient armor. As the chest and back plates and the guards on arms and shins were strapped into place, Corri felt the power and purpose of Varanna fall over her like a mantle. When she took up the mended sword, swirling it once before sliding it into the sheath, Takra's dark eyes went wide with surprise.

"Are you Sister-Friend or Varanna?" she asked, her eyes narrowing as she watched Corri's face. "I felt the ancient spirit of Varanna close beside you all during the journey to the bridge, and I feel her here now."

Corri's hand froze in its movement. "I am Corri," she answered. "But I feel Varanna's spirit so close beside me that her skills sometimes become mine." She bit her lip in confused thought. "What is happening to me, Takra?"

"The Tuonela tell of such things," the warrior woman answered. "To wear the armor of a dead warrior, to take up the weapon of one who has fallen in battle, gives one the power and skills of the fallen warrior." She placed one hand on Corri's shoulder. "Use what Varanna offers during this battle, Sister-Friend, but afterward lay it aside and be yourself. In some old tales, the warrior clung to the weapon and changed into the one who died."

I give my word; I will leave when the battle is done. Varanna's voice sounded by Corri's ear. *Do not fear our temporary joining. I have no wish to possess you as Jinniyah does this Kayth.*

A burst of hatred shot through Corri's mind at the mention of Jinniyah's name. *I will hold you to that promise, for I will be myself and no other!* Corri focussed on Takra, who now stood close, shaking her arm, concern sharp on her face.

"Varanna is with me," Corri said. "Do not fear that she would possess me, Takra. She has another purpose if this battle is won and we live." She threw one arm around Takra's waist and hugged her. "Keep yourself safe, Sister-Friend," she whispered. "And take care that your unborn daughter is safe."

"We shall grow old together, little thief, and tire our children's ears with tales of the great battle." Takra smiled and thumped Corri's back, but deep in her eyes shone the same uncertainty as was in Corri's.

"It is time to go." Imandoff's deep voice was soft in the pale darkness of early night.

The invaders made their way cautiously to the Tuonela side of the land-bridge, where they crouched in the darkness for some time, watching for torches of guards on the far side. The full moon hung in the velvet-black sky, its cold light gleaming on Varanna's ivory-colored armor, highlighting the scratched and worn scales of the strange sea beast from which it was made.

Corri took out the owl stone set in the band and wedged it down over the top of Varanna's helmet, like a crown. Then she brought the helmet slowly over her head, peering out through the eye-holes. "I am ready," she answered. "Now, sorcerer, how can we pass through the spells guarding the bridge? We have no magick box." She looked at Tirkul, Gadavar, and Takra, seeing their spirits glowing within them.

Imandoff opened his mouth to speak, then pointed wordlessly at the flickering across the end of the bridge. "The spells are weakening," he said, as he turned and strode toward the bridge. "The battle along the border has begun."

"Ride fair," Kulkar said softly.

With Corri at his side, the sorcerer stepped out onto the narrow bridge, turning once to look back at the others who followed. In the moonlight-splattered darkness, only the gleam of Zanitra's sejda ball and the quick flashes of light along sword blade marked where the Tuonela warriors waited.

Thidrick waited and watched from the alley behind the Bent Hook tavern. The city of Vum was quiet, not filled with the usual noise of busy people and rumbling carts, and this made him uneasy. His dagger was instantly out when the tavern maid opened the rear door and peered into the darkness.

"Come quickly," she hissed. He slid past her into the stuffy heat of the kitchen. "All here can be trusted."

He made his way into the common room, dagger still in hand. There, a sea of intent faces met his calculating glance, and on each breast gleamed a thin metal crescent moon. He drew a relieved breath.

"Have we your word that we do not fight against Fravashi, only against Volikvi and Trow?" The tall man who stepped to face Thidrick stood ready to strike him down, his dagger half-drawn.

"You have my word." Thidrick brought his clenched fist against his breast. "I told the Kirisani and Tuonela leaders I would not fight against my people."

"Then send out the word." The man turned and motioned to several men who disappeared silently through the tavern's front door. "We have made our own plans, Thidrick. Our men will interfere with the soldiers' march through the cities to the border. We will waylay and kill any Volikvi or Trow we can." His eyes sparked with fanaticism.

"Not all Volikvi and Trow hold their temple-position by choice," Thidrick said, his eyes narrowing. "Best you know where their heart lies before you spill needless blood."

"They are all evil!" The man's lips pulled back in a snarl. "I say they must all die!"

"I risked my life for this?" Thidrick sneered. "To exchange one fanatic for another?"

"He is right, Howan." Another man stepped forward. "My brother's son was taken against his will."

"This man is a traitor who worked for the Trow. You all know he was a guard in one of their temples. Die first, Trow-lover!" Howan grabbed at his dagger, then cried out as he fell forward, a trickle of blood dribbling from his mouth. The hilt of a dagger stood upright in his back.

The young man who had stood behind Howan reached down and pulled out his dagger, then turned to face the silent room. "You all know I do not agree with Howan's words. It is better that he die now than led others into destruction. We can sift the straw from the wheat as needed, but to make a river of blood, no." He turned to Thidrick. "We have no love for the Kirisani and Tuonela, nor do we trust them not to conquer our land. Yet we will aid their armies—not fight for them, but aid—until this battle is finished. When the power of the Fire Temple is crushed, they had best retreat into their own lands."

"That is all I ask." Thidrick's dark gaze scanned the room. "There are many groups like yours?"

"In every small town and city, every farm and seaport," came the answer.

Thidrick smiled grimly. "We must disrupt all supply caravans, harass any who march to join the soldiers and keep the Volikvis and Trows besieged in their temples. We will need swift messengers to go from one group to another so we know what happens. If it becomes necessary, even women and children must be prepared to fight with us. And here is how we will do this."

"They prepare to attack." The shape-shifter Hindjall narrowed his light-green eyes against the shimmering spells of the border. "Look! There is a Volikvi with one of their accursed black boxes."

"When the spells break, put a spear into him. I will destroy the box." Another shape-shifter hefted a heavy war-hammer as if its weight were nothing, his eyes never leaving the Volikvi who crouched beside the box. "Each of you, choose your targets well. Take out the leaders and priests first."

There was a murmur of agreement from the ten men who surrounded him. Already, each of the shape-shifters showed signs of change: a lift of lip, bared teeth, crooked and spiked-back fingers, a shrillness or deep rumble to the voice.

"Rider coming." Hindjall's voice rasped with the harsh croak of the hunting asperel.

The horse bearing a Tuonela warrior woman pounded out of the trees and skidded to a stop within reach of the unflinching warriors. "Border-spells are broken in four places now," she said. She showed no fear of these daunting men, who topped her tall figure by more than a head. "Try to kill as many as you can before the moon darkens and Kayth's power grows stronger." She cast a quick glance up at the full moon riding high above. "The Lady be with you!" She whirled the horse and rode back the way she had come.

The shape-shifters turned as one to the border as the spells broke apart. Their forms seemed to change as they surged forward to meet the invading Fravashi. Where there had been a man wearing a winged helmet with a jutting beak, now there moved a great asperel, its harsh scream riding above the Fravashi battle-cry. At its side, a snarling Rissa leaped forward, a war-hammer in its paws. A gigantic stallion reared, its bared teeth prepared to tear out throats, while other animal-forms surged forward around it.

The Rissa-like creature darted among the Fravashi and brought the hammer down with a crash on the black box, destroying it and leaving the invaders no way of resealing the border. Nearby, the Volikvi choked out his life under the rending claws of the asperel.

The battlefield quickly became slippery with blood and hazardous with dead and wounded under foot. Yet the shape-shifters fought on, determined to hold their piece of the border against the enemy or die.

How strange this is, Corri thought. She looked down upon her armored body crossing the land-bridge in perfect step with Imandoff. In the bright moonlight, she could clearly see her helmet, blackened and rent from eye-hole to cheek-piece on one side. *My spirit-body, my shadow-self, is separated from my body, yet I am not sleeping.*

Stay within your body and keep the dream-flying under control until it is time. Varanna's voice was clear in Corri's mind. *You must reach Kayth before you relax your control, and getting to him may take some doing. The Fire Temple swarms with priests.*

Are there no guards here? Corri asked, eyeing the deep shadows at the gate at the end of the stone bridge.

Kayth thinks all his enemies fear to cross into the Fire Temple. He has placed the guards at the gates leading into the city instead.

Corri gave a last look back at those left behind at the end of the bridge. Zanitra's black hair shone with a halo of moonlight, streams of energy pouring from the sejda ball in her hands. Beside her, Balqama bit her lip and clutched her hands together tightly, her eyes locked on Tirkul's broad shoulders as he crossed the bridge at Takra's side. Kulkar, Odran, and the Tuonela warriors faced outward around the women, their swords drawn, their eyes intent on the dark trees and rock-studded hills, ready to defend their position. Slowly, a misty veil of magick spread from the ball in Zanitra's hands to hide those who waited with her behind a scene of an empty landscape.

Corri felt a tug, then was aware that she once more inhabited her body. They were almost at the end of the bridge now, but no Fravashi had called out a challenge. She glanced from Imandoff's grim face to the closed gate at the end of the bridge.

"What now?" she murmured.

"It seems we are unexpected." The stone set in the top of Imandoff's tall staff became a scintillating ball of white light as the gate slowly opened. "But be prepared for a trap."

Corri felt the uneasiness and suspicion that rose in those who walked behind her. Her thief's instincts sharpened as she walked through the gate with Imandoff.

Whatever I must do, Varanna, show me how. She felt the burn of the ancient warrior woman's battle-anger, carefully banked and hoarded until the proper time.

What needs to be done, came the answer, *we will do together. Then I shall have earned my rest for a time, and you will be free to live and love.*

"Corri?" Imandoff's voice caught her attention. "Do you know where to find Kayth in this place?"

Corri's eyes narrowed as she saw a faint tendril of deep red retreat back into the darkness of a corridor to their right. *The mark of Kayth's life-energy!* "This way," she answered. Sword in hand, she ran into the black-shadowed corridor, her companions at her heels.

Chapter 18

The flotilla of ships rode the waters off the northern coast of Frav like great birds of prey on favorable winds. The protecting hills of the harbor of Vu-Kath, curved like crab pincers around the sheltered bay and topped by two watchtowers, showed no signs of unusual activity. The setting sun cast long shadows of the temple's spires across the city like clutching fingers.

"Can your men take the hillforts without alerting the authorities?" Kanlath stood beside the rough rail with the tall captain of the Sea Mist, his eyes fixed on the stone fortresses.

"We shall soon see." The captain folded his wind-browned arms across his chest and braced his long legs against the rolling swells as the ship turned and headed into the harbor mouth.

The fleet of ships was quiet except for the creak of rigging, the snap of sails, and the slap of waves against wooden hulls. Not a man spoke as the fishermen went about the business of sailing from the wind-ruffled Zivitua Sea into the calm of the harbor. Just as the first of the fleet passed between the open end of the claw-peaks and into the bay, a ball of fire shot from one of the fortresses. The fiery missile arced through the sky, dropping with deadly accuracy onto the roof of a warehouse that stood by itself, wide paved streets separating it from the other wharf-side storage buildings.

"They succeeded," the captain said, his white teeth bright in his tanned face. "A direct hit on the temple's central warehouse."

"What a use for tangleweed!" Kanlath watched the explosion of flames with appreciation. "The Asurans dry it and use it only for fertilizer."

"As you know, the problem with the wet weed is that it blisters the skin if touched." The captain motioned for the men to get into position as the sails were lowered and the ship edged in for docking. "We discovered its flame properties when we were attacked by a school of krynap up north. We fired the floating tangleweed by accident. Fortunately, the wind was away from us, or we would have lost the ships."

Kanlath shuddered as he pictured the giant krynap, its vicious red eyes peering over the rails and its huge claws scrabbling for a hold to get aboard. "A school of them? It is rare to see one at all, unless they wash up dead on the beach."

"They use a part of the northern edge of the Zivitua Sea as breeding grounds." The captain drew his curved gutting knife as he watched the priests milling around the burning building. "The krynap are uncommonly vicious and seem to like the taste of blood. Like the Volikvis, they lie in hiding, then attack without warning."

Another ball of fire sailed through the air, this time arcing farther into the city. It struck against one of the stone spires of the central temple and slid down the wall into the courtyard. A plume of smoke and flame roared skyward as the tangleweed exploded and set fire to wooden structures there.

"Good shooting." Kanlath brushed his thinning black hair out of his eyes and grinned at the captain. "Mayhap your men found some of the soldiers willing to join us. I never knew fishermen to use a catapult."

"Mayhap," the captain answered, grinning back. "Be ready," he called to the men at his back.

The anchor fell with a grating of chain and a splash; then fishermen quickly slid out the gangplank with a thud against the dock. The plank barely touched the dock before both the Asuran and Fravashi fishermen swarmed down it behind the captain and Kanlath. Men from the other ships joined them as they raced along the wharf toward the burning building.

The Volikvis, who shouted at their slaves and drove them with whips toward the fire, never saw the flash of gutting knives and glint of great hooks until it was too late. Caught between the determined sailors and the rebelling slaves, they died in a widening stream of blood that ran down the street and into the gutters.

The seamen's ranks were quickly swollen by others from the docks.

Their anger and hatred toward the Volikvis boiling to the surface, the milling mob started up the street toward the burning temple. Behind them, merchants organized water brigades to prevent the destruction of other warehouses, but no one went near the Volikvi bodies or made any attempt to rescue temple goods. A silent understanding swept through the dock area: let the Volikvis defend their own.

By the time the sailors and fishermen reached the great gates of the burning central temple, their ranks were swollen with people from the city. The two guards who stood before the gates backed against the wall. The eyes of the younger man were full of fear, but the officer beside him glared arrogantly at the crowd. From inside came the crackle of flames and the shouts of the priests as they tried to control the spreading fire.

"Wait!" the captain of the fishermen shouted as the crowd surged toward the guards. "We are here to kill only the Volikvis and those who sympathize with them." He turned toward the guards, his gutting knife tight in his hand. "Are you for the Volikvis or for the people?" he growled.

"The people!" cried the younger guard, and was felled by his officer's fist.

"Get back to your homes," ordered the officer, "or you will find yourself on the altars of Jevotan."

The fishermen stepped aside as, with a roar, the crowd surged forward, and the officer went down in a sea of fists and knives. Kanlath signaled to his men who, with the Fravashi fishermen, took up a position before the open temple gates.

"Let them roast in their own hell-fires," he growled, his lips pulled back in a snarl.

"Those who wished release from the Volikvis and Trows were warned," the captain said as he pushed his way to Kanlath's side. "Any still within are there by choice. Let none escape."

The people of Vu-Kath took over the guard-positions at the temple gates, freeing the seamen to return to the docks. Sparks from the warehouse blaze had set fire to several other storage buildings, but these were quickly brought under control. It was full night with the moon riding high when Kanlath, Gran, and the captain of the Fravashi fishermen finally sat down with their men in the Krynap's Claw, one of the dockside taverns.

"The word has come from other seaports," Kanlath said as he raised his mug of ale. "All the coast of Frav rebels. If the Lady wills, this night shall see you and your people free of Volikvi control."

"We call upon no Lady here." The captain's sinewy hands tightened around his mug, his knuckles white under the tanned skin. "We have had enough of priests and gods. We swear only by the winds and the sea and the fish in her."

"There is one thing we can all raise our ale to." Gran's gold tooth glinted in the light of the tallow rushes as his voice cut through the tense atmosphere. "No religion should control the lives of the people."

"Aye, that we can agree with." One corner of the captain's mouth lifted as he raised his ale. "But I think Asur is as bad as Frav, in its way."

"As I well know." Gran touched the patch over his eye. "Magni or Volikvi, there is little difference. That is why we do not return to the ports we have long used. Look for us now in the northern city of Zoc on the River Tho."

"There are Magni in Zoc," one Fravashi fishermen said, a sneer lifting his mouth.

"No longer," answered Kanlath. "That city drove them out before we left."

The captain threw back his head in a roar of laughter, and his men joined in. "Only a fisherman would have the sense to make such plans to ride out this religious storm and find himself cast up on a good shore."

"The moon darkens!" A barmaid ran from the door to cower beside the captain.

"A natural thing, girl," he said, pulling her into his lap.

"Natural in that the moon sometimes goes dark. But this time its natural power will be used for unnatural purposes. You say you pray to the sea?" Gran said, his mouth drawn in a firm line. "Then pray to her now. The Dream Warrior, the only hope we all have, is even now facing the greatest of powers in the Fire Temple."

A hush fell over the tavern as the sailor-merchants and fishermen in Vu-Kath waited and wondered what their future would be.

Kayth-Jinniyah held the black disk in both hands in Malya's shadowed room. *Who hid this here? Why was it not brought to me immediately?*

A deep frown creased his forehead as he raised his cold eyes to stare at Malya. His daughter stood in the semi-darkness, her dark eyes dreamy as she gazed back at him.

"Did you touch this?" he asked. "Did you take it from the bag and hold it in your hands?"

"No, I brought it as I found it, in the bag." Malya moved a step closer, one hand reaching seductively for his arm. "My dreams led me to it."

Kayth shrugged aside her hand and turned toward Zalmoxis, who hovered in the doorway of the room. "Why did the Volikvi Lukalus not bring this immediately to me, as I ordered?"

"I do not know, Jinniyah, for I did not see or talk to him after he returned." Zalmoxis stood very still under Kayth's scrutinizing stare. "He locked himself in his chamber and would not talk with me."

"You speak the truth," Kayth said after a long moment. Without another glance at either Malya or Zalmoxis, he left the chamber and headed down the corridor toward his secret altar-room, the torches dropping to mere sparks of light ahead of him.

"I do not understand." Malya stared at the retreating figure. "He barely looked at me, yet he has come to my chamber nightly."

"Let us go to your chamber now." Zalmoxis moved close to Malya and ran one finger down the side of her neck to her breasts.

Malya's eyes widened as understanding flooded through her. "It was not my father at all, but you!" she screamed and raked at the Volikvi's face with crooked fingers.

Zalmoxis caught her wrists, a smile on his cruel face. "And you will take me in your arms every night, if I so desire."

Malya kicked and twisted, but she was held tight. Zalmoxis forced her backward until her knees caught on the edge of her bed and she fell, the Volikvi on top of her.

"Strangers have entered the Fire Temple!" Xephena shut the door behind her. "My sources tell me the battle begins here, as well as out on the border. We have no time for this, Zalmoxis. She is too dangerous to keep alive." The Trow swayed to the side of the bed where the Volikvi still pinned Malya's twisting body. "Kill her and dispose of the body."

"When I am finished with her." Zalmoxis said.

"Now!" Xephena jerked out her dagger and slit Malya's throat before the priest could prevent it. "Do you not understand what I say?" the Trow hissed. "If you would wrest control from Kayth, you must move very soon."

Zalmoxis rose from the bed where the woman gurgled out her life. A row of scratches marked his flat face, and blood soaked the front of his robe. "Kayth has gone back to his secret place," he said. "We do not know where that is."

"I know where it is and how to get inside." Xephena cleaned her dagger on the bed-blanket, then tucked it back into the sheath. "I followed and watched while you dallied with the girl. We will go there and wait until Kayth has won the battle for us. Then we will kill him."

"I thought you had dreams of being his mistress." Zalmoxis' lip lifted in a sneer.

"Like that one," the Trow pointed to the body on the bed, "he is too dangerous to let live." She shrugged away the priest's hand as he reached for her arm. "I do not like the feel of the night, Zalmoxis. Something is wrong."

"You have jumped at shadows ever since the watcher you created rebounded and caused such havoc." The priest followed her out into the dimly lit hallway.

"I have reason to be wary," Xephena snapped. "I cannot sense this Dream Warrior. Bring the remaining Tuonela prisoners to the altar-chamber. I will call up the dark powers of Croyna to guide us."

The rock-hewn corridors were lit with flickering torches that cast the shadows of Corri and her companions as grotesque, rippling figures on the walls. Twice Corri had lost track of the deep red tentacle of Kayth's energy as they followed the labyrinthine tunnels deeper into the forbidding mountain. Now she stood, her friends at her back, on the platform overlooking the altar-cavern.

Gathered around the altar below were six Volikvi priests, their shrieking chant and boom of hand-drums echoing from the black walls and covering the screams of the man dying under a priest's sacrificial knife. Scattered along the edge of the great fuming crack in the ground like discarded firewood lay the bodies of the Jabed's followers.

"Kill them." Corri's whisper was understood only by Imandoff, who nodded to the others and pointed to the steps. They followed Corri down to the cavern floor at a run.

They caught the Volikvis by surprise, cutting them down without mercy where they stood about the bloody altar. Gadavar drove the sacrificial priest to the edge of the crack, his shining sword a dance of light against the man's bloody knife. With a cry of terror, the priest stepped back into empty space and fell into the fume-scented depths of the abyss.

"We can do nothing here," Imandoff said as he rose from examining that last of the bodies. "None live."

"Where is Kayth? And where are Zalmoxis and Xephena?" Corri felt Varanna's battle-rage boiling within her. She closed her eyes and reached out with her inner senses until she found the trail of the Trow priestess. "The Trow and Malya are this way." She headed back up the stairs into the tunnel. *Something is different about Malya's life-energy.*

"Corri, we must find Kayth." Imandoff grabbed her arm but could not stop her.

"Sister-Friend, to kill a tujyk you cut off its head." Takra moved up beside Corri and matched her fast pace up the corridor.

"The Trow has a source of hidden power. Kayth can draw upon it through her." Corri's eyes were hard as she forged ahead, her companions at her heels. "And Zalmoxis is too powerful to ignore. Kayth may have unholy power, but he is so caught up in his possession by Jinniyah that he thinks we dare not challenge him. At Zalmoxis' orders, though, all Volikvis and soldiers within this place will come against us."

"What will you do with Malya?" Imandoff's deep voice came over her shoulder as she paused at a junction of corridors.

"I do not know," Corri answered. *What should I do with my half-sister?* she thought, but no inner voices answered. She reached out for Malya's life-energy and found it weaker than before, more distant and rapidly fading away. *She is dead,* Corri thought, but found no pity within her heart.

His secret chamber is down this corridor," Xephena whispered, as she and Zalmoxis stood near a glassy-walled tunnel leading from the altar-chamber. "I cannot understand why he did not sense who killed the priests here." She pointed across the great crack to the carnage on the other side.

"Kayth is crazy, more so now than before. He might have killed them himself."

"But why?" Xephena tilted her head as she listened. "The prisoners come. Croyna will tell us what we wish to know."

She turned to go back across the bridge, but her feet refused to move. Beside her, Zalmoxis struggled to free himself from the invisible net that held him fast.

"Come to me."

The Volikvi and Trow turned back toward the dark tunnel, their eyes wide with fear as the voice compelled them against their will. Their shuffling walk brought them to the open panel leading into the hidden room where Kayth waited.

"You will do my will," Kayth-Jinniyah said as the panel closed behind them. His sly smile chilled Xephena's heart. "The loss of Malya is nothing to me, as your deaths will mean nothing." He stepped close, looking into each of their eyes. "You will do whatever I tell you. When I no longer have use for you, the death you gave others will be as nothing to the death I will give you."

Xephena gurgled, a scream locked in her throat; her heart pounded like the sacrificial drums in her ears. *No!* her mind cried, but she could do nothing but Kayth's will.

"Corri, wait!" Gadavar's voice broke into her thoughts and brought her to a halt. "Listen!"

From the altar-chamber behind them came the distinct clink of chains, the crack of whips, and the murmur of male voices. Suddenly, Tuonela war-cries of defiance ricocheted through the tunnel from the cavern.

"Tuonela!" Imandoff shouted. Takra grabbed Corri by the arm and whirled her around, forcing her to follow. They ran back the way they had come, the others at their heels.

I let my own hatred blind me, Corri thought as she dashed down the corridor at Takra's side. *I should have felt the Tuonela nearby. The Trow must wait.*

Corri and her companions barely paused on the platform before they were running down the steep steps to the chamber floor below. The two guards, caught in their surprise of dead priests among the slain Kirisani prisoners, did not see the invading warriors until they were upon them. They died instantly under the swords of the invaders.

"The keys!" The first man in the line of chained Tuonela prisoners scrabbled at the belt of one of the dead guards, finally holding up the keys in triumph. Quickly, he worked at the ankle and wrist shackles until they were all freed.

"We have no weapons for you. If you would aid us in the battle, take those." Imandoff gestured toward the dead priests.

"Gladly will we use their own weapons against them." The Tuonela warrior raised a gaunt face to the sorcerer. "We will guard your back, sending any Volikvis into the hell-fires they deserve!"

"We must go that way," Corri said in a low voice as she pointed to the far side of the shadowed chamber. She could hear the Singing Serpent clearly in her mind, its song begging her to remember her promise.

Gadavar raised his brows in question, yet he followed close upon Corri's heels as she quickly crossed the uneven cavern floor. They hurried over the narrow bridge and straight into the dark tunnel beyond. Corri felt a pull that led her on down the glassy-walled, black tunnel. She never paused until she stood on another platform, high over the dark and murky lake.

"This must be the Cave of the Footed Serpent." Imandoff's soft whisper echoed through the rocky chamber. "Why are we here?"

"A thing needs doing," Corri said. "I made a promise." *But how do I fulfill it?* she questioned. "Wait for me."

She cautiously made her way down the slippery steps, her eyes flicking back time and again to the black water of the lake. Just as she reached the narrow shoreline that curved about the edge of the water to a tunnel on the far side, the lake began to bubble, ripples moving out from the center to roll up on the shore's black sand.

Corri tugged at Varanna's ancient sword, but the blade seemed stuck in the sheath. There were cries of fear from her companions as she looked up into the scaly face of a huge monster. In her peripheral vision, she saw Gadavar start down the steps, the others at his heels.

A calmness settled over Corri as the great head on its long sinuous neck arched up, its taloned forefeet reaching for her. *I call for aid.* She sent her thoughts streaking into the Otherworld realms. *I call upon the Singing Serpent.*

A burst of light filled the cavern. The Footed Serpent reared back with a scream, clawing at the air about its head in pain. The light dimmed, then shimmered with rainbow colors as a slender serpentine form, fin-like protrusions along its backbone, slowly took shape. Singing filled the air as the creature bent its long, thin head toward the monster.

I must dream-fly! Corri stumbled back against the wall, aware that Gadavar now stood at her side. *Out!* she commanded, and her spirit-body soared free. *What must I do to help you?* she pleaded with the Singing Serpent.

The glowing ruby-red eyes held hers for an instant. *Rejoin us, Warrior of Shadows.* The rainbow serpent whipped its slender coils about the dark monstrosity from the lake. The muscles stood out like huge ropes as it continued to tighten its coils about its heaving opponent.

How? Corri's scream echoed through the Otherworlds and bounced back as a multitude of deep sighs against the cavern walls.

Death rejoins them, wanderer in my realm. At her side, Corri saw the strange man she had met in the shadow world. His tip-tilted eyes willed her to listen. *A death-blow split them apart. A death-blow will rejoin them. Strike now!*

How can I kill something so beautiful as the Singing Serpent?

Death is not an end, as you should know. The shadow-man moved closer. *Life-energy does not die. You dream-fly when your spirit-body separates from the physical. Are you then dead? Strike, girl, or lose the battle!*

Corri reached for the spectral form of Varanna's sword as she soared up over the entwined serpents who twisted and turned in their deadly dance in the lake. The spectral sword blade sparked with flames as she tried to strike the Footed Serpent, but the forms moved too quickly for her to get a clear blow. The water churned into great billows of white foam as the dark monster clamped its teeth into the white throat of the slender serpent.

No! Corri darted down, striking with the flaming blade. The sword pierced through the black spine and continued on into the white throat. *No!*

Corri flew to the body of the Singing Serpent where it rolled in the dark water, twisting from the waves with a faint parody of life. She dropped the sword and knelt on the black sand. *I did not mean for you to die, beautiful one.* Under her trembling hands, the slender white form began to dissolve into a sparkle of lights.

Why did you not help? Corri turned in anger toward the shadow-man, but he was gone. Only Gadavar stood on the shore, his mouth open in surprise, staring into the lake. Tears ran down her face as she held up her hands to the swirl of sparkling light that now danced in a column before her on the dark waters.

Rejoin us, warrior woman, came the whisper-soft plea.

Corri bent her head in sorrow and saw, on the sand by her knees, the shadow-pendant the strange man had promised her. She clutched it in her hand as she struggled to her feet.

Take what power it has, she said, and cast the shining pendant into the midst of the swirl of light.

The pendant hung suspended in the air above the lake, surrounded by the rainbow sparks. Then it dipped once into the black waters. As it rose again, a swirl of black lights followed it, joining with the rainbow colors—merging, dancing, reforming—until a great silver and black serpent hung there.

The two are one! The cry of triumph sang through the chamber. The great, flashing, red-flecked silver eyes held Corri's;

she felt a wave of joy and blessing pour into her spirit-body. *By freely offering a thing of power, a thing that could turn the tide of battle, you gave me whole life again. For such an offering, I give my blessing to your cause.* With a great swirl of water and light, the serpent vanished.

Corri fell backward into her physical body and opened her eyes to look into Gadavar's face.

"What happened?" Imandoff rushed down the steps with Takra and Tirkul close behind. "The Footed Serpent seemed to go into a frenzy and then suddenly disappeared."

Corri groped at her belt with her right hand and found Varanna's sword still in the sheath. She opened her other hand, but the shadow world pendant was gone.

"The enemy comes!" The Tuonela warriors on the platform rushed back into the tunnel.

"Where do we find Kayth?" Takra asked as they ran back up the stairs. "He could be anywhere in this pile of stone."

"Perhaps we have a way. Use the pendant Gadavar wears." At Imandoff's words, Gadavar jerked his pendant over his head and thrust it into Corri's hand. The warriors had forced the Volikvi priests back into the altar-chamber, where Tuonela war-cries shattered the air along with the screams of dying priests.

"Hold it by the chain and think upon Kayth," Imandoff said.

Corri dangled the pendant before her and centered her thoughts on her father. The pendant slowly began to move, swinging forward and backward, straight into the tunnel's darkness.

Chapter 19

The moon hung full and glowing overhead, its light slashed into ribbons by the thick trees surrounding the campsite. The air was hot and humid, the heat seeming to build upon itself as the night deepened.

The armies of Tuone and Kirisan were thinly spread along the border, healers with each group as a precaution. No one knew where the spells would weaken next.

Breela and the other women of Her Own ranged out into fighting position, between their healers and the open space that marked the border. Although untried in battle, the warrior women of the Temple were determined to hold their section of the border or die. On the Fravashi side of the border, facing them, stood the silent ranks of the enemy. Breela listened to the eerie quiet around her, alert for any warning sounds.

Why so quiet? she wondered. *Not even the cry of a night bird. Even the attacks of the shadow nightmares have ceased. It is as if all Sar Akka waits in suspense.* Only the creak of leather armor or the occasional click of metal against metal broke the silence. She wiped the perspiration out of her eyes with the back of her hand as she lifted her head to look at the night sky. Breela gasped as she saw the first black rim of darkness smudge the moon's face.

"It begins," said the High Priestess Vairya, who stood at Breela's side. "Whatever they do, they will do it now."

A section of the border-spells rippled and winked out of existence. Fravashi soldiers poured across the bare, rocky ground separating them from the armies of the Temple. Screaming with one voice, the warrior women of Her Own leaped forward, sword blades flashing like white molten fire in the moonlight. Although more than one woman fell in the first rush, the Fravashi wavered under the ferocious onslaught and began to give ground inch by inch.

The noise of battle was deafening as the healers frantically worked over the wounded. Merra looked up at her mother, seeing the High Clua's robes reddened with blood. Jehennette's face was calm as she moved quickly from one fallen warrior to another, her healing satchel swinging at her side.

"Beware!" Taillefer's voice rang out at Merra's side. The hissching of his sword as it left the sheath rang through the sounds of battle.

Merra kept the pressure on the bleeding wound of the warrior woman over whom she worked, but her heart pounded in her throat. Another healer hurried up with thread and needle to stitch the severed vein. A woman from Sadko, the healer did not spare a glance for the battle swirling closer to them, but only smiled encouragement to the frightened girl.

Taillefer's voice rose in a mighty war song as he thrust at the Fravashi soldiers who had broken through the defenses. The clash of mountain steel against Fravashi metal was a counterpoint to his voice.

Merra could not say later when her senses had recorded the turn of battle, only when Taillefer's singing suddenly stopped and he came to her side. She looked up from the wound she was bandaging to see him, dark hair in sweat-dampened strings about his face and two lightly bleeding wounds on his arms, where Fravashi blades had gotten through his lightning sword-play. Without a word, Merra rose and ran into his arms, heedless of the other healers and of her mother's soft smile.

"Have we won?" Dakhma sat close beside the Oracle, who cradled the sleeping Athdar.

"I think not yet," the young woman answered. She stared at the figure-strewn table before them. "Too many of the dark figures still stand." The Oracle glanced at the window, open to the hot, still night air, and saw the full moon half-swallowed in the eclipse.

"The Dream Warrior still stands, as do those who are with her."

"Yes, she still lives." The Oracle smiled at the girl and pulled her into the circle of her arm. "Try to sleep now."

The children quiet against her, the Oracle leaned her head back against the wall. She was so tired, yet sleep would not come. Her mind raced and would not be still.

The Dream Warrior should have faced Kayth by now, she thought. *Instead, she has done battle with others, as if this Kayth placed obstacles in her path at every turn. Those who are most dangerous to her and to the outcome of the battle still live. Help her, Goddess. The greatest battle of her life is still to come.*

"Mine!" Takra's harsh growl of war-challenge rang down the tunnel just as Xephena and Zalmoxis came into sight.

"And mine!" Tirkul shouted, as the Volikvi and Trow ran toward the altar-chamber, the Tuonela warriors at their heels.

"I smell Kayth's evil stench." Gadavar's soft words tore Corri's attention from the scene at the far end of the tunnel where Takra and Tirkul fought against Xephena and Zalmoxis.

"Kayth is somewhere in here. There is a secret catch to a hidden room there in the torch-holder." Corri moved close as Gadavar ran his hands over the wall. With a hiss of effort, he worked his strong fingers at the half-open edge of a panel in the slick tunnel wall. "No!" she cried as Gadavar yanked open the panel and plunged into the hidden room.

She darted in after him, Gadavar's pendant wrapped around one hand and Imandoff at her back. Inside, the candle-light was dimmed to only a spark. Calling up her inner senses, she saw Gadavar as a faint image, struggling for breath, his hands clawing at his own throat. Kayth stood near an altar, his pale face and hands exuding a luminescence like dead plants in a bog. In one hand, he held a black disk close to his breast, while the other hand crooked toward the struggling Green Man, as if he slowly choked off Gadavar's breathing.

"Kayth!" Imandoff's challenge rang through the rock-hewn chamber. Although the sorcerer's voice broke the red-haired man's attention, Kayth used his power to slam Gadavar against the stone wall before turning to Corri and Imandoff with a cold smile on his lips. The Green Man crumbled, dazed and half-conscious, to the cold floor.

Corri stared at Kayth's pale eyes, a flicker of fire in their depths. *He willingly shares his mind and body with another entity. I feel its evil thoughts reaching out and influencing all in this place.* She felt the owl stone's energy surge as it repelled the control Kayth sought to gain over her. For an instant, she saw a cruel face behind her father's, the face of a man who once reveled in the vilest practices. *So this is Jinniyah returned.*

"You! Varanna's helmet does not disguise your eyes, daughter. Come to me," Kayth ordered, beckoning to Corri.

Corri felt his summons slide off her mind like water off a smooth stone. "No," she answered and smiled as Kayth again tried to bring her under his control. "Even if you are my father, I will not obey you." Confident, she stood motionless but ready to leap into action as the power washed around her in black waves of energy, never affecting her mind or actions.

Kayth's voice changed into Jinniyah's arrogant voice. *I remember you, Varanna. I recall your eyes from the last time we fought. To reach me you must come into the Otherworlds.*

Do not fight him in the Otherworlds yet! Varanna cried. *Delay that as long as possible. His power will wane as the shadow over the moon wanes.*

Soon, you spawn of the abyss. Then I will throw you and this man Kayth into the hell-fires. Corri smiled as Jinniyah screamed in anger.

With a snarl, Kayth turned and slammed the black disk into a hollow in the front of the dark altar. Corri threw herself against him, knocking him to one side before she was thrust away. As she fell against the stone floor, she instinctively curled into a ball. Her helmet banged painfully against the wall.

Imandoff moved snake-fast, pressing the plaque he had carried for so long over the black disk.

"Too late." Kayth laughed. Corri grabbed at his legs, but he kicked her in the thigh, making her gasp with pain. "No one can defeat me. Sar Akka is now mine."

"I think not, Kayth." Imandoff's cold smile brought a deep frown to Kayth's face. "Look."

Kayth's cold eyes followed Imandoff's pointing finger to the altar where the plaque was boiling and bubbling, sealing the disk inside itself to the altar stones.

With a deep roar of rage, Kayth bent and snatched the band with the owl stone from Corri's helmet, where she lay half-dazed on the floor. "She is nothing without this," he said as he pushed the band onto his own head. His pale eyes reflected the dim light like red-tinged silver disks. "My power is now so great this stone cannot harm me, but must freely give its energy."

"No!" Corri tried to stand, her hurt leg cramping. She grabbed at Kayth, but he again shoved her away, laughing insanely.

With a shout, Imandoff drew his sword as he leaped at Kayth. With a flick of his hand, Kayth plunged the room into a thick darkness as he escaped through the door, slamming it shut behind him. The sorcerer snapped his fingers for light, but his magick was sucked up by the strange vibrations of the room.

"We must go after him." Corri's voice echoed in the room. She felt along the wall until she found Gadavar's groaning form, then helped the Green Man to his feet. "We cannot chase him through this maze forever." She slipped the Green Man's pendant over his head. "Take heart, for whatever Kayth-Jinniyah believes, I can and will find and kill him, even without the owl stone." She allowed Varanna's battle-fever to flood through her.

Imandoff fumbled against the wall until he found the unlocking lever and forced the door open. "He flees to the cavern," he said, his eyes narrowed in fury. "Takra and Tirkul cannot stand against him. If Kayth harms Takra, I will make him pray for death and not give it to him."

"It will be dangerous, but I alone must fight him there." Corri felt a core of coldness in the pit of her stomach and knew her words were truth. "He, and the entity Jinniyah from the abyss, will draw upon the tainted power of that filthy chamber. With that stolen power, Kayth will force the battle into the Otherworlds and I must go after him, Imandoff. This last task is why the Lady called me. No one else can go there but me."

She pushed past Imandoff and ran down the tunnel. She heard Gadavar's footsteps behind her. No longer hampered by the shield against magick inside the hidden room, Imandoff drew upon the power flooding through the Fire Temple, turning it from its evil path into Light. He shouted a word of power and an explosion rocked the tunnel, sealing the evil hidden room forever. Corri ignored everything around her, her thoughts locked on finding Kayth. *This battle spawned centuries ago must come to an end here and now,* she thought as she burst into the altar-cavern just as the hundreds of candles there dimmed to mere sparks of light.

"The moon is nearly covered." Kulkar's soft words to Charissa and the other Tuonela about him registered in Zanitra's mind, but she kept her gaze fixed on the sejda ball in her hands. Within the cold crystal, the pale wash of moonlight that had lit its depths faded. An inky cloud flowed through the sejda ball, gradually obliterating the pearly reflection.

"The Dream Warrior runs into the heart of danger," Zanitra said. What moonlight remained glistened on her long black hair and formed a halo about her. As the crystal turned completely black, she felt a cold wave of air rush over the land-bridge, as if a winter wind burst suddenly through the barrier of late summer heat. "Something comes!" she whispered.

The warriors who guarded the bridge moved quickly to form a barrier around her and the two healers, their nervous eyes flicking over the long black shadows creeping from rock and tree. The cold wind pulled at their pale braids and whipped up clouds of dry dust.

"Blessed Goddess, protect us," Zanitra said, her fear instinctively taking her into the death-litany of the Mystery School. She cupped the sejda ball to her breast with both hands, her dark eyes fastened on the land-bridge before her. "Grant me wisdom to do what must be done, to face what must be faced, with courage and faith. May my steps never falter, my heart ever cleave to You. For within Your hands are the powers of life and death."

"Look!" Charissa stared at the land-bridge, her eyes wide with fear. "A creature straight out of the hell-fires of Frav!"

Although the swords of the Tuonela warriors shook with dread, their hearts pounded and their mouths went dry as one they faced the terrifying apparition that glided toward them.

Zanitra's words never faltered. "Lord of Death, who gathers the dying for Your Lady, guide our feet away from the abyss of eternal Darkness and into Her Light. As the Maiden ripens with Your seed and becomes the Mother, so do we know She takes the face of age when She calls us to our rest." Zanitra raised her eyes from the sejda ball as the hideous figure stopped six paces away. The initiate stepped between the warriors to meet the fearsome image. "My heart knows no fear of Croyna, the Aged One, for Her loving arms will receive me at the last breath. Her heart and soul are pure love. Her hands bring the release of pain and suffering. In Her breast beats the loving comfort of the Mother."

The warriors held their places, yet their eyes were wide with terror, their faces pale, as the figure became clearer and clearer. As the last of the moon was smothered in the eclipse, the entity before Zanitra shone with a brilliant black light, every feature clear to their sight.

"I welcome Croyna." Zanitra took another step forward, the only sign of fear a sheen of perspiration on her pale face. "Croyna's love changes all. Suffering becomes peace. Fear becomes joy. Age is dissolved into a new seed, ready to be born at the Lady's will. I shall not fear the Aged One, for She is love at its best and brightest."

The air about the entity burst into a blaze of scintillating black light, illuminating every feature of the hideous face and every fold of the blood-stained robe. A tall, bone-thin hag stood on the bridge facing Zanitra. Her face was wrinkled, the teeth in the grinning mouth sharp and glistening. The long, matted hair hung in untidy strings about the evil-filled face. Malicious eyes raked across Zanitra as a hair-raising cackle crossed her thin lips.

"Fear me," Croyna hissed, crooking her taloned-fingers before Zanitra's face. "For I am death that does not end, torture eternal in the abyss. Give Me your fear, mortal, as I tear your flesh from your bones."

"You are Croyna, the Gatherer, the Aged One, who is also the loving Lady." Zanitra's sleeves shook from her trembling, yet she did not retreat from the nightmare figure. "Therefore, I cannot fear You, for I do not fear the Goddess."

"The Fravashi do not call upon the Lady, and the Peoples have forgotten Me." The hag's words were like snakes hissing in the night. "No more is My name called in their temples and Schools. Only these have remembered, and they have distorted the memory." A gaunt hand gestured back toward Frav.

"I grieve with You, Croyna. I feel Your sorrow and anger. But I have not forgotten You, nor have others who have the inner teachings. Look into my heart and soul." Zanitra lowered her hands from her breast, the sejda ball still clutched between them.

There was a hiss of breath from the Tuonela warriors as the hag moved closer to Zanitra, then fastened one blood-grimed hand in Zanitra's black hair. The evil eyes narrowed as the hag stared deep into Zanitra's mind. The initiate's body began to shake harder, until her robe flapped about her legs, but never once did Zanitra lower her eyes from the nightmare face that looked deep into her soul.

"I see the truth in your heart. In My anger, I forgot My true nature." The hag released her grip on Zanitra's hair and stroked it smooth. The figure whipped about to face Frav and raised both fists above her head. "They fed Me on blood and terror," the hag screamed. "They soiled My body and name, knowing full well what they did."

"Beloved Croyna." Zanitra's words cracked as the hag whirled to face her, the long strings of hair coiling like striking snakes about the wild, rage-filled face. "Well I know that You have the power and right to exact vengeance, but not all within Frav are evil, nor have they all misused You. I humbly ask You, have mercy upon the innocent and show to me the face of love I was taught to seek."

The hag hesitated, Her head tipped to one side as the glittering eyes tested the heart of each warrior who stood, unflinching but fearful, at Zanitra's side. "I am the Aged One, the Bringer of Death to all mortals. I am also the Dispenser of righteous judgment."

The hideous figure began to change, at first slowly, then faster and faster. The blood marks faded from the black robe, the sharp talons shrank, and her hair smoothed into silvery locks about a wrinkled but wisdom-filled face. The glittering eyes became deep, dark pools of love and sorrow that saw the cruelty and pain within the world, yet loved the erring mortals who lived upon it. On the land-bridge stood the bent-shouldered figure of an elderly woman, full of power and dignity.

"The truth in your heart and the love in your soul has stayed My hand," came the gentle voice as the figure began to fade. "Because of your faith, Zanitra, not all shall suffer My wrath this night."

The form of the Goddess broke into a thousand sparks of light as She disappeared from sight. The tiny pinpricks of brightness hung for a moment over the bridge, then winked out, leaving a momentary afterglow.

"Holy Mother of Mares, did my eyes and mind deceive me with phantoms?" Kulkar caught Zanitra in his strong arms as she staggered back against him.

"I think not," Zanitra answered as the Tuonela war-chief lowered her to the ground, her back against a boulder. "We each saw Croyna as the Fravashi priests and Trows made Her, hideous and bloodthirsty. Yet, we also saw Her change."

"Drink this." Charissa held a flask of mountain water to Zanitra's parched lips. The initiate choked down two swallows of the burning liquid before she pushed the flask away. "I thought my nightmares had taken life and stood before me," the warrior woman said as she sat back on her heels. "Then, the nightmare became a vision of holiness, like a great shakka." She shook her head, at a loss for words.

"I think we each saw the Aged One as our hearts led us to see Her." Zanitra's hands around the sejda ball were stiff and cramped as she opened them, letting the crystal fall into her lap. "But now I feel hope, where before I felt only barriers and opposition confronting the Dream Warrior. What twisted power the Fravashi called up from Croyna they no longer have. Only their Dark God and the evil ones from the abyss will aid them now."

"What can we do?" Kulkar asked.

"Wait," Zanitra answered with a sigh. "The Dream Warrior must enter the Eye of Darkness alone. If she and her companions survive, their retreat may be with death at their heels, with only your swords and my illusions between them and possible final defeat."

Thidrick sat at the worn table, his callused hands clasped together, his eyes intent on the sailor facing him.

"All the sea ports are in rebellion," the sailor said. "The temples that have not fallen are besieged, with no Volikvis or Trows able to leave. Those city officials who favored the religious fanatics have been imprisoned in their own dungeons." His mouth lifted in a half-smile, then turned down again. "But hear me well, Thidrick. We will not surrender to the Tuonela or Kirisani."

"No one asks that of the Fravashi people." Thidrick leaned back in his chair, the rush lights picking up red glints in his black hair. "The other Peoples say they do not want our land, and I believe them. All they want, all I want, is the breaking of the iron fist of the temples. No more men and women dragged away to be forced into service as Volikvi or Trow. No more plotting and ranting about the conquering of others in the name of Jevotan." He leaned forward and stared into the seaman's eyes. "I want peace," he said in a hard voice. "I want my people to worship as they each please, and the other Peoples as they please, and no more religious wars."

"And what does this Kayth who rules the Fire Temple say?" The seaman's mouth twisted in bitterness.

"If fortune aids us, he can say what he pleases as he burns forever in the hell-fires of the abyss."

"And if fortune goes against us?" The sailor turned his ale mug round and round in his hands.

"Then pray that you die quickly," Thidrick answered. "What the accursed priests did before will be as nothing if more power comes into their hands."

The altar-cavern was a swirl of fighting as Corri and Imandoff burst out of the tunnel into the vast open area. The rows upon rows of candles were dimmed to tiny sparks by Kayth's command. The sullen red glow from the immense crack that bisected the cave cast up enough light to see, a light that even Kayth could not quench.

Takra, Tirkul, and the remaining Tuonela warriors clustered together, surrounded by armed Volikvi priests and Trow priestesses. Imandoff's loud roar of anger echoed above the clash of swords and screams of defiance from the Fravashi as he attacked those who threatened the Tuonela warriors. His shiny Wella-made sword flashed like living fire as he cleaved a path to Takra's side.

Wait! Seek out Kayth, for he and Jinniyah give his followers strength. Varanna's voice was clear in Corri's mind.

Corri froze where she was, sword in hand, her eyes searching the shadow-filled chamber for her father. Her mind registered Gadavar's rush past her to join Imandoff, but she ignored the clash of weapons and the screams of the wounded and dying.

Where is he? she thought. *I feel his presence but I cannot see him.*

He cloaks himself with power from the abyss so you cannot find him. You must release your shadow-self in order to see him. Varanna's spirit moved close to Corri's back, raising the hair on the woman's neck. *Let me join with you, Warrior of Shadows, that my skills with the sword may be yours.*

Yes, it is time, Varanna, Corri answered. *But remember your promise to me.*

I gave my word. I will leave without protest when Kayth and Jinniyah are defeated. A brief glimpse of Takra crossed Corri's mind as if she saw through Varanna's eyes. *If the warrior woman lives, a new life awaits me. If she does not, then it will not matter.*

No, it will not matter, Corri thought. *For if Takra falls, we all fall.* She knew her thoughts were true as soon as they crossed her mind.

Enter, Varanna, and let us put an end to this strife. She opened her mind and felt Varanna step inside, as easily as if she had put on a piece of clothing. Then Corri's spirit-body slid free.

The two women melded together, like two streams of water entering the same pool. Corri looked around the chamber again, this time finding Kayth standing with one hand on the bloody altar-stone, a wavering shield of illusive magick around him to keep him unseen by the others. His lips were drawn back in a grimace of evil delight as one hand reached out to draw in the soul-power of the Fravashi priests and Trows as they fell wounded or dying under the invaders' deadly swords. The life-energies were ribbons of red-smudged light, flowing across the great crack to Kayth's outstretched hand, then melting into his body.

With a thought, Corri flew across the crack dividing the cavern. For an instant, she was aware of the deep fires far below in the heart of the earth. She raised Varanna's sword and brought it slashing down across the ribbons of life-energy, scattering fast-dying sparks into the dark air.

Do not interfere! Kayth's scream of anger struck Corri like a blow, but she forced it aside as she lowered her shadow-body to face him. *You cannot defeat me,* Kayth-Jinniyah said, his mouth twisted in anger. *I have great power, more power than you can guess.* He crooked his fingers at her, willing Corri to give him her strength, her mind, her very self.

What you call your power is that of others and nothing of yours. Without the evil entities possessing you, Kayth, you are nothing. Corri watched the rapidly appearing and disappearing forms of Minepa, Kayth, and finally the powerful Jinniyah within the man's aura.

You do not understand. Grimmel bound me to him, Kayth said, his words pleading for understanding but his eyes sly and watchful. *When he died, I was controlled by Minepa. Then the spirit of Jinniyah took control when I entered Frav. Help me, Corri, for I need your loving touch to free me.*

He lies! Varanna said. *Do not trust him.*

Corri narrowed her eyes as she stared again at Kayth's aura and the entities coiling and twisting within it. *Nothing you have ever said to me has been truth, Kayth. If you would truly be free of the entities, tell them to leave.*

That will not release me, Kayth answered. *I need your touch to free me.*

Corri shook her head. *No! You will not control me through pity.* She fought against the painful memories that Kayth dredged up from deep within her mind: the flow of sticky, sharp-smelling blood over her hands when she had killed Grimmel's man in the Valley of Whispers, Druk in the secret Cave. Then Varanna's strength joined with hers and the memories died away. *I will not be turned aside from what I must do by your petty games.*

Kayth's mocking laughter filled her ears, and she saw his true spirit laughing at her from behind Jinniyah's ghostly, cruel face.

What need had you of Jinniyah? Corri said with a grim smile as she watched the twist of anger on Kayth's lips when he could no longer affect her emotions. *Your heart and soul were already black with evil.*

A burst of deadly power struck her chest, deflected off the ancient armor, and broke into nightmare-colored sparks and images. Corri staggered backward, skidding to a stop with one booted heel on the edge of the great crack.

I welcome the power that now flows through me, Kayth said, his cold eyes filled with satisfaction at her inner turmoil of emotions. *The death of Malya means nothing when you are here. I shall rule all Sar Akka as I always planned, and you will be my slave.*

I see in your thoughts that you have a lover. Kayth's words were full of contempt. *You would not come to me, yet you let another man plow the field. What will you do if he dies, Corri? Do not think to deceive me, for you are like your mother in your pity. His death would cause you great pain, enough that you would lose all hope and will to live.* Kayth-Jinniyah's smile was cold and mocking, but it faded when he saw the determination in her face. *So be it. Watch him die then.*

A bolt of energy shot past Corri, striking to her right. She whirled as Gadavar screamed in pain and fell to the rocky floor beside her. He lay motionless and pale, his spirit beginning to form in a white vaporous cloud over his head. Kayth's mocking laughter rang through the great cavern.

Chapter 20

If I die, it will be of no account, Corri said through clenched teeth as she faced Kayth. *For I will take you into death with me. I fear no death where I will be with Gadavar. Who waits for you, Kayth? My mother, who you deserted? I think not. Your companions, who came with you on your sky-ship? Jinniyah? You deserve their loving attention.*

She rushed at Kayth, throwing her arms around him, and instantly willed herself into the darkest parts of the Otherworld. Face to face with him, she saw the startled fear in his eyes as he struggled to break her hold. Grimly, she held tight as he writhed and clawed at her.

You have taken from me my greatest reason for life, she said as she tightened her grip. *I will avenge Gadavar by throwing you into the hell-fires myself, even if I must go with you.*

The cavern disappeared from view and they hung in a dark void, a place filled with far-off flickers of deep red light, the odor of putrid flesh, and disembodied groans. At the same time, Corri was aware that, in the physical world, the black shadow across the face of the moon retreated, that one tiny sliver of bright silver once more lit the night sky.

I call upon you, man of the shadow world! she cried. *If the promised pendant will rid Sar Akka of both Jinniyah and Kayth, send it to me now, even though it means that I die!*

Kayth worked one arm free and struck a glancing blow against Corri's ancient helmet, sending her reeling in the thick air of the darkness. A whirring noise, like the staccato wing-beat of the grassland prairie hens, grew louder. Instinctively, Corri threw up one arm to shield her face, and the silver chain of the shadow pendant wrapped around her hand and arm with a stinging slap.

Listen to your instincts! Varanna cried in her mind. *Press your attack!*

All those who would aid me, come now! Corri shouted as she tried to reach Kayth. She slammed against an invisible barrier.

I know you well, Kayth-Jinniyah said. *You cannot break through this wall I have set to match your life-energy.*

But others can destroy it for me. Corri drew herself up tall and stared at her father. *If you steal power, you must always fight to keep it yours. At the slightest break in your concentration, that power not yours will slip away. Only power lent by friends and companions can be used without fear of loss. Minepa and Jinniyah are no friends.*

As Corri spoke, the spirit-form of the Rissa, who had befriended her in Ayron's cabin, appeared suddenly at her side. Its muzzle wrinkled with a silent snarl, the great fangs exposed. Its battle scream of fury filled the dark void and brought a startled, backward jerk from Kayth. With one lightning sweep of its sharp-clawed paw, it struck at Kayth, again and again, the claws opening great rents in the man's aura. Then the Rissa winked out of existence as quickly as it had come.

I know your weaknesses! Kayth screamed, half-bent over in pain. *You forget, girl, that you carry a child. I will torture that child until you yield!*

An angry wail sliced through the burst of fear Kayth-Jinniyah poured into her mind. For an instant, Corri saw a red-faced baby screaming in anger, its tiny fists beating at the air. *My son! A child cries defiance to the evil ones, the Wella woman said.* She snapped the link Kayth had formed and threw up a barrier against his evil influence. *There is one with me who will protect that child against you, whatever happens. If the child and I die, Varanna will see that the child does not fall into your evil hands, even though I may not escape. Make your move, Kayth, lest we hang here forever, locked in combat.*

From Kayth's opposite side, the singing of the Otherworld Serpent suddenly filled the void with a sound like crystal bells. Kayth clapped his hands over his ears and screamed with pain. The shimmering silver and black scales threw wildly flickering bursts of light around him. Corri's eyes were nearly blinded as she tried to watch the Serpent.

Strike! Varanna's words jerked Corri back into action. Without hesitation, she swung out with the pendant. The pearly, shimmering, moon-like stone struck the owl stone in the band around Kayth's head. Eye-blinding sparks flared from the owl stone, streaming outwards to enclose Kayth's form in a net of fiery lines that sucked off his power and released it to whip away into the darkness. An explosion of brilliance temporarily blinded Corri's sight. As she stood, arm thrown across her face, she heard Kayth scream, the sound spiraling up until his voice cracked with terror and pain.

Corri opened her streaming eyes to see Kayth hanging motionless in the dark atmosphere. His head lolled to one side, his mouth sagged open, and his eyes were rolled back in his head. The Serpent's singing still echoed through the void, but it was gone from sight.

Watching for any sudden movement, Corri carefully hung the pendant chain over the end of her sword sheath, then reached out to grab the owl stone band from Kayth's forehead.

Kayth's body began to jerk from side to side as he hung suspended in nothingness. The air beneath him cracked open to reveal a deep pit, where great black flames crackled. A cacophony of tortured sounds rose from the pit to beat against Corri's mind. Deep within the pit shown the sinister Eye of Darkness. She cringed back from the lip of the abyss and her skin went cold with horror.

First a groan, then a piercing scream of agony tore past Kayth's slack lips as his soul was torn from his body. Corri clearly saw Kayth's diseased and rotted soul hang for an instant above the pit. Beside him, and fighting as hard as Kayth to avoid the downward descent, were the souls of Jinniyah and Minepa. A whirlwind of black flame shot up, surrounding the struggling souls and, when it fell once more into the pit, sucked them down with it. The Eye continued its hypnotic stare at Corri, but she thrust aside its influence, feeling Varanna's strength backing her. But even with the ancient warrior's strength added to hers, Corri felt a great tiredness that weighed on her like lead.

Terror flashed through her mind as she felt the edges of the whirlwind catch at her shadow-self. She struggled against the pull but was helpless to extricate herself from the suction. Cold fear froze her thoughts as she began to slide downward, inch by inch.

Do you believe in the hell-fires? The Lady stood before Corri in a bright column of pure light.

No, I believe in You! As Corri looked into the Lady's eyes, she felt her shadow-self retreat from the sucking current. *I am a Goddess daughter. Hell-fires are not of Your making, Lady.*

The Lady smiled, and the thick darkness retreated, leaving Her figure and Corri's in a globe of warm clear light that allowed no encroachment by Darkness. *Your heart has taught you much, daughter. Hell-fires are created by the minds of mortals as an Otherworld retribution for what they deem to be sins. Although I am also Croyna, who dispenses justice,* the form changed into the figure of an elder woman, sickle in hand, *I take no delight in eternal punishment. There is love in My justice.*

I am so tired. Corri felt strength run from her shadow-self as if from a great wound. *Let me stay with you, Lady. I have never felt such weariness of spirit before.*

The choice is yours, Warrior of Shadows. Your task is finished, the geis is lifted. Whatever you desire, shall be.

Corri, where are you? Gadavar's faint voice wavered in the darkness. *Return to me, my love. Oh Lady of the Mountains, do not let her die. Take my life instead!*

Is the child not important to you? the Lady asked, her sun-bright eyes looking into Corri's soul.

Yes, my child is important, but what will I do without Gadavar? Corri cried. *What life could I offer a child alone?*

The Green Man lies near death, yet he sends you his strength, came the answer. *What would you give in return for his life?*

My own, Corri answered without hesitation. *Take me in his place.*

I will not take a life whose course is not run. Neither will I hinder a soul that strives for union with My light. Use your powers to stay or return, but the choice must be yours.

The Lady vanished from sight, as if a dark curtain had fallen about Her. Corri hung, exhausted and trembling, in the Otherworld blackness. Below her, the crack of the pit closed like a giant mouth over the hell-fires within it.

Corri! Gadavar's plea broke through her confused thoughts.

Clutching the owl stone in her hand, Corri tried to will herself back to the cavern in the Fravashi mountain. *I am so tired,* she thought as her strength continued to pour out like blood. *I have no power to return. How will I help him?*

"She is trapped!" Dakhma's scream jerked the Oracle and Athdar out of sleep. "Now is the time. We must help her, Oracle, or she will be lost forever!"

Tears streamed down the little girl's face as she ran to the table and grabbed up the grave-crystal. She squeezed her eyes shut and bit her lip as she tried to send strength to Corri across the barrier Between Worlds.

"I cannot reach her!" Dakhma was nearly hysterical as the Oracle and Athdar rushed to her side. "Tell me what to do," she begged.

"We must all try." Athdar's voice held a deep rumbling growl, his small face half-shifted under the stress he felt.

"Yes, we must all try," the Oracle said, as she and the little boy both laid their hands over Dakhma's on the crystal.

Zanitra broke out of her light slumber with a jerk, her dark eyes wide, her heart pounding. *What power comes through the sejda?* she thought. She clasped the ball with both hands and brought it to her forehead. A vision of the Oracle was clear in her mind. *The Warrior is trapped? Yes, we must save her!*

Zanitra's long-fingered hands burned as the power shot through the sejda ball and out across the barrier Between Worlds. She felt her breath catch in her throat, then stop, as she fought to keep the current flowing.

Fight, Corri! Use your powers to gain the victory!

For an instant, Zanitra saw Corri hanging in a place of thick darkness, then the still body of Gadavar on the floor of a great cavern. The pictures flicked back and forth until Zanitra's mind reeled under the onslaught.

There is no true victory until all who crossed the bridge into Frav return! she shouted, and saw Corri's head snap up, her hands lift to catch the flow of power, channeling it into her exhausted mind and spirit.

I come! Corri answered, then blinked out of sight.

Zanitra struggled out of her trance, gasping for breath, and found the Tuonela warriors gathered close about her. "Be ready," she whispered hoarsely. "If the battle is truly won, the Dream Warrior and her companions will soon be on the bridge. If it is lost, then we must fight for our lives."

"The Fravashi are retreating!" The High Priestess leaned against a tree, her bloody sword drooping in one hand, the other clutched to a wound in her thigh.

"Look behind them!" Breela pointed toward the moonlight-brightened clearing just beyond the retreating soldiers. "More Fravashi to swell their ranks! We can never defeat so many."

"Not soldiers, but the people of Frav themselves." Taillefer's soft voice sounded near Breela's side. "There are even children with them. And see, on their breasts, a moon symbol!"

The silent crowd of people moved steadily toward the soldiers, the moonlight glinting on the metal crescents they each wore. The leader of the soldiers shouted for his men to attack, but the men overpowered him, cutting him down in a flurry of blades.

"Peace! Peace!" The chant began to echo into the night as the Fravashi people continued to move forward. Although the border was no longer sealed by the ancient spells, they did not cross into Tuone. They stopped in a long line on the Frav side and chanted, while a lone figure walked toward the defending warriors.

"Thidrick!" The High Priestess started forward, but her wounded leg crumpled and she fell into Breela's arms.

"It is ended." Thidrick held out his empty hands, then gestured back to the chanting people and the dazed and exhausted Fravashi soldiers. "The Fravashi ask only that you not invade our land, that you leave us to work out our own destiny. The power of the Volikvis and Trows is broken. We have no desire to force our way of worship on you, nor will we allow you to do so to us."

"The terms are accepted." Jehennette stepped out of the shadows to stand before Thidrick. "See to your wounded. In seven days, have your new leaders meet with us at the land-bridge. There will be many things to discuss, Thidrick—the manner of trading, new protection of the border."

"My people have asked me to speak for them." Thidrick's face held doubt as he stared at the small woman who faced him. "Will the Peoples hold to your words of truce?"

"If they do not," Jehennette said, her voice crisp and full of authority, "I, myself, will take up a sword for the first time in my life and crack a few heads."

Thidrick grinned, and in his eyes was a flash of respect. He nodded, then turned and walked back to his own people.

Corri slammed back into her body and staggered backward until she hit the cavern wall with a bruising blow. She looked around wildly for Gadavar, then spotted his bloody form on the other side of the crack. A part of her mind registered that the candle flames were high, not the smoldering sparks left by Kayth. Imandoff stood over the Green Man, his sword dealing death to any Volikvi who dared venture too close. At his side, Takra shouted the Tuonela war-cry, Xephena's body at her feet. Blood covered them both, and Corri was unable to see if either was wounded. With them were most of the Tuonela warriors who had been freed.

The pendant! Corri fumbled at her sword sheath, then glanced quickly at the rock floor around her. The shadow pendant was nowhere in sight.

"Corri! To me!" Tirkul's shout sent her running toward the nearest bridge, where the tall Tuonela waited, sword in hand.

"We dared not move you when you were frozen in trance," he said as she plunged past him toward Gadavar. "We could only defend you until you returned from your Otherworld journey. Xephena and Zalmoxis are dead."

"As is Kayth." *Oh Goddess, let me not be too late!* she prayed as she ran straight toward the snarling priests who faced the sorcerer.

"She lives!" A Volikvi screamed in terror and pointed as he saw Corri's armored form bearing down upon him. Imandoff's sword took the priest in the throat.

There was mass confusion as the remaining Volikvis fled, driven by the deadly swords at their backs. Too late they realized their error. Screams of terror echoed off the cavern walls as they plunged down into the smoking crack.

"Gadavar, stay with me!" Corri knelt to cradle the Green Man's head in her arms. "Do not leave me. Now that I have found love with you, I do not want to be alone again. Our son should know both of us."

Corri realized that the owl stone band was still clutched tight in her left hand. As she loosened her fingers, pain shot through them; her palm and fingers were bright red, burned from the power she had channeled through the stone. Tears of pain trickling down her cheeks, Corri held the owl stone against Gadavar's chest. "Do not leave me." Her voice was choked as she willed healing into the wounded man.

"Does he still live?" Takra's quiet words came to Corri as if from a great distance.

"Corri, you did not tell me." Gadavar's voice was so faint that Corri had to lean close to hear him. He opened his eyes, blinking against the candlelight. "I heard the Lady of the Mountains speak of a child, our child."

"We must move him." Imandoff laid a hand on Corri's shoulder. "Kayth's power is broken, but not the strength of the Fire Temple's priests and soldiers. Soon they will lose their fear and cut off our retreat if they can."

Corri nodded as Tirkul and Takra helped Gadavar to his feet. Tirkul pulled one of the Green Man's arms across his shoulder, supporting the weakened man as much as he could.

Corri paused and looked back at the altar, where Kayth's body lay crumpled and twisted. His fingers were crooked into tearing claws in death, his mouth frozen in a grimace of terror.

He was my father, she thought. *My mind knows that Kayth was truly no father to me, but my heart feels a sense of wrongness that I had to kill anyone. But the greatest sorrow I feel is for the warriors who gave up their lives to stay free of evil.*

"We may have to fight our way free," Imandoff said, as he took the owl stone band from Corri's hand and fitted it back over the ancient helmet. "I will lead the way." He retrieved his staff from where it had fallen during the fierce battle.

"And I will be rear-guard," Takra answered and motioned the weakened Tuonela captives ahead of her. A thin trickle of blood dripped from beneath the bottom edge of her chain mail shirt. "I hate being underground. We cannot be out in the night air too soon." She scowled around the cavern as the sound of shouting voices faintly reached them.

With a cry of dismay, Corri called upon the power of the owl stone and pressed her hand over the chain mail in the area she guessed had the wound.

"No time," Takra said, pushing away Corri's hand. "If we win free, there will be time for healing. If we do not, it will not matter."

Reluctantly, Corri nodded.

"This way." Imandoff gestured with his blood-stained sword. They moved off down one of the tunnels, Imandoff leading, Takra and Corri at the rear behind Tirkul, the stumbling Gadavar, and the exhausted Tuonela.

Their flight through the tunnels of the Fire Temple seemed to take forever, but Corri's instincts told her they were nearing the surface. Twice they encountered small groups of Trow and temple servants, but there was no attempt made by anyone to halt their retreat.

"These are nothing to us," Imandoff said as a group of Trow priestesses fled screaming down a side-tunnel. "Our greatest danger will come from the remaining Volikvis and soldiers when they come after us, and they will."

Varanna? When Varanna answered, Corri was surprised to find the spirit-woman beside her and no longer sharing her body. *How much farther?*

Not long now. The evil priests have rallied and are coming fast behind you.

Soon the sorcerer led them into a small courtyard with an open gate. Above, the sky was still dark enough to see the pale, full face of the moon as it hung in the west. Through the portal Corri saw the land-bridge and, at the far end, shadowy figures.

"The nathlings are still on our trail!" Takra hissed as they hurried through the gate and onto the bridge over the deep Kratula Gorge. Behind them, Corri heard shouts like the baying of hunting dogs as the Volikvis ran through the tunnels after them.

Corri stumbled as she felt the pressure of the air about her thicken and change. Imandoff bit off a curse, but urged them on. At the end of the bridge, Zanitra stood, the sejda ball in her hands, eyes closed in concentration.

"Keep moving," Imandoff said, his deep voice barely audible. "My sister is covering us with illusion. The Fravashi will not be able to see us."

They plunged on across the bridge, gasping for breath. Gadavar groaned through clenched teeth as Tirkul dragged him clear of the bridge and into the shadows of the monolithic stones dotted along the Tuone side. Balqama gave the tall warrior a quick hug, her face full of joy, before she knelt beside the Green Man. The rescued Tuonela, weakened from long captivity and the fight, staggered into the shelter of the rocks before collapsing.

The waiting Tuonela warriors moved to guard the end of the bridge, but the Volikvi priests stopped at the far gate, confused by the illusions and seeing nothing.

"You are wounded!" Imandoff sheathed his sword with a sharp movement, then pulled Takra into his arms. She hung there, letting the sorcerer bear her weight as she fought to stay conscious. "I was so intent on getting everyone out, I was blind to your wound. Forgive me, Takra. Why did you not tell me?"

"I did not want you to know," Takra murmured softly. "You would have fluttered around me instead of concentrating on getting us out."

"Hold her steady, Imandoff, while I try to heal her." Corri took off the owl stone and pressed it against Takra's side. *Let the child live, Goddess. My Sister-Friend fought well in Your service, Lady. I would not have her pay the final price.*

She closed her eyes and bent her head until it touched Takra's shoulder. Under her hands, she felt the trickle of blood slow, then stop. The wound below the bottom of the chain mail shirt pulled together and healed. Corri jerked back in surprise at the unborn child's annoyed cry in her mind.

"She will be a warrior," Takra said softly. "She kicks like a horse, sorcerer." The warrior woman raised one hand to touch Corri's helmet. "Gadavar, does he still live?"

"He lives." Zanitra motioned Imandoff to help Takra to a blanket spread on the ground. "Rest now, or you may lose the child." She frowned at Imandoff. "Have you no sense, my wandering brother, than to let a child-bearing woman go into battle?"

Imandoff raised his eyebrows. "Do you think I could stop her? My words mean little. Takra Wind-Rider does as she pleases."

"A fine thing, two such stubborn people as parents." Zanitra fussed over Takra. "What life will the poor child have?"

"A life full of love," Takra murmured as she submitted to Zanitra's soothing hands.

Corri sat cross-legged beside Gadavar and reached out hesitantly to take one of his strong hands. "Are you angry that I did not tell you about our child?" she asked.

"I understand why you did not." Gadavar leaned his head back against the boulder, his eyes holding hers. "Would you have told me at all?"

"Yes, at some time." Corri brushed the dark hair off his face. "I did not know if you wanted a child, Gadavar, and I would not trap you in that way."

"The night I lay with you, my heart longed for a child between us," he answered. "I will not bind you to me, Corri. I promised not to cage you and I will not. Whatever you wish to do, do it. If you decide to leave the child with me, all I ask is that you come to see us when you can."

"I would never leave the child or you," Corri said. "I no longer look upon love as a cage, nor do I think raising a child would be such. I well know how it feels to be without mother or father. And I have no wish to go wandering, Gadavar, except with you."

"Then my heart is full." Gadavar gently pulled Corri to him. His mouth was soft and loving against hers.

"Take me home, Gadavar," she whispered. "Home to your mountains. I want our son to be born where the air smells of green trees and where the Rissa will protect him."

"If the child is a son," he murmured.

"It will be a son," Corri answered, feeling the steady beat of his heart under her hand.

"I saw your fight with Kayth." Gadavar's breath stirred her hair as he spoke. "It was as if I watched from a distance and I could not reach you. But I was there when you faced the Eye of Darkness, faced it and Kayth. I saw the Rissa and the strange serpent aid you and heard the Lady Herself speak to you. If you say the Rissa will protect our child, I know you speak the truth, though I do not understand."

I never thought to know such happiness, Corri thought. *When I fled with Imandoff from Grimmel's clutches, I could not foresee what my future would bring. If I had seen it, I know I would have feared to take it in both hands. I would have run from Gadavar's offering of love, believing it to be false and confining.* She blinked back tears. *And by running from the very thing I longed for, I would have cast aside a future that holds all I ever wanted.*

Corri lay against Gadavar, content to do nothing but listen to the murmured words between Imandoff and Takra, the whispers of the Tuonela warriors as they guarded the camp, and the click of Zanitra's prayer beads as the first streaks of dawn light colored the tall stones around them.

The Oracle tucked Dakhma and Athdar into her own bed. Dakhma had cried tears of frustration, and Athdar had locked his little arms firmly around one leg of the table, when she suggested they go to their rooms and sleep. The young woman smiled down at the drowsy children.

"When will the Dream Warrior return to us?" Dakhma asked in a sleepy voice.

"They will send word when they can. Sleep now, knowing she is safe."

The Oracle walked across the room toward the balcony doors. She stopped at the table and stared down at the disarray of figurines scattered across the chalk-drawn map on its dark surface. The overturned figures that had blackened were crumbling rapidly into piles of dust.

What strange omens came from the past to aid us, she thought as she carefully put the remaining whole figurines back into their box. *I must keep these safe, for no one can say they might not be of importance some far time in the future.*

The Oracle opened the doors and went to stand on the tiny balcony in the cool morning sunlight. She looked down upon the quiet courtyard, watching the dawn light creep across the worn stones like water.

The battle against Frav may be won, but the great work is just beginning. We cannot replace the broken spells at the border. Watchtowers must be built, guards must be posted. We must choose ambassadors to work out terms of trade and non-aggression. She sighed wearily as she stepped back into the room. *Everyone has changed, as have I. No longer will I have the solitude and quiet of my Cavern. As Oracle, I must find new paths for the Kirisani to follow, and to do that I must be among the Peoples.*

She curled up on a narrow divan, willing her busy mind to quiet and let her find a few moment's forgetfulness in sleep.

Chapter 21

The snows came late that year, giving the Peoples time to hastily build and man fortresses along the border with Frav. The more severely wounded were housed there until they could be safely moved by stages across the wind-swept grasslands in the coming spring.

Councils between the Peoples and the Fravashi were called even while the fortresses were being constructed. The Baba and the elder shakkas of the Clans came to represent the Tuonela, while the High Priestess and Jehennette of Leshy spoke for the people of Kirisan. Not one representative of the Asuran government came. Thidrick and his chosen aids were as adamant about the issue of religion as were the Kirisani and the Tuonela.

"The Fravashi religion must be completely destroyed!" Kulkar's booming voice echoed among the trees surrounding the campsite. "I would not fight this battle again."

"The choice must be ours alone," Thidrick snapped. "No outsiders must determine how we live."

The shakka Norya rose and gestured for silence. "If we deny the Fravashi the right to worship as they please, are we not like their Volikvis and Trows?" she asked, staring around the circle at the hard-eyed warriors. "Thidrick has given his word that the remaining Volikvis and Trows, those who still want the old ways to exist, have fled to the barbarous northern regions, outside the realm of Frav. Who are we to dictate the lives of the Fravashi people? There is enough dissent among us to occupy our time and purpose."

"What of the Asurans and those at Sadko?" The Baba stood, his young face solemn. "They deliberately withheld aid, thinking to negotiate with the Fire Temple should the battle fall that way."

Angry murmurs broke across the Baba's words. One of the Fravashi started to speak, but Thidrick held up his hand for silence.

"That is your concern," he said. "As we wish no interference in our affairs, so will we offer none in yours."

"The Asurans must be isolated, as will the Mystery School at Sadko." The High Priestess leaned against a rough-cut staff, her left thigh swathed in bandages. "The initiates of Sadko have isolated themselves. Let it remain so. The Asurans will continue their mistreatment of their women and their religious control of their people, as they always have, and which we have ignored until now. To avoid contamination with their ideas, I would see them isolated as well within their borders. Trade would be allowed, but only with select individuals and those kept under strict controls."

The Baba nodded. "Their leaders have become much like the old Fravashi rulers. I suggest forts built along the borders with Asur, so that all traffic and trade goods entering or leaving Asur are taxed. In that manner, their spies and peddlers of influence will be discouraged from entering Kirisan and Tuone."

"What of the Limna workers and those who harvest the sea?" Balqama hesitantly stepped forward, her chin held high in anticipation of rebuke. "They are not like the others."

"The Asuran fishermen and sailor-merchants have moved to the northern city of Zoc," the Baba said. "The Keffin of Zoc have expelled all Magni and refuse to allow the new religious laws within their area of influence. As for the Limna workers, they have long wished to become part of Kirisan. We should allow them exemption of the taxes and freedom to come and go. The Keffin of Zoc have already approached the Tuonela, asking to be allowed to go through Neeba on trading ventures."

His eyes held an impish grin as he looked at Balqama. "You were a traveling trader, Balqama. Why do you not be an intermediary with those of Zoc who come to Neeba? They could negotiate with you for sale of goods, and you could roam through Tuone and Kirisan, selling their merchandise for them. They have no wish to be gone long from their homes."

The girl's eyes brightened with interest, then she started to shake her head. Tirkul moved to her side and took her chin in his hand to look down into her eyes.

"Yes," he answered, and was rewarded with a dazzling smile. "If we can get a large Tuonela wagon and enough horses, trading for those of Zoc will be welcome."

"You shall have it," the Baba promised.

"Will you also trade for us?" Thidrick asked. "I do not think it wise for the Fravashi to be wandering about your lands, nor you through ours, with feelings still so high against us."

"We will do that." Balqama nodded as she and Tirkul walked away, their low voices full of plans for their wandering future.

"What of those at the Mystery School of Sadko?" The Baba turned to Vairya.

"Word has come that they have closed their gates and refuse to admit anyone, even the sick. We shall keep watch over them. The High Clua of Leshy has chosen healers to stay with the shakkas here at the border to tend the seriously wounded until they can return to their homes. And the Limna workers and some of the farmers of that region have petitioned to become part of Kirisan. We have granted their request."

"Then the important things are settled." Thidrick looked at his council; they all nodded agreement. "The forts will be built to safeguard both Tuone and Frav against fanatics causing more trouble. Frav is in a state of upheaval, and I must return at once to do what I can to bring about calm and peace. While any of this council or I live," he added, "you need not fear a return to power of the Volikvis. A death sentence hangs over the head of any who try to return. Many of the Volikvis and Trows were held against their will and did not approve of the sacrifices. We have asked these to cleanse the temples and create a new way of worshipping Jevotan, a way without blood and coercion."

Thidrick and the Fravashi with him left the gathering to ride back across the border.

"You will return to Kystan?" Norya asked Vairya, who nodded.

"And what of the warrior women of Her Own?" Jehennette looked up at the tall woman, her head tilted to one side.

"Some have asked to stay as guards. Breela will lead them." The High Priestess, limping heavily, walked with the two women back to the waiting warriors of Frayma's Mare. "And you, Norya, will you stay here with your warrior women?"

"Yes," the old shakka answered. "They have more need of me than does any Clan."

The first wagons from Leshy rolled out of the Mootma Mountains down onto the wide grasslands early the next morning. Taillefer rode alongside Merra's wagon, his deep voice lifted often in song as he composed and polished the great epic of the battle. Jehennette and her healers, many of them refugees from Sadko, tended the wounded who filled the bouncing wagons.

The slow journey took over three weeks for the wagons to reach the Mystery School at Leshy. By that time, the first cold winds were whipping across the Tuonela grasslands and the half-built forts along the border. The meppe trees on the lower slopes of the Barren Mountains and Deep Rising dropped their big purple leaves to carpet the ground for the coming winter.

Imandoff and Takra had kept much to themselves during the journey, except for seeking out Corri and Gadavar at the evening campsites. When the caravan entered the gates of the city of Leshy, a messenger from the Mystery School brought Corri's bag that held the Forgotten Ones' treasure from Ayron's cabin.

"For you," Corri said as she handed the leather bag to Imandoff. "Perhaps these things will occupy your mind during the coming winter and keep you from being too restless."

Gadavar, along with Corri and his fellow Green Men, turned aside toward the trails leading up into Deep Rising.

"I thought you would return to Kystan," Gadavar said as Imandoff and Takra reined their horses to follow him.

The sorcerer frowned and shook his head. "I am a wanderer, Gadavar, and really not welcome at the Temple. The Temple at Kystan is no place for me." He turned to smile at Takra, who rode by his side. "Or for the birth-place of our child. Is there a place for us among the Green Men?"

"Always!" Gadavar grinned. "Our children shall grow up together, sorcerer, and be friends, as we are friends."

"Corri?" Imandoff looked at her in surprise. "You have said little enough on this journey, but is there something you should have said to me?"

"Only that her secret is now out, Imandoff." Takra's contented smile made Imandoff's brows lift in surprise. "You never guessed, did you, old man? You have much to learn about women."

"I know I do," Imandoff murmured. "And like all men, I shall never learn enough."

The death of Green Men at the border left empty cabins in the forests of Deep Rising. One snug cabin of a man who had no surviving family was given to Imandoff and Takra, while Corri and Gadavar settled into his home not far away. Takra and Corri spent much time together, the Tuonela woman teaching the former thief from Hadliden how to sew skins and dry the meat brought home by the men.

"I thought you were a warrior," Corri said as they sat before the blazing hearth. "How do you know all this?" A glint of firelight caught on her earring, a gift from the dead Wella woman Nimuanni.

"The Tuonela all learn to care young for children, as we learn to take part in all other Clan work," Takra answered as she smoothed a treated skin across her knees. She arched her back to relieve the tired muscles, then went back to her careful stitching. "Children are cared for by all in a Clan. If a child is orphaned, another family takes it in. No child is without love or ever abandoned."

"Except Dakhma." Corri's tongue showed at one corner of her mouth as she struggled with her heavy needle.

"Except Dakhma." Takra sighed and arched her back again. "The girl is now safe and happy with the Oracle. The Mother of Mares works in Her own way."

"Do you think the High Clua will allow Merra to join Taillefer at the Temple in Kystan? Gadavar says that the songsmith has been summoned there by the Oracle to teach the ancient songs to the initiates." Corri jerked as the needle pricked her finger. "Merra loves him, you know."

"The High Clua will let her daughter follow her heart," Takra answered. "Did Jehennette not follow her own heart when she chose the fathers of her children?"

A gust of cold wind and snow burst into the cabin as Imandoff and Gadavar hurried inside, their arms full of moss.

"Surely this will be enough," the sorcerer said as he hung the moss over the drying racks Takra had placed near one side of the hearth. He bent down to kiss her cheek, then gently laid one hand on her swollen belly.

"Only if you wish me to use your fine robe to diaper your child." Takra took one fold of the robe in her fingers and scowled. "It will need a thorough washing, though." She wrinkled her nose.

"More moss, then, for Takra." Gadavar smiled at Corri. "The racks in our cabin are full to overflowing, although your time is months off yet."

"Our daughter's cradle is finished and ready," Imandoff said as he pulled a stool to Takra's side. "In the spring, I will make a cradle-saddle, so when the child is old enough to hold her seat, she will be safe whenever we travel."

Gadavar's head jerked up as a call came from outside the door.

"Thalassa of Tree-Home." Corri identified the voice before Gadavar opened the door.

"My time is near," Takra said, rubbing her aching back. "She promised to come. I did not think these men would be much help when the birthing starts."

Thalassa hurried inside, shaking fine snowflakes from her cloak as Gadavar shut the door against the winter cold. Her green eyes were bright as she came to Takra's side. Leaning forward, her waist-length braid falling across Takra's knees, the feya woman gently felt the swollen belly and nodded to herself.

"Very soon now, perhaps within a day or two," she said. From the pouch at her belt, Thalassa pulled out the little priestess statue Corri had taken from the under-mountain Cave of the Maidens. "Before the high snows fell, I visited Willa of High Limna. She sends this to you as promised, with her blessings for the child."

Takra took the glassy black statue in her hand, stroking it with one finger. "Yes, as she promised. The time has come, my daughter, to be born."

Thalassa looked from Corri to Takra, her mouth pursed in thought. "Enough sewing for one day," she ordered. "Time for these two to rest. Uzza of Springwell is even now on her way here, and none too soon I think. I understand there will soon be other new mothers among the Green Men."

Corri and Gadavar made their way through the thick forest to their cabin, leaving Thalassa and Imandoff to fuss over a protesting Takra. Night fell quickly, and the snow drifted down in thick flakes to cover the tree limbs and sift through to the ground beneath.

Corri lay unsleeping at Gadavar's side, the blankets and fur robes heavy and warm over her. The crackle of the low fire and Gadavar's soft breathing were the only sounds within the darkened cabin. She felt in a curious, light state, almost floating, yet there was no separation of body and shadow-self. Her mind was clear of thoughts as she watched the fire's reflection on the beams overhead.

Warrior of Shadows, so we meet again. The air beside the bed rippled slightly as the man from the shadow realm materialized. *Your journeys have been most eventful since last we met.* His slightly-tilted eyes were the warm brown Corri remembered, his silvery hair just as bright.

My thanks for aiding me. Corri sat up slowly so as not to waken Gadavar. *Why have you come?* she asked, then shivered as her thoughts darted to Takra. *Is my Sister-Friend in danger?*

The man shook his head, his hair sweeping the sides of his sharp-chinned face. *She is in no danger, nor are you.* He held out his hand. The firelight glinted on the silver threads in his green cloak and the red stones in the hilt of the sword at his side. *You gave no thought of possessing the pendant when you returned to your world,* the man said, a smile lifting his mouth. *It returned to my hand.*

He opened his fingers and there, on his pale palm, rested the pendant Corri had used to defeat Kayth.

I could not keep what was not mine. Corri's hands tightened in the creases of the blankets as she looked at the shimmering stone on its silver chain.

Once you would have kept it without a thought. Truly, you were the best thief in Hadliden.

How do you know this? Corri frowned up at the strange Otherworld man.

The adepts of my world come and go as they wish, where they wish, he answered, letting the chain slip through his fingers until it hung by one link. *We each have a pendant such as this to aid us in our cross-time, cross-world travels. It is our task to help keep the balance of all the worlds. This is my gift to you, Warrior of Shadows. It will aid you in your search for knowledge and truth.*

You are saying that I will have to go through more dangerous adventures, that some other geis will be laid upon me?

The man smiled. *No. However, I understand your restless, inquiring spirit well, Corri Farblood. You cannot resist being curious about new and unknown things.*

Mayhap I have no desire to go traveling through other realms again. Corri clasped her fingers tighter in the blankets, fighting a deep desire to take up the pendant.

Then keep it for your child. Teach him its use, as you must teach him many things about the powers with which he will be born.

What powers will my son have? Corri laid her hand on her belly. *And how can I know how to use this pendant?*

Curiosity already raises its head. The man from the shadow world held the pendant closer, enticing Corri to take it. *You will know your son's powers when you see them. As for the pendant, you can only learn its magick if you use it.*

Corri reached up to touch the silver chain, and the pendant flipped into her hand as if an inner attraction drew it to her.

Will I see you again? She looked up into the brown eyes so intent upon her face. *I think you have things to teach that I may need to learn.*

My heart tells me we will speak again. The man turned his head, as if listening. *Your warrior friend needs you now,* he said, and faded from sight.

Corri slipped the pendant chain over her head, then bent down to shake Gadavar awake. "Takra's child comes," she said softly. "I must go to her."

Gadavar rubbed the sleep from his eyes as he sat up, tousled dark hair framing his face. "The snow is getting worse," he said as he sniffed the air. "Dress warmly, while I get the snowshoes."

The half-mile trek through the snowy, dark woods seemed over-long to Corri as she impatiently walked beside Gadavar. One strong hand on her arm to keep her from falling, he admonished her over and over to walk slower lest she come to harm. When the cabin's light came into view through the trees, she nearly dragged Gadavar in her rush for the door.

The room was warm, with a crackling fire roaring on the hearth. The dividing curtains were drawn back and a ball of magick light hung over the big bed where Thalassa held Takra's sweating hands. The table was strewn with Ayron's collection of Forgotten Ones' treasure, but Imandoff paced nervously back and forth before the fire. He jumped in surprise when Corri threw open the door and rushed inside.

"You did not mind-call me." Corri stood in front of the sorcerer, hands on hips, a frown on her face.

"You need your rest, and Thalassa is here," he answered, and breathed a sigh of relief when Gadavar came in, stamping the snow from his boots. "At least I am not the only man in this cabin now."

While the two men stood talking in low voices by the hearth, Corri went to Takra's side. The warrior woman writhed as each pain rippled through her, perspiration running down her face, her teeth biting into her lower lip.

"Flow with the pain, as you would flow with your sword in battle." In a low voice, Thalassa soothed and encouraged the laboring woman. "Greet the child. Welcome your daughter."

The night wore on, with Takra's pains coming faster and faster. Corri stayed by her side, only leaving to fetch cold water to moisten Takra's dry lips.

I must endure this, she thought, but suddenly realized that for once she did not fear the pain she knew would come. *All mothers endure this pain, most with joy, knowing they are creating a new life.* She felt a flow of love and bonding for the mother she could not remember. *May the Goddess bless you and your new daughter, Takra.* Corri smiled as she felt the presence of Varanna enter the room and move closer to Takra. *It is time,* she said to the ancient warrior woman. *Let her agony be finished. Welcome, Varanna.*

The child was born as the first rays of dawn broke across the sharp mountain peaks, the light cascading through the straight boles of the forest, the faint heat releasing the scent of fir and pine into the still air.

Imandoff took up his daughter in his big hands, tears of joy and awe in his eyes. The baby waved one hand, and her tiny fingers caught in his beard.

"What will you name her?" he asked Takra, as Thalassa took away the bloody birthing cloths.

"Varanna Star-Seeker." Takra's eyes were bruised with fatigue, but a glowing light shown deep within them.

How did she know? Corri thought in surprise. *I did not tell her.*

Her heart and soul knew, the Lady's voice whispered inside Corri's mind. *In her own way, Takra Wind-Rider hears Me.*

"Welcome, Varanna." Imandoff bent to kiss the baby's black hair. The amber eyes opened as the child blinked at the world around her. "I have no doubt you will be as talented as your mother, little one, and just as wild. But I would not have it otherwise."

Thalassa shrugged into her cloak as a knock sounded, and the door opened to reveal another Green Man. "Another child is being born this night. I am needed there. You must rest, Takra."

Thalassa nodded to them and left with the Green Man.

"No doubt the child will also inherit her father's talent for nosiness and calling up fire." Corri leaned back into the curve of Gadavar's arm.

"And a thirst for wandering," Gadavar added with a smile. He looked down at Corri. "The Green Men talk of setting up patrols in the Takto Range to the far east after the next winter. If I am asked to go, will you go with me?"

"Do not think to leave me behind," Corri answered. "Our son will be old enough to travel by then."

"The Taktos? The one place I have not explored." Imandoff laid the baby by Takra's side, then turned to Gadavar, his eyes alight with interest. "Do the Green Men think that the powers of the Silent Towers may weaken as did the border spells?"

"It is possible," Gadavar answered. "Come spring and the snows thin on the mountains, some of us will go there and build cabins in preparation."

"The Taktos have long been forbidden land." Takra cuddled the baby close as she leaned back on the pillows. "Are there ruins of the Forgotten Ones there, or underground tunnels?" She frowned up at Imandoff. "I really hate tunnels."

"We know little of the Taktos," Gadavar said. "No one but Green Men and a few Tuonela have ever set foot in those mountains."

"Besides," Corri murmured, "it will be far from the Temple at Kystan and any attempts to keep me in their service."

"So I thought when I said I would go." Gadavar tightened his arm about her shoulders. "I promised that you would never be caged, my love, and that I meant."

"The same thoughts have crossed my mind." Imandoff laid a protective hand on Takra's arm. "The Temple will be watching both our children for signs of talent. Distance will give the little ones time to grow in their own way, without interference."

"No daughter of mine goes into any Temple," Takra snapped, and the baby gave a protesting squall of agreement.

"Then we journey soon into new adventures." Imandoff strode across the room to get a jug of cider and four wooden mugs. He filled each cup with the amber liquid, then raised his in a toast. "To our daughter Varanna, and to new adventures and warm friendships."

"You are as bad as Imandoff, hankering after adventures," Corri said. Gadavar grinned and kissed her cheek. "I know I am companying with crazies," she said to Takra, "but I think I have finally become one of you."

Takra raised her cup, a grin on her tired face, then took only a tiny sip. The baby grunted and yawned.

"All life is an adventure to the Tuonela," Takra said. "And our children will live the wildest adventures of all."

Taillefer's Song

I sing of prophecies come alive from old,
of battles fierce and warriors bold.

I sing of sorrows deep and duties strong,
of a time of dread and an evil long,

When the gateless wall broke and fell,
releasing those from the bottom-most hell

To threaten our freedom and our Light
by covering all in an endless night.

But a woman arose with hair like flame
to champion us. Dream Warrior her name.

Leaving all she loved behind,
she used the powers of her mind

To protect the Peoples with her life.
Her shining sword cut down the strife.

Her battle raged in other worlds,
while at the border back we hurled

The flood of invaders in crimson tide.
Many fought and many died.

The moon turned black, but evil fell.
Dream Warrior returned from the gates of hell.

Victorious, this woman of the flame
was christened with a proud new name—

Warrior of Shadows!

One of the songs written by Taillefer the song-smith after the Great Battle.

About the Author

I was born on a Beltane Full Moon with a total lunar eclipse, one of the hottest days of that year. Although there were natural psychics on both sides of the family, such matters were rarely discussed. I seriously began my quest for knowledge in the occult fields more than thirty-five years ago. Incidentally, I don't "claim" my heart lies with the Pagan field; I *know* it does.

I have always been close to Nature and insatiably curious about everything. My reading covers vast areas of history, the magickal arts, philosophy, customs, mythology, folklore and fantasy. I have studied every aspect of the New Age religions, from Eastern philosophy to Wicca. I hope I never stop learning and expanding.

Although I have lived in areas of this country from one coast to the other, the West Coast is my home. I am not fond of large crowds or speaking in public.

I live a rather quiet life with my husband and our six cats, with occasional visits with my children and grandchildren. I collect statues of dragons and wizards, crystals and other stones, and of course books. Most of my time is spent researching and writing. All in all, I am just an ordinary Pagan person.

To Write to the Author

If you wish to contact the author or would like more information about this book, please write to the author in care of Llewellyn Worldwide and we will forward your request. Both the author and publisher appreciate hearing from you and learning of your enjoyment of this book. Llewellyn Worldwide cannot guarantee that every letter written to the author can be answered, but all will be forwarded. Please write to:

D. J. Conway
℅ Llewellyn Worldwide
P.O. Box 64383, Dept. K178-3
St. Paul, MN 55164-0383, U.S.A.

Please enclose a self-addressed stamped envelope for reply, or $1.00 to cover costs. If outside U.S.A., enclose international postal reply coupon.

Stay in Touch . . .

Llewellyn publishes hundreds of books on your favorite subjects. On the following pages you will find listed some books now available on related subjects. Your local bookstore stocks most of these and will stock new Llewellyn titles as they become available. We urge your patronage.

Order by Phone

Call toll-free within the U.S. and Canada, 1–800–THE MOON.
In Minnesota, call (612) 291–1970.
We accept Visa, MasterCard, and American Express.

Order by Mail

Send the full price of your order (MN residents add 7% sales tax) in U.S. funds to:

> Llewellyn Worldwide
> P.O. Box 64383, Dept. K178-3
> St. Paul, MN 55164-0383, U.S.A.

Postage and Handling

- $4.00 for orders $15 and under
- $5.00 for orders over $15
- No charge for orders over $100

We ship UPS in the continental United States. We cannot ship to P.O. boxes. Orders shipped to Alaska, Hawaii, Canada, Mexico, and Puerto Rico will be sent first-class mail.
International orders: Airmail—Add freight equal to price of each book to the total price of order, plus $5.00 for each non-book item (audiotapes, etc.). Surface mail—Add $1.00 per item.
Allow 4–6 weeks delivery on all orders. Postage and handling rates subject to change.

Group Discounts

We offer a 20% quantity discount to group leaders or agents. You must order a minimum of 5 copies of the same book to get our special quantity price.

Dream Warrior

D. J. Conway

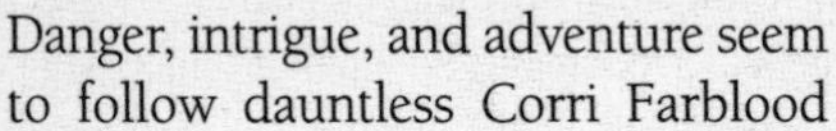

Danger, intrigue, and adventure seem to follow dauntless Corri Farblood wherever she goes. Sold as a child to the grotesque and sinister master thief Grimmel, Corri was forced into thievery at a young age. In fact, at eighteen, she's the best thief in the city of Hadliden—but she also possesses an ability to travel the astral plane, called dream-flying, that makes her even more unique. Her talents make her a valuable commodity to Grimmel, who forces her into marriage so she will bear a child carrying both her special powers and his. But before the marriage can be consummated, Corri escapes with the aid of a traveling sorcerer, who has a quest of his own to pursue. . . .

Journey across the wide land of Sar Akka with Corri, the sorcerer Imandoff Silverhair, and the warrior Takra Wind-Rider as they search for an ancient place of power. As Grimmel's assassins relentlessly pursue her, Corri battles against time and her enemies to solve the mystery of her heritage and to gain control over her potent clairvoyant gifts . . . to learn the meaning of companionship and love . . . and to finally confront a fate that will test her powers and courage to the limit.

1-56718-169-4, 320 pp., 5¼ x 8, softcover $14.95

To order, call 1-800-THE MOON

Prices subject to change without notice

Soothslayer

D. J. Conway

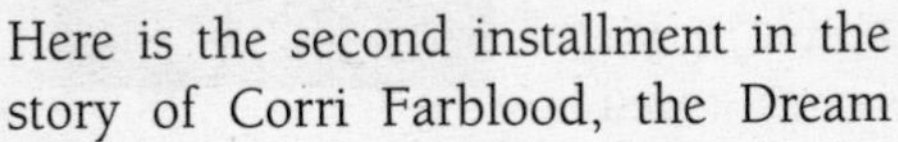

Here is the second installment in the story of Corri Farblood, the Dream Warrior, a young girl-thief who battles for the Goddess in a time of great unrest. The plot centers around Corrie and her friends—Takra Windrider, her warrior sister, and Imandoff, the sorcerer who saved Corri from the lusts of the Master Thief. Together, these three prepare to stand against the evil onslaught of the rulers of Frav, a country bordering their own, and the worshippers of a condemning god.

An ancient prophecy warns against the Soothslayer, a man who will try to destroy the Peoples. But just who is the Soothslayer? Can Corri prevent the religious war declared against the Peoples by the priests of Frav, led by her own father? Will her psychic powers be strong enough for her to save her people and the man she loves?

Soothslayer abounds with magick and intrigue, diabolical plans and well-plotted twists.

1-56718-162-7, 400 pp., 5¼ x 8, softcover $9.95

To order, call 1-800-THE MOON

Prices subject to change without notice

Lilith

D. A. Heeley

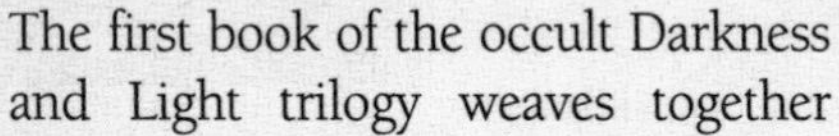

The first book of the occult Darkness and Light trilogy weaves together authentic magickal techniques and teachings of the Hebrew Qabalah with the suspenseful story of the spiritual evolution of Malak, an Adept of the White School of Magick.

Malak and his fellow magicians from the White, Yellow, and Black Schools of Magick live on Enya, the lower astral plane of the Qabalistic Tree of Life. Malak's brother and arch-rival, Dethen, is an Adept of the Black School. Dethen plots a coup to destroy the White School completely and begin a reign of terror on Enya—with the hope of destroying the Tree of Life and the world—and a colossal battle between Good and Evil ensues. As the Black Adepts summon the Arch-demon Lilith into Enya, Malak is faced with a terrible choice: should he barter with the ultimate evil to free his wife's soul, even if freeing her condemns other innocent souls forever?

The second half of *Lilith* takes place 1,000 years later, in feudal Japan. Malak has been reincarnated as Shadrack, who struggles with an inner demon who will not be denied. He must conquer Lilith's evil or there will be a bloody rampage amid the Shogun's Royal Guard. . . .

1-56718-355-7, 256 pp., 6 x 9, softcover $10.00

To order, call 1-800-THE MOON
Prices subject to change without notice

Cardinal's Sin

Raymond Buckland

Magical secrets found in an ancient grimoire hidden away in the Vatican Library . . . an insanely vengeful and ambitious Cardinal . . . fierce magical storms that take America hostage . . . sounds like another case for the Committee!

The story begins in the United States, where coastal hurricanes, flooding rains, and tornados have cost the country billions of dollars and thousands of lives. As it becomes clear that these storms are not natural, the Committee—a covert group of psychically talented people formed by the U.S. government to neutralize malignant paranormal forces—joins minds to determine how and why these devastating, magical storms are being caused—and by whom.

Enter Patrizio Ganganelli, a crazed Roman Cardinal obsessed with avenging his mother's rape during WWII by American soldiers. As the Cardinal plunders the Vatican's secret magic library to evoke demonic forces against the United States, the Committee joins forces with a Wiccan Priestess to counter the Cardinal's attack. But the Goddess alone may not be able to defeat this evil entity—someone needs to die. . . .

1-56178-102-3, 336 pp., mass market, softcover $5.99

To order, call 1-800-THE MOON

Prices subject to change without notice

Beneath a Mountain Moon

Silver RavenWolf

Welcome to Whiskey Springs, Pennsylvania, birthplace of magick, mayhem, and murder! The generations-old battle between two powerful occult families rages anew when young Elizabeyta Belladonna journeys from Oklahoma to the small town of Whiskey Springs—a place her family had left years before to escape the predatory Blackthorn family—to solve the mystery of her grandmother's death.

Endowed with her own magickal heritage of Scotch-Irish Witchcraft, Elizabeyta stands alone against the dark powers and twisted desires of Jason Blackthorn and his gang of Dark Men. But Elizabeyta isn't the only one pursued by unseen forces and the fallout from a past life. As Blackthorn manipulates the town's inhabitants through occult means, a great battle for mastery ensues between the forces of darkness and light—a battle that involves a crackpot preacher, a blue ghost, the town gossip, and an old country healer—and the local funeral parlor begins to overflow with victims. Is there anyone who can end the Blackthorns' reign of terror and right the cosmic balance?

1-56718-722-6, 360 pp., 6 x 9, softcover $15.95

To order, call 1-800-THE MOON

Prices subject to change without notice

Flying Without a Broom

D. J. Conway

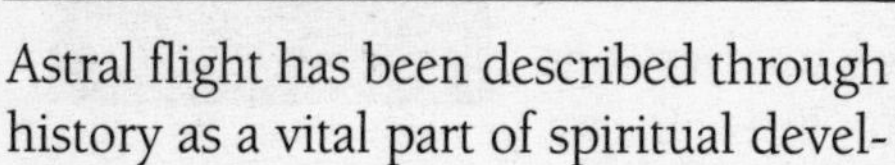

Astral flight has been described through history as a vital part of spiritual development and a powerful aid to magickal workings. In this remarkable volume, respected author D. J. Conway shows how anyone can have the keys to a profound astral experience. Not only is astral travel safe and simple, she shows in clear and accessible terms how this natural part of our psychic make-up can be cultivated to enhance both spiritual and daily life.

This complete how-to includes historical lore, a groundwork of astral plane basics, and a simplified learning process to get you "off the ground." You'll learn simple exercises to strengthen your astral abilities as well as a variety of astral techniques—including bilocation and time travel. After the basics, use the astral planes to work magick and healings; contact teachers, guides, or lovers; and visit past lives. You'll also learn how to protect yourself and others from the low-level entities inevitably encountered in the astral.

Through astral travel you will expand your spiritual growth, strengthen your spiritual efforts, and bring your daily life to a new level of integration and satisfaction.

1-56718-164-3, 224 pp., 6 x 9, softcover $13.00

To order, call 1-800-THE MOON

Prices subject to change without notice

Moon Magick

D. J. Conway

No creature on this planet is unaffected by the power of the Moon. Its effects range from making us feel energetic or adventurous to tense and despondent. By putting excess Moon energy to work for you, you can learn to plan projects, work and travel at the optimum times.

Moon Magick explains how each of the 13 lunar months is directly connected with a different type of seasonal energy flow and provides modern rituals and spells for tapping this energy and celebrating the Moon phases. Each chapter describes new Pagan rituals—79 in all—related to that particular Moon, plus related Moon lore, ancient holidays, spells, meditations and suggestions for foods, drinks and decorations to accompany your Moon rituals. This book includes two thorough dictionaries of Moon deities and symbols.

By moving through the year according to the 13 lunar months, you can become more attuned to the seasons, the Earth and your inner self. *Moon Magick* will show you how to let your life flow with the power and rhythms of the Moon to benefit your physical, emotional and spiritual well-being.

1-56718-167-8, 7 x 10, 320 pp., illus., softcover $14.95

To order, call 1-800-THE MOON

Prices subject to change without notice

Perfect Love

D. J. Conway

Here is a clear and complete system for developing your ability to astral travel. *Perfect Love* takes you beyond the world of mortals into the greatest adventure you will ever know. Learn how to develop a lasting relationship with an astral lover who will offer you emotional support and even help you to find a physical partner who is right for you. Meld chakras with divine beings in the ultimate sexual encounter. Boost your self-esteem through the healing effects of a relationship with a higher-level astral being who really cares about you.

Forging a personal relationship on the astral plane will enhance your life, filling it with love, compassion, understanding, and positive energy. Astral sex can even help you establish a stronger connection with the Divine and open new avenues of magick. Even if you choose not to be sexually active on the astral planes, you can establish strong, warm friendships with high-level beings to enhance your magick and spiritual advancement.

1-56718-181-3, 6 x 9, 192 pp., illus., softcover $12.95